THE LAST RIGHTS

Geoff Cook

Published by Rotercracker Copyrights, 2020
Copyright © Geoff Cook, 2020
Geoff Cook has asserted his right under the Copyright,
Designs and Patents Act 1988 to be identified
as the author of this work

This novel is a work of fiction. Names and characters
are the product of the author's imagination and any
resemblance to persons living or dead is entirely coincidental

First published in Great Britain in 2020 by Rotercracker Copyrights
Pacific Heights South, 16 Golden Gate Way, Eastbourne,
East Sussex, BN23 5PU

Paperback ISBN 9789899730069

A CIP catalogue record for this book is available
from the British Library

For more information on Rotercracker Copyrights,
books and plays, please visit
www.geoff-cook.com
https://www.facebook.com/novelgeoffcook/

For Rita

PART ONE - THE GIRL

BULLETS AND BREAD DOUGH

ONE
VEVEY, SWITZERLAND
December 2018

He walked on tiptoe across the darkened room, picking his way carefully between the sofas and armchairs. The solitary figure was sitting with her back to him, facing the bay window. The source of light was a solitary standard lamp set next to the wheelchair. Strands of frayed golden braid, partially detached from the fabric of the lampshade, caused the insipid yellow glow to cast uneven fingers of light and dark across the floor until they were absorbed into the surrounding blackness.

Closer now, he could make out the distorted reflection of her face in the window, eyes transfixed on a point in time that was not the present as she stared straight ahead at the swirling cloud of snowflakes that filled the night sky beyond the glass.

'I've been expecting you,' she said, finally. Her frail voice was laboured, the words expelled from her mouth on a current of exhaled breath.

'You have?'

'For the last seventy-five years.' A staccato cough growled in her throat. She was laughing. 'But we were too careful to let you catch us.'

He went to move forward, to face her, but a thin bare arm, wrinkled skin hanging limp with scarcely any bone to cover, lifted to tell him to stop. And he did.

'I have no wish to see your face,' she said, amidst a stuttered intake of breath. 'Do what you have to do, but I choose not to witness my executioner.'

'You mistake my intentions. My mission was simply to find you, to seek your cooperation.'

'Seek my cooperation—' Another cough, a dry, jagged bark that propelled her head forward and scattered spots of blood on the handkerchief she had drawn to her mouth. 'You are suggesting the assassin needs the victim's help?'

'I mean you no harm.'

She raised her hand again, this time to entice him nearer. Her eyes followed his to rest on the fungus that had blackened the nails on her skeletal fingers. 'Not a pretty sight, am I?'

He treated the question as rhetorical. There were no words of comfort. Perchance, he glanced at the reflection of his expression in the window and hoped she had not seen it.

Silence prevailed. Slowly, she raised her head to study him. 'Do you believe in natural justice?' she asked.

Her eyes were blue, untinged by age and still vital, as if the final blooms on a withering plant. They were interrogating him.

'I don't know.'

The dismissive shrug told him the answer was inadequate, not what she expected to hear. 'It's natural justice that keeps me alive.' She stopped to recharge her breath. 'It has condemned me not only for all the wrongs I have done, but for all the wrongs done to me that I have condoned. And its sentence' – she fought for air and inhaled afresh – 'its sentence is to keep me breathing so that I am obliged to witness this physical decay. It knows I will not seek my own end. My punishment is to survive in pain.' There was another pause. 'Yet, with every passing day as the body succumbs, my mind grows stronger, the memories more vivid. Do you know what hell is? You shake your head. Then I will tell you. Hell is not being able to forget the past.' A grimace, and then, 'And now you come.'

'Me?'

'You say you were sent to find me. Do you come to demand satisfaction or bring absolution?'

'Absolution? Isn't that in God's gift?'

Her hand beckoned him nearer still, her stale breath warming his cheek. 'Ah, God. I wondered when he would make an appearance.' She pointed to his cheek. 'You have a cut. It will leave a scar.'

'I was playing with my grandchildren and got a little too overenthusiastic. Hide-and-seek. Do you know the game?'

Her mouth creased into a weak smile. The giggle was no more than a rattle in her throat. 'I have been playing it all my life, but I cheated. You are supposed to play by the rules and, eventually, allow yourself to get caught. I never did. One step in front of the hunter is never enough. It can be a vicious game if one side or the other abandons the rules.'

'In that case, maybe God will be the arbiter.'

'There you go again, about God.' Her body stiffened. He could tell she was angry, losing patience. 'Don't you think I know? There is no God. God is an illusion, created by those who fear death; a panacea to provide a safety net for the lost souls who tip over the abyss of life into the unknown. Only the net is not really there, so you keep falling into the darkness for eternity.'

'You seem so certain. How can you know?'

'I just do. Your God is benign, all powerful. Correct? Don't nod your head. Say yes or no with conviction.'

'Yes.'

Her eyes closed. 'A lie. If your God existed, he would not let the innocent suffer at the hands of evil.'

'Can the denial of innocence be reason enough to reject your faith?'

'You ask too many naïve questions. What is it you want of me?'

'You avoid an answer.'

There was a long pause as she appeared to be stilling herself, organising her thoughts. 'We must acknowledge that the innocents have no choice but to abandon their faith when they realise their cry for hope has been ignored. Most succumb to evil, and perish in body or spirit at its hand. Those who manage to survive do so by discovering their innocence is replaced with malevolence as great as, or even greater than, the evil inflicting their suffering.'

'And you survived. I need you to tell me everything that happened.'

Was that another attempt at a laugh? He wasn't sure.

'There is not enough breath left in my body to speak of my life … much beyond the time spent in my mother's womb.'

He placed his hand on hers. 'I cannot conceive you did not make provision for this day.'

'I must sleep now. Tomorrow, it will end.'

Before he had time to reply, her eyes closed. In sleep, her breathing was laboured and uneven. Yet, as the minutes passed, she did not breathe her last. As her eyelids flickered, her pulse was regular and colour had returned to her cheeks. Her eyes opened wide and alert, as if reacting to the sound of a trap closing on the ensnared creature.

In her world, there had been no break in their conversation. She held his gaze once more, as if giving weight to his last remark. 'Are you certain you really wish to know? You will be signing your own death warrant.'

'I have no choice.'

She withdrew her hand from his and pointed a wavering finger. 'The cupboard. There is a file. It's all in there.' Another bout of coughing overcame her. Heavier spots of blood peppered the cloth.

He returned with a small leather-bound document case. She had used sheets from a writing pad, hundred upon hundred filled in small, neat handwriting; a fine nib in black ink. There was a musty scent about the case which suggested the narrative had lain unread for many years.

She shook her head. 'You have now been cursed with the burden, and I, by the same token, relieved.'

'How come?'

'If it is not your intent to silence me, they will surely know of your coming. Death, I will welcome, but no more torture. I will tell them that someone came for the file, and they will seek you out. They will not stop until the truth is extinguished.'

He took out the black leather gloves from his overcoat pocket and put them on, interlocking the fingers tightly. Two steps and he stood behind the wheelchair, his hand releasing the brake.

'I am beholden to you,' he said with a smile.

TWO
FORT VII, POZNAN, POLAND
January 1944

She dreamed about Josef last night. At least, she thinks it was last night. Her brother was whispering, but she could not make out what he was saying or from where the sound of his voice came. She needed to know he was safe. She pleaded then demanded he come out from wherever he was hiding. Didn't he realise nobody can play those games any more? If she could just touch his face, say how much she loved him. No! No! She would never tell another living soul she had seen him. If she could just touch his baby skin. His secret would always be safe with her. Even if they tortured her, she would never betray him by telling how she had forced him into the space between the floorboards. No, she hadn't said that out loud, had she? Heil Hitler. She was telling the truth, Herr Hitler. She did not know where Josef was. How could she?

Her heart is beating faster than she can count, One, two, three – six – nine. Don't stop. Keep counting. Twelve – fourteen. The candle is flickering. She recognises the voice of the ragman's wife. Why does this kind lady look so troubled? Why are there such creases on her forehead? What makes her stare at me that way? Does she understand everything there is to know about life and death?

'She's waking up. Do you think she'll remember what happened?' The ragman's wife watches as her husband shuffles to stand alongside her in the cramped storeroom.

The girl tries to shake her head, to shout out it was all a dream. There is no need to remember anything. No sound leaves her lips; not a muscle of her body moves.

'She's so hot,' the woman says. 'I'll wipe her face.' She shakes out the damp piece of cloth and wrings it into a tight knot.

A petrified stare follows the woman's every move. She holds the cloth out towards the girl. The scream shatters the silence.

It is so cold. Her eyes open. Every limb in her body is shaking, yet inside she is calm, strangely entranced by the wondrous symmetrical pattern frozen on the inside of the single windowpane beyond the iron bars. It glistens like fairy dust as watery sunlight traces a passage across the piles of garments covering the stone floor. She blinks. Her tongue traces a line around cracked lips. She is parched.

'How do you feel, girl?' She recognises the strange southern lilt of Yodel, the ragman who runs the tailor's attic. He is her friend. 'Here, drink some water.'

She claws at the tin bowl he holds out to her, fighting for breath in between the savage gulps of water.

'Steady. No need to rush. Water is the only thing we do have in plenty.'

His wife is fussing around nervously. The girl doesn't know the woman's name. Nobody does. Yodel always called her Mother, so they all just accept it. 'Can't she stand up yet?' She tut-tuts. 'They will be making their rounds in a little while. God help her if she's not back at her table when they arrive. She will be transported.'

'Be quiet, Mother. Can't you see she's in agony?' He smiles softly as he moves towards her. 'You need to get up, Rita, just for a short while.'

The girl puts a frail, childlike hand between her legs. 'It hurts so much. Like there's a fire burning inside me.' Tears are streaming down her cheeks.

As she struggles to her feet, Yodel removes the coat he had spread on the cutting table for her to lie on. He had chosen a red one on purpose, but the blood was darker, clotted. It had left a deep stain. She must have lost a great deal, he thinks, but if she could avoid infection, age was on her side. What would she be? Thirteen, fourteen? Her breasts and hips are already well developed. Too well developed for such a sensitive, innocent soul.

Yodel busies himself, allocating tasks amongst the inmates. Three suits have to be ready today; a hundred blankets for consignment to the Eastern Front. He looks at his workforce. Gaunt, blank faces stare back. Starving and inexperienced, few have kept the spark, the vision to survive beyond the sixteen hours at their stations and the paltry rations that follow.

The girl is different, an enigma. Beyond her worldly naivety is a calculating, fiery character with a sense of self-preservation. In this place, choices are few, the mood can change rapidly, but she is sensitive to the

6

warped personality changes that incarceration produces in those around her. Wasn't it she who prewarned Yodel about the woman who would try to kill him with the tailor's shears on the day he had criticised her work?

He steadies the girl as she grips firmly on the edge of the table, her body swaying, her eyes tight shut. The quicker the commandant appears, the sooner he can find a place for her to lie down again. She cannot go back to the women's quarters in her parlous state. The cavernous, brick-clad, arched chamber is below ground with no natural light. The driving rain of recent weeks has swept through the metal gratings. Human excrement washed from the inner recesses floats upon the puddles that have formed on the uneven floor. The straw on which the women sleep is damp and, although nobody speaks of it beyond a hurried whisper, rumour has it that Icchak, formerly a vet, now the self-appointed physician, is treating an outbreak of typhus.

There is an eerie silence. Just for a second, as if in an intake of breath, the nervous tension grows until it overpowers the rag room. Yodel and Mother scurry to their positions.

The commandant comes to a halt by one of the sewing machines, cursorily examines a stitched blanket before discarding it onto the floor. 'Which of these are the two girls?' he barks at the *SS-Helferin* who stands stiffly to attention behind him. The female guard moves to the area where the bobbins are wound with yarn and roughly ushers a young girl to stand, head bowed, before the commandant.

'Let me see your face, girl.' His gloved fist under her chin pushes up her head. 'Your name?'

'Samir,' she stutters. 'Rachel Samir.'

'Herr Commandant!' the guard barks.

'Rachel Samir, Herr Commandant,' the girl repeats.

'Turn around. Hold your hands out. Not that way! Palms up! Now your teeth.' He pokes a nicotine-stained index finger around inside her mouth. 'She will leave tomorrow.' The *SS-Helferin* bows her head in acknowledgement. 'Send her to my quarters this evening. Where is the other one?'

Mother gives Rita a smile of encouragement and silently mouths the words 'Be brave', but the girl still recoils as the guard approaches, a look of horror on her face. This is one of the two *Helferin* who held her down last

7

night. The nightmare has come alive in her head. This woman forced the dirty rag into her mouth and told her to bite hard. The serious-looking man in the white coat forced her legs apart, sweating as he guided the burning iron into her. His gaze, unfeeling and distant, met hers as he finished the task. She will never forget his face. The flicker of his satisfied smile is transformed into a moment of startled surprise as she screams, expelling the rag from her mouth. He curses as the iron tumbles onto the floor, close to his feet. The *Helferin* strikes her hard around the face. All about her is the smell of scorched flesh. The girl slips into the darkness.

'She is unwell,' the commandant pronounces.

The guard crosses her arms, moving her legs apart in a defiant stance. 'She was uncooperative. She tried to move during the procedure and suffered internal burns.'

'Is she disfigured?' He studies the girl's face. 'If there is any doubt, pick another and put this one on the purification list.'

'Apparently, not. In fact, Herr Doktor Sommer pronounced that when the wound cauterises, it will provide a rather pleasant intercourse experience.'

The commandant laughs as he pulls her arm towards him, twisting it to read the digits branded on her forearm. 'There you are, KZ409875.' He leans forward, breathing stale cigar breath onto her. 'Not only have we ensured no Jewish bastards come into the world through your legs, we have also endowed you with the means to give added pleasure to all those heroes of the Reich who will fuck and come inside you. Aren't you just the lucky girl?'

* * *

The girl is well again. Outside, the snows have gone with the transition of the seasons, but in the rag room the routine is constant. The pile of clothes never grows smaller; the sound of the sewing machines, busy sixteen hours every day; the faces of the inmates ever-changing, but all with one thing in common – a sense of foreboding and hopelessness.

Yodel is officially appointed a *kapo*, a trusted inmate. This is his story as told to the girl.

8

From now on, he is in charge of all clothing and shoe manufacture. The position allows him to enjoy the meagre privileges awarded to the *Judenrat*, the members of the Jewish council who work for the Nazis, more rations and the chance to leave the camp for escorted visits to the ghettos in which the remaining Jewish population is confined. Once there, he recommends to the commandant's second in command, *Obersturmführer* Kirchner, suitable candidates to replace workers whose fate has seen them removed from the rag room. He tells Mother he would take them all if he could. Every week, there are at least a dozen confused souls, dazed and beaten, punished for failing to meet the curfew, many by just a few minutes. Yodel is a kind man and makes a case to take them all, complaining that the demands on him are such that he must have a bigger workforce. Kirchner laughs. He treats Yodel's solemn and respectful pleadings as a game, a ploy intended to save those rejected from the firing squad. He plays his part in a charade, pretending to give these pleadings serious consideration, but, finally, after seeming to acquiesce, he denies the request and ensures Yodel is in the yard when the rifles are aimed and the bullets find their mark.

But today is different. Kirchner pulls the ragman to one side. 'Do you have one of your girls who you can trust to do exactly as I tell her?'

It is Yodel's turn to play his game. 'I will give your command serious consideration, *Obersturmführer*.'

Kirchner pins the ragman to the wall, his gloved hands pressing on Yodel's shoulders. Their noses are almost touching. 'Don't take too long, *kapo*. I am not a patient man. I am relying on you to find me someone who can keep to the instructions I give her and repeat them, if necessary under duress, to whoever may subsequently interrogate her. It is a simple question. Do you have such a female in your section?'

Yodel adopts his thoughtful posture, smiling to himself, head leaning to one side, avoiding the officer's threatening stare. Kirchner is going out on a limb, talking to him like this. Starting to put his trust in a Jew worker is a risk no SS officer would take lest he were desperate. It was important for Yodel to secure an advantage. He must not commit himself. 'As I said, *Obersturmführer,* I must make an assessment. You require somebody of outstanding fortitude.' And then, conspiratorially, 'We both need to be sure.' And, to leave the door open, 'There may be a suitable candidate ...'

A week passes and they are together again in the ghetto. Yodel has a plan. Firstly, he must ensure this is not some plot to compromise his allegiance as a newly promoted *kapo*. Today, he insists on recruiting the entire bedraggled bunch of would-be victims of the firing squad. The claim is that the outbreak of typhus has ravaged his group. The official position is to insist no such outbreak has occurred, but Kirchner does not react. Ten confused souls unsure of their fate stand before them. Only four, perhaps five, will be any use to Yodel, but it is his one act of defiance, a gesture to any god who cares to witness a single good deed in the face of such adversity. True to form, Kirchner objects, but on this one, solitary occasion, it is a foregone conclusion. Yodel prevails.

As the new intake is loaded onto the lorry, Kirchner pulls him to one side. 'So, you have found me someone?' He points to the group of men and women. 'There is still time for me to change my mind.'

Yodel ignores the threat. 'I have been thinking.' He gestures for the officer to come closer. It is his turn to play games. Yodel once had six tailor shops in Warsaw and Krakow and knows all about business deals. Kirchner is a young man, early twenties, who knows nothing but the thuggery of the Brownshirts before he joined the regular army. He is so obviously desperate.

'You say the chosen one will be subject to some difficult interrogation. Having the willpower to resist such harsh treatment is beyond many. Could I respectfully suggest you promise such a reward as to make it impossible for her to fail?'

'A reward? You are talking about money?'

Yodel holds out his arms, as if in frustrated despair. 'What good is money to us? No, I mean two promises: one for her and one for me.'

'Go on. More provisions?'

He shakes his head. 'If it is the girl I have in mind, I will tell her you agree to give her news about the whereabouts and condition of her father. He was taken to one of the camps. Perhaps a letter from him? Her desire to know he is alive will guarantee her compliance.' Yodel raises his head to look the taller man in the eye. 'I have no way of verifying what you tell her, but I would humbly beg you to find out the truth and not lie to her.'

'And, if he is dead?'

'You agree to take her to the place where he is buried.'

'But—'

'I know what you are going to say. A suitable site, a simple cross. I know it is within your power. She will need closure and the dead will not betray your deception.'

'And your reward. What is that to be?'

'Within the next few months, we know she will be taken to the place you call the Dolls' House, to serve the needs of your men. I would like your word you will keep an eye on her, see she comes to no harm until she develops the mental strength to survive on her own.'

'She is a relative?'

'No, but we have a special place in our hearts for her. She is a good worker, but young and very innocent. We will prepare her as best we can. We fear for her life when confronted with the experiences she will be expected to endure.'

'We are not savages. Are you suggesting we are?'

Yodel retreats at the threatening gesture. 'Whatever side they are on, men who have fought on the front line display many pent-up emotions, some seeking love and compassion, others bent on releasing the fury of war that lives inside them. I listened when my father talked of the last conflict.'

Kirchner appears to accept the explanation. 'I still do not understand why she is so important to you.'

'My wife and I have no children. This girl has filled a gap. She eats at our table, so to speak.'

There is a shake of the head. 'If she is as tender as you suggest, how could she stand interrogation?'

Yodel nods at the logic. 'She may have no idea of the ways of the world, but she reminds me of my wife when she was a girl. There is a will of iron that cannot be broken.'

'Yet you fear for her safety when away from here?'

'I do. I think she has the strength of character to take her own life if she feels no reason to carry on. No father, not even an adopted one, wants to see his child suffer.'

11

The girl appears to understand everything required of her. She listens carefully and asks few questions, for her task is simple. Mother is troubled and the girl understands why. The gravity of what she is being asked to do, if it were to go wrong, does not bear contemplating. On this aspect, the girl appears unmoved. It is either dangerous naivety or resolute self-belief. Mother knows both she and her husband have put their lives at risk, their fate very much intertwined with hers; dare she say, totally dependent upon the conviction of this child's performance. Yet this tender young girl is not without emotion. There is a driving force that heightens the sense of anticipation in her voice. Once she has answered all of the questions, satisfied the testing examination of the interrogators, there will be news of her father, maybe even a letter. Yodel has promised. There is no way she will fail. Mother has to believe this to be true. God will help them.

The days pass. They pass without changing.

It is to be today, whatever day this day is. Today is different.

Yodel watches the girl as she takes another overcoat from the floor and deftly begins to unpick the hems and seams with the curved knife he sharpened for her just hours before. In the space of two minutes she has reduced the garment to strips of cloth ready for the *kapo* to inspect. Slicing beyond the stitching into the material would earn a reprimand and, if repeated, a transfer to work on the stinking dye vat. Yodel has no concerns on this score. She is proficient and never makes a mistake.

Yodel cannot pretend to know much about jewellery, but the bracelet he has just passed to her must be worth a king's ransom. The rubies and diamonds are set alternately in a solid gold setting with a safety clasp embossed with the hallmark of one of the most prestigious goldsmiths in pre-war Paris. Now, it sits on the bench in front of her.

The commandant is looking unwell. His hair, long and untidy, is smarmed back with either brilliantine or perspiration. His face is sallower, his features more strained and pallid than usual. Yodel told Mother there was talk amongst the *Judenrat* that he is suffering from gonorrhoea. No surprise, Mother said, considering all the whores he beds. She looked around at the girl, but there was no sign she had been following the conversation.

Now is the time. He nears her bench. The female guards are hanging back, a sure sign he is in a bad mood. His eyes are drawn to the bracelet. This trinket, he says dismissively, his hand covering the bracelet. Where did she find it? The girl looks confused. In the lining of the coat she was stripping, of course, as with anything she finds. She places it in the well at the front of the bench. These are her orders. The *kapo* will write on her day sheet and take whatever she has found when he comes to collect the garments.

The commandant grabs and twists her arm to read her KZ number. She lowers her gaze. The bracelet is no longer on the bench. If she values her life, she is to forget the trinket and not to mention it to anyone. It is a cheap imitation with no value and the commandant will ensure it is dealt with appropriately. He swings around to face the nearest female guard. 'This one is working well,' he says. 'Extra bread ration.'

Yodel smiles at her as he gives a slight nod of his head. Mother looks anxious. She knows the worst is yet to come.

***

The girl sits upright in a high-backed chair in front of the three men in their black uniforms and polished faces. They are very serious, with the same stern expressions she recalls Rabbi Zanvil adopted when she forgot the words to the fifteen steps of the Passover Seder; only the rabbi was scarier than these men.

This is the first time she has seen Commandant Dressler with his shirt collar done up and the iron cross at his throat. He lounges in a chair behind a table with several sheets of paper spread before him. He looks unconcerned but he is perspiring heavily, and even from where she is sitting she can detect the stench of fear she knows so well. Next to him sits the *Helferin*, who bows her head to the floor as one of the three men state she is charged with aiding and abetting the commandant, whatever that means. That must be why the woman forced her, arm behind her back, into the cellar last night, threatening another session with the hot iron if she did not cooperate. All the girl has to remember is that she has never seen the

13

bracelet, never spoken of it to anyone nor has any idea what they are talking about. Say anything else and her life will not be worth living.

The man in the centre asks for her KZ number. Another female guard reads it out. The man is speaking again as he twirls the bracelet around between his fingers. Has she ever seen it before? She says she finds things from time to time in the lining of the garments she strips, things people have been hiding and which the reception guards have failed to locate. Can she see it, please, to be sure? She pretends to study it, but she is looking straight past it at the commandant. The sinews in his neck are taut. His shirt is drenched. This is her moment. He is suffering and she longs to let the suffering last forever.

'Well?' The man recognises she is anxious.

She puts the bracelet on her lap and shakes her head violently. She knows her voice will sound full of fear, but only she will realise how much control she will feel over her every word. She shakes her head again. The commandant is starting to look relieved.

'Speak up. You understand the question. Answer it.'

She shakes her head for the third time. 'The *Helferin* told me I would be tortured if I said I had seen the bracelet, but, forgive me' – she begins to sob – 'I cannot lie before God, for his punishment will be even greater.' Her look is one of panic.

'Go on,' the man encourages. 'Tell us what happened.'

'I found it in a greatcoat and left it for the *kapo* to collect from the table, just like I was told, but the commandant took it instead.'

'Did he say anything?'

She hunches her shoulders. 'He told me to say nothing. It was a trinket and worthless.'

'He said that? Anything else?'

She takes a deep breath. 'He said I could have extra bread.'

Everyone in the room begins to talk at once. The man with the moustache is angry, his face twisted into that look Yodel calls contempt. He accuses her of lying to make problems for the commandant. If there had been a bracelet on her bench, she would want to hide it and keep it for herself.

The girl knows how to look confused. She used to put on the expression when her mother chastised her for a chore she had not done in the house. They asked for the truth, she told the man. She had spoken the truth, before God.

The man's expression softens. Is she not misunderstanding what happened? Perhaps she did not find it in the lining of the coat. Is it not the case that someone gave her the bracelet to place on the bench for the commandant to find? He waits for an answer. The look of innocence; a simple no, it was exactly as she had explained. She holds the man's gaze briefly before lowering her eyes.

His mood changes again as he turns to face his fellow officers. This Jew bitch is full of deceit, deliberately lying to discredit an outstanding officer of the *Wehrmacht*. How could anyone believe a word she says? He wheels around to address her.

She feels a strength she has never known before. This is the first man who has ever been afraid of her. Could he repeat the question? She does not understand. No, she has never found anything that substantial before in the lining of an overcoat. Many things are found, normally small items and folded money.

How is it possible the reception officers could have missed such a thing?

How can she say? They are human, too, are they not? But his question was not intended for her. She understands that.

The girl is bundled to the back of the room whilst Yodel is roughly pushed into her place before the three men. His appearance is brief. Yes, the girl did tell him of the find and who had taken it. As it was the commandant, he did not see the need to make a note in his daily report. After all, he had seen nothing.

***

Three weeks pass and everything appears normal; as normal as life can ever be amongst this tide of human flotsam where there is no sense of the passage of time, a sea of expressionless faces with no belief in a future beyond these walls. Yet, it seems to her that every day there are fewer people around the

15

camp. Lorries line up to take inmates away but bring no new faces to replace them. Mother says they are evacuating the place, yet the rag room is as busy as ever. Requisitions arrive daily for warm clothing, mainly from the east. Yodel looks troubled. Their working day has been extended to eighteen hours. Some fall asleep standing up and are harshly treated by the *Helferin*.

Yodel has kept a close eye on the girl since the interrogation. Events taking place amongst the camp hierarchy are the fuel of rumours now the commandant no longer makes his daily rounds. In fact, few can remember seeing him recently. Directly following the aftermath of the investigation over the bracelet, there were threats of retaliation against the girl, but none were carried through. During the last week, there has been a calm, almost cautious reaction amongst the guards, who no longer spend idle time wandering through the rag room, harassing the workers, feeding their sadistic interplay with threats of intimidation. Their inspections are cursory, their visits brief. Mother says God be praised. She never thought to be grateful for the sensation they were in quarantine with some deadly contagious disease.

On a Thursday – Yodel says he knows it was a Thursday because that is the day they all stand naked in the ablution chamber and are hosed down with ice-cold water – he and the girl are escorted to the top floor of the tower where the commandant has his quarters. Fear grips their hearts. They cannot bear to look at one another.

The guard gives a respectful, single tap and opens the door. It creaks on its hinges.

Kirchner looks up from the desk, a blank expression on his face, as if seeing them for the first time. The guard recites her PZ number and is dismissed.

The room is silent. The girl shuffles nervously. Kirchner is reading from a single sheet of paper. 'You are Rita Krakowski, daughter of Malka and Solomon Krakowski?'

She cannot contain herself. 'You have news of my mother and father?'

Yodel presses his foot hard on hers. It hurts and she understands what it means. Control yourself. This man is not our friend. He is our enemy, and a more powerful enemy than he was three weeks ago.

16

But the innocent bonds of a child are too powerful to hold in check. She starts to weep, sobbing beyond Yodel's pleas to cease, all the pent-up emotions released in a torrent of tears that run down her flushed cheeks. Kirchner draws a freshly folded handkerchief from his breast pocket which he passes to her. Through the tears, she notices the strange expression on his face, not sympathetic, more quizzical, as if he is making a judgement. Yodel fusses around, drying her face, chiding her to stop and not to waste the commandant's precious time. The man is staring at her. His eyes are a piercing blue. She blows her nose hard. A glimmer of a smile crosses Kirchner's mouth. He has very few eyelashes, she notices. They are blonde, almost turning to white, like his pencil-thin eyebrows.

'Your father is detained in the centre at Potulice. He was a cobbler by trade, I understand?'

She hands the handkerchief back to him. She appears calmer now, though her heart is pounding inside her chest. 'He prefers to be known as a shoemaker,' she states defiantly.

Kirchner laughs out loud and Yodel follows suit with an understanding smile. 'Of course he does. He works in the shoe shop and has written you this letter.' He passes a heavily folded sheet of brown paper with grease marks along the crease lines. The large, uneven black lettering looks as if it were written with the tip of a piece of coal. She tucks the paper unread between the folds of a skirt she fashioned from scraps of material. It is far too precious to squander with a casual glance in front of anybody else. She will read every word in private a thousand times until they are scorched into her very being.

'Do you have news of my mother?'

Kirchner gives a stern look to the *kapo*. She knows the subject is closed. 'Please be still,' Yodel says. He stands in front of her.

'I wish to thank you for your concern, sir. May I take it that *Herr Obersturmführer* is now our commandant?'

'You were present at the inquiry. Did you not draw your own conclusions?'

'We were removed before the questioning was concluded.'

'Commandant Dressler was convicted of theft; the appropriation of treasures belonging to the Reich for personal gain. It is a very serious

17

offence. He was stripped of his post and his rank. As to the rest, I have no knowledge.' He shakes his head slowly. 'It is a very valuable piece your girl here discovered. Over three hundred thousand *Reichsmarks*, I am told. You are dismissed.' He shouts for the guard to return.

Yodel holds his ground. 'You will recall the second matter we discussed?'

'Do not tax my patience, *kapo*. Neither my memory nor my obligations require your prompting. As it happens, this KZ is on the list for transportation to Berlin next week. You had best prepare her.'

***

'Come in.'

There is a small room next to the blanket store which Yodel and Mother have made their own. The stone wall is always cold and damp to the touch, but at least the material offcuts stitched together into a carpet take the chill off the floor. Wooden boxes serve as a table and chairs and also as a support to raise the paltry straw mattress from the ground.

Yodel sits forward on one of the boxes with another either side of him. He beckons the girl to sit and calls for his wife to join them. Mother has rolled up her sleeves, tying the material around her forearm as if about to make pastry, just like the girl's own mother used to. For a moment, she can imagine the smell of fresh baked bread.

Yodel smiles with his mouth, but his eyes are sad. 'Did your parents ever talk to you about the way a man and a woman have physical contact?'

The girl doesn't answer.

He tries again. 'Did your mother explain why you bleed every month?'

She looks up. 'I used to bleed. I don't any more, not in the same way.'

'I know, but did she?'

'No. She said my time would come.'

'And your father?'

'He is a very private man. He never talks of intimate things.'

'And in the ghetto or in here? What have you learnt?'

18

There is an anxious look on her face. She shrugs her shoulders. 'The women talk. Some have had experiences and tell of things before the tears come. Some things I understand; some things I pretend to understand and laugh if they laugh, look sad if they look sad.'

'After tomorrow, who knows what will happen to us all? Soon, they will come to take you from here to another place. It is what I want to talk to you about.'

She nods. 'I have heard the guards talk. They call it the Dolls' House. I will be expected to go with men.' It was spoken as a matter of fact.

'I want to make sure you understand from Mother and I, the people who care about you, the difference between having sex and making love. You must never confuse the two.' Yodel stands, releasing the rope tied around his trousers and lowering the long johns to his knees. He manoeuvres his testicles and penis as far forward as he can between his open legs.

The girl looks fleetingly at Mother's expression which displays no reaction. Her cheeks are burning as she turns her face to the wall.

'Have you seen this before, Rita?'

She shakes her head, keeping her gaze fixed on the wall.

'Never?' He waits. 'Answer me. I asked you a question.'

'I opened the door once when my father was dressing. He was very angry.'

'Is that all? Turn around and look at me, please.'

'I used to change Josef's napkin, if that counts.' Her eyes meet his.

'Look at where my finger is pointing. Look, I said. That's better.'

Her face is crimson, but he can tell she is starting to become intrigued.

'Do not be embarrassed and do not resist. Do you know God played a joke on us humans? He put the sexual and reproductive tools we humans use in the same place as the parts of our body we use to rid ourselves of waste material. Mischievous, wasn't it? Tell me, what is this part called?'

She glances at Mother for reassurance but gets none. 'A penis.'

'Good. Now touch it.'

She hesitates.

'I told you to touch it!'

Gingerly, her hand moves forward and her index finger brushes the flaccid flesh.

'Leave it there. What does it feel like? Speak. The first thing that comes into your head.'

She looks at Mother's bare arms and remembers. 'Like the bread dough that Malka used to make.'

'Bread dough, that's good. Now, all men have one of these. Circumcision is demanded by our faith, so we have this hat arrangement at the top, but most of the men you will meet do not. Their bread dough goes from top to bottom. When a man is not aroused, the bread dough sits happily on top of the two little cakes, shall we call them?'

He adjusts his sitting position on the box. 'Now, Mother, if you please.'

Mother smiles at him and plants the softest of kisses on his lips. Her hand fixes around his penis which distends almost immediately and remains rigid as she gently holds it between her fingers.

'Rita! Watch, please. Two things have now happened. The first is my body feeling a physical urge, the basic animal need in us all to reproduce. So, my penis becomes firm. The second is that because I am in love with the person who has sexually aroused me, the urge I feel is positive and healthy, full of my love in return. Feel it, please.'

Mother guides the girl's hand to grip tight.

'Now, what does it feel like? Don't look away. Your face is the colour of red cabbage.' He laughs to relieve the tension. 'Come on. Don't think about it. Tell me what it feels like.'

She looks steadfastly into his eyes. 'A piece of hot iron like father used to use on the fire.'

'Good. Let's call it the barrel of a gun, because the sex act will end for you when the man fires his sperm. Now listen, this is the most important thing I will ever tell you. You will not feel love for any of the men who come to you, or they for you. Sex without love can be harsh and brutal. You will be there simply to serve their sexual desires and fantasies. Soldiers play a rough game, and you will be treated as an object to relieve their frustrations. Remember what I tell you: sex without love is meaningless. The result will be washed away like the waste from your body. All you are

20

dealing with is a ball of bread dough and, when it is inside you, nothing more than the barrel of a revolver with no sense or feeling for you. Do you understand?'

She nods, still holding his gaze, her lips pressed tightly together.

'There will be days, many days, when you feel despair; times when you feel you cannot carry on. Although Mother and I will not be with you, we will talk to you inside your head, and you with us. Always think to yourself, what would Yodel do? What would Mother say? Cling to life as hard as you can. Let the hatred and the war of others wash over you. Always move on until tomorrow, because one day that special tomorrow will finally come when all this suffering and misery will be over. Someday, Rita will know happiness.'

THREE
POTULICE CONCENTRATION CAMP, POLAND
September 1944

So, the rumour is true. The camp at Poznan is closing. Most have already left. The place is like a mausoleum; hardly a sound can be heard. No longer the gentle hum of the generators pacing their daily existence. No longer the sadistic laughter of the guards as they force their captives to heave boulders up the stairway of death, only to knock the heavy load from bleeding hands as the lost souls clamber to the top and are, once again, commanded to repeat the ordeal. No longer the cries and prayers of the condemned, now; just the constant reminder of death from the nauseous stench of rotting bodies dumped into the trenches just beyond the compound.

The fifty or so workers who manned the rag room will be the last to leave. With heads bowed, they stand aimlessly around the lorry waiting for the guard to drop the tailgate. Alongside, the stock and machinery is packed, ready for shipment. Word has it that the two vehicles parked alongside the perimeter wall and covered by tarpaulins are the *einsatzwagens*, the mobile gas chambers.

Yodel and Mother stand apart from the main group, their possessions wrapped in two bundles. It is not cold, yet Yodel stamps from one foot to the other; his expression, a fixed smile, conveys nothing. The girl stands facing him, her eyes pleading, moving to Mother and back to Yodel, waiting for a sign that does not come.

'You will remember everything I told you?' Yodel prompts.

Tears well in her eyes. 'Why can't I come? What did I do wrong? Was it when he gave me the letter?' She pats the pocket of her apron where she guards her father's words. 'Was I wrong to want to ask about my mother?'

Yodel takes her hand. 'No. You have done nothing wrong. The commandant has saved you from the Dolls' House. You will stay here with him and when he goes, you will go too. Perhaps we will be together again in another place.'

'Am I to love him?' There is fear in her voice.

23

'Remember what I told you. There is no love. I doubt he is capable. He will have needs and you will provide them. That is all, just like we told you. Do not ask for favours, news about your family. He is not a postman. He is our enemy and very dangerous, more so now than ever, because we know something about him that is a secret from the rest of the world. He will see this as a weakness in his armour, and if we try to use it against him for our own advantage, he will crush us like flies.' He pats her on the head. 'Be thankful for your father's letter. Cherish his words and pray to God we live through this hell.'

The two guards march purposefully towards the group. One grabs the girl by the arm and starts to lead her away. She starts to resist, but Yodel frowns his disapproval. He mouths a kiss, blowing it towards her, and turns sharply towards Mother, a hand covering his eyes. 'We will start a new adventure, Mother,' he says. 'Probably at another rag room in another city. God give us strength.'

These are the last words she will hear Yodel speak. The guards are talking as they lead her back to the commandant's quarters. One laughs as he turns and watches the group bundled into the lorry. His companion says something about being a good deal more comfortable in the lorry than they will be when they arrive at Chelmno. Their fate is sealed.

Yodel and Mother; this girl will never forget you.

***

Next, comes the sound of children. Not playing, excited, happy, expectant; voices unsure, hesitant, scared and abandoned. Where is her brother now?

They used to sound like children should, she and Josef. He is hiding and she is coming to look for him. Of course, as he is almost five years her junior, they cannot play proper hide-and-seek. He will choose one of the five places he always goes to, and when she finds him, she will tickle his stomach until, amidst his giggles, he pleads for her to stop. That is, until the last time. The men come to take them from the ghetto. The tickling stops. Josef wets himself. Then, she makes him hide for real. She knows a place between the cellar steps and the landing floor. Provided he holds his hands out in front of him, he can just manage to slide in.

Their father whispers to him. Wait until night comes. Find Rabbi Zanvil. He will look after him until his parents return. Josef will be safe. Was it not the rabbi who had warned her father to send Josef away? With the sickness in his lungs, the boy's chance of survival in a German camp was very bleak. She did not understand 'bleak' then, but she does now.

The commandant who took her away from Yodel and Mother is in charge of this place. She heard one of the *Helferin* describe Potulice as a *dreckloch*. She must be lucky. In the corner of the tiny room in which she is held is a toilet made of tin, just like the one they had at home. She does not have to shit in a hole. The *Helferin* laughs at her. The woman is fat with black hairs on her chin. She spits as she talks. Why Kirchner wants such a simple girl, the woman cannot understand. There are better things to be doing in a war than watching over some little bitch waiting for intimacy training.

There is a small window in the room, facing the central square where the work brigades assemble every morning at dawn and are discharged at sunset, just after the punishments are meted out. None of the children who line up every day ever laugh. They are too afraid. Day in, day out, they are forced to carry heavy loads, stones, cement, building materials, until their hands are red raw. Beaten if they plead for food, they are forced to stand in bare feet for hours as the rain pours, waiting for the commandant to attend the roll call. He shows no regard, no pity, no compassion. The boys who stole the potatoes must have been hungry. She watches along with all the children as the guards are ordered to beat them and drive red-hot pokers through their hands. The *Helferin* says it will teach them not to steal again.

Once a week, the lorry arrives to bring the women to the camp. This is her favourite time, when Tillie comes to visit, maybe for as long as an hour before she has to go and 'attend to the miserable bastards with their smelly bums'. Matylda, or Tillie, as she insists on being called, has been ordered to instruct her in the art of satisfying a man, to teach her the tricks of the trade, as she calls them. Not only does Tillie describe and play-act every manoeuvre with a subtlety and skill that she can only watch in amazement, but with a sense of humour which, for the first time as long as she can remember, makes the girl laugh out loud. She must promise, cross her heart, never to repeat anything Tillie says to her.

'If you can learn how to handle men, their weaknesses, the chinks in their make-believe armour, being a whore in wartime is not such a bad deal as many a poor sod would have you believe.' She strokes the girl's matted, unwashed hair. 'I have a theory why men go to war. Do you want to know?'

Of course she did. Anything Tillie had to say was gold dust.

'They go to war to re-establish their authority over women. During peacetime, women gradually begin to gain control, to deal with a man's pathetic excuses, handle the domestic finances, twist him around their little finger and apply the capacity for emotional blackmail with which all women are born. Just before he accepts the surrender to our superiority, a sixth sense tells him to pick a fight with someone weaker so that he can tell us, the female of the species, to crawl back into our shells whilst they go off and play with their guns. Once again, men rule and we are reduced to below waist level, obliged to worship their cocks as we pretend to be Cleopatra to their Mark Antony.'

'You know a lot of words I don't understand, don't you, Tillie?'

'Not enough to keep me out of this war. I was a university student in Warsaw, looking forward to becoming a doctor one day and curing the world, but I had the misfortune to have a grandmother who was born a Jew. As my purity is now in doubt, I hope I infect the whole fucking lot of them.'

It is as she is waiting for Tillie to arrive, just as the sun is setting, that she finds herself studying the faces of the two boys who are about to be punished in the square. Their hands and mouths are stained red from the berries they have eaten whilst on harvesting detail outside the camp. All the inmates are summoned to watch. First, comes a beating with a leather horsewhip; then, a red-hot iron is branded onto the first boy's leg. He screams for his mother and father before collapsing unconscious onto the ground. Yet the second boy stares at his aggressor as he receives his punishment, his body barely faltering as blood seeps from the wound.

She knows the boy from somewhere. An image of his face, stoic and unbowed, plays on her mind. As Tillie enters the room, the memory comes flooding back. This is the boy whose magnificent bar mitzvah she attended at the synagogue ... when was it? The spring of 1939. This is Malik Wiesel. His family is very important. Something to do with the railways, she remembers. Her father made shoes for Malik's father and uncle. He would

26

speak of how important the family was, building locomotives and carriages, describing enthusiastically their properties and riches. How come such a boy is here, in this place, accepting such cruel punishment without speaking a word? She poses the question to Tillie.

A shrug of the shoulders. 'Strange things happen in wars and all sorts of people get caught in the confusion. Probably in the wrong place at the wrong time and got rounded up. He wouldn't want to let on who he really was in case he brought his family into focus and under suspicion. I doubt his parents even know he is here. Money can buy lots of things, but sometimes all the money in the world can do no good at all.'

Tillie is not in such a good mood today. The girl has never seen her so short-tempered, the atmosphere between them tense and far more subdued than normal. Eventually, Tillie vents her frustration. Her baby is unwell, probably a sickness caught from the old woman in the ghetto who cares for the infant at night and never stops coughing. She needs to appeal to the commandant to spare her for one or two days and let her comfort her daughter. There has to be a way.

The girl listens open-mouthed. There can only be six or seven years between their ages, yet there is a lifetime of experience and hardship between them. There is a baby to consider. How come? Who would consider bringing a child into this world in the midst of all this suffering and hate? She has a burning desire to ask questions, to know who and why, yet she is afraid to delve into Tillie's world for fear of provoking that volatile temper. Her Tillie is the quick-witted, self-confident optimist who brings humour and irreverence into her scared little girl existence; not a fragile, vulnerable woman like all the others who traipsed through the rag shop, scarred and defeated.

'Why not bring your baby in here? I'll look after her. I'm good with babies.'

A mixture of anger and fear flares up in Tillie's face. 'Are you really that stupid or just totally naïve? Have you learnt nothing from me?'

'I don't understand,' the girl stammers.

'Think about it. If my baby once entered this camp, she would never leave alive. Any living creature unable to work is useless to them, a liability and disposable in the blink of an eye. You would do well to remember this

27

for your own good. Right now, you're Kirchner's Christmas present, his promise for the future. He holds you out at arm's length like the promise of a fine cognac he has yet to taste. He fantasises about the pleasure it will give him, just as he does you, the virgin maiden whose only role in life is to satisfy his imagination.'

'You said "my own good"?'

Tillie's mood softens. She grasps the girl's shoulders. 'Listen, Rita, his fantasy will pass. Unless you play your cards right, in a day, a week, you will be the same as me – just another whore. Your survival will depend on the ability to keep him interested.'

'How do I do that?'

'I can't give you any guarantees. Men are men, good and bad, but all soldiers fighting a war are bastards. Your hope is to remember everything I have taught you. Every trick you have learnt is a card in your hand. You have all the cards facing you so he cannot see them. You play one and wait. When he has seen that card, you play the next and so on, until you have shown him all of your cards. All you can do then is read his mind, understand what cards he reacts to best and vary your play: today, this one; tomorrow, another; maybe two at once. Keep him interested, on tenterhooks, never knowing what to expect. Above all, get to know and understand him, his gestures, his likes and dislikes. Once you get inside his head, there's a good chance you'll stay there long enough to find your own escape route. Do you understand what I'm saying?'

'I think so.'

'As the days pass, show him the person inside you he is looking for. Let him crave the real Rita, an intelligent, bright and inventive girl with a personality he wants as much as the body he takes. He will never show or admit it. That would be a sign of weakness. He will continue to treat you like shit, but you will recognise when the time has come. Just pray that by then the war is over and the bastard is dead and cannot harm you any more.'

The next week, Tillie does not come. When the door opens later that evening, it is the commandant who stands before her. Has the time finally arrived? Is it tonight she must react as Tillie has described? Act naturally, but with self-confidence. Do not be a doll conceding to his every gesture. Tantalise. Suggest, and then delay. Tease a little, but not too much. A hundred instructions course around inside her head, but all she knows at that moment is panic.

But he does not recognise the fear in her eyes. He holds her arms firmly to her side and pushes her backwards to sit in a chair. Does she start to make some suggestive advances? Imagine it's Tillie who is holding her down and play the role she has been taught.

He backs off and stands, studying her features, a smile crossing his thin lips. He starts to laugh. 'Not now,' he says. 'I want information, no more. Not tonight. Perhaps tomorrow.'

She looks at him out of the corner of her eye, just like Tillie said to do: 'Give him the occasional sideways glance. It's suggestive.'

He shakes his head. 'You look like some eighteenth-century harlot. Come here.' He pulls her roughly by the neck towards him and kisses her hard, full on the lips.

She remembers lesson six very well. Tillie had kissed her, a long lingering kiss with her tongue moving gently inside the girl's mouth. It had made her downstairs feel all funny. She does as she was taught. The sensation registers in his eyes. It doesn't feel the same as kissing Tillie. Not as nice. He tastes of stale beer and cheese. At least, it's what she remembers cheese tastes like. Look into his eyes, was the instruction. Make it appear you have enjoyed the kiss, then spit it out when he has gone. You would be better off gargling with your own piss than leaving the taste of these animals in your mouth. She banishes the memory as he pulls away to speak.

'Listen, I want you to tell me something. You know one of the boys who was punished in the square last week, don't you?'

It could only be Tillie who told him. She has not mentioned it to another living soul.

'I don't remember.'

'There is nothing to fear. You could help him return to his parents.'

'You talk of Malik. We both studied under Rabbi Zanvil at the synagogue. Malik is three years older than me.'

'You know his parents?'

She nods. 'I met them once. My father makes shoes for them.'

'Ah, yes. Your father.' She senses his hesitation is giving him time to come to a decision. 'You would like to know how he is, I imagine?'

29

Her heart is pounding against the letter which is always pressed close to her chest. 'Could I?' All the breath leaves her body in a long sigh.

'It may be possible. No promises, but you did something for me once. Do you remember? Good. Now, I want you to help Malik see his parents again. You can do this.'

He takes her hand and leads her through the door into his office. 'I will explain to you how it will be.'

FOUR
VEVEY, SWITZERLAND
December 2018

He awoke with a start, instantly aware of the hand resting on his shoulder. The woman in the starched white uniform took a hasty step back, shocked at his sudden movement. Some of the pages he had been reading slid off his lap onto the floor. He hastily retrieved them and shuffled the pack back into the document case.

'Sorry, I must have nodded off,' Marchal said. 'Have I been asleep long?'

The woman ignored his question. 'You know, we do have guest bedrooms. It is only necessary for madame to ask and we can accommodate you.'

'I arrived late. Nobody apart from the concierge was around.'

'Quite so. Madame has very individualistic habits and requirements. She prefers to remaining awake at night and sleeping into the morning. I have to tell you she is now able to receive you in her room. I will accompany you. She has asked that breakfast be provided for you, although, quite frankly' – she looked at the fob watch pinned to her pinafore – 'at this hour ...'

'Thank you. Most kind. I am hungry.'

Madame's room was more a suite than a bedroom – Marchal put it in the executive suite, five-star hotel category. 'This is the most upmarket nursing home I could ever imagine,' he said, a whistle in his voice. 'It must cost a small fortune to stay here.'

The old lady was propped up in an armchair, her legs and lower body covered by a rug in a muted tartan design. Somebody had decorated her with a jet-black wig and made her up with mascara eyeliner, a pallid white foundation, and ruby lipstick that extended beyond the line of her lips. Her eyes followed him as he made his way to the settee next to her.

'You don't approve,' she said, her voice stronger than on the previous night.

'To be honest, I prefer the natural look. I hope you're not offended.'

31

'I meant about staying in a high-class nursing home, but you obviously reacted to what is uppermost in your mind. You speak as if you intend to defer with smooth innuendoes to my age and physical condition. I'd rather you didn't. It doesn't suit your personality. You were a policeman, you told me. Presumably, you have a tough, no-nonsense streak?'

'I had. My grandchildren are knocking it out of me, I think.'

'I doubt that.' She held up her hand whilst she coughed. 'As to my luxury accommodation, I invested in a founder's bond when they were building the place. The quid pro quo is they look after me until I pass on.'

'And the make-up? Is there a reason for that?'

'Of course—' A knock on the door announced the arrival of a young Asian waiter with a tray comprising a continental-style breakfast which was set down beside Marchal.

'Is that satisfactory?' the old lady asked, watching the door close behind the waiter as he left.

'Better than I get at home, by a long way.' He started on the orange juice and exotic fruit cocktail. 'You were saying?'

'I've forgotten. Oh, yes, the make-up. We are expecting visitors, maybe today, maybe tomorrow. They will be coming for a certain document.' She pointed to the document couched in his arm. 'If they read that, I don't want them to see me as a demure, nondescript old lady. They have another image of me. I don't want to disappoint them. I was branded many years ago as a malevolent sadist, capable of the most heinous crimes. The least I can do is to project the persona of some fucking evil old hag. By the look on your face as you came in, I have certainly succeeded.'

'I promised my partner I would look after you until he arrives. He will have a plan, I'm sure. In the meantime, I will see no harm comes to either of us.'

'You are the purveyor of the harm. They follow René Marchal to seek me out. And when they do? You are one and they are many, and they desperately want the document they assume is in that case.' She smiled. 'It may well be beyond your power to stop them.'

'I'll do my best. Who are these people you talk of?'

'How much did you read?'

'You are still young and innocent when I fell asleep.'

32

'The girl, you mean. Was she ever young and innocent? I don't recall the instant, for that's all it could have been.' She was lost in thought. 'Oh, yes, your question. You will read about them. They call themselves *Der Kreis* – The Circle. The faces change, but just like a circle, there is no beginning, no end.'

'And the pages I am reading could harm this Circle?'

A shaking hand pulled up the tartan rug that had slipped from her lap. 'My story simply tells the truth, a truth to put everything right for me and, in the process, expose the evils I have witnessed. Others will be prepared to sacrifice both our lives and, perhaps, theirs, to see this truth die with us.'

She smiled, a grotesque smile. Lipstick the colour of venous blood was smudged across her teeth.

'One aspect of your writing intrigues me,' he said. 'You write of yourself in the third person, "the girl" or "she", rather than adopting the narrative as your own. Why is that?'

'Because I don't recognise that girl as me, a precursor to the woman I became. Her attitudes, her actions, are so foreign to me now. I see her as a stranger, a person full of disruptive emotions, capable of foolhardy acts without regard to her own safety. She was lucky to survive. What came afterwards was a woman bereft of the capacity to feel close to any living soul, unable to relish the one emotion so precious to our species: the ability to love.'

'You are saying the woman talking to me now cannot relate to the girl she once was?'

'She knew how to love. I do not.'

FIVE
POTULICE CONCENTRATION CAMP, POLAND
September 1944

He pulls at the skirt of her new dress to straighten the hem and twirls her around, holding her hands above her head. 'Do you like your new clothes?' A smile briefly crosses his lips.

The girl nods. The dress and petticoat may be new to her, but they belonged until recently to someone called Berta, the name stitched into the material just below the collar. She wonders where Berta is now. As her mind dwells fleetingly on the answer, he starts to talk again, repeating once more the instructions she has heard a dozen times before. Wait for it; here comes the threat.

'Do not even think about trying to run away. I will catch you for sure and make you watch as I put your father to death. You will do anything to avoid that happening, won't you?' The grip on her arms tightens as he waits for her to raise her bowed head and nod.

He still hasn't touched her. At least, not in the way Tillie said he would. Apart from that one rough kiss, he has resisted her, turning away whenever she sees the look in his eyes that says he has the urge. It's as though he's saving the experience for a day when his mind is in tune with the lump in his trousers. Somehow, she can tell he wants it to be special.

Malik also has new clothes and is strangely clean. He stands to attention in front of the commandant and looks handsome. She had expected to see him with a mouth stained red from the berries he had eaten and signs of the bruises suffered from the beating he had taken. That was two weeks ago. Why does she think his mouth would still show traces of his crime? Perhaps, she accepts, in this place the victims bear the marks of their suffering and punishment for ever as a matter of course.

They listen intently as the commandant explains the task before them. Malik is only handsome on the outside. Unusually for somebody living on their meagre rations, his body is muscular and he is tall with short, curly mid-brown hair. They must have soaped and hosed him down, for his hair is no longer matted with blood and dirt. The shape of his head reminds her of three sides of a rectangle, a figure she recalls from lessons at the village school a lifetime ago. From the cheeks down, his face tapers into a more pointed chin. With those full lips and the shallow eyes with the permanent sad look, Tillie would have said he had a sensuous appeal. But she sees something else. Behind the placid expression, there is a callous and ruthless countenance with a barely disguised arrogance he does well to hide from the commandant.

Of course, a young and inexperienced girl cannot put into words the description she has just given. She has a feeling, an impression of what a person is like, and the words come later as the weight of experience and understanding provide the means of expression. But it is right to tell everything about Malik because her fate and his will forever be intertwined.

The expressions of the boys and girls on work detail waiting in the yard are a mix of confusion and amazement. The girl and Malik are led to a saloon car where a portly driver in baggy civilian clothes ushers them into the rear seats. She is confused and apprehensive, not at what is happening at that surreal moment or the importance of the task ahead, but at the attitude displayed just now by Malik in the commandant's office. After one final recital of their orders, he waves them away. As Malik reaches the door, he turns, attempts to click the heels of his soft-soled shoes together and thrusts his right arm forward. 'Heil Hitler,' he shouts. She steps past him, her eyes transfixed on the soulless expression on his face. It is inconceivable to imagine an inmate making such a gesture, even in mockery, let alone somebody who has been badly beaten in the name of the oppressor he now salutes.

As the car makes its way slowly south on pot-holed roads to begin its one-hundred-kilometre journey to Poznan, he stares straight ahead and says little in answer to her questions. It's as though he wants to ignore her presence altogether.

'How old are you?'

'Sixteen.'

'How did you come to end up in the camp?'

'They caught me trying to escape from the ghetto.'

'Why did they not know your name?'

'I gave a false one. My papers were forged.'

'Why?'

36

'You ask too many questions. Why don't you shut up?'

'I won't. I asked you why.'

He grits his teeth. 'You're stupid. My family planned my escape. I will not let them suffer.'

'Don't you remember me? I was at your bar mitzvah. My father makes shoes for your family.'

He turns his head slowly towards her, his mouth twisted as if he had just tasted sour milk. 'I do not know you and I do not want to. As far as we in the camp are concerned, you are just a Jew whore, one of the bitches who lies and cheats on their own kind and gives her body so that she can stay alive. You would be better off dead.' He looks away, seemingly offended by the sight of her.

The driver gives an amused chuckle.

'You are right about one thing and one thing only, Malik Wiesel.' There is both anger and distress in her voice. 'You do not know me, you, with your fancy heel-clicking and Jew-hating salute.'

They sit in a hostile silence until the car reaches its destination, trundling slowly along the cobbled streets of a silent Poznan towards the ghetto. The journey takes five hours. On two occasions, they are halted at checkpoints, the driver's documents and authorisation meticulously checked before the two passengers are subjected to a rough body search by bad-tempered *kapos*.

The driver eventually brings the car to a stop at the southern end of the ghetto alongside a row of two-storey terraced houses out of keeping with the endless blocks of tenement buildings they passed on the way in. Surely this cannot be the place, she thinks.

An old lady in a blue housecoat is brushing the front step. She chances a glance at the official-looking car as she pretends to adjust the tie around her waist. The driver orders them to get out. The woman fishes for a pair of glasses in her pocket, straining as she does so to see who is approaching. The brush falls from her hand and she screams.

The girl is ignored as a cluster of people emerge from along the street to embrace and fuss around Malik. Tears of joy, sounds of 'We never thought we would see you again' or the more positive 'I always knew you were safe and would come back to us' fill the evening air. She knows religion was bound to rear its head. 'God has spoken and delivered our son back to his family,' recites the old lady who had first spotted her grandson.

'Your god, maybe,' the girl says to herself. 'If I had a god, my Josef would be here next to me.'

Jealousy tugs at her heart as, still unannounced and irrelevant to the homecoming, she follows the group back into the house. Oh, that this were her home and these were her relatives welcoming her back. She thinks of her father. She is doing this for him. She must succeed.

They are all gathered in a first-floor room with high ceilings and tall windows. The walls may be unpainted and missing plaster in some areas; the floorboards may be bare with gaps between the joints; this house may be in the ghetto, yet it is more splendid than any in which she or any of her relatives has ever lived.

An attractive woman of around her mother's age breaks away from the group and walks towards her, arms extended. 'And who are you, my child? What brings you here with Malik, little one?'

The girl is confused. She looks around to see if there is, in fact, a child standing behind her. No, the woman is addressing her.

Malik approaches before she can answer. 'Where is Father?'

The woman turns and smiles, her long jet-black hair obscuring one side of her face as she does so. She is very beautiful. 'They will bring him back soon. He goes to the factory every day. They need him.'

Malik coughs. 'This is Rita Krakowski.' He breathes in deeply. The girl knows he is readying the script in which they had both been thoroughly versed by the commandant. 'I would prefer Father were here with you and we had some privacy before you hear our story.'

His mother is confused, the girl can tell, and goes to speak but thinks better of it and simply smiles an acknowledgement. She even sets about reassuring family members and friends as they disburse that they will be brought up to date with Malik's news as soon as he has had a chance to speak with his father. Everyone is sensitive to the proximity of the daily curfew and the dangers of being on the streets once the patrols are underway. Within minutes the large room is empty but for the girl, Malik, his mother and grandmother.

For almost an hour and well into the curfew, the four sit and make small talk, Malik and his mother holding hands on a worn sofa, the grandmother, her legs covered in a blanket, moving to and fro in an old rocking chair. Her eyes rarely leave the girl's face, watching every expression as if she expects the answers to a hundred unspoken questions which pollute the atmosphere. They talk of Malik's bar mitzvah, but not of the people present. Asking how is X or where is Y can do nothing but provoke sad and awkward silences as they search their minds for other topics, but there are none to speak of which avoid arriving at the same horrific dead end. And so, they stay in an aura of forced silence, waiting for someone to break the spell.

Malik's sister has tired of playing chords on an upright piano in the adjoining room. Just as well, the girl thinks. The discordant sound of a novice incessantly repeating the same thing on an out-of-tune piano is like torture, except nobody else appears to notice or take exception to the ghastly noise.

Yetta Eliza plays piano so well for a girl who is just seven, her mother announces, placing the child strategically between herself and Malik. Yetta stands there like a doll, with a porcelain white face, bows in her hair and dressed in a stained and dirty silk party dress. She is still pouting, a sour expression to tell everyone, for the first time in the four months since Malik left, she is not the centre of attention. She seems confused rather than happy to see her brother home again.

The girl looks longingly through the open doorway at the aged upright piano. How come a piano? Nothing in this house fits in the world in which she is trying to survive. It is years since she was able to practice her scales on the piano used to accompany the ladies on the Shabbat when they sang the *zemirot* for the townsfolk to enjoy. Father had promised that one day, when they were rich and everybody wanted to buy his shoes, she would have her own piano.

Nothing fits any more.

Malik's father arrives after the curfew in a car with a swastika painted on the door. He is like her commandant. Did she say 'her'? She meant 'the'. Not in looks; they are very different in appearance, but in the way they both take charge of a room the moment they walk in. They both show no emotion, no feelings, just the need to be in control. To simply shake Malik's hand and tell him he looks well as if he had last seen his son that morning on his way to work is heartless and explains why his son acts so abruptly and appears so cold. He greets Magda, his wife, with respect but no affection, and her mother with a cursory nod. Yet, when Yetta launches herself into his arms, he melts, cuddling and caressing her, smiling and whispering in her ear.

Lew Wiesel is shorter than the commandant, with dark brown hair, cropped and severely trimmed around the ears. Unlike the commandant, he wears thick-rimmed glasses, but their eyes are very similar, blue and piercing with the tendency to stare, as if into a void, and to frighten in the process.

Malik's father is much older than the commandant and likes to talk about himself. He is respected by his German counterparts and was surprised he was not informed his son was being held in Potulice. When Malik failed to make contact, he strongly suspected the boy had been captured and he began to make some discreet enquiries, as he put it. He made it sound as casual as booking seats on a train rather than a paternal urge to protect his offspring, and nods benignly as Malik explains how he used his forged identity papers to ensure his family were not implicated.

Magda suggests they carry on talking over their evening meal. It's a stew of sorts, the remnants of some meat from an earlier meal and a few root vegetables in a watery stock. Every mouthful is eaten.

Malik's father has been patient, just like the commandant. Apart from shaking the girl's hand when he arrived and asking her name with the merest bow of his head as he did so, he has said nothing to her, nor asked how they came to be there. He wipes his mouth with a cloth napkin and looks from one to the other. 'I am intrigued,' he says. 'People go into the camps. They do not come out, especially in chauffeur-driven cars. Do tell me how you have managed to achieve such a feat.'

Malik glances at his mother and raises his eyebrows. She mutters something about the dishes and putting Yetta to bed, and ushers her mother and daughter out of the room.

'Commandant Kirchner is in charge of the work camp at Potulice,' Malik says. 'Rita Krakowski is his woman. Indirectly, she is responsible for revealing my true identity and, indirectly, the reason why I am back with you today.' He is speaking so softly, it is hard for her to believe he is play-acting.

'I don't know whether that means I should be grateful or not.' For the first time, Malik's father looks critically at her. 'In what context exactly are you his woman? You are but a slip of a girl.'

'I am nearly fifteen and a Jew whore.' She transfers her stare from father to son. 'I was to be transferred to the Dolls' House – you know what that is, don't you?' The father bows his head. 'Commandant Kirchner ordered that I be reserved for him, and I live in a storeroom next to his quarters.'

'I see.'

'No, you do not see, Herr Wiesel,' she retorts. 'I had no choice in the matter, but it gives me food and drink, more than is available to Malik and his brethren.' The commandant had said this tone would start to gain her some respect and credibility, and he appears to be right. She would press her advantage.

'I recognised Malik when he was being punished for eating the berries he had been picking. I mentioned it to someone who told the commandant. When he asked me, I told him Malik's family had been wealthy. He said they would probably know where to find the money to ensure his safety in the future.'

Lew Wiesel shakes his head in disbelief. 'You told him this? Why? We have nothing now but our name.' He falls silent and appears to study the floor. 'What does "safety in the future" mean?' he asks, eventually.

'You must ask him yourself. We are messengers and cannot know his intentions. It may mean escape to another country where there is no war against the Jews. I can only guess.'

There is no sign of emotion on Malik's face. He says nothing.

'How could I ask him myself? We are all captives in one way or another. I have no freedom of movement beyond the ghetto and the factory gates.'

'You are an important man in running the railways, I understand.' She continues without waiting for confirmation. 'The commandant cannot seek you out. It is too dangerous and he would not take the risk. He will make a written request to Railway Command asking for attention to a problem with the rail cars in the sidings at Potulice. You will intercept the request and suggest you go to the camp to resolve the problem. Tell me how to phrase the wording so that you are seen as the person best placed to deal with the matter. You can do that?'

'Possibly.'

'When you are there, you can speak freely with him.'

There are creases in his forehead. 'These are not your words, are they? You are too young to talk in such a way. I find it difficult to take you seriously.'

As clever as Malik's father must be, she has a grudging admiration for the commandant. He calculated all the possible avenues this conversation could have taken and prepared a response for each. 'I am young, I know, but I left my memories of childhood a long time ago and I face the prospect of death every day if I, like Malik, cease to be of use to our captors. If the messenger has no pen, no paper, he must rely on a good memory. Does that satisfy you?'

They will put a mattress on the floor in Yetta's bedroom. The girl can sleep there tonight. Tomorrow, they will talk again.

Magda puts an arm around her shoulder as she is ushered into the room. Closing her eyes tight and concentrating, she can imagine it is her father's arm.

'I am sorry about Yetta,' Magda says. 'She sings herself to sleep. She is very musical with a strong voice. Just tell her to be quiet if you can't get to sleep.'

But she doesn't. Yetta does have a lovely voice, sweet and innocent. She sings in German. The music is so powerful and the girl has heard it before, somewhere locked in her memory. The next morning, she asks Magda. It is a piece Yetta is learning at her Germanisation classes, from a poem by Friedrich Schiller based on Beethoven's Ninth Symphony and called 'Ode to Joy'. She smiles. It is so appropriate. Malik has come home to them and they are joyful. Magda doesn't realise because Malik hasn't told her. Tomorrow, they must return to Potulice.

Malik's father asks her many questions, to all of which she can only give one answer: 'Only the commandant can tell you what you want to know.' The repetition starts to annoy him. 'Has your commandant considered I might go to his superiors and denounce his plan?'

She had been told he might say something like this and knows exactly how to reply. 'He will deny it and shame you by describing Malik's presence here as a gesture of his goodwill. When he found out who Malik really was, he considered it might help the war effort if he made the gesture. Malik and I are bound to confirm the story if we value our lives. But I know it will only be a temporary respite. If we are unable to convince you, we will have failed. The commandant has no powers to release your boy, and we serve no further purpose.' She lets the last sentence hang in the air.

'I see,' he says softly.

'Do you? Malik has admitted his family were complicit in his attempt to escape from the ghetto. They would have to be dealt with accordingly.'

'Your commandant leaves me little option.'

'It may all turn out for the better as far as Malik is concerned.'

Another day passes and now the women of the household are beside themselves with sadness. Malik has told them he has to return the following day to Potulice. He understands this and accepts it. Besides, to flee would be futile. They would capture and bring him back for execution in front of all the inmates, his body fed to the pigs. Malik knows the commandant's intention was always to give his family the shortest and sweetest taste of a reunion, to create a longing so great that when he was taken from them, there would be intense pressure on his father to do anything to secure the boy's safety. The commandant knows how to manipulate people and get what he wants. Look how he controls the girl.

She has no sympathy for the older women, wailing and moaning as if Malik were dead. Why cry when there is a real prospect the boy will survive in another, safer land? Oh that Josef and her father were in the same position. Her tears would be tears of joy.

Yetta is better company. She acts as if she is oblivious to everything and everybody whenever no attention is paid to her. Does Yetta mind if she joins her at the piano? Yetta places a piece of music on the rack and she tries to keep up, her fingers fumbling over the keys. Both frustrated at herself and annoyed with Yetta for laughing, she stops, grabs the child by the shoulders and pulls her roughly towards her. She hisses in Polish, 'You may be a talented child, but you are still a Jewess living in a cocoon that will disappear when you have to face the fate we all suffer.'

Yetta has understood nothing. There are tears in those fearful eyes, her porcelain chin quivering. 'You're hurting me. Don't you like me any more?'

The girl turns around to find Malik watching them from the doorway.

The next day, Malik and the girl are sitting together on the sofa, waiting for the transport to arrive. From somewhere, Malik has found some precious sheets of paper and a pencil. She watches as he sketches the face of a man with a moustache and deep-set staring eyes. He is very good. The image is so lifelike, the shadows accentuating the smile lines around a nose with flared nostrils and a thin top lip.

'You should be an artist,' she says. 'I wish I had such talents.'

He turns and looks into her eyes, his head tilted as if trying to reach a decision. For the first time, she realises that although his eyes are hazel, one has a distinct ring of blue circling the pupil, very precise when close up, but losing its effect as she moves back.

He still has a funny look. 'What's wrong?' she says.

He shakes his head. 'You must have many talents,' he says.

The women are away from the house on laundry duty. As she had foreseen, it was a tearful goodbye. Yetta is at her Germanisation class. Herr Wiesel shook his son's hand when he left for work this morning; no emotion, just a final nod of the head as if to say he would make it right.

Malik rounds on her, his chest heaving as he blurts out the words. 'Today, I am the commandant.' He grabs her forcibly by the waist, pushing her close to him. 'And you are my Jewess whore.' His hands move to her hair and he thrusts his lips hard against hers.

Her first thought is a curious one. Rather than resent the assault, she realises he is not using his tongue in the same penetrating way the commandant did. Instead, it is wiggling about frantically like a fish on the end of a line. She reacts as he forces his hand inside her skirt, tearing at the petticoat and the thigh-length knickers Magda had given her. He pulls them down around her knees, causing her to fall back onto the bare floorboards. Winded, she cries, imploring him to stop as she feels his flesh upon hers. But he is much stronger, pinning her to the floor with one hand as he finally releases the buttons on his trousers, his penis thrusting wildly as he tries to enter. It's like Yodel's and his words fill her head. It is only the barrel of a gun steadying to fire its bullets.

With his knees he forces her legs further apart, releasing one of the arms pressed to the floor. She is gasping for breath. One last effort, a clawed hand tears at the flesh on his cheek, but the blow knocks her almost senseless. Remember Tillie's words, she thinks. Do not resist. It will hurt even more. If you make it nice for them, the bastards come quicker and it's all over. So, she stops her resistance and moves into him. Sure enough, after ten seconds of pushing and gasping comes a long moan as she feels the three quick spasms inside her. He retreats from her, wiping the saliva from his mouth and shuffling what is now an image of Yodel's bread dough back into his trousers.

Neither speaks on the way back to the camp. He folds the sketch of the man's face into a small square of paper and hands it to her without looking. She tries to pass it back. She wants nothing from him, but his hand is clasped around hers, tight, hurting, so that she cannot let go of the paper. What's the point? There is nothing in her world but sadness and the sensation of his semen seeping out of her into those nice new frilly knickers with the jagged tear down one side.

From that day on, she never sees Malik again.

SIX
POTULICE CONCENTRATION CAMP, POLAND
November 1944

Once the stain of Malik's semen is cleansed from her body, memories of the incident and the boy begin to fade from her mind. She will remain a virgin because to truly lose her maidenhood would mean giving her whole body willingly to somebody whom she is capable of loving. That will never happen, and as Tillie would have told her – where is Tillie now, when she needs her? – she will remain a virgin in her head forever, whatever the acts to which her body is subjected.

The commandant has been in a good mood since she returned from the ghetto. Her expectation grows, but to remind him of her request would be bound to anger him. Why does he delay the meeting with her father she craves so much? Surely, it cannot be long. She considers praying to God, but no sooner is she on her knees with hands clasped than she begins to chide herself for the futility of what she proposes. What does God have to do with this place? Does he listen to the cries of the starving children, shivering as they lie on the straw soiled with the excrement from their own bodies? Does he do anything about the cries of anguish, loneliness and pain? Can he feel their desolation? You have deserted us all, she mouths under her breath. I hate you, you betrayer.

Her prison is the room next to the commandant's office. She spends hours, sometimes whole days, without seeing a living soul. From time to time, the interconnecting door is opened and a hand feeds a plate of thin soup or boiled vegetables onto the floor before the door is closed and locked again. She amuses herself, sometimes daydreaming, at other times trying to make sense of the snatches of conversation she hears from next door. Her excitement heightens as she recalls a story told by Yetta's grandmother. As a young girl, she had wanted to overhear what her parents were saying in the adjoining bedroom. All she did was put a glass to the wall and her ear to the glass. It really worked, something to do with sound waves, Yetta's grandmother had explained, although she urged caution. There was nothing wrong in being curious about everything, but the time comes when a person loses interest in wondering about the world around them and in learning new things. Now she is old and has heard too much; so much that it hurts. She puts her hand to her heart. Just here, she says.

The girl hides the glass under the bed, afraid that somebody will ask where it is and punish her when she confesses to the deception. But nobody does. A *Helferin* fills her water jug once a day and changes the bucket which she uses as a toilet. Once a week, they make her strip and douse her body with cold water, always boisterously impatient to finish the distasteful chore of attending to the commandant's whore.

There is a voice she recognises in the commandant's office. It is Herr Wiesel, Yetta's father. The glass is soon pressed tight against the wall. Whereas the commandant is talking in his loud and serious voice, Yetta's father is speaking softly, with cautious reserve, nothing like the way he talks in his own home. She has difficulty in making out what he is saying. Several times, she catches the name of his son and references to Yetta, various numbers and the names of people she does not recognise. There is talk of 'Carmo' and 'Lisbon'. Are they family members she has not met? They talk of railways, place names. Sometimes they laugh together, but most of the time the conversation is serious. Two hours pass and she tires of holding the glass against the wall and the sting of the chafing around her ear as she presses hard to make out the words. Finally, they say their goodbyes, friendly and courteous. 'Heil Hitler,' Yetta's father says, only loudly this time.

As the weeks pass, she is sent twice more to the ghetto, both times on her own, always with specific instructions as to how she must act, step-by-step details, repeated and repeated until she is sick of his voice.

The driver takes her to Yetta's house. Magda is waiting for her, arms outstretched, treating her like a favourite daughter with hugs and kisses; such relief and happiness in her face. She looks ten years younger than the girl remembers. Here is the explanation – a photograph of Malik, smiling and relaxed, waving at the camera, dressed in casual clothes, and standing between an elderly couple in front of a grand building with a flag flying from the central spire.

Magda asks if Rita knows where it is. She has no idea. Can she guess? Warsaw? No, silly, spoken with so much laughter in Magda's voice. This is the town hall in Malmo. Where? Sweden. Has she heard of Sweden?

48

Yes, in a hesitant voice. It's far away, isn't it? Across the sea? No, it is not so far. But Sweden is not in the war. It is a neutral country and, more important, Malik is alive and safe and FREEEEEE! The word hangs on her lips until her breath runs out. The old couple work for a refugee agency. They wrote a letter to Magda. As soon as transportation can be arranged, Malik will join his aunt and uncle in Chicago, in America. Can she believe it?

She is taken to another place. These are Magda's friends, Feliks and Irena Gorski. They look sad and anxious, just like Magda used to. Their rooms are not as big as in Magda's house, nor are there so many. Still, hackles of jealousy begin to rise in her. Why should she help them? Feliks might have a factory to smelt aluminium, whatever that is, but what about her father? He is a shoemaker, which is just as important. Soldiers cannot go to war in bare feet.

It seems their daughter, Agata, has been taken to Potulice. They feel it is so unjust. Even if they are trapped inside the ghetto, Agata's parents remain at liberty whilst the child is forced to work and suffer in the camp. Feliks is a thin man who looks grey and ill and talks in a slow, precise way, always with a limp smile on his lips. He seems kind as he gently explains how the children are kept in the camp to ensure the parents, who must strive for the Reich, do not think of themselves and try to escape or work with no purpose. The parents must do everything they are told, or the children will suffer.

He nods understandingly when she tells him her instructions are for Agata's father to come in secret to Potulice to talk about repairs to the railway sidings. Yetta's father will tell him what is involved, but they must come soon. The commandant is very insistent. Time is running out.

Feliks puts his finger to his lip. He will tell her something she must never repeat to another living soul. She remembers Yodel and tells Feliks she has kept promises before. He whispers into her ear. The Germans are losing the war. Men with the power who are able to think and act for themselves are planning to use the confusion that will ensue as the fighting stops to accumulate as much wealth as possible before they plan their escape. Perhaps her commandant thinks this way and, if he does, the girl must start to worry about her own survival if he is no longer there to protect

49

her. His only concern will be his own safety, and should she become a liability, well – Feliks gives a shrug – the solution is simple.

She thinks about what he has said. For Feliks to take the risk of telling her such things, he must believe she, too, is important and must be protected, just like his own daughter.

It has made her see the commandant in a different light. She watches him whenever he comes to her room to kiss and fondle her, looking for the signs of disaffection and rejection, but there are none. He quizzes her on why she looks at him in that fashion. There are no words, but she knows he finds it disarming and uncomfortable. 'What are you looking for?' he asked once. 'Trying to see into my soul?' He still has made no move to take her like Yetta's brother did, but she can sense the time is approaching.

She has been back one last time to the ghetto, this time to speak with Jerzy and Laura Sowka. They treat her with such respect as if she were a queen. They tell a similar story to the others. Here is a photograph of their ten-year-old son, Roman. She recognises the boy from the work detail during daily assembly in the square. His hair and face are filthy now, his eyes permanently red from crying, but she can still tell it is the same smiling and cheeky blonde-haired boy from the creased photograph.

Can she use her influence to help save Roman, like she did for Yetta's brother and Agata? So, Agata made it too, did she? Is there a picture of her smiling face in, where was it? Oh, yes, Sweden. She looks into the pleading faces and yearns to say, 'Fuck Sweden, fuck Agata, fuck Malik, fuck all of you.' That's what Tillie would say. Where is the picture that says 'There is Rita, Josef and her mother and father in Sweden'? Nowhere. Because it does not exist and never will. Instead, she says she will do her best, but they must do something for her commandant.

Laura Sowka is an artist who, before the occupation, owned an important gallery for fine art and antiquities in Warsaw. In a few weeks, she will be summoned to visit the commandant. Next February, it will be the birthday of the Führer's companion, Eva Braun, and Laura is to paint a family portrait from a photograph as a surprise present from the commandant. When she has completed this commission, they will discuss Roman's future.

There is a strange mood around the camp. Not amongst the inmates; for them, nothing changes. They walk, heads cast towards the ground, shunted by short-tempered guards to their allotted workstations in the factories and mines where, for the next fourteen hours, they will slave relentlessly. Most are children, their lives stripped of meaning, every day a painful repetition of the day before. Thankfully, for the good of their own sanity and will to survive, they are unaware that in less than two weeks it will be Christmas, a time of unreal memories of presents and people laughing.

She overhears the mess kitchen staff talking of the Russian advance and what to expect if they do not get out in time. Tales of the atrocities inflicted on the German forces, whether true or exaggerated, are talked of in hushed whispers of dread and amazement, as if somehow of a scale far more excessive than the inhumanities which are practised in this place.

Daylight passes quickly into darkness. She likes the dark, a time of constant, subdued noises, the humming of machinery in the background, so different from the brash, violent sounds of the day. The interconnecting door to his office opens and stays ajar. She can see the table with all the chairs around, so many more than is normal. The blackout curtains have been drawn closed. Will there be an air raid? There have been no sirens.

He stands facing her on the other side of the half-open door, saying nothing, just staring through her. There is something different about him: latent excitement, nervous anticipation. His breathing carries the scent of schnapps as he starts to speak. His tone is threatening. Tonight, for her own good, she must be very quiet. Important people will be coming and he does not want evidence of her presence.

The door is locked and the darkness returns to comfort her, to let her sleep and re-enter the world of her parents and Josef. Strange voices interrupt her dreams, angry exchanges and then a shushing noise obviously intended to return the conversation to an even tenor. It reminds her of schooldays and the sound of children urged to keep secrets.

She presses the glass to the wall. All those chairs she saw must be occupied because many people are trying to speak at once, yet, apart from the commandant, there is only one voice she recognises. He speaks German with an accent that comes from the throat like a gargle. He has visited the

51

commandant many times in recent months. Somebody refers to him as Herr Falscher, Mr Forger, and everybody laughs.

Most of the conversation is audible, but she understands little of what is being said and her mind starts to wander from listening to a heated exchange about rail routes and personnel disbursement. Somebody mentions the name Wiesel. Now, she strains to hear. There will be a vivid red mark around her ear. For a few seconds, there is complete silence, followed by noises of disapproval which stop abruptly when the commandant speaks above the rest. His voice is loud but weary, a little slurred by alcohol. 'He knows how to present the rolling stock and vary the route as circumstances dictate. His involvement is indispensable.' Nobody argues.

It is late into the night when the door crashes open and wakes her from another dream-filled sleep. He is alone, the room behind him deserted as daylight strains through the now open blackout curtains. He is rocking on his feet, appearing larger than he has ever done before as he sways menacingly in front of her. His tunic is unbuttoned, the coarse-knit undervest stained and damp with a mix of sweat and spilled alcohol. She is pulled roughly towards him as he demands a proper kiss like the bitch taught her. Like an automaton with sleep in her eyes, she does just that, an overpowering resentment rising within her as she savours the grouts of chewed cigars and his foul breath in her mouth. He reaches for a chair and collapses awkwardly into it, legs apart, his eyes straining to focus on her. 'What do you see when you look at me? Tell the truth. I'll know if you're lying.'

She feels amazingly calm, even though the answer to his question may well determine her future, whether she will live or die. If she is truthful, and she knows how to put thoughts into words, she would say what? On the surface, you are a ruthless and sadistic megalomaniac. Even your own despicable kind calls you 'Jew Killer' behind your back. You deserve to burn eternally in hell, and maybe, if you believe in these things, you will. Yet, underneath this evil veneer you are a lost little boy, insecure, craving the respect of others but with no self-respect, demanding attention by perpetrating outrageous deeds. You see virtue in guile and cunning, deceiving friend and foe alike. You need the praise of others, even though all the time realising such praise is false. You do not deserve to survive, to experience the prospect of change, yet you will; for I, who is no more than a 'she' to you, intend to change you.

'Come on,' he urged. 'What's there to think about?'

'I see a powerful man who knows how to get everything he wants.'

He explodes with laughter, spittle spattering the floor in front of him. 'It must be wonderful to be so innocent, so untouched by the world. You haven't got a fucking clue what is going on, have you?'

He doesn't wait for an answer. 'You've never heard of Robert Steinbacher, have you? He is the Spider, a great man, and he was here tonight. Are you listening to me?' He is angry and moves towards her as she recoils.

'What is the Spider?' she asks in desperation.

'Good question.' He gives a facetious clap of the hands. 'I'll tell you. Bring the bottle from the table.'

It's the first time she's been into his office unaccompanied. Through the dirt-encrusted windows, she can see that assembly has been called. Inmates are shuffling into position in the half light. Around her, the air is heavy with tobacco smoke. On every flat surface there are glasses, mostly empty, some with cigarette butts floating in them. Ashtrays are full to overflowing. In one, a half-eaten sandwich has been crushed into the base. Empty bottles lie discarded over the floor. A black cigarette, barely smoked, tinged with traces of dark red lipstick, has left a trail of ash and burnt varnish on the edge of his desk. She did not hear a woman's voice.

The girl returns with the remains of a bottle of brandy that he snatches from her hand and thrusts to his lips. 'Our beloved Germany is losing the war,' he says. 'Some astute men, me included, are already thinking about the Fourth Reich; the obligation to keep our best men alive to plan for its coming in the future.' He wheels his arm around in a circle. 'The flame must never be extinguished.' He closes his eyes, head weaving slowly side to side and back to front. 'You, my ignorant little Jewess, tell me: what do spiders have?'

'Eight legs?'

He laughs and claps again. 'Good,' he says, a smile still on his lips, eyes staying closed. 'What else do spiders have?'

'I don't know.'

'Of course you do, you fucking idiot. I'll give you a clue. Where do they live?'

'In a web.'

'Brilliant,' he shouts. 'That's it. The man's a genius. The spider has eight legs and a web. Don't you see?'

She is silent. What is she supposed to say? He's talking in riddles.

He jerks forward, pushing the chair onto its two front legs as he leans towards her. The slap across her face leaves a stark red mark. 'Answer me! Don't sit there and ignore me. I asked you a question.' He goes to hit her again, but the brandy bottle slips from his grasp, he loses his balance and the chair rocks back onto all four legs. He recovers the bottle and puts his index finger over his lips. His voice is now a whisper. 'I'm going to tell you a secret. I have a plan which the Führer will approve because ...' He draws a long breath. 'Tonight I have the last piece of the jigsaw. You mustn't breathe a word. Every web will have a spider at its centre, controlling each one of the eight legs. None of the legs ever comes into contact with another, each working independently through the centre. Steinhauser has the Ratlines all set up through Draganovich, running from Italy to North and South America. Genius, is it not?'

'Yes,' she says. Better to answer than tell the truth. She does not understand one word.

'What day is it today?' he mumbles, opening one eye to focus on her. 'Whatever. On Saturday, we leave this shithole for Berlin. I am to be second in command at Sachsenhausen, the jewel of all the camps as far as the Führer is concerned. Finally, *Sturmbannführer* Heinrich Kirchner will meet and present his plan to the great man.' He slumps back in his chair, his breathing regular as his eyes close once more and he begins to sleep.

As he spoke, a block of ice formed around her heart. She fights for breath. She can feel a pounding in her head. Her fists pummel at his chest. 'What about my father?' she stammers. 'You said I could see my father. When can I see him?'

The question, shouted now, forces a retreat from drunken slumber. He tries to stand, to defend himself from the punches that have now ceased, but his movements are so uncoordinated he falls back into the chair. He is blinking hard, trying to understand what happened, to focus on his assailant.

'I asked when can I see my father?'

'Your father?' He begins to grasp the meaning. 'You can meet up with him in hell. He's dead.' There was no sentiment in his voice.

The words are jumbled in her head. My father is not well? No, that's not what he said. It doesn't matter if he's not well, as long as he's not ... Did he say dead?

'When?'

Head bowed, eyes fluttering, his hands massage his forehead. 'I don't know.' He is becoming irritable. 'Did you hit me? You risk your life for the sake of what?' His lips pout in a dismissive gesture, forming bubbles of saliva. 'You expect me to remember when everybody dies? I have more important issues on my mind.'

'I said "when".'

The ferocity in her voice seems to sober him. His eyes open wide. 'Two weeks ago. He had been ill, unable to work. Satisfied?'

Two weeks ago, she had been in the ghetto, helping Laura Sowka to save her son, whilst all the time her father had been dying and she was not there to comfort him. 'You promised,' she cries, but there are no tears.

'You promised for me. I do not make deals with your kind. Some miracles I can perform. Stilling the passage of time and resurrecting the dead are not amongst them.' He finds his comment humorous and makes another attempt to stand up, this time hoisting himself by gripping the arm of the chair until the tendons in his arms can be seen in relief as his legs strive to gain purchase. He sways unsteadily towards her but stands in his tracks, rocking to and fro as he senses her hostility. 'Got a will of your own, have you? Not knocked it out of you yet? That's what I like about you. You have no fear.' His shoulders shake as he laughs. 'Even fancy your chances against a drunken man, do you?'

She holds his gaze, a look of contempt on her face. Slowly, she shakes her head. 'You promised,' she repeats, only this time, softly.

'I did make enquiries,' he says, as though offering an excuse. Quick to recognise the weakness in his retort, he reacts. 'We have no food to keep invalids who cannot work alive. His death was quick and painless.'

'You killed him.' His expression recognises the loathing she has conveyed in those three words.

He checks around him to see where the door is and edges towards it, supporting himself with one hand on whatever piece of furniture is available. The adrenalin and stimulants in his body have lost any effect and have been replaced by fatigue and exhaustion.

His stooped body is framed in the doorway as he hesitates and turns to appraise her. The expression on his face, a mixture of disappointment and indecision, alarms her. The words of caution from Feliks ring in her ears. She must be wary.

She has no words to explain why or how she reacted at the time, the sudden realisation of the stark choice she was about to face. Yet, with the benefit of hindsight and the passage of time, these sentiments come to be defined. Surely, the man who controlled her fate is two people: the ruthless, unfeeling monster who could squash her like a fly with one command – that's exactly what she sees in him at that moment; but, somewhere deeper, the scared little boy, shunned and disregarded by his family, abandoned into a world of solitude and immature self-determination, easy prey for the preachers of fascism and disciples seeking the purity of the *Volk*. He craves the respect of others, a false hope if there is no self-respect and misunderstood if he deludes himself into believing it can be imposed on her. During these past months, she has been there as a prop for him, somebody with something he needs that he cannot define but cannot be without. That is why he has not taken her bodily, for that would surely do no more than define her as one of the whores he fucks whenever he feels like it. This is the paradox. He wants her to offer more, but how can a captive slave girl ever be expected to meet this challenge?

He can tell from her expression; it says he understands there is no respect, only contempt for him, and he can no longer permit such a reaction to test his fragility. Her future is in the balance. Tonight, he has fashioned a block of ice around her heart that will never melt, impenetrable to his word or deed, threat or favour, never vulnerable to words of love or hate from any man. He has fashioned her in his own image. No longer will she ever see him as the commandant. From now on, he will always be recognised by her as Kirchner or, simply, as 'he'. He has no rank as far as she is concerned, no status other than a slave master.

56

Her only objective is to stay alive, to do everything possible to survive until her time comes.

'I'm sorry,' she says. 'I do understand, and I will get over the loss I feel.'

He looks at her again, intently, as if processing the meaning of her words. 'Do you mean that?' He sounds almost relieved.

She nods and gives him a smile.

'Thank you,' he whispers, and closes the door.

SEVEN
SACHSENHAUSEN-ORANIENBURG, GERMANY
February 1945

She has never seen anything like this in her life. So much activity, so many people milling around, day and night. This is Germany, near Berlin, he tells her, but just a suburb and so much smaller than the capital city. Can anything really be busier than this?

The main camp is as big as a town in Poland, with a ring of smaller camps set like feeder birds alongside enormous factories with dark, sinister chimneys, their tops obscured by the masses of black smoke swirling around and billowing up into the sky in menacing clouds that hide the weak winter sun from view. At the circumference of all this activity sits a complex of concrete bunkers, highly fortified with camouflaged anti-aircraft gun emplacements, replete with lines of enormous searchlights that illuminate the night sky whenever the sirens sound and the drone of aircraft can be heard in the distance. In the time she has been there, the sirens now ring out their low moan more often, the sky illuminated for nights on end, the dull thud of bombs exploding in stark flashes, lines of tracer fire arcing into the darkness, a macabre firework display bent on creating carnage and destruction.

Prisoners in their striped uniforms are everywhere, a never-ending stream of humanity trudging along the pot-holed roads like sad wind-up dolls nearly unwound. The guards are of the same breed as in the last place and the place before that, uncaring, snarling as they urge their charges forward. But the faces of the inmates are different. In previous camps they were mainly Poles from Jewish families, or Romanies. So far, she has seen nobody she could say looked similar. These people all have square faces and stony expressions she associates with the immigrants from the east and the Russian prisoners of war. She asks him where they are from and he just says all over, mostly rounded up during the glorious advance towards Moscow.

He has been allocated quarters next to a women's camp near the south-western perimeter of the main camp. There are fewer factories in this area, mainly agricultural land, now unworked, trodden into a muddy bog by the brigades of workers excavating the underground fortifications on the road to Berlin. She sleeps in a storeroom with no window, crammed with leather offcuts, shoe lasts, straps and shelves of tins with tacks. The smell is one she recognises, one with which she is comfortable. Every night, as she drifts into sleep, her father talks to her, remembering days of what seemed like perpetual summer as they walked through the countryside, pushing Josef in his pram, laughing and counting the rabbits as they darted across the fields. If she closes her eyes really tight, with arms outstretched she can grasp a hand of each one, recognise the gnarled skin of her father, the soft touch of a baby. When she awakes, they have gone, but she is comforted because she knows tonight they will be back.

Two days every week, she accompanies Kirchner to the main camp. These are the days when the commandant is absent and Kirchner is in charge. She is made to sit in a side room and watch the roll call in the vast central area shaped like a triangle.

There are so many people crammed together with barely room for them all to stand. Some can't – the weak and dying, propped up by their fellow inmates – and for what? The privilege of living a few more minutes? For, as the able form into work parties and trudge in lines towards the gate at the apex of the triangle, watched by guards in machine gun towers with weapons trained, those with no strength left fall to the ground. There are maybe twenty poor souls left, some kneeling, some collapsed, a few standing but swaying as if buffeted by the wind. They must feel so alone and deserted by their god, yet they mumble and clasp their hands together.

The officer of the day walks between them, carefully shooting each one in the back of the head. The bodies twitch in their death throes, but she can breathe out. Now, they are at peace.

For one or two men filtering towards the exit, the sound of gunfire behind them outstrips their capacity to think and act rationally. They break from the ranks and run towards the perimeter fence. Do they realise they are committing suicide or has desperation overcome them? Once someone steps into the neutral zone – they call it the death strip – the guards will shoot to kill. Should these poor souls reach the fence, they are electrocuted, and if by some miracle the fence is scaled, as they run towards the perimeter wall the dogs will tear them to pieces.

A dozen inmates appear from the shadows below her. These are some of the Russian soldiers taken prisoner on the front about to make their final gesture to the war effort. Do they realise this? They don't appear to. Their job is to drag the corpses from the assembly area to the ditches behind the barracks, where they are unceremoniously dumped into a mass grave. Task completed, the prisoners of war stand to attention as the door opens and a machine gun rattles, tossing them backwards as if marionettes, arms and legs flailing at unnatural angles, to join the bodies they have just deposited.

Once, not long ago, she would have shuddered at the sound of every round of gunfire. Now, she feels nothing.

There is rarely a day when he does not make time to come to the storeroom and use her as his sounding board. She says this because he does not want her to participate beyond an understanding nod of the head or a complimentary comment; in truth, she grasps precious little from the disjointed non-sequiturs he utters as he attempts to explain the passage of events which have shaped his day. It's like he's doing mental filing, opening the drawers, allocating decisions and occurrences to various folders, and glancing in her direction for confirmation before he closes the drawer and opens the next. Sometimes he lets off steam, like those infernal trains he constantly talks about, slamming the drawer shut with a loud expletive or a disgruntled snort.

When the sirens sound, they sit in the darkness in silence, listening to the constant hum of planes flying above them, the whine of engines accelerating as they begin to dive and the repeated dull thump as bombs land and explode, the sound like hailstones as gunshot follows in its wake. He smiles at her reassuringly. The war is coming to an end, he affirms. Unfortunately, Germany is losing. The camps at Sobibor and Belzec in Poland have already been overrun by the Red Army. It is only a question of time.

Things have to be tidied up at Sachsenhausen, he tells her. He is critical of Commandant Kaindl, who should be cremating the documents in the filing cabinets rather than the bodies of the ten thousand Russian prisoners of war he massacred. Kaindl is a fool. Why herd them into a warehouse with some pathetic trickery that they were about to be measured for new uniforms and slaughter them by gunfire through holes in the wall? Not one survived. Kaindl will feel the hangman's noose when all this is over.

She must not concern herself. It is true she and he have done bad things, but the Spider and his *Ratlines* will see them safe. What does he mean? Why is he including her? She has thought bad thoughts, but she has not done any bad things. Perhaps being his Jew whore, like the guards call her, is a bad thing in the eyes of those who will judge her.

On some days, he is exhilarated. There is more talk of railways and the involvement of Lew Wiesel; praise for the man called the forger; references to something called the Reischbank and Operation Bernhard; his conversations with the Führer's staff; and gold. He is obsessed with gold and what he calls wondrous treasures; the need for money known as foreign currency to be deposited in safe havens in Switzerland and Portugal. She has never heard of safe havens. It was banks, she understood, where you keep your money. When he is like this, he never stops talking, rambling on until she cannot listen and starts to dream of another world, of orchards full of apples and children always laughing.

It is Saturday the third of February. She knows because he keeps repeating the date. He is so angry, lashing out at everyone around him like the spoilt child she has witnessed on occasions before. Somebody has wrecked his plans and we are all to blame, those within the gaze of his mad eyes and acerbic tongue. He keeps asking the same rhetorical question. Why did they have to drop their fucking bombs on Anhalter? It was part of the plan and now it's all been ruined. He has photographs. The station has been blasted to smithereens, platforms destroyed and rails twisted into coarse, jagged lumps of metal, bent into almost statuesque images.

He sits in silence, head in hands, repeating over and over one thing: Wiesel insists it has to be Anhalter.

A week passes and she does not see him. It is cold, but the sky has been clear and she has taken to sitting on a chair outside the storeroom door during the brief daylight hours. There are fewer factories now within her line of sight. Most of the tall chimneys are no longer and only the occasional pall of smoke dims the horizon. She can stay for hours and watch others move around now she can wrap up warm with all the spare blankets no longer requisitioned for the front.

Some of the *Helferin* display signs of nerves. Gone is the arrogant self-assurance that once characterised their attitude to the inmates. One in particular, a small, blonde young woman named Katarina, sees the girl as a cross between a confidante and a mother confessor with power to absolve her sins. The girl has no idea how to react. The best she can offer are non-committal replies and a smile, the only answer to so many searching questions about lost souls and repentance. Suddenly, the woman sinks to her knees with hands clasped together so tightly that they turn white, and begs for salvation. The girl's instinctive reaction is to place her hand gently on the woman's head and pat it as she would if it were the family dog. The woman rises slowly, grasps the girl's head between those two blood-starved hands and kisses her full on the lips as the tears begin to flow.

Words pour out, the pent-up confessional of a woman desperate for forgiveness and a peace of mind she will never enjoy. For Katarina has done and condoned ungodly things. In staggered breath between a mixture of gulps and sobs, she talks of life as a *Helferin* in the experimental centre at Sachsenhausen where Dr Wirth did terrible experiments on inmates with chemical weapon and psychoactive compounds; where Dr Sommer developed the work he had started with the children at Potulice on something called cognitive neuroscience. She had watched children under hypnosis giggle mischievously as they hacked each other into pieces with knives, embracing as the blades dug into their backs. There was more, much more, and however many words of contrition or forgiveness existed, both of them knew in their hearts that no god could ever forgive Katarina her sins. Rabbi Zanvil used to say redemption was always possible for those who repented, but he was wrong. Katarina was bound for the eternal fires of hell.

Their final meeting is one of contrasting moods. The girl tells of her news, a move to the centre of Berlin where he can finalise a plan which now has the Führer's consent. They will live in a requisitioned house near the *Führerbunker* so that he can be close to the people who matter.

She is talking fast and trying to keep the excitement out of her voice, but Katarina is hardly listening. Her mood is sombre. All the inmates in the Sachsenhausen camps are to leave and begin forced marches across the country. She has received orders to go north with one of the groups of women. It's crazy, she says. Word has it there are sixty-five thousand male and thirteen thousand female prisoners in all the camps. How could they be expected to move that many people? Where will they go?

She makes sympathetic noises, but Katarina deserves her fate, and, forgive the girl, dear Father, her mind is elsewhere.

They have a terraced house with three floors on Goeringstrasse. It is big and so grand, with much more space than the house which the Wiesel family occupy in the ghetto. She is very proud.

All the rooms on the ground floor have been turned into offices, which are strictly out of bounds to her. She has been given civilian clothes and is free to come and go during daylight hours, but on re-entering the building she must use the staircase direct to the first floor and under no circumstances enter the door marked '*Zutritt Verboten*'.

It is of no consequence. There are two lounges on the first floor, overlooking the park. The windows are decked with full-length velvet curtains in a rich, deep purple, held open by matching ties with tassels that are so comforting to hold and make her smile as the strands tickle her palm.

To the rear is a dining room with elegant high-backed chairs in a varnished, dark wood and a matching table with space for, perhaps, twenty people. He insists she must learn how to be the lady of the house and to stop acting like a servant when guests are present. She does try, but on the one occasion when there is a dinner party, all ten guests are men, mostly in uniform, and they all laugh loudly whenever she opens her mouth to speak. All the derisory chuckles and sideways smirks with fellow guests make her feel like the court jester. He doesn't help. He's drunk and just joins in with his crude innuendoes.

But she has learnt to put all this aside. These men with their feeble little bits of bread dough tucked inside their trousers; they can laugh, but there is something troubling in their eyes, as if they longed for tonight, this moment, the very here and now, to be their reality as opposed to horrors which will confront them when the dawn breaks. If the rumours are true, one day, and it will be soon, they will stand naked, stripped of their fancy uniforms and tin medals, heads cast down looking at their fat white stomachs as judgement is pronounced. She yearns for that day to come.

The evenings she prefers are when there are just the two of them. He sits at the head of the table with her alongside to his right whilst dinner is served by a tired-looking old lady who speaks little German. She cooks and cleans well and leaves when the plates are cleared. Only when the woman has gone does he start to talk, and does so long into the night. He is never angry or short-tempered with her now and, if he has not had too much to drink, shows a softer side to his nature as he speaks.

Tonight is a special night. He opens the small leather case as they sit at the table. For one moment, her heart leaps. Fear. Excitement. Apprehension. But, it's not for her. Earlier today, the Führer presented him with a medal, the Civil Service Faithful Service Medal. It's not a glamorous name, he admits, but it is an honour now rarely gifted and only presented to special people who have demonstrated loyal and faithful service to the Führer. There are tears in his eyes as he speaks, and she smiles back at him. She knows now it will be tonight.

For the first time, they share the double bed in the largest of the four bedrooms on the top floor. If she means to secure her future, remember Tillie's advice. Act as a lover, never the whore. But remember, do not be confused. Her demonstration of need and adulation is a necessary act of self-preservation, not one of affection or even simple kindness. It must signify nothing. Live by the mantras of Yodel and Tillie she recites in her head as the foreplay is exhausted and he craves to mount her. His eyes are wide open, staring into hers, searching for something she does not comprehend. He freezes and hovers above her, his penis brushing her thigh. A shudder of rejection runs through her body.

He has something important to say and she must listen. God, please don't let it be words that speak of feelings or, worst of all, love. But she has nothing to fear. What is the significance of a speech, especially one that, at the time, seems meaningless to her? He needs her to understand that if he were to treat her as a whore, he would get up when the sex was over and leave the bed. Tomorrow, when they both awake, they will be in the same bed together. Does she see what he means? She nods, but she did not expect anything different, so why say it?

Five minutes must have passed since he began to rise and fall on top of her, first with an urgency, now slower, his breathing laboured. She can sense his barrel is not so firm any more. What would Tillie do? She raises and folds her legs around his waist, gripping tight, feeling his barrel react. The pushing gathers speed. An image of Malik comes into her head and she can sense that this man is now close too. In what is more like a cry of anguish, he cries out through gritted teeth and, with two violent shudders of his body, comes inside her. She feels the bullets leave his barrel and relaxes her grip.

Tillie told her to expect the man to move off her in total silence, turn over, stick his bottom in her face and go straight to sleep, but it isn't like that. He reaches for his cigarettes, lies on his back and pulls her head onto his chest. He does not speak. Every time he pulls on the cigarette, the glow from the embers allows her a fleeting image of the intricate stucco design around the central light fitting.

He says he wants to give up smoking, perhaps grow a moustache; not one like the Führer's; one like the American film star, Errol Flynn. She doesn't know who Errol Flynn is. She will, he claims.

For once, he doesn't talk about *Die Letzen Rechte*, the pet project that absorbs most of his waking hours. He briefly touches on personal aspects, things he has never said before. Can he only be twenty-four, just nine years older than she? Why, even the age difference between her father and mother was seven years. He looks and sounds so much older. More sights and experiences in a few short years, he says, than most people would experience in a dozen lifetimes. His parents, along with a younger sister, were killed in an air raid on Dusseldorf in the early months of the war. She asks about his sister, but he avoids the topic, preferring to detail his experiences in the Führer's youth movement, joining the army and his transfer into the SS.

Eventually, the words meander and he drifts into sleep whilst she lays awake, imagining the stucco design on the ceiling until daybreak comes and the confusion in her head ceases.

* * *

I feel I should write the next paragraphs in block capitals or change the colour of the ink or print heavily, but I won't.

I entered his bed as 'the girl', a 'she' and a 'her', the person who was never in control of her own destiny, taught, manipulated, coerced and fashioned by others, never responsible for her own actions. Up to this point, I could always relate the good and bad in my life to someone else, look around for an explanation, an excuse, even forgiveness. I was no one beyond a stand-in for whomever lacked in someone else's life – a sister for poor Josef; a child for childless Yodel and Mother; a project for Tillie; a priest for Katarina; an innocent partner in Kirchner's crimes. All I rightfully ask is that blame should not be cast upon a child for the sins of those around her.

I awoke this morning as 'I', 'me', 'Rita', a person in my own right, accepting that from hereon in, my decisions, my reactions, my obligations, are all on my shoulders. If I commit a crime, you can rightfully punish me. I will not seek to blame others for my choices whether they prove right or wrong, good or bad. Whether I remain under someone's physical control or not, I am my own person.

Today, and for the rest of my life, I am Rita Krakowski.

PART TWO - RITA

THE CATERPILLAR

EIGHT
VEVEY, SWITZERLAND
December 2018

'Josef is still alive, you know?'

She cocked her head and raised what was once an eyebrow in apparent surprise at the remark. 'I know,' she replied, contradicting the expression. 'What of it?' She was sitting in the same armchair in which he had found her the night he arrived. Her gaze was still fixed on a scene far beyond the picture-postcard panorama, as rays of a watery sun glistened and played on the snow-capped trees.

'Wouldn't you like to see him before …'

She interrupted her daydream to savour his embarrassment, the dead end with no escape into which a kind and sympathetic soul walks; that same wide avenue that brooks no problem for the callous and insensitive. 'Before he forgets who I am. Is that what you meant to say?'

Marchal smiled. 'Something like that.'

'You know, I have taken a liking to you, René Marchal. I shall be …' She smiled to herself. This time, she was the one in danger of entering a dead end.

'Sad?' he volunteered.

'I have no recollection of what sadness feels like. It is an emotion expunged from my being an eternity ago.'

'I can believe it.' He reached for her hand. She grasped his fingertips.

'I was about to say, rephrase perhaps, the statement that I shall be forever conscious that you have reintroduced me to an aspect of manhood I have known only once in my life. I am grateful to you for rekindling such vivid memories.'

He pointed to the document case. 'Will this aspect be apparent to me from your manuscript?'

She pushed his hand away. 'Manuscript! That's a grand word for my scribblings. I'm surprised you haven't reached that section. You must be a very slow reader.'

It brought his mind back to the concluding sentence of one of her scenes. 'You say you never saw Malik again. Do you know what happened to him? Perhaps he is still alive as well. You could meet up.'

The old lady slowly shook her head. 'That will not occur in this world.'

'And Josef?'

Again, she shook her head. 'It would be as if two strangers were meeting for the first time. Anything we felt as children is no longer. If I so chose – which I rush to say, I do not – to provide him with excuses and explanations, I might talk until the cows come home. He would extend no mitigation for my actions. I would always be the traitor who betrayed the Polish people and the Jewish faith.'

'I must be almost halfway through your narrative and I have read nothing which could brand you in these terms.' His anxious look searched for an explanation in her face but found nothing but resignation.

'Well, for one thing, I never left or betrayed him, did I?'

'Who?'

'Kirchner.'

Marchal turned his head at the sound of the door opening behind him.

There was a cackle like the sound of a hen in the throes of strangulation. 'Did you think that was him?' she crowed. 'Still alive and creeping up behind you?' The laugh turned into a cough. The carer placed the tray of tea on the side table and began to massage the old lady's back.

'Don't excite her,' the woman said in French. 'It overexerts; puts too much pressure on her system.'

Marchal put on his sympathetic face.

The coughing stopped and the carer was waved away.

'We were interrupted,' she said.

'Have you heard of the Stockholm Syndrome?'

She put up her hand. 'Please don't make me laugh again. You are being absurdly humorous. If you mean did I become obsessed, infatuated, madly in love with my captor, forget it. I loathed the man for what he was from the first day I clapped eyes upon him until the last day I ever saw him alive.'

'How do you explain your actions?'

She savoured the question before answering. 'Have you ever needed someone and, at the same time, been needed by that someone, René?'

Memories trailed through his mind, but somehow he managed to suppress the desire to answer a question to which she wasn't expecting a reply.

'Some people walk through life leaning inwards,' she went on. 'It's the only way they know how. Their head rests for support upon the shoulder of the person walking alongside them. It's uncomfortable if that person is standing upright. After a while, the one doing the leaning tires or loses their balance; the one supporting becomes ever more conscious of the weight upon them. However, when the other person is also leaning inwards, the way forward is easier to negotiate. They are both exerting a similar pressure and deriving equal comfort from each other. The feeling is one of relief, not exertion. Does that make sense?'

'I know exactly what you mean.' And he did. Françoise had been taken away from him suddenly, just at that time of life when they could begin to relax into each other's company beyond the demands of parentage. Their only daughter, Monique, had set her course in life; then in her final year of training to become a veterinary surgeon, a fiancée with prospects and a deposit on a terraced house in Lille. She didn't need them; at least, until grandparenting duties came along. Marchal was to ask for a transfer out of detective work to a desk job, a ten-year wind-down before the earliest date he could retire on full pension. Françoise would cut back her locum work as a professor of philosophy at whichever Paris university was shorthanded. Together, they would do all those things career and family had precluded. There was a bucket list as long as his arm. He was so excited.

And then, one summer's day, when the countryside and a picnic beckoned, she had a stroke so profound it left her imploring her family to help end the suffering. Both father and daughter resisted, though when the end came, Marchal was convinced that somehow Monique had been involved. Certainly, she had never been as emotionally stable after her mother's death and whether through guilt or distress, her volatile temper had eventually contributed to the breakdown of her own marriage.

'Your cheeks are flushed,' the old lady said. 'Have I exposed a raw nerve?'

'Shame, I'm afraid,' he managed to say. 'My wife died tragically, very suddenly. Her body was not even cold when I vented my frustration.'

'You did?'

'I'm not proud. She had robbed me of my support, the one person who could see through my mood swings, rationalise my tendency to dwell on the daily horrors of life as a homicide detective, bring me round to see sense and recognise the wonderful thing we had together. She had abandoned me to solitude in a dark place and I felt impotent without her.'

'But, you learnt to stand up straight again?'

'Is that what you did?'

'The truth is we were two lost souls looking for a life raft. Kirchner was a thug, a bully and totally ruthless. But, inside, he lacked any self-belief. Instilling fear and oppression in the weak and defenceless to further the only worthwhile cause, the purity of the *Volk*, the German race, was his attempt to harness what he believed was respect. As the trains pulled in and he stood on the ramp, legs astride, body erect, motioning the confused and petrified souls, most to the right and a short, stumbling walk to the gas chambers, some to the left to work as slaves and starve until their bodies could stand no more – playing God was how he deemed his comrades and superiors would determine his worth.'

She sank back in her chair and breathed heavily, the exertion of talking apparent. She coughed intermittently and Marchal noticed the specks of blood on the cloth she used to cover her face.

'Do you want to rest?'

She shook her head violently. 'Tell me how you survived.'

He could tell she needed him to talk while she regained her strength. 'Using your words, I never realised just how much I was leaning over onto Françoise's shoulder when she was alive. For a while I became submerged in a mire of resentment and self-pity, blaming everyone and everything for my sorry state. My superiors wanted me to take a leave of absence, time to grieve. That was worse than a prison sentence. I thought about becoming a serious drinker, an alcoholic, but, to be honest, beyond a glass of red at dinner, I get little satisfaction out of alcohol. So, I went back to work as soon as I could, busied myself in all the gruesome details of the latest murder and kept to my one glass of wine.' He finished the remnants of his tea and looked down at the wizened features and glassy eyes staring back at him. 'You sure you want to hear this?'

She shrugged her shoulders. 'You talk to the dead, as well?'

His smile was one of submission. 'Guess you know me better than I know myself. Whenever I needed guidance, I talked it over with her, calculated what she would have said. It steered me into a better place, one where I can enjoy the solitude of my existence without needing anyone by my side.'

'Do you still talk to her?'

'Only in my head and only when I think it's something she would have liked to talk about.' He hesitated, uncertain whether he should pursue the conversation. Talking had plainly tired her, but she still appeared engaged enough to want to listen. 'We seem to have spent more time talking about my life than allowing me to get a better understanding of the person about whom I am reading. Is there anything else you would like to know? Otherwise, I'll leave you in peace and try to speed up my reading technique.'

She drew a crumpled paper tissue to her face in a trembling hand and pressed it against her lips before withdrawing it into her palm to study. 'I need to go to my room and apply fresh make-up. It could be tonight we have visitors.'

'I understand my partner will arrive tomorrow,' he said. 'We will ensure your safety.'

She shook her head. 'This colleague you talk about. Is he like you? Is he sensitive and understanding?'

The hesitation wasn't intentional, but he knew she would react angrily if he slipped into platitudes and clichés. 'His background is very different to mine and we tend to complement each other and approach problems from a different perspective rather than come at them from the same angle. Chas was a career soldier, an officer in British special forces, mainly during the troubles in the Falklands and, later, in the former Yugoslavia. I cannot imagine the horrors he has witnessed, possibly even perpetrated. Doubtless he is ruthless, although his subsequent career in royal security has rounded some of the rough edges and introduced a degree of diplomacy into a mentality based on order and obedience.'

'He is single, I take it?'

'I've never talked with him about relationships, be it mine or his. He's a very private person. I don't believe he ever married. He told me once it would be unfair to subject any woman to the stress of waiting for a knock on the door to find out if it was him standing there or somebody else with news of his death. And even if he had returned, would it be the same person who had said goodbye all those months or years earlier?'

'Strange how men don't talk about these things. If you've ever been in a ladies toilet, you'll understand that relationship issues are the bread and butter of most conversations. There is obviously something about this man you find compelling?'

He glanced up at the ceiling, his mind wrestling with the word 'compelling'. What was Marchal's motivation in developing his relationship with Broadhurst? 'Compelling' suggested some form of attraction, an emotional driver. Their meeting of minds was far more pragmatic. 'Above all, I trust him,' he said. 'He listens and makes informed judgements. I enjoy his company. Is that compelling?'

He turned to face her and smiled. He had taken too long to answer. Her eyes were closed and her chest barely moved with those shallow, regular breaths as she slept.

NINE
BERLIN, GERMANY
March 1945

In retrospect, I might have expected my lasting impression of those two brief months in Goeringstrasse to be defined by the subtle change in my relationship with Kirchner. My big test was over and I had passed. As satisfying as he found the occasional and well-choreographed visit to my bed to fuck with my body, I could sense his real objective was to conquer and dominate my person. I would never allow such a thing.

The paradox was that in the attempt to disarm me, his inner sentiments became exposed, chinks maybe, but just enough for me to start to exert my personality in some small measure. Of course, this reasoning comes to me many years after the actual passage of that brief period. At the time, I handled the physical side with my bread dough and bullet philosophy, as upgraded by what I had come to call in my mind 'Tillie's tricks'. What was going on in my head at the time could better be described by my dear mother's words of a strong-willed little girl determined to make a point.

Yet, for all these minor empirical achievements in strengthening my relationship with Kirchner, I will always associate that house in the street next to Hitler's bunker with the fondness I felt for a man named Richard Meier.

He appears as a dinner guest one night in March. A rather nondescript individual, thin, with slightly rounded shoulders, a slender face creased with heavy lines, he wears wire-framed glasses perched on the end of his nose through which his eyes dart around the room with the look of a startled bird. His manner in front of Kirchner is a strange mixture of humility, respect and an acquired arrogance which I think he feels befits his rank and reputation. They must be of similar age; perhaps Meier is a year or two older.

My first reaction is one of amusement. I really think I am beginning to understand men or, at least, the German soldier extension. From his first stolen glance at my face, the formal click of the heels, rigid outstretched hand and stilted greeting, I can tell he is besotted. '*Oberleutnant* Richard

Meier,' he announces, his eyes for once transfixed on somewhere around my chin. As I take his hand, he raises his eyes and I feel a gush of emotion, a warmth and kindness I had forgotten existed. The moment is almost nothing, passing in a fraction of a second, yet I sense Kirchner has picked up on it too, so skilfully does he deflect the other man's attention.

As dinner progresses, I do my best to avoid eye contact with our guest, not to still my blushes, but more to avoid his embarrassment and the ease with which his cheeks redden when he looks in my direction. As he converses with his senior officer, it is apparent to me that Meier's background and progression through the ranks of the military are at odds with the disciplines of a fighting soldier.

Kirchner is on his way to getting drunk. The meal is over and the two men are swirling brandies around in ostentatious balloon glasses as if practising some dominant male social ritual. There is a break in the conversation and I wonder if he sees Meier as a threat.

I felt during the meal he made one or two juvenile attempts to belittle the man. He certainly shows Meier little respect, appearing to find his guest amusing. As the alcohol blunts his professional approach, he treats the man as if he were a freak show at a circus rather than a comrade-in-arms.

Kirchner grabs my arm and leans forward as if about to impart a secret. 'You will not credit this,' he says, with strained incredulity in his voice. 'Until less than a year ago, Meier here was a lowly *gefreiter*, a pen pusher, working in the Reischbank. What was the department in which you worked?' He studies me carefully as he taps an index finger on the side of his nose. 'You will never believe the name they gave it.'

'The APD – the Appropriations Registration Department,' Meier says slowly.

Kirchner bangs his fist on the table and guffaws. 'That's it. Isn't it classic? Tell me, Rita, what do you think the appropriations registration department does? This will make you laugh.'

'I should clear the table.' I start to get up. Meier is plainly uneasy.

'Leave it and sit down. I asked you a question.'

I do sit down, but very slowly, not in the mould of his men downstairs who react like frightened rabbits whenever an order leaves his lips. 'How would you expect a simple farm girl to know what such things mean?'

He glares at me. 'You're about to learn.' He takes a long swig of his brandy, scrapes his chair backwards along the floor to allow him to thrust his jackboots onto the table. 'Go on, Meier. Tell her. Chop, chop.'

'My job was to record and categorise all the monies, goods and chattels confiscated from the internees taken to the camps.' He looks down at the table as he speaks.

'What he means is he listed all the possessions you Jews were trying to hide from us.' He gives me a fake, overripe smile. 'You will probably find on one of his lists the candelabra we confiscated from your father. Won't she, Meier?'

Why does he feel it necessary to focus on me, Rita Krakowski, whenever he wants to attack my faith? I feel vulnerable. Does he feel ashamed in front of others that he shares his bed with a neutered Jewess?

'My family is' – I nearly say 'was' and catch my breath – 'poor. We have no candel*brasas* or whatever you called them.'

He laughs and shakes his head in dismay. 'Candelabras,' he corrects me. 'Candelabras sit on furniture and hold candles.'

'It's like a menorah,' Meier explains. 'It's the candleholder I think you associate with the Hanukkah holiday in your faith.'

'My, my,' Kirchner says. 'We have an educated man in our midst. You just have to look at his lily-white hands to appreciate his background. No trace of gunpowder residue on those delicate digits.'

Flashes, like out-of-focus photographs, of the synagogue, Rabbi Zanvil and Josef pass in front of me and my eyes fill with tears. Without thinking, I reach across the table for the remaining slice of coarse bread and knead it between my palms into a tube, wrapping my fist around it to maintain the shape. 'When we light a candle, as the wax begins to melt' – I turn my clenched fist downwards – 'we let it drip onto the bare wood, and then' – I slam the tubular form so forcefully onto the table that the sound rings around the silent room – 'we stand it in the molten wax until it has hardened.'

For a few seconds, the tube of bread remains upright, and then starts to slowly unfold. I stand and start to remove the debris along with the surrounding dirty crockery, and shake my head. 'We do not need cande*labra*.'

'Temper, temper,' he chides, banging his boots on the table and smirking in Meier's direction. 'I suspect your father had lots of candelabra or similar, as do most devious and calculating Jews, hidden safely away. You try and trick the Reich by pretending to be poor.'

'We are poor,' I insist.

'Rot!' I know he is tiring of the conversation and his target is not me. 'Is it not true, Meier?'

The poor man had not looked up once during the outburst, his gaze firmly fixed on the plate in front of him. All he can do is react to the question with a puzzled frown as if the topic is too private for him to comment.

'I said, do you not agree, Meier?' he insists. 'My uncle always used to impress upon me that you will never see a poor or honest man praying to his god on a Saturday. Wise words, don't you think?'

'It's time I cleared these things away. It's getting late.' God, how I wanted to deflect the attention away from this trapped animal. I can feel his patience and subservience are wearing thin. He will be playing right into Kirchner's hands if he explodes. I walk around the table and flick an imaginary speck of dust from Kirchner's wine-stained tunic. 'Wouldn't it be wonderful to imagine that all of us who pray to their god, whatever the day, will aspire to honesty and riches?' I smile warmly at him.

'Yes, it would.' Thankfully, Meier recognises my tactic.

'Sit down and leave things where they are. *Oberleutnant* Meier has something to tell us.' I'm afraid he's bent on provoking a reaction, but at least my gesture seems to have disturbed his thought pattern. I return to my seat.

'Meier here is going to tell you how, in the space of a mere twelve months, he has managed to rise from a mere *gefreiter* to wear the uniform of an *Oberleutnant* in the *Wehrmacht*. I am sure we are about to hear a commanding story of bravery in front of the enemy and of loyalty to his fellow comrades.'

He gives a princely wave to indicate Meier should commence just as the knock on the door interrupts the performance. His adjutant, whose real name I do not recall as in my head he will always be Hase – Bunny – stammers an apology for interrupting. I have listened to the man on a number of occasions. He lives in fear Kirchner will display one of the violent temper tantrums to which he has often been subjected, more frequently now than ever. As his project nears realisation, there is a frustration and impatience in Kirchner which he finds impossible to control. He has said as much to me. So many things can go wrong, like the bombing of the Anhalter station or a change of mind at High Command. He is desperate for success.

Hase is almost lost for words. He would never have interrupted had it not been for the telephone call currently on hold in the office downstairs. He did explain the *Sturmbannführer* could not be interrupted, but the secretary to the Führer, Reichsminister Bormann, was insistent. In the circumstances, he felt it appropriate that the man who sits at Herr Hitler's right hand should be obeyed.

As Kirchner stands, the effect of the alcohol appears to fall from him. He pushes the adjutant to one side and makes for the door, stopping abruptly in his stride. 'You had better come with me, Meier. It may well concern you.' He glances at me and then at Meier. The look says it all.

Of course, our paths are bound to cross whilst Meier is working in the same house in which I am living.

As March nears its end, I am returning from a walk and about to climb the stairs when he strides out of the ground floor office. Unlike the rest of Kirchner's uniformed staff, who, at best, ignore me and, at worst, treat me with their silent looks of contempt or whispered obscenities, Meier clicks his heels together and bows his head. I laugh inside as the head-bowing is obviously to avoid me seeing the blush on his cheeks.

'It's freezing outside,' I say. 'I have some tea upstairs; no coffee, I'm afraid. Do you fancy a cup?' Both of us are aware Kirchner has gone to Anhalter for the day to discuss some technical details regarding the train.

Meier sits there looking at me, saying nothing, his fingers embracing the cup as if enjoying the warmth. Of course, he is silent. What pleasantries could he exchange with me? 'How are things going?' to a camp inmate with a captive present, an uncertain future and a destiny outside of her control? Or, 'tell me about your family' to a Jewess whose loved ones are probably lying with their skulls crushed, tossed into a mass grave in some cold and lonely outpost?

Of course not. So instead, I ask him what his family does. His parents have a mixed farm close to Magdeburg and the River Elbe.

'You don't have farmer's hands,' I say.

He looks down as if studying his palms for the first time. He seems relieved to be able to break the silence. 'Don't you start,' he laughs. 'I had enough with the *Sturmbannführer* commenting on my fingers the other night.'

'Sorry. I forgot. Tell me a little about yourself.'

He does. Growing up on a smallholding in the heart of the country, he found the delicate balance of nature fascinating as he developed an appreciation for all the interwoven components of society, be it insects, animals or humans. 'The natural world evolves,' he says, 'and we must nurture, not destroy; understand, not rebuff. Every living thing has a part to play in the complex world we live in. That's what growing up on the land has taught me.'

I had never experienced anybody talk to me in this way before, not my parents, teachers or even Rabbi Zanvil. It is intoxicating and yet it sounds so obscene coming from the lips of a man dressed as a German soldier.

'Our farm is beautiful, but too small to provide anything but a hand-to-mouth existence for those of my family prepared to contribute, to literally get their hands dirty. I couldn't. I had a chronic inherited asthma disorder which, thankfully, seems to be improving as I get older.'

He talks of his parents, his three sisters, with such love and affection that I begin to feel and show my pain. I have to beg him to speak just of himself. He smiles his understanding and tells me how study became his world, from high school to university, a degree course in anthropology, so cruelly interrupted before fulfilment by the start of the war and conscription. His health condition precluded active service and with his academic background, the rank of *gefreiter* and a civilian role as a clerk in the Reischbank in Berlin was a logical placement.

'I guess I must have impressed my superiors with my commitment and application.' He stops and gives himself a make-believe punch on the chin. 'That's being a little naïve, isn't it? With fit and healthy men assigned to active service, there were few secondments of young men to the bank. I became a bigger fish in a smaller pond and, as you heard so forcibly the last time we spoke, my job is to record all possessions confiscated from transferees to the camps.' He is deliberately careful with his choice of words and studies my face to ensure I understand what he means.

He begins to warm to his narrative. 'Within the bank, I was noticed for my diligence and application by the senior personnel and promoted to *Obergefreiter* in 1943. Last July, the bank's president, Dr Walter Funk, summoned me to his office to discuss a highly confidential role which he felt would suit a talented employee.'

I suppose, in retrospect, his attitude has changed slightly to reflect the arrogance he had assumed, but I feel so honoured that he is prepared to confide in someone like me what I believe are secrets, I do not pick up on the change of inflection in his voice. Of course, the fact is that by the time he was telling me all this, his activities were common knowledge amongst his fellow soldiers and I was not the confidante I considered myself to be.

As the tide of the war began to turn and the prospect of defeat grew, so Dr Funk became aware of a disturbing development. Information had come into his hands and into those of his counterpart at the head of the economic department of the SS, *Obergruppenführer* Pohl, indicating certain senior *Wehrmacht* and SS personnel in charge of the internment camps were failing to channel all of the appropriations taken from the inmates back to the Reischbank.

'Funk banged his fist on the table,' Meier says. 'I had never seen this mild-mannered man so close to losing his temper. I recall his exact words: "These traitors are hoarding vast sums in the hope of securing their futures. When the time is right, they will try to flee. To deal with these common criminals, you, my loyal Meier, will be our secret weapon."'

Pohl had conceived a strategy, sanctioned by none other than Secretary Bormann and signed off by the Führer himself, whereby Meier was instructed to visit every camp on a surprise basis to audit the records, interrogate personnel and identify the culprits. To strengthen Meier's hand

and give him the status to deal with senior camp officials, he was rapidly promoted through the ranks to commissioned officer level. In addition, he would carry direct orders signed by Bormann and be accompanied by an elite group of SS troops, commanded by an experienced officer, who would lock down the camp's administrative operation whilst Meier completed his investigation. To Meier's chagrin, the SS officer was to dispense to the guilty parties what the orders obliquely described as summary justice.

'Was it effective?' I ask.

'In one respect, yes. Within six months, I had recovered from various camp officials a fortune in cash, jewels and gold' – he hesitates – 'mainly fillings in teeth extracted from the corpses and wedding rings.' There is another pause. 'As a deterrent, I was also obliged to witness the execution of a dozen men and women by firing squad,' he adds softly.

I nod, not as a reaction to his statement, more an understanding of the undertones present when Kirchner had attempted to goad him.

It is as though Meier reads my thoughts. 'You can perhaps now understand why I have a difficult relationship with the *Sturmbannführer*. In the space of a year, I achieved not only the rank of *Oberleutnant,* but I became the most hated man in Germany to wear this uniform.' He shrugs and shakes his head. 'Like all rumours, news of my activities spread like wildfire and are exaggerated with every telling. I recently heard that, at the last count, I had condemned over a hundred loyal comrades to the firing squad and personally dispatched over thirty. I have never fired a gun in anger in my life.' He chokes back a grunt. 'I could even see the funny side of this folklore if it was not so damn apparent that all the servicemen with whom I come into contact find these ridiculous exaggerations totally credible.'

We lapse into silence, pretending to concentrate on our tea. He has so many little nervous habits, those darting eyes, periodic bouts of hand-rubbing, legs agitated. They did that in Potulice – the kids; the lost souls who don't understand what is happening to them. They arrive as confused children and to survive they must grow up fast. There is no in-between. Meier is just like one of those wretched children. One day he is protecting the butterfly that it might fly away; the next he is watching his own kind in their ritual kill-and-die throes. He may yet be lucky and make the transition.

More likely, he will become one of us; we who travel onwards with all the outward signs of maturity whilst fighting a constant battle inside us to overcome the fears and insecurities of our childhood. I don't need to look into a mirror and see the reflection when I can look into his eyes and see the same thing.

'What are you doing here?' I ask.

The spell is broken. He is not privy to my thoughts and believes I am asking something else. The intimacy between us has passed.

He cannot answer the question. His work is of the highest secrecy and as much as he insists he would like to confide in me, this would be to disobey his orders. Thank you for the tea, he says, and the chance to spend a few sociable minutes away from his desk. He hopes we can do it again.

And so do I.

TEN
ANHALTER BAHNHOF, BERLIN, GERMANY
13 April 1945

'*Schlaumeier*!'

The summons echoes around the hollow ruins of the deserted concourse. Way above our heads, birds nesting in the remains of what was once a majestic arched structure spanning the entire building are startled into flight. As their wings flutter, shards of glass cascade onto the floor not metres away from where we shelter. Meier places his arm protectively over my head in an attempt to shield me from any stray fallout from the downpour. As he does so, he loses his balance and falls awkwardly into a crater where there had once been a platform. I try to look concerned, but, in truth, when I see he has come to no harm, I find we are both laughing with relief.

'*Schlaumeier*!' The birds have all taken wing and no more glass falls. There is an eerie silence while we both wait for the next summons which fails to come.

'You are an SS bastard, Kirchner,' Meier is mumbling to himself. 'And as you well know, my name is not *Schlaumeier*. It's just Meier, and I am proud of it. *Oberleutnant* – yes, you facetious sonofabitch – *Oberleutnant* Richard Meier.' His voice is becoming louder and higher in pitch. I smile and gesture for him to lower his voice. It is not cowardice but self-preservation to pray the tirade is lost on the spring breeze long before it reaches the ears of the man who issues the command.

Meier's lips are moving again, mouthing words in a convoluted mix of anger and frustration, his eyes ablaze, tormented by both hatred and impotence.

'Can you hear me, Kirchner?'

'Of course he can't,' I say to myself. 'You are whispering now, thank God.'

'I am not prepared to tolerate your insults any longer. It is you who thinks he is the *schlaumeier,* the wise guy, the know-it-all. Not me. You wait. My time will come.'

He stands and brushes himself down, careful to remove every speck of grime. It is a pointless task. The uniform of which he is so proud may be new to him and freshly pressed by his own hand, but the fate of the previous inhabitant is recorded by the poorly darned repair around the bullet hole on the breast pocket. It is a size too big for his slender stature, but the bagginess around the chest and waist has not diminished his pride in the dress regalia. He flaunts the distinctive epaulettes, the white plaid braid cast in a loop up to the shiny brass button and the red and gold badges adorning his lapels, tarnished by age, perhaps, but still a reminder of his position as a senior officer in the Wehrmacht.

Since Kirchner learnt that whenever absent at a meeting somewhere, Meier was regularly inviting himself to take tea with me in Goeringstrasse, their relationship has deteriorated even further. Meier understands this, even told me as much, but says he is unable to resist the temptation. He calls it his informal time, when he finds my company refreshing and stimulating. Nobody has ever said that to me before, or since, come to that.

Unfortunately, nobody likes Meier and the people downstairs gossip. That's how Kirchner came to find out. He wasn't angry with me. I told him the truth. I don't invite Meier – at least, not since that first occasion – and it's not my place to object to his presence. Kirchner says I shouldn't worry. They are obliged to put up with the man because he was appointed by Dr Walter Funk himself. I try to look blank as he explains how Funk is the Führer's trusted money man, president of the Reischbank. He says we won't have to suffer Meier for much longer. I intended to ask him what he meant by that, but the opportunity passed.

He questioned me. Had Meier touched me? Again, I could be truthful. There has been no physical contact between us, except once as he was leaving. His lips were centimetres from my cheek and his intention was apparent. I drew back. No man has rights over me, no claims on my body whenever he feels the need; that is, for as long as I have a choice. As to my feelings for Meier, I am simply complicit in a shared opportunity for companionship with someone who treats me like a real person and talks of things about which I can only wonder. I hesitate to say I am treated as his equal. It is not in the make-up of a soldier indoctrinated for a decade with the virus of racial purity to discard such a mindset, but Meier comes as close as it gets. At times, he likes to boast in roundabout terms of his contribution to the project. At least, I know it is definitely called DLR, *Die Letzen Rechte* – The Last Rights – and, how out of the disaster all around us, things might just work out.

On our last 'informal time', two days before we all quit the house in Goeringstrasse and moved to Anhalter Bahnhof, he came to the lounge with a flask of clear liquid he claimed was a fruit brandy made by his father from the medronho tree. Even the smell offended me, but he put a large dose in his cup of tea and just laughed when I refused. By the time good sense should have prevailed, he had abandoned all pretence of 'flavouring the tea' and was taking swigs direct from the flask. Instead of getting up to leave, he slumped back in the chair.

'It's about time you knew a little of what is going on. It is not right he keeps you in the dark. I am going to trust you with a secret because I know you will never betray me.'

I wished I was as sure as he was.

'Do you remember the day just over two months ago, on the third of February, when so many bombs fell? I can see you are uncertain. I know there are so many air raids, but this one was more intense than usual.'

I said I recalled the day Kirchner was so angry about the station being bombed.

'I was working at my desk in the Reischbank when the sirens started, and we made our way to the underground shelter. Even though it was a Saturday, there were five thousand of us, so you can imagine the cavernous space necessary to house everybody. Two hours later, with Dr Funk at our head, we emerged, making our way through piles of debris to witness a scene of total devastation. It was all around us. The buildings had been razed to the ground.'

He was talking quickly, reliving the sights and sounds of the experience. The grandiose, turn-of-the-century building in which he worked had been virtually flattened, exposing the basement and vaults. Later reports say the building suffered twenty-one direct hits and the sky had darkened as a thousand Flying Fortress bombers passed overhead and dropped two thousand tons of bombs on the city. Many important buildings had been targeted, including the rail terminal at Anhalter.

'It was the scale of the devastation which finally determined the Führer's order to Goering to implement a plan for the transfer of Germany's gold and currency reserves from Berlin to safe havens in Bavaria and the Tyrolean Alps.'

Meier's chest literally expanded as he talked of receiving his last promotion in the billiard room of Funk's country house. The assignment with which he was about to be entrusted would be the most important task the *Oberleutnant* would ever undertake and, as described by Funk, his last as a soldier of the Third Reich.

'You will be on your own, Funk told me, with the weight of securing the future of the Fatherland on my shoulders. I was to be second in command to *Sturmbannführer* Kirchner, the man who had conceived the original plan and in whom Funk had no confidence. He insisted I watch him with the eyes of a hawk, the name he had assigned to the project.'

As the two men shook hands for the last time, Funk offered one final piece of advice. The war was over and the reality was that Germany had lost. 'He said what he was about to tell me was not treachery, but the simple truth. Once we had reached our destination and completed the assignment, I must report to his colleague in Munich, Dr Schwedler, where I would receive my discharge papers. I should burn my uniform, change into civilian clothes and disappear. I recall his exact words. "Your enemies, Meier, are regrettably not just the forces against whom we wage war. There are many amongst your own ranks who would wish to see you dead."'

I must have been daydreaming. An angry shout brings me to my senses. I look up and realise Kirchner has caught sight of us across the concourse and is waving for us to return. Alongside him is *Oberschütze* Freiberg, one of the small group of sycophants who hang on his every word and do his bidding. Freiberg is struggling to contain the German shepherd dog which is up on its hind legs, desperate to be free and begin the chase. Words pass between the two men and both start to laugh as they look in our direction.

We start to clamber through the mounds and caverns of jagged concrete slabs, around the twisted railway track forged by the searing heat of the bomb blasts into eerie statuesque forms. Meier indicates a sheltered spot, hidden from view by a partially destroyed wall and a rusting metal sign indicating we have reached what was once the 'Ladies Waiting Room'. A concrete bench is still intact and he gestures for me to sit.

'We should get back,' I say. 'He knows we're here. He is not a patient man.'

'I don't care. Let him wait.'

I have tried to impress upon him the danger we face. Just before we left Goeringstrasse, I insisted he should not seek me out again. His energies should be totally committed to the project and to fulfilling Funk's orders. Kirchner is a deadly serpent who bides his time before he strikes, an insidious opponent prepared to stalk and bait his prey. He has created an aura of tacit acceptance designed to instil false confidence in Meier. And, it has worked. Meier decided to ignore my protests, seemingly emboldened by Kirchner's apparent indifference to our association. His invitations for me to join him became more brazen, his insistence that we be seen together more forceful than ever. But I fear his main objective is to use me to get at Kirchner. Whatever his true feelings towards me, he is consumed by a passion; the wrong kind of passion; the negative kind. And Kirchner just laughs as if we are two naughty children exploring some juvenile infatuation.

Today, Meier is close to breaking. He is perspiring, talking incessantly, mainly mumbling to himself. He is losing control. I sit there afraid, hands clasped, imprisoned between my legs to stop them shaking. He leaves a space between us as if making room for an invisible third party, his gaze transfixed on the gap.

'Do you know why we are here? Do you understand what will happen?' he says.

'I'm not stupid. I use my eyes and ears.' Without realising, I look beyond the concourse to where we are presently billeted. At the eastern end of the station complex, concealed under a corrugated iron roof and miraculously unscathed by the bombardment, is an area that was once the train marshalling and repair yard. In the siding a solitary steam locomotive stands at the head of three coal wagons and ten passenger coaches, around which a troop of soldiers and two gangs of civilians have been at work ever since we arrived. The whole area has been sealed off by barriers and a shroud of camouflage material, with armed guards patrolling the perimeter at all times.

Temporary accommodation is in the second and third carriages, officers in one and the team of soldiers in the other. We have an individual compartment, formerly for ladies only, in the second carriage, with an adjoining toilet. The rest of the carriage is now open-plan, totally stripped of internal partition walls and seats. It is where the officers sleep on bunk beds and share a toilet. God knows how the soldiers fare in the third carriage. It must be like fish crammed into a tin.

I spend most of my days looking out of the windows, watching Lew Wiesel gesticulating and giving orders to the civilians. Kirchner let slip it was Wiesel who found the train, organised its return to Berlin and planned its conversion to strip it of all unnecessary weight. On two occasions, during the hours when I am allowed to leave my makeshift prison or Meier insists I accompany him, Wiesel has seen me, but he avoids eye contact and chooses to walk straight past me; the girl who helped save his son. What right does he have to ignore me?

Beyond the sleeping accommodation, the work taking place in the forward seven carriages is truly amazing; a magical illusion, as Kirchner described it to Freiberg when they were about to start.

Every carriage has been stripped bare. Internal walls of thin sheets of wood have been installed lengthways along each carriage, leaving a gap by each window for a single passenger seat to be inserted. There is a large door built into each wooden panel at one end of the carriage. The illusion has been created by a group of elderly stagehands seconded from the long-defunct Berlin Opera House, who work from dawn to dusk painting onto large canvas sections. Laid on the floor, the perspective of the images looks all wrong, but as soon as the artwork is attached to the internal walls, it makes perfect sense. They are really talented individuals. If I survive the war, I will take up painting.

A senior Gestapo official was here two days ago, shown around by Kirchner. I was made to stand in the middle of the group of civilian workers, who held their hats against their stomachs and bowed their heads in respect.

'Imagine,' Kirchner says to the visitor, 'you open any carriage door and either side of you is a seat with a real person sitting down as in a normal train. Alongside them is a wooden partition with a painted canvas attached. Forget the image is painted and, from afar, you see a train full of wounded civilians, some sitting, others on stretchers. The people seated alongside the windows will be dressed as nurses or hospital orderlies, and red crosses will be painted on the roofs of the carriages. Hidden between the walls will be the precious cargo we are moving to a safer location.'

'You expect to fool people with this imagery?' The Gestapo official waves his hand casually at the artwork.

Kirchner frowns. 'Whilst it may not deceive a bystander at close quarters, from a distance or, more importantly, from the air, which is our main concern, it will appear a civilian passenger train crammed with suffering refugees and, hopefully, avoid further attention.'

The officer nods. 'I will report back to the Führer's office.'

'May I know your findings?'

Heels click together. 'Given the circumstances, time and manpower available, you have done an impressive job. My recommendation will be that you leave on the morning of April the fourteenth. I have inspected the diversionary arrangements. They will also be ready to depart. There is no time to lose. A hostile pincer movement is closing in on Berlin.'

Meier listens as I tell him what I know. He appears calmer now and impressed by the extent of my understanding. 'You have a right to know the facts, Rita,' he says. I cannot recall him using my name before. 'You not only have a right to emerge from behind Kirchner's shadow, but, I believe, from what I have seen, you may be the one person who will have the power to influence him.'

'Me?' I gulp in air. 'He pays no attention to what I say or think.'

'You will see,' he said. 'Perhaps you cannot see what others can.'

We have started walking again. The figure of Kirchner looms nearer, arms crossed and legs apart, looking towards us, Freiberg alongside with the dog straining and salivating at his heels. Looking back, that image is a cliché for all the evil, hatred and barbarism of Nazi rule and is forged into my memory forever.

'What happens now?' I ask.

'Over the past weeks, I have listed and separated the most valuable assets held by the Reischbank that have convertibility – how can I put it? – a lasting international value beyond our borders and the war. I'm talking about gold, foreign currencies, precious jewels, pieces of exquisite art. These things are coveted by all mankind. Today, these treasures, and I'm talking of more wealth than you or I could ever imagine, are held in vaults. Tonight, they will be loaded into the compartments of this train, and tomorrow, will be under the sole control of Kirchner as we attempt to make our way south to Berchtesgaden where the Führer will establish a second headquarters.'

'Are you afraid we may not arrive?'

The mad, desperate look is back in his eyes. 'I have two fears,' he says. He raises his arm to acknowledge he has seen Kirchner's beckoning gesture. We are fifty metres away now, but still picking our way carefully through the chaos. 'The Americans have reached the River Elbe to the west; the Russians have crossed the Oder and Neisse to the east. Eventually they will meet up. We have to beat them to it. Wiesel tells us our only hope is to take a long diversionary sweep to the south-east through Saxony and Czechoslovakia before turning back west. It will be touch and go.'

'You said two fears?'

He stops and turns to look at me. His eyes are bloodshot, underscored by wrinkles of black flesh. He has had little sleep. 'I do not doubt Kirchner's loyalty to the Führer, but I know his self-interest is much greater. I suspect he has two plans: one, we all know about, and another' – his mouth crimps – 'that he alone has prepared and does not include you or me and perhaps many others.'

ELEVEN
ANHALTER BAHNHOF, BERLIN, GERMANY
14 April 1945

I am hurting down there. It is the first time such a sharp pain has returned since that man butchered me in the camp. Last night, it brought back all those vivid memories, and the little time I slept was filled with … were they nightmares, or perhaps just snapshots of the past? I am too tired to think.

It's cold this morning, a damp mist in the air mixed with the smell of smoke curling in the distance from the chimney of the locomotive as it tries to escape upwards, away from the camouflage shield which envelops us all in a cocoon. Daylight is still an hour away as a barrage of arc lights concentrates on the groups of soldiers manhandling crate after crate into the central voids of each carriage.

Kirchner made me stand with a group of new arrivals, men and women, some I recognise as inmates from Sachsenhausen, all, like me, with numbers tattooed on their forearms. We were told to stand with our backs to the train and not to turn around or look at what was taking place behind us on pain of death. I don't need to disobey. Now I have my precious mirror, I can see what is taking place.

Yesterday, he forced me to listen as he tried to goad Meier into reacting by treating him as a miscreant child who fails to obey his elders. 'What will I do with you?' or 'I should make you stand in the corner,' or 'I'll have you sit in the naughty chair.' He used Freiberg as a conduit for his remarks, looking over and with a shake of the head, saying, 'This just won't do, will it, Freiberg?' or some other sarcastic put-down.

He knew the effect it was having. The sinews in Meier's neck stood out, the flesh bright red; his fists contracted and released at an ever-increasing speed and his chest heaved inside the ill-fitting uniform. Meier has no idea how to deal with the perpetual barrage of insinuations intended to condemn him as unfit for purpose and a liability to the project. Even so, he has managed to hold in check the one reaction Kirchner would love to provoke. If he could get Meier to assault him, the man's career as a soldier would come to a summary and dishonourable end.

In an instant, Kirchner's attitude can change. He pokes Meier in the chest repeatedly with his index finger. Two non-commissioned officers are summoned to join him. 'We leave tomorrow morning, so you pull yourself together and get your job done, Meier. Tonight, you supervise the delivery and loading of the cargo.' He withdraws his finger. 'Understood?'

Meier looks down at the ground and nods faintly.

Kirchner turns to address his men. 'Everything is going to plan. All prying eyes are on the stations at Michendorf and Lichterfelde-West and nobody is paying us any attention.'

I know what he is talking about. Earlier, as we cowered in the remains of the Ladies' Waiting Room, I asked Meier what 'diversionary arrangements' meant.

To keep the project at Anhalter a secret involved distracting the attention of foreign intelligence services to activity elsewhere. In the southern suburbs of Berlin, at two stations that had escaped major bomb damage, a similar operation, yet one far more visible, was underway. Two trains, code-named *Adler* and *Dohle*, were standing with steam up, awaiting the signal to depart. In their baggage cars was a hoard of treasures, coupled with over five hundred million Reichsmarks in notes and coins.

'If you think about it,' Meier said, 'whilst it seems a great deal of money to be prepared to sacrifice, when the war ends Germany will eventually have a new currency, and all this paper held in stock will simply be worthless and destroyed.'

Although the trains were to be heavily guarded, no changes had been made to their appearance, and it was envisaged that Doctors Funk and Schwedler, along with senior Reischbank staff, would openly travel as custodians until they reached their intended destination at the bank's branch in Munich. As an added distraction, a road convoy carrying bullion and printing plates was also coordinated to set off for the same destination.

'If we can focus hostile attention on those two fleeing birds, *Adler*, the Eagle, and *Dohle*, the Jackdaw, then our *Falke*, the Hawk, can escape undetected and unscathed into the National Redoubt.'

'And if the train doesn't make it?'

Meier closed his eyes. 'It's not something I'm prepared to contemplate.'

Kirchner finishes his informal briefing. He seems to have forgotten I am standing directly behind him. Meier starts to walk away, but stops in his tracks.

'I don't remember giving the order to dismiss, *Schlaumeier*. I haven't finished.'

'You know my name. Either use it or my rank' – he hesitates, fists pumping again – '*Sturmbannführer*.' Meier spits out the word as if it were a deadly infection.

As Kirchner turns, he realises I am there and orders me back to the compartment. He takes a step to stand directly in front of Meier, centimetres away, a bemused look on his face. His fingers reach for the braided loop on Meier's uniform. He pulls it gently, releasing the tack stitching under the shoulder epaulette, allowing the braid to fall and dangle at waist level. He massages the braid between his fingers. 'Like your uniform, you are a fake, a fraud. But you are a clever fake, clever enough to get your boss to look after his little protégé. I'd say that is worthy of a *schlaumeier*, a wise guy capable of conning his superiors, wouldn't you?'

Meier says nothing.

'And now, your fucking boss has once again interfered with my arrangements. You are to move from the officer's billet to the last compartment in the first carriage which will be your private domain. He obviously believes the other officers' – he turns to indicate the three men standing next to him – 'are not suitable company for somebody with such delicate sensibilities.'

There is suppressed laughter from the men.

'Fear not. I shall be moving to the adjacent compartment, so if you do have any trouble sleeping, you only have to tap on the wall.'

This time, the laughter is loud and derisory.

'The rest of the first carriage is out of bounds. We are facilitating the travel arrangements of some important people who will join us just before we depart. They will not be disturbed under any circumstances during our journey, and Freiberg here will be responsible for catering for their every need and the only person, other than myself, to enter the area.'

97

As I walk away, at least part of the puzzle has been answered. Ever since we arrived, I have wondered what was going on with the first carriage. It was stripped and refurbished by the civilian construction gang before anything else, with pulled-down blinds painted with the Red Cross symbol. Speculation will now be rife. Before the day is out, I guarantee rumours of the Führer or Bormann or Goering joining the train will be repeated as the gospel truth.

A lorry has just arrived and disgorged a collection of dazed-looking individuals alongside the marshalling yard. They stand around aimlessly waiting for someone to direct them, looking cautiously at each other, not a word passing between them. *Fahnenjunker* Kimmel, one of Kirchner's favoured knot of sycophants, pushes past me and begins to order them into line. Another soldier from the carriage preparation detail rushes to join him and they begin to herd the arrivals towards a collection of cardboard boxes at the end of the yard. Kimmel makes a beeline for a woman holding back from the group as she looks into a small compact mirror to straighten her hair and check her appearance. The swagger stick catches her on the wrist, knocking the mirror from her hand to break into two pieces on the ground. She catches the next blow from the leather strap around the cheek, breaking the skin in a long, thin red line.

'What the …' Her head lifts as she speaks. 'I was only trying to look pretty for you boys when the party starts.' She obviously has no idea why she is here.

I recognise her. 'Tillie!' I call out.

She turns to face me, her expression one of total confusion.

'Move,' Kimmel says.

She is rooted to the spot. 'Rita.' She is crying from the pain as blood starts to ooze from the wound.

Kimmel has the stick raised to strike again as I walk towards her just as a hand reaches past me and stops the blow on its downward arc. The action unbalances Kimmel who falls to the floor on one knee. His first reaction is to believe it is I who stopped him. The look on his face says he is preparing to kill me.

Meier fills the space between us. 'What do you think you're doing, Kimmel?'

I can tell Kimmel is looking back beyond us to where Kirchner is standing as he watches the scene play out. He makes no move.

Kimmel is back on his feet. 'What's it got to do with you?' he says, his tone one of uncertain bravado.

'I am an *Oberleutnant*, Kimmel. I am not "you". Now ask the question again.'

Kimmel's eyes are pleading for Kirchner to intercede, but I know him well enough to understand this reaction is exactly how he can engender the hatred of his men towards Meier.

Kimmel looks around at Tillie and back to Meier. 'You would protect a Jewish whore?' There is even less assuredness in his voice.

Meier pulls the swagger stick from the other man's grasp, clenches his fist around the hilt and pushes it hard into Kimmel's chest. He holds it there. 'I said, ask the question again, *Fahnenjunker* Kimmel.'

Kimmel hesitates, but there is no respite from another quarter. Reluctantly, he relents. 'I asked what it has got to do with the *Oberleutnant*.' His expression is a confused mix of hatred and despair.

'I'll tell you what it's got to do with me, shall I? You are putting this whole project in jeopardy by your irresponsible actions. Tomorrow, this woman will sit in the window of a train, attired as a nurse. I don't want her looking like some fucking battered wife a little sadist has had a go at. Now, get off with you.'

Meier bends to pick up the two pieces of the mirror, ushering Kimmel in front of him and giving neither Tillie nor I a second glance.

Tillie's fingers are feeling around her cheek as I help her to her feet. 'What's going on?' she asks. 'I thought—'

'I know what you thought,' I say, 'and it's nothing like that. I'll tell you later. You had better join the others before there's trouble.'

'I thought he was going to kill me.'

'You picked the wrong one,' I say. 'He may look like the Aryan dream, blue eyes, blonde hair and a figure like Adonis, but this particular member of the master race prefers males; the younger the better, so talk has it.'

Tillie tries to smile. 'I see you've grown into a woman since I last saw you.'

'Either that or die,' I reply.

'That's my girl,' Tillie mumbles, her cheek visibly swelling around the wound.

I smile back, but I can see through the façade, a vain attempt to project the Tillie of old, irreverent, brash and self-assured. If I have learnt one thing in this harsh world, it is that the eyes do not know how to lie. And there is such a deep sadness in hers. As she leaves, she begs me to seek her out tomorrow. I sense the one-time pupil has become the teacher.

Meier has already relocated to his berth in the first carriage and two civilians are moving Kirchner's belongings into the adjacent compartment. I retrieve a small, battered suitcase I have managed to keep with me since my internment, fill it with my few clothes and walk towards my new prison cell.

Meier opens his compartment door. 'I thought you might like this,' he says, smiling broadly and handing me the compact mirror. He has joined the two sections with the tape they used to attach the canvas scenery to the wooden partitions, restoring it to its original shape, save the gash across the face where it had broken. He must have scissors – I hadn't seen a pair since the days of dear Yodel and Mother. Where were they now? – And how thoughtful of him to trim the tape so precisely around the circular form of the mirror.

Kirchner comes into the compartment long after dark. He has been drinking and stands there, swaying and appraising me with bloodshot eyes, barely able to focus.

I don't want to talk about that night in detail. Kirchner takes me ferociously. I try to resist, but it just makes him more determined. It isn't even sex, just the manifestation of anger, frustration, and what I have come to realise is the singular intention to provoke. Whispering in my ear to gasp, grunt and scream with delight as loud as I can has but one aim. A flimsy partition away will be Meier's bunk. He will hear and be in no doubt as to what is taking place. Although I imagine the sudden noise is our bunk reacting to Kirchner's gyrations, I realise later it is Meier pounding on the partition wall. The distress he has suffered as witness to Kirchner's act of rape is etched on his face the next day. If I didn't hurt so much from the wound where I had been torn; if I had the means and opportunity to comfort him, which I do not; if, perhaps beyond comprehension and above all else, I hadn't felt what I can only describe as pity for Kirchner, I could have come to terms with the urge to strike back at something, someone – I don't know what or who or how.

Now, we are standing with our backs to the train. I'm next to Tillie, holding her hand and, with the other, moving the mirror to see what is going on behind us. She said I could have it. Tillie looks good dressed as a nurse, and as she pretends to take my temperature, we start to giggle, but sharp looks from some in our group shut us up. None of the guards are paying any attention to us, concentrating instead on the evolving situation around the train.

A large black car drew up about fifteen minutes ago with blinds drawn down over the windows. The Gestapo officer who was here a few days ago got out from the front passenger seat and entered into a lengthy conversation with Kirchner. There was a great deal of gesticulating and finger pointing. Meier tells me later it was to do with the shunting around of the carriages which Kirchner had ordered the previous evening. Carriages two and three, housing the officers and enlisted men accompanying the shipment, have been taken from the front and attached to the rear of the train. When the blinds of these carriages are now drawn, underneath the Red Cross symbol the word *Leichenhalle* – mortuary – has been added. Kirchner says it adds authenticity to the character of the train and avoids a question mark over two carriages with blinds almost permanently down.

There is activity around the car. I reposition the mirror. The rear door nearest the train has opened and I see two pairs of children's legs scampering towards the first carriage. A pair of shapely legs wearing dark brown stockings with a thick black seam follows. The woman's figure comes into view, bowed with head and shoulders covered by a blanket. A well-dressed man follows, similarly disguised. Their carriage door shuts and we are ordered to turn back to face the train.

The instructions are straightforward. Most of the inmates who arrived yesterday have now been decked out in some form of medical uniform or smart civilian clothes. They are to all take one of the window seats in the eight cargo carriages and remain in situ until given orders to the contrary. Instructions are that they will be allowed out for food and a toilet break twice per day. When given the order to draw down their blinds, they will do so immediately and the blinds are to remain down until the order is given to open them. No attempt must be made to look through gaps or take notice of any activity outside the train when blinds are drawn. Guards will be stationed in the cargo areas between the partition walls and have been ordered to shoot on sight should there be any disobedience.

Everybody acknowledges the command and we all walk towards the train.

Kirchner and I are sitting in silence in our compartment. He checks his watch and smiles. Nine in the morning, and the carriage shudders and stutters forward as our journey into the unknown begins.

TWELVE
PROTIVEC, CZECHOSLOVAKIA
29 April 1945

We have stopped again. It has been six hours since Kirchner set out to complete a reconnaissance of the branch line the train is on as it traces a circuitous route into Czechoslovakia and then back to the frontier with Germany just beyond Cheb. This information, as with everything I get to know about this journey and its significance, comes from Meier. He talks freely now and is happier than I have ever seen him. I think he believes the war is as good as over and he will soon be back with his family in Magdeburg. It sounds like a beautiful place to live, very old with many historic buildings.

As the train headed south on the first leg of the journey, we passed within a hundred kilometres of his city, so he explained. He was excited and passionate as he described the scenery around where his family lives.

It was Meier who told me Wiesel was on the train. I hadn't seen him since the preparations were completed and I assumed he had left and gone elsewhere. All the time, he was up in the locomotive, working with the train drivers. Apparently, they have bunks in a space next to the first coal tender, and all three are supposed to work a four-hour shift on, four off, day and night. Unfortunately, it hasn't worked out that way.

Wiesel had said it would take between two to three days to reach the destination, but it depended upon the intelligence received on hostile troop movements. Kirchner was naturally cautious. Food supplies took up valuable space otherwise available for cargo, but even so, he ordered a ten-day supply. We were now into day sixteen and, as loose talk had it, still hundreds of kilometres from our final destination.

The initial euphoria I felt at what seemed like escaping from the Nazi stronghold quickly turned to concern and apprehension. The first three days to me were like leaving on holiday. There was a sense of anticipation even amongst the officers and guards as we made reasonable time, albeit with numerous stops and starts, towards Leipzig and onwards to Dresden.

That was when it all started to unravel. We were stopped on the line north of the city for six hours. I overhead Kirchner explaining to a junior officer that the main line had been destroyed by the bombing in February and orders to restore a single track had not been completed. We were trying to find a branch line to enable the train to detour the city to the west and it proved to be a horrendous experience.

For long stretches, the rail line ran parallel to a main road or through a suburb. The countryside was packed with refugees, many with a few possessions strapped to their backs, moving slowly on foot, heading south and westward to escape the advancing Russian forces. The more fortunate children walked alongside their parents, but many struggled on alone. In their midst were soldiers in tattered uniforms, many wounded; sometimes a group of camp inmates in their striped uniforms, herded like cattle by guards with pointed rifles and desolate expressions. The scene was one of misery and it never ceased. Many a soul would cast a glance across the wire fence at the train and turn quickly back when they caught sight of Kirchner's troop, positioned at intervals on the carriage roofs, guns trained. Every so often, the line of people would be scattered like ants underfoot as the horns of lone vehicles or convoys demanded passage through the throng.

Even so, the presence of life, however desperate and distressed, was a more tenable option than the view from the other side of the train. To the east, the scene of devastation was unimaginable. Meier explained how the mid-February bombing of Dresden had literally razed the city to the ground. You just had to look at the jagged remains of a skyline to realise the extent of the devastation, and it turned my stomach. Even though I would have been more than willing to see every German held to account for the evil they had unleashed onto the world, the reality that such a fearful, crushing and indiscriminate revenge could be inflicted I would not have believed possible. Maybe, the sight of such devastation made a lasting impact on me.

We wait for hours on end, stopped outside a station, a halt or level crossing until it is cleared so we can pass through at speed. Kirchner's nightmare is the prospect of the train stopping somewhere where people have access to board. To halt a stampede towards the train would mean either mass murder or being overwhelmed. Two machine guns and a dozen rifles will not hold back a desperate mass until the wall of bodies is too high to scale or the pool of blood too deep to cross. This cannot happen.

And so we move on, painfully, kilometre by kilometre. Our break stops have developed a sort of ritual. The train always halts alongside a deserted, wooded area. The passengers are separated by sex and accompanied by the guards in groups for toilet relief and, whenever there is a stream nearby, the chance to wash and freshen up. Once the meagre field rations have been distributed, they are shunted back into their places and blinds drawn. The following ten minutes provide a chance for the officers and men to eat, relax and chat amongst themselves before they, too, are ordered to return to their carriages and blinds are drawn. Only Kirchner and Freiberg remain outside to ensure total compliance.

At this point, I have to make a confession. All the carriage windows had been sealed shut with an industrial glue, so the civilian worker at Anhalter had told me, a type used in shoemaking. I recognised the smell and I had often seen my father loosening particularly difficult strands of glue that had hardened on his workbench with a mixture of vinegar and cooking oil. I had no access to vinegar, but a little cooking oil from the camping stove in the kitchen area at Anhalter was easily secreted in an old chipped cup.

Whenever the hours of solitude had seemed never-ending and with Kirchner elsewhere on the train, I would set to my work. The main window was out of the question. Apart from the enormity of the task, under normal conditions it was made to obey gravity and stay in the down position until a leather strap with holes at various intervals was pulled to raise it and then fixed to a metal stud protruding from the door frame to hold it in position. If I was surprised by someone's presence with the window in the open position, I would never have time enough to release the strap and pull it closed.

However, the small ventilation window at the top of the door was a different proposition. It was no bigger than the side of a house brick, and slid sideways to the open position. It required no more than a simple movement of the hand.

Over two days, I chafed each strand of glue with a dinner knife, applied the oil and waited until the adhesive had softened sufficiently for me to scrape part of it off with a teaspoon. I hid the redundant glue in my tea mug and disposed of it when washing up the crockery. Finally, this time using some of the oil as a lubricant, I forced the window open.

It was a godsend. If I sat close to the blind, I could hear all normal conversation within a ten-metre radius and much further beyond if people were shouting. And the two special children did like to shout.

Once everyone is locked away behind their window blinds, Freiberg will open the door to the area reserved for our secret guests. The children rush out and scream and shout as they play together. I've worked out they must be close in age. He is Anders and she is Gretchen. On one occasion, the wind blew my window blind backwards and I caught a view of the pair of them. She seemed to be looking straight at me, but nothing happened. I'd put them at eleven or twelve.

I have never seen the parents, but I like the sound of the woman's voice. It is always soft and appealing. I have imagined her as tall with flowing ginger hair and I see her as gentle. His voice is like all German men, cold and harsh, even when he's talking to the children. I think he must be small with tight features and fish eyes. I don't like him, especially the laugh; it seems vaguely familiar and unpleasant.

The secret guests spend ten minutes or so outside, and then Freiberg escorts them back to their quarters. They are right next to us, taking up three-quarters of the carriage, but I rarely hear them through the partition wall. One or other of the children plays the violin; at least, it sounds something like a violin. He or she is very good. The parents clap sometimes and the father says 'well done'.

On days like today, when Kirchner is away and we are held up for hours on end, Meier orders the guards to allow the inmates to disembark and laze in the area to one side of the train. Freiberg is to let the guests know they are welcome to disembark on the other side, out of view of the rest of us. They rarely do, I understand.

Meier's actions give me the opportunity to meet up with Tillie and talk. She is always full of questions I cannot answer, the repetitive one being 'what is going to happen to us?' I ask Meier and he shrugs with his 'what do you think?' expression. I say I don't know.

'Look at it this way,' he says, solemnly. 'When we get to where we are going, their usefulness is over as far as Kirchner is concerned. I doubt there is a camp for them to go to. If he releases them, they could tell people what little they know, or have guessed, and set rumours afoot. Now, what do you think?'

'They will be put to death?' I must sound like the wondrous schoolgirl.

Tillie is in no way naïve. I try to suggest when we near or reach our destination, with all the confusion likely to ensue, it might be best if she tried to get away. She understands what I'm trying to say and gives me a vacant smile. I think she has lost the will to fight for survival. Her baby died. Pneumonia, she said, but there are no tears in her eyes when she talks of her daughter. Maybe I'm wrong. I really hope so.

Today, as we wait for Kirchner and Wiesel to return from their scouting trip, we are all lazing on a grassy knoll. The sun is unusually hot for so early in the year and the sky is a violent blue with not a cloud in sight. Meier says it's because we're getting further south every day, and something about heat and land mass. I can't be bothered to listen. There are just two guards sitting at a distance from each other on the carriage steps, rifles resting on their knees, their faces turned towards the sun. Most of the other men have stripped off their tunics and are lying in a group away from the inmates, displaying their vests and the braces holding up their trousers with legs rolled up as they take advantage of the warmth.

Meier asks me if I would like to visit his parent's farm when the war is over. Strange how some people pose the question they really want answered by asking something different. And people answer in the same fashion, which is exactly what I did by saying my first objective was to return to the family home in Poland and I just couldn't make further plans.

There is hardly any breeze and few people talk. The only noise is the sound of the birds in the copse communicating with each other. In such a scene, it is impossible to imagine the din and horror of war. Everything is at peace and conflict no longer exists.

The sound is like the hum of a bee. You hear it before you see it, before it comes out of the sun towards you. The hum grows louder. The soldiers are the first to move, struggling to their feet and heading for the train. The guards shout for us to return and disappear into the nearest carriage.

On two occasions so far, the train has been buzzed by enemy aircraft; once an American Mustang, and the day before yesterday by a Russian MiG. On both occasions the aircraft made one or more passes, dived for a closer look and departed. The Mustang even wiggled its wings in response to the false waves of the so-called passengers.

This time, one of the men shouted out that it was Russian, a Yak-3. The plane comes in from the south-west, dives to just over tree height and makes a pass across the adjacent cornfield. Shouts come for us to wave, and we do. There is no wing wiggle as the Yak disappears into the distance.

People begin to shuffle back to the carriages and their allotted places. All the guards are already inside. Out of the corner of my eye, I catch sight of the two of them, unmistakably Tillie and the man who sits opposite her in the carriage. They are running along the knoll to even ground and into the cornfield. Two fields across, you can see there is an unmade road weaving through the countryside and into the hills and forest beyond. They are making a break for freedom. I pray they succeed.

This time the sound is horrendous. With no time to clamber into the nearest carriage, we run to hide underneath the train. It sounds like a rainstorm. The fighter plane comes in this time directly from the west and broadside on to the train. Bullets strafe through the cornfield and rattle against the gravel alongside the track and close enough to send stones spinning into Meier's face. A volley of bullets thunders into the underside of the train. Fortunately, the aircraft has to pull up over the copse before it is at an angle to do any damage to the superstructure or take out the windows.

The sound of its engine disappears into the distance and silence returns.

As the sun is setting, Meier knocks on my compartment door. He's holding his peaked cap against his chest and he acts like an interrogator. Tillie is dead. The bullets nearly severed her into two, he says bluntly. From the person I have come to respect, the comment is strangely lacking in sensitivity. The man with whom Tillie fled was seriously wounded. Yes, I did hear the single gunshot.

Kirchner returns at daybreak, tired but elated. The way through to their destination is clear. I have never known his conversation with me to be so unguarded. We are heading for somewhere called the National Redoubt. I ask whether it's a camp and he laughs. Apparently, the German forces and High Command are to relocate to this place with the peculiar name and, from there, to forge a new Reich stretching from Bavaria through Austria and into northern Italy.

I feel a different kind of sadness. Tillie died in vain. Meier was wrong. He is to blame. She would not have been executed. Kirchner explains the intention is to keep thirty-five thousand prisoners as hostages to work on the land and to be offered in exchange for guarantees once negotiations start with the Americans and their allies. For him to tell me all this detail indicates a new phase in our relationship. Or so I imagine.

As the train pulls away, I make a promise to myself to return to this place and lay flowers in memory of a dear friend who taught me some valuable lessons in the struggle to survive. It is to my eternal regret I never can fulfil my pledge.

THIRTEEN
NEAR OBERAU, GERMAN–AUSTRIAN BORDER
7 p.m., 30 April 1945

The last station we passed was called Hallein and I have been allowed to look out of the window. I assume we have been travelling through Germany, but Kirchner tells me we were only briefly in the homeland before crossing into Austria. They must speak the same language here because all the signs I see are in German.

Somewhere along the route, we joined the main line which has taken us through towns rather than skirting around them, with no sign of the level of destruction we witnessed further north. The scenery is now mountainous with dense pine forests and luscious green valleys. It's beautiful, so like the images on the paintings you could buy in the old market square on Sundays in my home town. From Hallein, we crossed a river and have now come to a stop with darkness all around, save the millions of stars that shine in the sky.

Wiesel is outside the compartment calling for Kirchner to join him. 'We are too early,' I hear him say through my open window. I have now done something else. I used the rest of the oil to loosen some of the glue at the base of the main window and wedged one end of a small, thin stick into the gluey compound. It stuck as if into plasticine, and I can move it to and fro without it coming loose. The other end of the stick I prop against the bottom of the blind when it's down, forcing it back slightly from the glass and allowing a space through which I can see what is going on.

Kirchner checks his watch. 'How much longer to the drop-off?'

'Ten, fifteen minutes.' It's the first time I've caught sight of Wiesel for days. His face is black with coal dust. Even in the cool of night, his face is laced with beads of sweat.

'I ordered everybody to assemble in the last two carriages at eight ready to disembark. Let's say it takes five minutes to move the prisoners along the train, we should leave here at seven forty. That gives us thirty minutes to prepare.'

They walk away out of earshot.

Meier must have been watching them as well. He appears at the carriage door almost immediately. I gesture for him to open it, which can only be done by using the external handle.

His face is flushed, his voice stammering, very much like the first time he came into my life. 'This is it,' he says. 'By daybreak it will all be over, the cargo unloaded, the train gone, and I will be a civilian again, out of this wretched uniform for ever.' He looks at me, his eyes pleading. 'Please say you will come and find me when it's all over.'

There's the crackle of a field radio from the compartment allocated to the secret guests. I can hear the man's voice, not distinctly, not the words he is speaking, just the sound of his voice. I know it from somewhere I cannot recall and it scares me.

'Of course,' I say blindly, my head totally absorbed by the voice. The man stops talking and says something in a softer tone, to his wife, I presume.

Meier ploughs on. 'Do you know where you are going after this?'

I return my attention to him. 'He said something once about a *Ratlines*, whatever that is, and joining a circle. Where or if I go is not a choice I have to make.'

'Really?' He sounds astonished. 'It means there is an escape route and point of contact. Listen!' There is the approaching sound of boots on gravel. 'If you make it, there will be a chance somewhere, sometime, for you to escape. I'll help you, and I'll be waiting.' He takes a piece of toilet paper from his pocket. 'Hide this. It's my parents' telephone number. Ring and I'll come for you.' Hurriedly, he closes my door and retreats back to his compartment.

From this moment on, my night is full of fear and confusion, incomprehension and despair. Images will live in my memory for ever. I cannot truthfully explain my appreciation of what was happening at the time, but I have long since pieced it all together in my mind and I provide a dispassionate recounting of these events.

I am alone in the darkness. There is no light in the compartment or in the surrounding countryside. Kirchner has not returned. It was Kimmel whose footfall we heard as he approached, ordering blinds to be shut and remain firmly closed until further notice. Even so, my stick does the trick

112

and I can see in a line, either forwards or back along the train, as I oscillate the blind one way or the other. I slide the small window to the open position, sit on the edge of my seat and wait. I can feel the piece of paper Meier gave me rub against the sole of my foot.

The train edges forward. We glide slowly through a deserted and lightless station. I make out the name. Oberau. Onwards we go.

A light flashes in front of us. Someone is on the line waving a lantern. The train brakes with a screech, vibrating the carriages as it stops. There is activity behind. Hurriedly, I change the position of the blind and move to the opposite seat. We are on a deserted stretch of track. The carriage jerks forward and back; then, the sound of metal clanging in the distance. There is another forward movement and the train advances a hundred or so metres before it again stops. I look back from where the noises came. I can see nothing. The train whistle gives a short single blast. Carriage doors are being opened in the distance, feet trampling on gravel.

Arc lights explode to life around us. The sensation is macabre, the intensity unnatural, as if we are participating in some strange theatre, illuminated until the scene has played out.

The train has stopped on a long, sweeping curve, enabling me to see what happens at the rear of the train.

The last two carriages have been decoupled from the rest of the train and stand isolated some distance behind us. Soldiers and inmates alike are milling around on the ground in front of the carriages.

The sound is unmistakable. Machine-gun fire. I've watched and heard a single gun mow down a group of helpless victims before. It's nothing like this. Whichever way they turn – men, women, officers, soldiers – no one escapes the hail of bullets coming from all directions. Bodies are flung into the air to fall to the ground like puppets with the strings sliced. Flashes of gunfire, even brighter than the lights that penetrate the night, hang in the air as if they were fairy lights at a bar mitzvah. Soldiers who raise their arms to return fire are butchered before they have time to aim. Some run, but never manage more than a few steps before they are cut to pieces.

There is silence. I hear voices, words I don't understand, nervous laughing, what sounds like orders being shouted out. Three men in uniform are walking between the fallen bodies. An occasional single gunshot from a revolver breaks this new silence.

The train whistle sounds one more blast and we move forwards. We are entering a tunnel. The noise is unbearable. Black smoke is curling in through my open window. I slide it shut. I want to see what is in front of us, but I am sitting in the wrong seat. The blind is set for me to look behind and I daren't touch it. Once again, we have stopped and people are moving around alongside the carriages, dark, shadowy figures, saying nothing, just hurrying past.

To the rear of the train, everything is in darkness, but I can tell that lights have come on somewhere in front. I can't see what is going on. All of a sudden, the answer comes to me. The compact mirror. Tillie's mirror. It's hidden amongst the feathers in one of my pillows.

Things are happening I can't see. There is that noise again: the sound of metal and banging. The train lurches again momentarily and I nearly drop the mirror onto the floor, just managing to tighten the grip with the tips of my fingers before it slips through. I hold it at an angle in the gap between the blind and the window. It's magic. I can now make out what is happening.

The sudden noise is of the locomotive gaining steam; are we about to move again? There is a bank of three lights on a stand. I don't recognise the uniforms of the soldiers hurrying around. The colour is a drab olive and the leggings above brown boots make their trousers crease into folds at the calf. Some have cross belts around their shoulders and I see two men wearing armbands with the letters 'MP' stamped on them. If I wasn't so terrified at what might happen, I could laugh. Nearly all of them are chewing something, like cattle in a field, a constant, precise movement, never stopping.

They take little notice of Kirchner who is standing alongside the locomotive, talking to Kimmel. The noise of the engine is deafening. Kimmel nods, receives a pat on the back and goes to raise his arm in salute. Kirchner hurriedly grabs it and pushes his hand back down. Two of the soldiers standing nearby begin to laugh. Kimmel jumps onto the step, grasping the handrail as Wiesel's head appears. He nods at Kirchner, pulls

Kimmel up onto the footplate and the engine starts to move forward along the tunnel.

We are not moving. The noise I heard must have been the engine uncoupling from the rest of the train. I can see now the locomotive has gone that we are close to the exit to the tunnel. If I swivel the mirror just a little, I can make out stars in the night sky beyond the arch.

Soldiers are standing to attention, making a strange-looking salute and ceasing to chew. Freiberg rushes past and I hear him say to someone, 'He's here.' A carriage door opens and I sense the family walk carefully past my compartment, emerging out of the darkness to stand grouped close to the bank of lights. They have their backs to me, facing a procession of three people who have just entered the tunnel. The man in the middle wears a short brown military jacket and a funny little hat that sits on top of his head. He returns a salute that looks like he is pointing at his ear whilst displaying the palm of his gloved hand. I assume he must be the commandant.

The secret guests shuffle forwards and the man holds out his hand towards the commandant, who calls Kirchner over and speaks to him with some words in a language I recall vaguely from my school days.

Kirchner turns to the secret guest and speaks in German. 'This is General Franklin Williams, joint commander of the US Fifth Army deployment in Bavaria.' The general steps forward and briefly grasps the man's fingers with his gloved hand. 'The general is commanding a small expeditionary force sent to escort you to Munich, which I can confirm is now under the control of the Americans and their allies.'

The man clicks his heels together and bows his head. 'Please tell the general, on behalf of myself and my family, I am grateful for his intervention.' He turns to Kirchner. 'And to you, Heinrich' – that's the first time I've ever heard anybody call him by his first name – 'for liaising with the Americans over these past weeks to enable us to escape this wretched war.' He coughs. 'Can you also tell the general I have it on good authority from former military associates in Berlin that earlier today, Herr Hitler and his wife, Eva, along with a number of personal staff, were pronounced dead by the resident physician.'

Kirchner returns to address the general and the two adjutants who flank him. Their conversation fades in and out of earshot as I detect the sound of men at work at the rear of the train. American soldiers have started to dismantle the partition walls in the last of the eight carriages and are moving the crates of cargo onto large handcarts which are ferried to the mouth of the tunnel. There must be at least fifty men at work.

Kirchner is talking in German again. 'The general has heard the same rumour and is awaiting official confirmation. Within the hour, we will move from this location in convoy to begin the eighty-kilometre journey north to Munich. Your family, Doctor Sommer, will travel in separate armed vehicles. Progress will be uncertain. This whole area is a no man's land, neither controlled by the US nor the Wehrmacht. The roads are packed with refugees and members of the German armed forces who have surrendered their arms and are trying to escape from the advancing Russian forces. Of more concern are a number of Wehrmacht battalions roaming the countryside with orders to head for Berchtesgaden and the *Kehlsteinhaus* – it's what the general calls the Eagle's Nest – to mount a defensive operation. If we encounter one of these groups en route, the fighting could be heavy.'

The name, Doctor Sommer, means nothing to me. I have heard his name mentioned, but I don't remember when. He must be important to warrant all this special, secretive treatment.

'Closer to Munich, intelligence suggests retreating forces could prove especially difficult to avoid and their appetite to fight impossible to gauge. Our convoy will split into three more mobile units and take different routes, converging from both east and west into areas of the city where we have established control zones.'

One of the men standing alongside the general asks a question. Kirchner turns back to Sommer and smiles. 'Colonel Hadley is curious. He says his Texas origins are founded on straight-talking and no bullshit answers. Their orders were hurriedly drawn and issued with no explanatory or background content, which is unusual. The confidential instruction is to collect the contents of the train and prepare you and your family for onward transmission to the United States. He would like to know what makes you so important to warrant this special treatment. We have time. It will be twenty minutes before they finish the cargo transfer onto the trucks.'

There is the laugh I recognise. Sommer half turns to face the colonel and the mirror falls from my trembling hand. This is the man who put the

116

iron inside me at the first camp. I close my eyes and feel the sweat on my face, the comforting words of Yodel, the pressure to hurry from Mother, the smirk on the face of the *Helferin*. The mirror is in my lap. I try to replace it with shaking hands. I have seen this man's contemptuous expression in my nightmares, heard that self-satisfied laugh a million times.

In my haste, the mirror taps against the glass of the window, not loud enough for them to hear, but the girl, Gretchen, turns and looks in my direction. Our eyes seem to meet through the prism of the mirror, but it can't be. Her gaze is fixed, yet she says nothing and turns back when her arm is tugged by her brother. They are both tall for their ages. Her hair is auburn, cut short and close to the chin in the style of most of those Hitler Youth posters. But the eyes are her most stunning feature; a clear blue almost turning to grey, large pupils and a stare that could transfix a cobra. They make me draw breath in fear.

'The objective of war is to overcome and suppress your enemy, occupy and control his territory as your own.' Sommer stops at frequent intervals for Kirchner to translate into English. 'We do this by killing people, thereby creating amongst other things the need for revenge, which, in turn, we overcome by instilling fear and retribution. We also do it by destroying property which we then have to replace, using precious resources in the process. My professional life is dedicated to developing a means of ensuring mass capitulation and acceptance which would avoid death and destruction whilst achieving the same aims as using physical force.'

Hadley guffaws and says something which causes General Franklin to smile. Kirchner reacts to Sommer's quizzical expression.

'He said you want to see the military out of a job by using what, hypnotism? In his view, you are living in a world of science fiction.'

Sommer addresses Hadley directly, his tone serious, and ignores the fact he is speaking in a language the other man does not understand. Kirchner's sporadic translation sounds like an echo as Sommer talks without stopping. 'Science, yes. Fiction? Who knows. The science is predicated on two elements, both in an embryo stage, I admit, but with some degree of initial success. Numerous tests have been carried out and the progression is to move the trials from one or two people to a large number; say, the population of a major city.'

'You wanna brainwash a whole city at once? It's been proven people can't be hypnotised into doing things they consider bad or against their instincts.' Hadley chokes on the words. 'You sound crazy, man.' He leaves a second between every word, as subsequently mimicked by Kirchner's interpretation.

Sommer is unfazed. 'Absolutely. You must condition people to believe in your concept of what you describe as bad and against their instincts. If you can convince them a heinous crime is a virtue and will benefit society, their judgement will be altered accordingly.'

Franklin turns to Hadley. 'Like brainwashing a whole society to accept it's all right to exterminate a few million Jews. Maybe he's got a point.'

Sommer nods as he acknowledges the translation. 'If you like. I might take issue with the analogy, but maybe I've been brainwashed too, though I don't like the term. I prefer to think of it as an electrician applying a circuit breaker and rewiring certain functions to react in a different way.' He holds up his arm to dissuade any further break in his discourse.

'My colleagues have been testing a low radio frequency to simultaneously transmit a subliminal message to make all but the least susceptible responsive to certain reactions when key words are broadcast on air. Such a technique will be employed in conjunction with the use of a hallucinatory, relaxing stimulant to alter the state of mind of the subject and increase receptivity of the message.'

He waits again for Kirchner to relay his words, but leaves no opportunity for a rejoinder.

'To anticipate your next question, tests have been carried out using airborne transmission attached to a virus, thus far with unsatisfactory results, or, more promisingly, with a variant that slowly dissolves in the mains water supply. We have a great deal more work to do.' He motions to Kirchner. 'Perhaps now is the time for the practical demonstration we discussed to show these blockheads what I mean.'

Kirchner smiles. 'My pleasure.'

There is a lull in the exchanges as orders are relayed between the Americans. Several check their watches. I calculate the unloading has now reached the forward carriages and they are close to removing the remaining

118

cargo. Kirchner moves out of my sightline to return minutes later dressed as a civilian in used, ill-fitting clothes. Freiberg stands next to him, similarly dressed.

Everybody I can see, all the Americans, officers and men, has stopped what they are doing to look. A dishevelled-looking Meier, stripped to his underpants, appears from in front of the carriage. There are cuts and bruises right across his torso. He is forced to his knees in front of Sommer's family and restrained by two of the soldiers with 'MP' on their arms. Meier looks up at Kirchner, confused and exhausted, and, without his glasses, seemingly unable to focus.

His head moves unsteadily. 'Your new uniform suits you, traitor Kirchner.' He manages a weak smile.

Kirchner motions for the two guards to move back and walks across to Meier. A food can is in his hand, an opener in the other. He carefully cuts into the lid, almost detaching it, and holds out the can for Meier to see the label. 'The condemned man deserves a final meal, Meier. The Americans have these wonderful B-Rations with all sorts of nourishing ingredients. I chose beef for you.' He twists off the jagged lid and passes over the tin which Meier takes between cuffed hands, a look of boyish incomprehension on his face.

'I regret this isn't quite the celebratory meal you might have imagined on the completion of your assignment, nor indeed can your protector, Dr Funk, be with us to celebrate, although I expect you will be reunited with him before too long. Do enjoy it, Meier.' He picks up the lid from the floor and hands it to Sommer.

Kirchner exchanges remarks with the general and Hadley, and returns his attention to Meier who is still kneeling with the can wedged between his hands. His eyes look around, searching for a friendly point of reference, but there is no sympathy in the expressions of any of those who stand by and watch on. How I wish I could hold out my hand to him.

Sommer whispers into the ear of his daughter. Gretchen's body straightens as he talks. She looks over in my direction, but I sense her attention is somewhere far distant. She walks over to where Meier is kneeling and smiles at him. Somehow, he manages a brief smile in return and shifts position slightly. The two guards stiffen, their hands on the leather holsters holding their small arms.

Gretchen holds out her left hand to take the tin he is clasping. 'Have you had enough?' she asks, again with a smile. He extends forward to let her remove the tin which she places on the floor. I am watching, transfixed by the spectacle. And then, I see it just before Meier does.

'*Ren*,' Sommer says precisely.

Reindeer, I ask myself. What does that mean?

Grasped between the tiny fingers of a child is the top of the tin. With one thrust, an equally tiny hand draws the jagged edge across Meier's exposed throat. He looks at her in disbelief, his Adam's apple swallowing as he senses the cut.

There is a collective gasp from those watching the scene play out.

Meier's hand is at his throat. Ten seconds pass as he tries to get to his feet. Blood starts to seep out between his fingers; at first, a trickle of arterial blood, then, enough to fill a cup seeping past his hand every time his heart beats and onto the gravel at his feet. As he turns to face our carriage, time stands still. One hand still pressing uselessly against his neck, the other, half-raised in what I like to remember as a gesture of parting to me, he pitches forward, his body twitching on the ground until it eventually lies still.

Gretchen remains standing in the position from where she put the can. With careful precision, she replaces the lid to cover the exposed food.

Two soldiers remove the body and carry it somewhere out of sight.

Sommer calls his daughter over to whisper in her ear. Her shoulders visibly relax and she turns around to talk to her brother. She doesn't seem to show any reaction to what has just taken place and, equally, nor does he.

I can't look any more. It's too much to take in. I am desperate to cry, to scream out, but I cannot. Beyond the horror, the tragedy, the sheer waste of life I have witnessed over the last few hours, I can feel sorry and disappointed to be deprived of Meier's company, the only man who has ever treated me as a real person, sharing my opinions, my feelings and my dreams. Maybe so, although I now know myself well enough to recognise a 'but' is coming.

The 'but' is this. However much I long to want to reject violence and the evils of war, as this day draws to an end the stark truth is all I really care about is that I am still alive and, in spite of his many virtues, Meier, the Nazi soldier, his Führer and many more like him are dead. Good riddance.

FOURTEEN
MOVING TOWARDS 1962 AND VALPARAISO, CHILE

I could write a travelogue detailing all of the places I have seen in three continents over the last forty-three years. Alternatively, I could try to explain how a relationship could remain intact over such a long period when it had grown out of fear and loathing and has never experienced a stronger emotion on my part beyond pity and the intimacy of the bond of two fugitives forever on the run.

It would be logical to question why I never chose to make my escape, to leave him and return to pick up my roots in a homeland I barely remember. I did try once and I'll come to that, but whilst I will always see myself as the victim, others see me as a collaborator, the co-perpetrator of terrible crimes. I accept, from their standpoint and based on the apparent facts, this is the only conclusion they could reach.

Over the years, columns of newsprint have been dedicated to analysing the reasons for my actions. It was fashionable, at one time, to speculate I had experienced the Stockholm syndrome, to suggest I had formed an alliance and developed positive feelings towards my captor. Nothing could be further from the truth.

But, first things first.

Near Oberau – 30 April–1 May 1945
It is nearly an hour since the Sommer family and the general and his entourage left. Freiberg releases me from the compartment and takes me to a dirt cutting above the mouth of the tunnel. His hand feels around my bottom as he pretends to help me up onto the tailgate of a waiting truck. He leers at me as he sniffs his fingers. I turn my head and ignore the profanity he utters.

There is a wooden crate to sit on, and with the canvas backdrop tied up I can watch what is going on inside the tunnel.

Kirchner spends most of his time liaising with an American who has three inverted triangles stitched to the sleeve of his uniform and who, whenever he sees me, winks and whistles two notes through nicotine-stained teeth. Kirchner seems to find the man amusing. Together, they have organised the dispatch of a dozen trucks, transporting the cargo and most of the soldiers.

I've counted six soldiers still around. Three appear to be running wires around the perimeter of the tunnel exit. The other three appeared from inside the tunnel, carrying a similar roll of wire, and are now lounging on the grass laughing, joking and watching the others at work. Freiberg was driven off in an open-top military vehicle accompanied by one of the MP soldiers.

Kirchner looks worried, forehead creased and his attention distracted whenever the headlights of a vehicle appear on the main road beyond the cutting. Of the few vehicles that pass, nobody appears to stop or slow down to fathom the glow from the arc lights at the bottom of the embankment. Perhaps they do but are too sensible to satisfy their curiosity.

The arc lights go out. Kirchner is in the driving seat of the truck and shouts for me to join him. He points to the passenger seat, pulls the starter and waits for the engine to catch and fire into life.

'Freiberg should be where you are. What the fuck has happened to Kimmel? If we're stopped, pretend you're ill. Moan with pain.' At least the truck seems to have heeded his command and makes a series of groans and whining noises as he wrestles with the steering wheel. Eventually, with sweat dotting his forehead, he manages to get the truck to face back down the cutting, its headlights now illuminating the pathway.

I can see the Americans have finished and are making their way back up the cutting. That's clever. They've just reached a thicket and are removing foliage from around two of those military vehicles hidden from sight. It is so well done, I never would have guessed they were there. One of the men bends on one knee and presses down on something. There are two mighty explosions, one in the distance and another close at hand. The exit to the tunnel caves in along with the surrounding embankment. There is another detonation. Tons of earth collapse in on the mass of bricks already displaced by the explosion and cover the rail lines for a distance of fifty metres beyond what was once the tunnel exit. The carriages and Meier have been buried together.

One of the American soldiers claps slowly and says something to one of the others. For the first time, Kirchner smiles. I look at him and raise my eyebrows.

'He said to his companion, you couldn't even blow up your mother-in-law if you got her to sit on a stick of dynamite.' He recognises my incomprehension. 'American humour,' he says dismissively, and puts the truck into reverse to back up the pathway.

What is left of the night we spend sleeping in a barn near Ettal, right on the edge of the forest. The adjoining farm is owned by a rosy-cheeked woman and her husband, who had been expecting us. In the morning we are provided with a breakfast of boiled eggs, rough bread and, for me, a mug of fresh milk. I will remember this meal for as long as I live. For three years I had not seen an egg, let alone eaten one. Butter? I've heard the name. I don't think I've ever tasted anything so glorious. As for fresh milk, what can I say, but the ache in my stomach is not from the food – at least, not yet – it's the association of the taste with memories of happier times in another place with a family full of love. Funny how a taste, a phrase from a song, a stanza from a poem or a book creates a reflex somewhere in your mind, like turning to a page in a photo album you had forgotten existed.

Am I ill? The face of the farmer's wife shows her concern as I vomit repeatedly into the mixing bowl she rushes to hand me once I express the first wave onto the stone floor. I feel like death, but all Kirchner can do is laugh. He says I've been eating swill for so long, my body can't take normal food yet. He is treating me like a child, which I can't abide. I can't stand. The dizziness comes in waves as I collapse back into the kitchen chair. Through my distress, I long to wipe the smile off his face. Happily, Freiberg does that for me.

He arrives mid-morning, unshaven and dishevelled. The farmer explains they have to get on with their daily chores. The farm won't run itself. His wife casts a rueful glance over her shoulder at me as they leave. I must look a sorry sight, sitting there like a zombie, an empty mixing bowl propped in my lap.

There is no more pretence at confidentiality or, to my surprise, of rank. 'Well?' Kirchner says.

'He got away.'

'Who got away?'

'Wiesel. Who do you think?' he adds testily.

'How?'

'I'm guessing. He must have realised why you sent Kimmel. He had it all planned.'

'What do you mean "planned", for God's sake? You're talking in riddles.' Saliva clung to the corners of his mouth.

'You told me the intention was to leave the locomotive and tenders at the sidings in Hallein. He did not do that.'

'Go on.'

'He took it on to the freight yard south of Salzburg. There must be a hundred units laid up there. It took me thirty minutes to find it. The driver and his mate were in the coal tender, bullet holes in the back of their heads. Kimmel was on the footplate. The blade edge of the coal shovel had almost severed the head from his body. He was taken from behind. No sign of Wiesel. The place is chaos. American forces are advancing towards the city. The roads are clogged with refugees. It won't be long before this area is occupied. We need to go.'

The next few days are a blur to me. From somewhere, Kirchner gets hold of an old Volkswagen car and we move slowly westward. The farmer's wife had provided us with a selection of dried foodstuffs, flagons of water and two amazing meat pies she has baked. Kirchner rails at the muck, as he describes it, calling it unfit for pigs to eat. To me, it's like a banquet now my stomach is getting used again to something other than gruel.

We avoid towns and sleep in abandoned buildings or alongside the car in the open air. The spring weather is unusually warm and it's no hardship to wake up in the morning with an aching back so long as the birds are singing and the breeze is fanning the trees.

The first day, Freiberg travels with us in the front passenger seat. Kirchner has been in a bad mood since he found out about Wiesel, and the two of them bicker a lot about plans and tactics, as they call it. That night, we sleep in the waiting room of an abandoned railway station, and by the time Kirchner shakes me awake the next morning, there is no sign of Freiberg. All I get is a grunt when I ask where he's gone and his name is never mentioned again.

Eventually, we reach our destination, a large farm near Ravensburg. As we briefly rejoin the main road, a fallen sign indicates we are forty kilometres from the frontier with Switzerland.

We are greeted without ceremony by the landowner, Albert Pfenning, who insists we hide the car in the barn immediately. American soldiers are in the area rounding up the remaining Wehrmacht stragglers. They have a list of fifty names of SS officers of special interest to them who need to be located. Kirchner's name is on it.

Although he looks foreboding with an eyepatch over his left eye, a gruff voice and a penchant for saying whatever first comes into his mind, however offensive or dismissive, I grow to like old man Pfenning's company over the four months we spend at the farm. The veteran soldier of the First World War lives on an army pension which he supposes no longer will be paid. He will have to concentrate on the farm, an inherited responsibility following his brother's sudden death three months earlier. He openly admits he knows bugger all about farming and leaves most of the day-to-day work to Vido, an Italian immigrant who has worked for his brother for over twenty years. Pfenning claims the man is dumb and mentally retarded, though I've heard Vido humming a tune and he seems to react normally when we tackle some chore around the place. He certainly knows how to show his frustration whenever Pfenning tries to order him to do something against his will.

For the first time in years, I wake up looking forward to the day in front of me. Vido teaches me so much about the life cycles of plants, when and where to grow them, how to look after them and the right time to harvest the various crops. With the animals, I play my part. There are six cows, a bull, four sows and fifty or more chickens. I learn to milk the cows, swill out and feed the pigs, and attend to the unholy mess made by the chickens. Every day, twelve hours a day, I play my part on the farm and although Pfenning says he'll be glad to see the back of us, I know he values my contribution. My feeling of self-fulfilment is carefully masked to reflect the frustration I know Vido feels but cannot express. I have become his mouthpiece by constantly complaining about the lack of this or that, whatever is needed to make the farm run better. Pfenning's stock answer is that it wouldn't be that way if Germany had won the war.

127

As far as Kirchner is concerned, this small interlude in his life is akin to purgatory. He has never done a day's manual labour in his life and it shows. For the sake of appearances, he has to be seen to be making an effort and I openly laugh sometimes along with Vido at his ineptitude. I even think he's scared of the ageing bull, a totally docile animal when amongst the cows, even when one or other is in season. Of course, it's an anathema for someone who has lived their life controlling others by fear to be the butt of another's humour, especially when the person he has deemed his possession is the one to recognise his failings. I react spontaneously, always within bounds and with kindness, a combination which blunts his temper and frustration. I have seen his violent and sadistic side too often and I am still afraid to provoke him. Even so, I know he annoys Pfenning with his persistent demands to pressure the old man's *Ratlines* contact for a date when we can leave.

Pfenning is a small link in a very complex chain, I have learnt. A man called Steinhauser, who lives in Switzerland, handles the passage of fleeing Nazis as far as Italy. He recruited Pfenning to receive and house named individuals and pays a fee to the old man in Swiss Francs for each human consignment. When we leave, someone else will arrive. That's the way the *Ratlines* work.

On two occasions, we are visited by American soldiers, accompanied by a German in a civilian police uniform. Kirchner has a hiding place under the floor of the barn and I have forged papers as a refugee from Czechoslovakia. I am a casual farm worker, Pfenning explains to the German and then launches forth into a tirade about needing all the help he can get and expecting nothing from these gum-chewing usurpers. He sounds eccentric and the men leave with a smile on their faces, the Americans, as ever, chewing what I now know as gum. I have given all the cows American names I read in a book, which Pfenning found funny and gave me a big hug.

We leave one day in late August. Kirchner is elated as we say goodbye. Vido and I weep as we embrace. The old man is wiping his eyes with a sleeve and mumbling about how he can't wait to see the back of me.

To Genoa, Italy – August 1945–September 1947

I have never seen, visited and stayed in so many church buildings in my life. A few are grand and ornate, the majority, simple and bare, many damaged, seemingly almost beyond repair. Who wilfully destroys a church?

I expect our escape route to be through Switzerland, given our proximity to the border, but the lorry transporting both the empty beer barrels and us returns eastward and into Austria. After laying up in Innsbruck until early evening, we travel for an hour, arriving at the tiny villa of Gries am Brenner just before nightfall. I recall that night and the following day as if they were yesterday.

The driver lets us off, motioning towards the lights of a tavern in the middle of the only street I can see. Kirchner asks where the border is, receiving a snort in return and a finger pointing across a field towards a hillside and forest to the south. Of the few people in the bar, nobody takes any notice of us as we order two beers and take a corner seat, as instructed. The pendulum clock startles me as it strikes the half hour, as if to announce the arrival of our guide. I think of Josef and how he must be now. This lad cannot be much older but acts like a seasoned adult, dropping his voice to hide the alto lilt as he hands us the temporary travel permits granting us passage to visit a sick relative across the border in Sterzing, or Vipiteno, to give its Italian name. The presence of transient strangers and the arrival of our guide must be such a common occurrence that not a single head in the tavern turns to look as we leave.

You need to be a mountain goat to negotiate the terrain. By the time we struggle to keep up with this young athlete, avoid two roving patrols of Italian border guards and cross a stream, I'm covered in pine leaves and my inadequate shoes are saturated. Kirchner doesn't look any better, but as our imperturbable guide waves us goodbye, we brush each other down, make ourselves look as respectable as possible and wait for the train to take us down from the Brenner Pass to the medieval town standing on the Eisack river in the disputed territory of the South Tyrol, or, as the Italians insist on calling it, Alto Adige.

We make our home in the Golden Cross Inn in Sterzing, waiting for someone to make contact. Day after day, I watch Kirchner grow more and more impatient. Whilst I accept inactivity must be difficult to handle for somebody used to snapping their fingers to get things done, the fact is he is living in relative comfort. I remind him of the horror stories coming from the east of torture and execution of thousands of German officers and soldiers by the Russians. He actually once said he wished he'd stayed and taken his chances – anything better than being forgotten in this shithole. I called him a liar and he didn't even react.

Two weeks into our stay and who turns up but the German known as 'the forger' at the meetings in Kirchner's office. He explains his role is to provide us with identity documents and, for the reason he outlines, why it is best he claims our origins are in the South Tyrol.

At the start of the war, a history of territorial claims and counterclaims between Germany and Italy over the rights of the German-speaking population of the South Tyrol was settled by a referendum, whereby those concerned could decide which nationality to adopt. Those choosing the German option would be relocated to Austria or Bavaria. Of the quarter of a million who determined their allegiance with Germany, only seventy-five thousand had managed to relocate by the end of the war. The remainder were effectively stateless, ignored by Italy and allied to a defeated nation. As no documents had been issued to this group since 1943, Italy was obliged to accept old identification cards as some form of verification. The forger had got hold of a collection of blank identification cards, courtesy of a disgruntled mayor removed from his post, and was selling new identities to the highest bidder. Kirchner must have influential friends. Somebody in Switzerland was prepared to pay the forger's asking price.

Photographs are taken and forty-eight hours later, we are in possession of two authentic looking documents with the surname of Taube, first names, Angela and Leonard. Strangely, although I have used many surnames over the years, I always come back to using the Taube identity whenever it has been possible. Angela Taube is a comfortable name, my first as an adult in my own right, perhaps the identity of a person free to go and do as they please. Perhaps not.

Kirchner is elated. The workmanship is first class, he claims. 'Are you surprised?' I ask. He gives a knowing laugh.

'Why should I be?' he says. 'The man has done some outstanding work in the past, good enough to fool all those who looked ... including you.'

Identity documents apart, it is still dangerous for us to move freely. Kirchner's name is on a hundred wanted lists and I have seen his photo amongst the rows and rows of small images recorded in the supplements of newspapers. Underneath each photo is an amount of money to be paid for information leading to capture. Kirchner is highly valued.

Guides take us from church to church on our journey south, never the same guide for more than a single journey. Sometimes we stay within the church precinct, sometimes an adjacent building or barn, occasionally the home of a sacerdote or a monastery. Sometimes the stay is just one night, other times for various days. The longest, nearly two weeks, is in Tuscany, to the south of Grosetto, in an abandoned church with a wondrous view overlooking the sea.

As we travel, I learn more and more about the complex system Kirchner calls the *Ratlines*. Apparently sanctioned by the Vatican and encouraged by someone called General Peron, ex-Nazis and fascist collaborators are channelled from various points in Europe through Rome and onto Italian ports where vessels dock on their way to a safe country known as Argentina. I have never heard of it before. There is a sophisticated network from Austria into Italy run by a Croatian, Father Draganovich, a member of the Franciscan order based in Rome, which is where we eventually end up, or, more precisely, in a friary in the beautiful countryside around Civitavecchia.

Kirchner advises me not to settle in and make friends with the friars as we will shortly be moving on to our final destination within days. Seventeen months later and we are still in the friary. It begins with what the French call déjà vu, a repeat of our stay with Pfenning, but the differences this time being an extended period and with little chance of summary arrest. I find I am intrigued by the attitude of the friars to the land, nature and what God's gifts offer, not just to survive but to benefit the local community in which they are exceptionally active. I learn so much.

Poverty and hardship in the area is rife. There is barely enough food to go around and medicines are almost non-existent. This is where the friars step in to help. In the field named after Father Giacomo, there are row upon row of hives. The bees are bigger than the ones I remember, with alternate bands of brownish yellow and dark brown around their bodies. They produce a light and delicate-flavoured honey with a floral aroma from the many flowers and plants grown in the three outer fields, also named after past friars who are now with their Lord. In the outhouse, most of the honey is mixed with water, a little yeast and some berries from the hedgerow to produce a wonderful drink they call mead. The friar I call Annusamiele Silvino, because he always smells of honey, tells me I make a good brew. One glass and it certainly goes to my head.

With virtually no beer and only rough wine, mead is a popular drink in the local bars and by far the product most in demand from the friary. It provides the finances for the many other social activities.

I spend every possible waking hour attending to the plants in the medicinal garden or in the orchard of fruit trees, occasionally in the vegetable garden. At dusk, I join the brethren at prayer, not because I have found God, but to enjoy the hot meal served in the refectory afterwards and only available to those who have toiled in the name of the Lord.

Work is no chore. Understanding the qualities of each plant is like touching the stars. I mix the stalks of poppies with honey to make a plaster to heal open wounds; anise for coughs, asthma and bronchitis; chamomile for colds and inflammation; juniper for the digestion; cotton thistle for cancer and ulcers; common broom for heart problems; and so it goes on, a seemingly never-ending list of plants with healing properties. These compounds are provided to the local residents free of charge and there is often a queue at the gate waiting for the appearance of Medico Mauricio, as they and I call the friar with the lazy eye.

As the end of our second August nears and we begin to harvest the apples, Kirchner's mood improves as my fears grow. I could stay here forever, but I know we will soon leave. After months of frustration and his eternal moaning about the Croatians having long since forgotten about us and only assisting the Ustase from Zagreb to escape, he now tells me we have the green light. Since the spring I have put on some weight, about ten kilos, mainly around my stomach and buttocks, the reason, I assume, for his loss of interest in my company. He often risks going into the village to eat and drink with the locals, or so he says. It's true he never has many hot meals at the friary because he rarely shows up to work. But I often smell scent on his shirts when I wash them and I plead silently with God during evening prayers to let him have found another woman so that I may stay here forever.

I'm getting used to saying goodbye to people. I weep for the loss of these wonderful human beings inside my head, yet nothing but a smile, a blown kiss, a fatalistic nod is all they see from the outside. I can tell from the expression on the faces of a few who really understand me that they can see inside my head.

Thanks to the friar known as ParlaTutto Roberto, I have become reasonably proficient in Italian and he has taught me the basics of the English language. It's much more difficult than all the others. I practice with Kirchner who learnt as a young boy from a South African uncle with whom he used to stay during his summer holidays. He speaks it with a strange accent. In stark contrast, his Italian is limited to gutter words and phrases he has picked up in the bars and God knows where else. His accent is dreadful, so he lets me do most of the talking.

Nobody at the Swiss Consulate in Genoa seems remotely surprised by the request I make in halting Italian. The man at the door nods and waves us inside. The woman says, 'Speak in German, if you like. I know why you are here.' Kirchner tries to look simple and in some sort of trance, so I carry on doing the talking, but it's hardly necessary.

'The new regulations from the Red Cross allow us to help, without extensive background checks, all those stateless South Tyrolean citizens to whom neither Italy nor Germany can issue a passport.' She holds out her hand to take the photographs I clutch in mine. 'Your identity cards serve this purpose. Wait over there.'

Before the consulate closes for the day, we hold two passports and tickets for passage on a refrigerated cargo ship running meat supplies between Argentina and Europe. It has passenger accommodation and facilities for two dozen people. Every cabin is occupied. Transporting people as well as cargo is a clever ploy by the ship operators as it allows us to bypass all the waiting cargo-only vessels and dock in any port with priority status.

It's six in the morning on the twenty-ninth of September when we step off the ship onto the dockside at Buenos Aires. It's still winter and the air is cold and humid. Breathe deeply, Rita. A new day. A new continent.

From Buenos Aires, Argentina – September 1947, to Cairns, Queensland, Australia – June 1953

There are Union Jacks everywhere. Far away in England they are crowning a new queen, Elizabeth. You would think she were here in Brisbane by the way people are acting with processions and street parties. She looks beautiful in that long-flowing robe. It's only the second time I've watched moving pictures on a television screen. The first was a week ago. A man called Wiesenthal from Linz was being interviewed. He said Australia was not doing enough to assist in bringing ex-Nazis to justice. He showed a photograph of Kirchner in his uniform as assistant commandant at Sachsenhausen. He doesn't look like that now. The man in the studio mentioned my name, as well, but there was no photograph. That's why we are on the run again.

But let me explain how we came to be in Australia.

Life was far from settled in Argentina. In spite of Kirchner's assurances that our Circle was now closed around a central hub with spokes extending individually around the Americas, we still had to keep one step ahead of betrayal. Kirchner's contact in the centre was called Kurt Bauer. They had been comrades at some stage during the war and Kirchner felt Bauer, as controller of the Circle, would 'make sure we are his priority consideration'. I have no idea from where Bauer operated. If references to the Web or TELA mean anything to anybody, I leave them out there, and if 'priority consideration' means letting us know literally minutes before possible capture, then the term is well served.

Clandestine groups operate in South America from time to time, supposedly financed by the Israeli or German governments. With little chance of successful legal extradition, the groups resort to kidnapping suspected Nazi war criminals and transporting them secretly back to Europe or Israel. Whenever a suspect resists or responds with force, they are prepared to kill the target and return to their paymasters with proof of death.

134

This said, for the most part life is a strange mix of normality, yet learning to trust no one and forever looking over your shoulder. Our 'alien identity cards' show us as brother and sister, Ronald and Ingrid Lehmann. The German community is large and spread throughout the country, a wide but closely knit fellowship set to enjoy, once again, the good life of theatres, concerts, restaurants and a surprisingly wide variety of cultural pastimes. Parties were frequent, rowdy and charged with depraved sexual behaviour, but Ingrid manages to look on at a distance while Ronald takes full advantage.

Money seems to be readily available and Kirchner's arrogance has reasserted itself, suppressed no longer by the sense of insecurity and uncertainty which hung over him like a cloud during our time in Italy. He works as the personnel officer in a company making and exporting engineering parts to Europe and has surrounded himself with a group of fascist thugs who work on the factory floor. There was an incident with a local banker of Jewish descent, found butchered in his office. Apparently, he had friends in high places and the local police are keen to question Ronald Lehmann.

Time to move on again.

It is 1951 and we are now the Williamsons, man and wife, living in the Barossa Valley outside Adelaide in South Australia. I like it here. Over the years, I have discovered a real penchant for picking up languages. I define fluency not as speaking like a native, but the ability to think and write in a language and the ultimate ability of being able to tell a joke with appropriate inflections. I can do that in five languages and my talents are heavily in demand. The company I work for as secretary and translator sells wine produced in this lush and beautiful valley. Export markets are a novelty as economies start to recover after the war and I deal with importers throughout the western hemisphere. I work alongside Akari, a Japanese girl who also speaks Mandarin and deals with the Asian markets. She and her family, a mother and father, are very private and she rarely talks about the past. From what morsels of information I can gather, her father fled Japan after the war. I've met him once. He has eyes like Kirchner's; not physical similarities, but the cold, unfeeling look of somebody who has dealt extreme violence. He scared me.

Kirchner hasn't got a job. He's been offered a few labouring opportunities – it's what the economy needs in this area, but he considers they demean his status. We live on my salary while he spends most days drinking or playing cards with his German-speaking buddies in the area. If I can find him some positive avenue for his talents, that will suit me. I want to stay here forever and be Mrs Katherine Williamson, living the Australian dream. I feel nothing now but pity for Kirchner. If he has no desire to make the most of life, I wish he would die.

There is a bar brawl. Kirchner is arrested and charged with affray. The picture in the local newspaper is of the two of us leaving the courthouse, and it all starts again. This time, I know Bauer and the Circle are less than sympathetic. We are being hunted, Bauer tells him, and we have to move fast. I make a stand. He can go, but I'm staying put. He shakes his head. No way. It's now us they are after, not just him. Rita Krakowski is wanted as a collaborator. Then he says something which shakes me to the core. Willing or otherwise, members of the Circle are bound until death. He made the commitment for both of us. I have no option but to go with him or face the consequences.

The two-thousand-kilometre journey through the outback from Adelaide to Brisbane turns into a nightmare. What he estimates as a three-day journey takes a week, not only because of stretches of difficult terrain but the inability to travel once night has fallen. It's too dangerous. As we drive, there are literally hundreds of kangaroos bounding across the barren landscape and easily prone to change direction in an instant and collide with the car. If not kangaroos, there are herds of goats or emus; even one day a plague of locusts that leaves the car looking like a dung heap.

I don't like the look of Blanchard from the moment we meet him in the crowded hotel bar in Brisbane. Unshaven, he has a large, oval face with a high forehead and swept-back, greasy black hair. You can't see his tiny ears from the front; they're pressed back against his head and his eyes are permanently casting around the bar, never once fixing on Kirchner as he talks to him. As I play no part in their negotiation to secure our passage from Cairns to Papua New Guinea on the tramp steamer Blanchard skippers, I spend my time following his eyes around the room. They seem to settle too frequently, albeit momentarily, on three men who are seated, one at the bar; the other two, one at either exit to the place.

Kirchner finally agrees on a price, shakes the older man's gnarled hand, and we watch as he hobbles slowly from the bar.

Kirchner stoops to whisper in my ear. 'What did he mean at the end when I said, "We have a deal," and he said, "That's kosher"?'

'I pricked my ears up at that,' I say. 'It's slang for "that's good" or "okay", but strange he should use the term in the circumstances. Perhaps it's a phrase the English use.'

He looks askance when I suggest we leave by separate exits, but I insist. The first to find a taxi waits with the door open for the other. As I wind my way through the crowd towards the exit of the bar, I play at being a little worse for wear and bump heavily into the table at which one of the men is sitting. His fresh beer wobbles and tips into his lap. 'Jesus,' I say in my best Australian accent, 'I'm really sorry, mate. Had one too many.' He looks at me, uncomprehending, as I fish for some loose change in my handbag and put it on the table. 'Here. Dry off your pants and get another on me. Gotta get back to the kid.' Before he can react, I am at the door.

Kirchner thinks I am being paranoiac. In his eyes, Blanchard is sound, selected through Bauer, and I've just assaulted an innocent stranger having a quiet drink. Look, nobody is tailing us.

It will take four days' sailing for Blanchard to cover the seventeen hundred kilometres from Brisbane to Cairns, allowing for loading cargo en route, whilst we make our way by road to the northern port city. We will meet with Blanchard at Ports North, eleven p.m. sharp on Saturday the sixth of June, to be smuggled onto his vessel, leaving at daybreak. Two days later, we will reach our destination.

Throughout our trip north, I plead with Kirchner to turn back. I sense it's a trap, but he won't listen. Above all else, his faith in the Circle and Bauer is total. They would not set him up. Maybe not intentionally, I plead, but they can't know everybody.

He says I'm driving him crazy. He calls me a fucking dripping tap, but in the end I get my own way, or rather, we reach what he calls a compromise. We arrive early and leave the car in Kenny Street, close to the naval base. There is a footpath into the port. It's much smaller than I imagine, and finding somewhere to hide close enough to Blanchard's vessel, *Barrier Reef*, is not easy. In the end, we opt for a gap between two large piles of timber planks, no more than fifty metres from the quayside.

It's past eleven and Blanchard is marching up and down impatiently, forever checking his watch. The only light is from a spotlight on the bridge of the vessel. There is no breeze, no sound other than the lapping of the sea against the harbour wall.

Midnight. A church bell strikes. Kirchner goes to stand up, make his presence known. I tug at his coat to pull him back. A figure appears on the gangplank. 'They're not coming,' the man says in German as he comes within the beam of light. He is one of the men from the bar.

I see the veins in Kirchner's neck stand out as Blanchard replies in German. 'You had best send Walter to find out. They arrived this morning. Eiger tailed them here. It's the woman. She sussed us at the hotel. It was no accident Eiger ended up with the beer in his lap.'

Kirchner is fishing for the revolver he hides tucked into the back of his trousers. I place a restraining hand. 'What warped parents name their child after a Swiss mountain?' I whisper into his ear. He turns and looks at me in a way he has never looked before. To me, it seems like a mix of gratitude and respect. He smiles as his hand releases the gun back into its hiding place.

'I should have listened,' he says. 'I must remember to stop treating you like a girl and start treating you like the intelligent woman you have become.'

From Darwin, Australia – July 1953, to Valparaiso, Chile – February 1962

He sells a diamond in Darwin. I don't know where it came from or how he got it, but it pays for flights to Jakarta and on to Cape Town. For the time being, he says, he would rather Bauer not know where we are, just in case the intended ambush in Cairns was sanctioned. We have ditched the Williamson identities and are travelling on our Argentinian passports as the Lehmanns again.

He leaves me on my own in Cape Town for a week while he travels to Europe to, in his words, 'put an insurance policy in place'. I do contemplate making a run for it while he's gone, but I have little money, enough to survive for a week but not to get out of South Africa and disappear. I comfort myself with the prospect that my time will come. And it does.

I'll fast forward the nine years, five back in Mendoza, Argentina, and then to Asunción, Paraguay, where he becomes involved in the sale of falsified spirits, whiskey, rum and vodka. Through his illicit dealings, a German called Paul Schafer comes onto the scene. It's New Year's Eve, 1961, and we are planning to join Schafer at a commune he is developing in Chile. The idea suits Kirchner. To expand, his illegal business needs an outlet on the Pacific coast once the contraband has been smuggled across the border. He sees Schafer's project, Colonia Dignidad, in a remote area of Maule, central Chile, as an ideal staging post to transit the merchandise. He couldn't be more wrong. Colonia Dignidad is like being back in a camp, barbed wire fences, a watchtower, searchlights, and armed guards with dogs. The place is full of right-wing Chileans and low-level, Nazi German thugs, escapees from Europe who try to recreate a world they recognise but does not exist any more. Thankfully, Kirchner can't stand it either.

Three weeks later and we are in the port city of Valparaiso, which is where *Mayor* Carlos Duran comes into my life.

As a woman in her mid-thirties, I wouldn't say I was conventionally beautiful, not having that fashionable voluptuous look of the time, but, in the eyes of some men, I have an appeal which stimulates an infatuation, even bordering on obsession. Meier fell into this rare category and so does a high-ranking Chilean *carabinero* who, I discover, is working undercover.

By this time, Kirchner's shady dealings have attracted plenty of equally shady characters with pseudonyms taken from North and South American gangsters. I come across Al, Bugsy, Baby Face and El Loco amongst many others, all part of a lucrative industry smuggling God knows what onto cargo ships bound for Asia and the west coast of America. But the guy named Chico is different to the others. As blunt and aggressive as he tries to appear, whenever he is around our penthouse apartment I can turn to catch him looking at me with those puppy-dog eyes and an expression a long, long way from indifferent.

If there were any problems with Bauer, they appear to have been resolved and I now have identity documents in the name of Renata Strauss, an Austrian citizen. Kirchner is my husband, Friedrich, an ideal name for somebody so addicted to power and control. An unlimited supply of wealth has restored all the negative aspects of his character, and sex with high-class whores is obviously high on the list of habits reacquired. I have to say, whatever his many shortcomings, he is courteous and respectful to me and prefers to distance himself rather than force me to witness the traits I despise in him. The trouble is, it's easy for others to read this distancing as his losing interest in me, and that can be dangerous.

I have got to know Chico quite well. He is handsome and well-educated with a seductive, baritone lilt to his voice. On several occasions, I have accompanied him to the port. We go in the guise of tourist sightseers whilst he plots the movement of the security patrols around the dockside. Our visits always end with a drink together in a local bar or café.

On this occasion, he straight out asks me what my real name is as he knows it's not Renata Strauss. I play with him and laughingly say I will if he tells me his. He agrees and to my amazement and lasting regret, I actually tell him the truth. I am Rita Krakowski, a Polish citizen on the run for my wartime collaboration with Friedrich. I stop at giving him Kirchner's name, though I suspect, knowing mine, he could easily discover the truth.

Out of the blue, he confesses to being Carlos Duran, a major with the Chilean police on undercover assignment to infiltrate the network in which Kirchner is just a small cog, however important he would like everybody to think he is. Carlos tells me he has fallen under my spell and wants me to run away and hide until it is safe, until the ringleaders are rounded up and he can join me. In retrospect, I was stupid in agreeing to go back to his apartment and letting him make love to me, although, as I recall, it was an enjoyable experience.

The pressure grows. Carlos is totally besotted and extremely persistent and persuasive. I should tell Kirchner I am leaving and go to the authorities. Carlos will ensure I'm protected somewhere I cannot be located by this mysterious Circle. Collaborators who were forced to cooperate with the Nazis, he tells me, are treated with leniency by the authorities and he sees no reason why I should be looked upon any differently.

It's the twenty-second of February and I have finally plucked up the courage to do it. Carlos has given me his service revolver, just in case Kirchner reacts physically. He shows me how to fire the gun, but cautions against using it other than as a threat.

I have a case packed by the front door as Kirchner comes down to breakfast, and I tell him I'm leaving for good. He laughs and busies himself fishing around in the refrigerator.

'I'm serious. I've had enough of running. I've decided I want stability in my life.'

'Who put you up to this? Let me guess. Who looks at you with doe eyes every time you walk into the room?' He sounds bored with the subject matter. 'You are not going anywhere.'

'I said I've made up my mind, and nobody has put me up to it. It's something I've been serious about doing for years, if you recall.' I finger the revolver in my coat pocket. 'You won't stop me.'

He sits on a stool at the counter, a plate of cereal in front of him. 'I wouldn't dream of it. Where are you planning on going?'

'I'm hardly likely to tell you.'

He looks up, the spoon hovering in his hand, halfway towards his mouth. 'You'll end up in a German prison for the rest of your life, and I expect there will be plenty of inmates willing to shorten that for you.'

'As I say, I'll take my chance.'

'Just give me ten minutes before you leave, will you?' He calmly finishes the cereal, drains the remnants of milk by lifting the bowl to his lips, goes into his office and returns with two sheets of paper stapled together. He throws them at me. I miss the catch and they fall to the floor at my feet. 'Best read that first,' he says. 'Time for coffee. Big day today.'

'What is it?' I ask, making no effort to retrieve the papers.

'I'm sure you remember Lew Wiesel?' He waits for my nod. 'He returned to Poland in the nineteen fifties to try to locate his family and was picked up by the police and sent to Germany to stand trial as a collaborator. He pleaded duress and provided a statement which was supported by a letter

141

from his late brother-in–law in the United States shortly after the war and just before he died. You should read the statement.'

'What's it got to do with me? I had nothing to do with Wiesel other than to help get his son freed.' I'm staring at the pages on the floor, but unable to pick them up.

'It's damning evidence, also corroborated by relatives of Agata Gorski and Roman Sowka.'

'What do you mean, "damning evidence"? All the children ended up in Sweden. I saw the photographs.' I can tell he recognises the fear in my eyes and has planned for this moment.

'I regret the statement clearly states you attempted to extort money and valuables from Wiesel in exchange for a promise of safe passage for the children to Sweden, knowing full well they would never reach their destination.'

I hear the words, but they don't make sense. All I manage to say is 'What?'

He busies himself making a coffee, plainly relishing the suspense. 'You are going to refer to the photographs again? A man before his time, our forger, don't you think? The adults in the pictures were sympathisers, living in Sweden, both hanged after the war. They took a number of photos in front of the Swedish parliament building in Stockholm, careful to leave a space between them. The negatives were sent on to our forger friend who expertly inserted the image of the relevant child. The result fooled everybody … until the war ended.'

My legs turn to jelly. I grip the counter for support. 'The photos weren't real?' I can't believe I'm asking the question. 'But I didn't do anything. I just followed orders. Your orders.'

'Wiesel's brother-in-law wrote to him shortly after the war ended to confirm Malik had never made it to the States. Similar stories for the other two.'

'You knew all along what would happen.' My grip closes around the pistol in my coat pocket. 'You used me.'

He shrugs his shoulders. 'The war was ending. I knew as soon as the Americans joined in that our days were numbered. Everybody was using everybody to try and make sure their future was secure. You were just a pawn.' He turns his back on me to take the percolator from the stove.

I point the gun at him and release the safety. 'What happened to the children?'

He is still facing the stove. 'I don't think you want to know that.'

'I asked you what happened to Malik, Agata and Roman.'

'Ah,' he says, seemingly nonplussed at the sight of the gun in my hand. 'A FAMAE Colt 32, if I'm not mistaken; standard Chilean *carabinero* issue. That explains a great deal.'

'Answer the question!'

'The children never left Potulice. How could they? Dr Sommer requested their transfer to his experimental unit to participate in some tests he was working on. They stayed there until the mothers could be brought in to complete his trials.' He slowly pours a coffee. 'Now, hand the gun to me before you do some damage.'

I move back from his extended arm, tightening my finger around the trigger. 'Where are they now?'

He retreats and takes a sip of coffee. I am not quick enough. The contents of his cup, boiling coffee, douses my cheek. I raise my hand and the retort as the gun fires sends it even higher. Flakes of plaster cascade from the ceiling. He rips the gun from my hand and slaps me hard across the face, exactly where the coffee has scalded my skin. I collapse to the floor. The pain is unbearable. I just want to die.

He is standing over me. 'You silly bitch,' he says. 'Why did you go and make me do that? Get it into your head. We are going nowhere unless it's together. Of course' – he kicks at the pages on the floor – 'I am indicted for the same crimes and a great deal more.'

'You are a monster,' I manage to say.

His teeth grind together as he goes to speak. 'If you really want to know, I'll tell you what a monster looks like. It's a man who puts Malik in a room while his mother is watching, provides a knife so that the drugged-up juvenile can start to hack himself to pieces, and puts enough shit into his mother so she thinks the whole thing is highly amusing. Conditioning people to accept what they abhor is his life's work and is what the Americans consider is worthwhile preserving, important enough to have him smuggled out of the war zone. That's a monster for you.' He steps over me, retrieves the broken cup and gestures for one of his bodyguards to enter. 'Find a first aid kit and take her to her room. Lock the door.'

Three days pass and I see no one nor stomach any of the food left on a tray inside the door. I have lost the will to live. Even the photograph slipped under the door has little impact. I have caused the two men who really cared for me to suffer brutal deaths: Meier, his throat cut by a slip of a girl; Carlos, a bullet in the centre of his forehead. My vow is to never let another man get close enough to me to suffer the same fate. The scar on the left side of my face will never heal, a constant reminder of the havoc I have wrought on those to whom I have shown friendship.

As it turns out, the *carabineros* are a lot closer to splitting Kirchner's cartel wide open than Carlos had me believe. The tip-off comes an hour before the raid, just time enough to pack a few things into a suitcase and flee back to Paraguay, and onwards to only God and Bauer know where.

FIFTEEN
THE ALGARVE, PORTUGAL
TOWARDS 1988

Twenty-seven years in one place, a smallholding in the hills above the central Algarve, an idyllic and peaceful setting, memories of constant sunshine, summer heat and the joy of a garden to produce exactly what I choose to grow.

Living again as Angela and Leonard Taube, we arrive on the flight from São Paulo as tourists, eventually achieve foreign residence status and, little by little, gain acceptance from neighbours, of whom there are few, and the local traders in the village. According to my closest neighbour who lives in a ramshackle single-storey house some hundred metres further on along the dirt road, the locals see us as a courteous couple, very private, originally from Belgium – I don't know how that came about – and always willing to try to speak Portuguese. 'I tell them you have green fingers,' Anna Paula says, 'with all those wonderful plants and the bees as well. Tosé from the mini-market says he'll buy all the honey you can spare.'

Kirchner counsels against contact with the locals. 'Her husband's a policeman, a member of the GNR and who knows what else. We live in a dictatorship and the last thing we need is to attract the attention of PIDE, the Portuguese secret police. Don't be so sociable.'

But it is difficult. Anna Paula lost her mother as a child and craves someone to take up the parent mantle from time to time. She finds any excuse to appear at the front gate, anxious to seek advice for her current preoccupation, and I cannot walk away like he does. Besides, talking to Anna Paula helps improve my Portuguese with the practical conversation my Linguaphone course recommends as desirable to supplement the recorded sessions. Spanish helps, of course, and within six months of our arrival, I class myself as fluent.

Two things happen, two years apart, but closely interrelated. It starts in the late summer of 1968.

Kirchner is away for the day, one of his many excursions on what he describes as Circle business. I have learnt a great deal about the organisation known as TELA and the various Circles, all in dribs and drabs from him when he's either talkative, excited about some occurrence or drunk.

Of the twelve trucks that set off from the fated train with their cargo of Nazi treasures, part of the deal with the Americans was for two trucks to be diverted towards Switzerland, received by Steinhauser and associates for safekeeping and subsequent conversion. Once laundered, there is a trickle-feed arrangement to fund a newly formed investment banking corporation. With part of this money, the TELA network was established and, through it, the funding of seven independent Circles. Each of the Circles is a stand-alone organisation with up to twenty spokes, at the end of each an individual beneficiary, normally an escapee from Nazi Germany. In the centre of each Circle is a supervisor or controller, Bauer in our case, who monitors the well-being of each beneficiary and reports to an overseeing committee who make the major decisions.

Kirchner reckons that allowing for death, capture and assassination, there are now only ten spokes remaining on Bauer's Circle. The deal is for the Circle to provide support and information until the death of the beneficiary, who, in turn, agrees to be bound by the orders he or she receives.

Anyway, back to 1968 and a glass of lemonade with Anna Paula in the garden. She is tearful. After years of trying for a child, she and husband Pedro decided to try adoption. The rules are strict, opportunities are few and they have just been rejected by the authorities on the grounds of insufficient means of support. I think for a minute she is about to ask me for money, but I misjudge her. She has never journeyed outside Portugal and imagines I have seen many countries where adoption procedures are simpler and offer them more of a chance. If there is the chance of a family, they are willing to emigrate.

I try to be non-committal and say I'll think about it, hoping she doesn't bring the subject up again. In fact, because I can't get her predicament out of my mind, I actually go out of my way to avoid her over the following months. She never does speak of it any more. I think Pedro might have said something to her about involving other people in their business.

Fortunately, Pedro and Kirchner have discovered, as neighbours, they have a number of common interests. With trees and shrubland around us, there are worries about forest fires and the precautions we all need to take. One evening, Kirchner is in a rare receptive mood and invites Pedro indoors for a drink. I hear laughter and animated conversation from the room he uses as his study. 'It's good to get a policeman on your side,' he says after Pedro has left. 'You never know when you might need one.'

It is now September 1969 and Kirchner is away in Lisbon again. He talks about the Banco do Carmo and things he has to do. If everything goes to plan, he should be back by the weekend.

Anna Paula has their car today and I ask if she would mind running me to see the local doctor, not hers but one I had picked from the phonebook, in Faro. I complain of a pain in my stomach. I tell her not to wait around for me. I intend to do some shopping and I can get the bus back to Bolequeime.

The doctor, whom I tell Anna Paula is a specialist in digestive complaints, prods and pokes, asks for a urine sample and calls for his nurse to be present whilst he does an internal examination. I'm starting to get worried. There's nothing wrong with my lady parts, I tell him, so why the examination? Just precautionary, he replies, and the nurse gives me a supportive smile that says he knows what he's doing. He wants an X-ray. That's at the facility over the road and it's just as well I didn't ask Anna Paula to wait. I've already spent well over an hour in his consulting room and it's another hour before I return with an envelope to hand him.

'Sit down, Senhora Taube,' he says. 'You don't have regular periods, I imagine.'

'No. The occasional discharge of blood, but I was operated on as a girl and have never had real periods. Why?'

'You have to understand, this is a confidential conversation and anything said will never go beyond this room. You may believe the Portuguese go around denouncing each other, but it's not true, and especially so for someone who has sworn the Hippocratic Oath.'

'It never crossed my mind.'

147

'Good. Somebody tried to sterilise you and made a botch of it, correct? I'm not asking where, when or under what circumstances, but you do have a number tattooed on your wrist.'

'Carry on.' I am holding my breath.

'One side of the uterus has been cauterised along with one of your Fallopian tubes. The left-hand side is mostly undamaged, and although the tube is partially closed, it can tear open, which is probably the pain you suffer. A combination of events have occurred which have resulted in the fertilisation of an egg and the tube opening at just the right moment for the fertilised egg to reach the uterus and attach itself to the wall. In other words, fortunate or otherwise, you are pregnant.'

At the age of forty with a damaged womb and possible complications, he recommends abortion; not in Portugal, where it is extremely difficult to obtain authorisation, but, possibly, the UK, where the law was changed in 1968 to facilitate conditions such as mine. If I do try to go the distance, as he puts it, the birth will have to be a caesarean as a natural birth would be far too painful and, quite possibly, life-threatening.

I listen to all this in a daze, disbelieving, ready to challenge this ludicrous assertion. Yet, female intuition tells me he's absolutely right and that's why I came here this morning. After all, who believes obstetricians deal with digestive problems?

By the time I reach home, I have made my decision. With the clever use of homemade clothes – memories of my time with Yodel never leave me – and some astute social distancing, I manage to obscure the lump until nearly seven months and the possibility of legal abortion is no longer a threat. Kirchner takes the news, initially with total incredulity and subsequently with his normal analytical approach. I dread at one stage he is actually considering suggesting we keep the child, but he is just working through the various options and, in the end, agrees with my proposal.

As far as the locals are concerned, I am taking a holiday in the Alentejo countryside, some two hundred kilometres north of the Algarve. I never did return to the doctor in Faro and now rely on a fresh-faced young man who works in a private clinic in Evora. I bring my own handmade smocks, all with long sleeves, and refuse to use the standard wear provided by the clinic. I have a few troublesome occurrences when it looks as though there might be a terminal problem with the pregnancy, but timely and efficient treatment means that on the twenty-ninth of June, 1970, I give birth to a beautiful baby boy weighing three and a half kilos.

Two weeks later, I leave the clinic with my bundle of joy and return home. Money has changed hands and the detail of my attendance at the clinic and the birth is expunged from the records. This gurgling little bundle does not exist as far as the rest of the world is concerned.

To avoid any suggestion of coincidence, I keep the boy hidden at home for another two weeks before I make my move. Anna Paula doesn't come around as much as she used to. I think she feels the months of me distancing myself from her mean I don't seek her friendship any more. It's natural and something I can easily put right.

It's Saturday, the first of August. I wait until her car passes in the afternoon. Pedro has worked the early shift and she is going to pick him up. I pack the baby into a basket along with a cool bag with four bottles of milk I have expressed and walk along to their house. I thought I might cry, but I don't. As I leave him in their porch, I feel both relief and concern, not sadness or regret. The prospect of us having to flee once again, but this time with a baby in tow, is unthinkable. Besides, he would be branded forever as 'the son of' and not a person in his own right. I couldn't live with myself. I just pray Pedro and Anna Paula are devious and selfish enough to take advantage of the situation. They will give him the most wonderful home.

I don't need to worry. A month passes before I get a visit from a flush-faced Anna Paula who has come to tell me her wonderful news. They have managed to adopt a child. It's very hush-hush because they couldn't do it legally in Portugal. The baby came from Brazil and is registered as a natural home birth at her aunt's address in Setubal. I must never tell anyone. Pedro is over the moon at having a son. When she tells me his name is Daniel Moises, I chuckle inside.

As I hoped, I see a great deal of Daniel as he grows up. By the time we are into the eighties, he is quite a little man, spending hours helping me in the garden, attending to the hives and bossing me around by reciting the instructions I have just given him as if they originate from him. I can see strains of Kirchner's arrogance in his make-up, which I try to counter with subtle lessons on humility. Only time will tell.

We love each other's company, the mutual enjoyment of a shared passion for nature and a bond which I understand perfectly and which he unconsciously accepts by calling me *Tia*, or aunt. He also gets on well with Kirchner. Amazingly, Daniel has convinced him to buy a dog, something which I believed he would never contemplate, given the transient nature of our existence. Knowing Kirchner so well, I knew it would have to be a German shepherd, and so it is. What started off as a bundle of fur is now a fully grown guard dog with a bad attitude as far as strangers are concerned.

Kirchner is visibly ageing. He has started to cough a great deal and has lost the voracious appetite he has had most of his life. He is far less impetuous now and tires easily. Next year will be 1988, Kirchner will be sixty-eight and Daniel will be eighteen and off to university in Coimbra. I will miss him.

Pedro came by last night. I haven't seen much of him since the New Year celebrations and we now have the first blooms of spring. He said he didn't want to concern us, but yesterday and the day before, as he was leaving for work on the night shift at the local station, he spotted someone watching our house. He suspects it might be a thief, casing the house for future reference, as he put it. Thieves tend to follow the exodus of Portuguese from Lisbon and Porto to the Algarve during the summer months, looking for rich pickings from holiday-minded tourists. Kirchner thanked him.

We sleep in separate bedrooms now, but I attend to the cleaning. I notice he now has a pair of binoculars on the bedside table and a loaded handgun in the drawer.

SIXTEEN
THE ALGARVE, PORTUGAL
1988–1989

Something has really upset him. I don't exactly know what it is, probably an issue with the Circle, but he's become very introspective and wary. He told me Bauer retired as controller some months ago when they decided to amalgamate three of the Circles into one. There are very few beneficiaries left now and it makes sense to consolidate their resources. The new controller is someone called Richter and, as far as Kirchner is concerned, the chemistry definitely does not work. I hear his raised voice on the telephone in the office. I'm tempted to lift up the extension in the hall to find out what is going on, but he can detect a click on the line if I do it once he is listening on his receiver. My hand has hovered over the telephone on a number of occasions, but I don't have the courage to go through with it.

The other change in his behaviour is his insistence to be the one to collect the post. Outside of the town, postmen do not visit individual residences but leave the mail in personalised postboxes grouped together in a single metal structure at the end of the road, opposite the mini-market. It's a good kilometre away from the house and the unspoken agreement is I collect whatever it is, normally a utility bill or circular, whenever I go to the mini-market. Now, he insists on being the one and has even tried to confiscate my key. I told him no. If he wants to collect the post, it's fine by me, but he has to get the shopping at the same time.

One particular telephone call in May really gets to him. He is agitated for hours afterwards and I hear him padding around in his bedroom into the small hours. The next day, he announces he is off to Lisbon. Over the past year, his visits to the capital have been restricted to one per month, normally around the twentieth. This time, it's out of sequence and, by his state of mind, to address a problem he won't tell me about. He has locked the door of the lounge and is, inexplicably, moving the furniture around.

When he's gone, I notice the sofa is out of position. It's left an imprint in the dust on the tiled floor and, along with provoking my curiosity, I have a very domestic reaction; it's time to do a spring clean.

Our dog, Raus, now full-grown and a real handful, seems to find the base of the sofa really interesting and sniffs loudly around the large wooden ball feet, exposed now I have tipped the sofa on its back. As I finish cleaning and go to right it, one of the front feet dislodges and comes away in my hand. It has not been screwed back on properly and the thread has been crossed. I can see why. The inside of the wooden ball has been expertly hollowed out to provide a hiding place big enough for ... what? A set of keys? There is just one. The devious bastard has taken the postbox key from my ring and hidden it. He has a woodworking kit in the lean-to in the garden and, most definitely, the proficiency to perform the operation.

I intend to challenge him, but when he returns later the following day, seemingly more relaxed than when he left, he hands me a copy of *Time* magazine and suggests I'll find the cover story interesting. Thoughts of keys and hiding places evaporate the moment I see the name under the sketch drawing of a middle-aged man, wearing dark glasses and a *shtreimel*, the fur hat favoured by Hassidic Jews. 'The Nazi Catcher' runs the cover title. I am looking at the image of my brother, Josef Krakowski.

The story deals with his part in the investigation of the famed 'Angel of Death', Dr Josef Mengele, the Nazi war criminal who escaped to South America. It is timed to coincide with the report about to be issued by the OSI, the US Office of Special Investigations, to close the case surrounding the exhumed remains of the corpse which it concludes is that of Mengele, 'beyond all reasonable doubt'. Whilst the Israelis still have their concerns, Josef is lauded for his part in the process and the many other successful captures he has masterminded over the last two decades. The closing paragraph is especially telling. Asked if there are any important Nazi war criminals left to apprehend, Josef is quoted as saying he will not cease his endeavours until he has discovered the whereabouts or the fate of two particular fugitives whose crimes need to be exposed in an open court, and who, if they are still alive, must be brought to justice. The identities are not revealed, but I am left in no doubt.

By the time summer arrives, I can more or less memorise every word of the article. I have read it so many times and never a day or night passes when thoughts of Josef are not uppermost in my mind. I create so many scenarios of what I will say when, one day, we meet, how I will explain myself, how he will react. It always ends badly.

My escape from the nightmare comes from the almost daily visits of Daniel to help me in the allotment. He is off to university in a few weeks and appears to find, as I do, the temporary cure for nervous apprehension is a few hours spent with the plants or watching the bees. I teach him how to make mead and how a glass can sooth away all the problems of the day. He jokes and says I'm turning him into an alcoholic even before he gets to uni. We have an unspoken bond and I'm glad I did what I did, bringing him into the world and providing a family with immeasurable happiness. It's the one good thing I've done in my life by using my initiative and I am so proud of him. He adores his parents.

Kirchner's health is failing. He is all skin and bone; he is forgetful and loses concentration easily. The traits I wish he would lose are his bad temper and the bouts of irritability when he curses the world and then sinks into a deep depression. I am fairly certain these trips to Lisbon are for regular medical consultations and chemotherapy. He is bald now and wears a baseball cap almost every waking hour. I wouldn't be surprised if he sleeps with it on.

Easter 1989 comes early, at the end of March. Daniel has a two-week break and visits almost every day to help me for an hour or so. He says his girlfriend is coming down to the Algarve from Braga next week and he is keen for me to meet her. Pedro is fretting, apparently. He said he would make up a bed for her in their study, but Daniel told him not to bother as they would be staying in his room. I laugh. The thought of soft, kind-hearted Pedro laying down moral guidelines to his son is beyond amusing. I want to hug them both.

It's Good Friday and the phone rings. I instinctively know it's important and lift the extension in the hall before Kirchner reaches the office. My hand is shaking as it covers the mouthpiece.

There are no introductory niceties.

'As you requested, we have the second opinion.' Richter's voice is much younger than I imagined. He sounds about Daniel's age, but he must be older.

'And?' Kirchner sounds nervous, his voice shaky.

153

'It concurs with your original diagnosis. The cancer has spread from your lungs to your stomach and other organs. It's terminal.' His harsh and brash manner suggests he's almost glad.

'How long?'

'Irrelevant, I'm afraid. We've talked about this and we agreed. Next Wednesday. Finish by nine and I'll have the sanitation unit in place.'

'Is that necessary? There is somebody here to take care of things.'

'That's what I wanted to talk to you about. The Jew bitch goes as well. We can't have her hanging around after you're dead.'

The phone trembles in my hand.

'I can't have that. It's totally unnecessary. She knows nothing and will never talk to anybody. She can be trusted. Why can't you people see that?'

'It's a decision from above. No negotiation, I'm afraid.'

'I won't do it. I need to speak with the person who took the decision.'

'Not possible. Don't argue with me. You've both had a good run. If it wasn't for the Circle, you'd have both been strung up at Nuremberg.'

'You're making a mistake and I won't do it. It's my wife you are talking about.'

'If you don't do it, we will. Next Wednesday. It's been nice knowing you.'

The line goes dead. I hear Kirchner curse the man in his mouthpiece before he replaces the receiver.

He appears in the lounge five minutes later. 'Everything all right?' I ask.

'You know,' he said, 'some people should be shot at birth.'

'Are you talking about yourself?' I joke.

He turns to look at me and smiles. 'Maybe,' he says. 'It wouldn't have been a bad thing. What do you think?'

SEVENTEEN
THE ALGARVE, PORTUGAL
Wednesday, 29 March 1989

An early dinner, he suggests. Easter has passed and he feels like a little celebration. After all, we have a great deal to be grateful for, and splashing out a little of our now meagre resources on a special bottle is fully justified.

Do we have a great deal to be grateful for? Do we have anything to be grateful for? Tonight, he intends to kill me and commit suicide. The bottle of bubbly, nothing more than the means to administer the sleeping draught or whatever he has put in my glass to make sure I pass out before the dreaded moment. It's not death I fear, but I don't want to be unconscious throughout whatever method he chooses to finish me. Fortunately, we have a strange ritual whereby Raus eats when we do, and his bowl alongside the table is handily placed for me to tip in my glass of bubbly whilst Kirchner is absent from the table. On his return, I ask for a top-up, confident that as he's drinking from the same bottle, whatever drug he used was already in my glass and is now in the dog.

The die is cast. He cannot bring himself to look up from the table. Head bowed, he pretends to concentrate on dissecting the salad. I know him too well. If he allows himself to meet my gaze, he believes I will see right into his soul and lay it bare. No comment is needed, no question implied. He cannot allow this to happen, even if it means imposing his will over me until the end.

He has not sought my agreement to mark this day as our last on earth together as ... what? A man and a woman, conqueror and vanquished, master and mistress, allies in survival, an unholy partnership ... how does he see it? He often refers to me in front of others as his wife, but such a relationship implies a freedom of choice I have never had and a range of emotions rarely felt and never expressed. Do I really mean something to him? It certainly sounded that way on the phone call with Richter, or were his protestations the simple manifestation of guilt? I cannot allow myself to dwell on this tender notion without exposing a weakness in myself. Tears now would serve no purpose, nor asking questions that might weaken his resolve.

The caterpillar spares us such a confrontation. Almost indistinguishable from the lettuce leaf from under which it appears, the tiny creature contracts and extends its body as it moves across his plate; the colouring, the detail, the sheer perfection of its form. Strangely, it gives me a sense of well-being about what is to come. Whatever science may dictate, however logical the explanation, how can we doubt the presence of a dimension beyond our comprehension capable of structuring such a perfect equilibrium between the creatures, plants and environment in which we all co-exist? Perhaps, at the moment of death we will discover the answer. Perhaps, in a blinding flash of realisation it will all be so apparent, a simplicity so obvious, yet beyond the understanding of mere mortals.

What slides across his plate and occupies his attention is a symbol of the intricate and delicate balance of co-existence which he and millions like him had tried to change and failed.

It is too late now. The experiment ended in disaster, years of anguish and wasted lives he would excuse as in the pursuit of a noble cause. He raises his fork and takes the last mouthful of salad. Is this to be his final act of defiance, a pointless demonstration as the end approaches to show that the destiny of this helpless insect is at the whim of the man who once held in his hands the fate of tens of thousands?

With no cover left under which to hide, the caterpillar appears confused, changing direction, but finding nothing before him but a flat expanse of white porcelain.

He smiles to himself. Flicking over the caterpillar, he slices it into two, spikes both pieces onto his fork and puts them into his mouth. The cutlery is placed neatly together in the centre of the empty plate.

For the first time, he looks up and sees I am smiling too. 'Did you enjoy that?' I ask.

It is nearly eight. As I suspected, the dog is fast asleep, snoring and breaking wind in random order. I am playing my part, apparent doziness transcending into crafted unconsciousness. How am I to die? He gathers me up from the couch with more difficulty than I imagine, even considering his poor state of health and my portly figure. Exhaling loudly, he lays me on the rug, carefully arranging me and placing my right hand in a closed fist against my stomach. So, it is to be a knife. I hear the sound of metal on glass as he places the weapon on the side table which he then pulls towards him.

'Shit,' he says. He raises himself from his knees, steadies himself and walks into the hall to retrieve the phone. From somewhere he has produced an extension lead and is bringing the handset over to the side table. He checks for a dialling tone and grunts his satisfaction.

Raus is stirring with a sort of whining noise and jerky paw movements. I can see him from the floor, my head turned away from Kirchner. The dog is in my direct line of sight. From the reflection on the copper coal scuttle, I can watch Kirchner without him realising my eyes are partially open. He takes the long, thin-bladed knife from the table and studies it. The handle is rubbed clean with a handkerchief which he then ties around the blade, just above the hilt. He kneels over me, prising my fist apart just enough to force the handle between my fingers to rest in my palm. The handkerchief he has used to complete this manoeuvre is unwound from around the blade. My eyes close as he wheels my head around to face him and the last thing I see is the small blue cross inked onto the vest he is now wearing. From now on, I can rely only on my hearing.

He is much thinner and lighter than he used to be, but the weight as he goes to lie on top of me takes me by surprise and the breath out of my body. Involuntarily, I gasp.

'Through the sternum,' I hear him say to himself. 'Penetrate the right ventricle with a five millimetre wound and sever the right coronary vein. Five minutes to bleed out.'

He clasps his hand around my fist and forces himself down onto me. The blade shudders as it penetrates skin and bone. He cries out in pain. The blade slides further in until his chest is flat against mine. The sigh is like a child's and I start to feel the warm, sticky sensation seeping through the dress fabric onto my skin.

He rolls off me and reaches for the handset. I can see the handle of the knife protruding from his chest. He must have put the phone onto speed dial. 'Sergeant Pedro Rodrigues. It's urgent.' The Portuguese is rehearsed. Even after all these years, his grasp of the language is little more than basic. 'He's where? Tell him it's Senhor Kirchner, his neighbour. Tell him to come quickly. My wife is trying to kill me. She has a knife. Oh no! She is going to stab me! Please!' He presses the 'call end' button and collapses onto his back.

My reflex action is to reach for his hand and hold it tight. He is trying to speak. Blood seeps from between his lips. 'It's the only way,' he says, strands of red spittle between his lips as he forces out the words. 'If the police arrest you, Richter won't be able to get to you. It's the only thing I could think of to do.' He is fighting for breath. 'Whatever you think of me, I really do care about you. I always have. Without you, my life has never had any meaning.' He stops, and starts to raise his arm. 'We have to make it look authentic, a fight.' He closes his hand into a fist and before I can react, it is swinging towards my head.

Raus is barking. I awake with a start, my jaw feeling swollen and hurting like hell. There is a noise outside the garage. It is night and the house is in darkness. For a moment, I think it must be Pedro with a colleague, but the whispered words are in Spanish, asking about the dog. Two voices; one a woman's. 'Perhaps he did do it,' she says.

Kirchner had drilled me many times on what to do if strangers tried to break in. I reach the mains box in the hall and prise out the porcelain fuse. With Raus barking frantically and pawing the door to be let out, I move into the rear yard, towards the tarpaulin covering the wood pile we never use. I take out the six logs with the dab of white paint and crawl into the hollow, carefully replacing the logs to cover the entrance, this time with the white flash pointing inwards. I am now cocooned under what appears from the outside to be a solid pile of logs. Noise percolates through to me. Raus is going berserk. I guess he's leaping up at gate, attempting to reach the intruders in the drive. One way or the other, his presence has slowed down whoever is trying to get into the house.

Two minutes later, I hear him thundering past the wood pile on his way to the back door. They must be inside the house. He is still barking frantically, so loud I would not be surprised if the neighbours could hear.

A man's voice; a startled cry of pain; a solitary gunshot shattering the silence and the whimpering of a dog, getting louder and nearer to where I am in hiding.

'Are you hurt?' the woman asks.

158

'My arm. The fucking thing went for my throat. You arrived just in time. It would have killed me. Was she upstairs?'

'No. She can't be far. My guess is amongst those trees. You go round to the left. I'll come in from the right.'

'Just a minute,' he says. 'Look at the dog.'

I can sense Raus must be edging towards my hiding place, his snout almost touching the tarpaulin. I can hear the hurried intake of breath. He's looking for me to comfort him.

'Let me check this out.' The sound of feet is close by.

The noise of a diesel vehicle engine thunders into the drive. I recognise the clank it makes. Pedro has arrived.

The voices disappear back into the house. The whimpering from the dog is getting louder. Pedro has come into the garden through the gate. 'Jesus, Raus. What's happened to you?' There is a noise of china breaking inside the house. That table lamp was never very stable. There was no groove in the base to channel the electric cable and it wobbled.

Pedro is shouting. 'Come out where I can see you with your hands up.' He is moving towards the back door. There is an exchange of gunfire, several shots, muffled shouts and the sound of feet running, one dragging heavily on the gravel.

'There's no time for that.' It's the woman's voice. 'He called for support before I shot him. They will be all over the place. Let it be. We'll find her.' Her voice is fading into the distance. 'You need a doctor.'

I pull away the six logs. Raus lies unconscious or dead just to my right. A full moon casts an eerie glow over the house. The beam from a torch in the lounge is pointing up at the ceiling. Pedro is sitting on the floor alongside Kirchner's body, his back propped against the sofa, his hand pressed against the red stain on the pocket of his blue police shirt. The material is still soaking up blood like blotting paper. He is barely conscious. I go to grab the telephone Kirchner was using, but Pedro shakes his head. 'On their way,' he manages to say. 'Did you do that?' His eyes flutter in the direction of the hilt of the knife.

'It's a long story,' I say. 'One I'll tell you when you're mended and ready to listen.'

We both know the words are nothing more than a placebo. Within five minutes the shallow breathing has stopped and his head sinks onto his chest. Yet another dear man has died because of me.

There is a callous, calculating side to my nature, a desire for self-preservation I thought had been discarded when I accepted I was about to die alongside Kirchner. As I look down at his body, I have to say I feel only numbness, no genuine emotion. I wipe the handle of the knife clean, pocket the handkerchief and lie down on the bloodstained rug. The crack he gave me on the chin is proof enough I was assaulted.

As people begin to mill around, I feign unconsciousness. The fact is it's not far from the truth. I'm feeling faint. The effect of the adrenalin is fast receding and I begin to shake uncontrollably. I vaguely recall seeing Anna Paula's incredulous expression, the intensely moving sobs and the suspicious look on Daniel's face. He is taking in the whole scene, looking around, as if he is recording every single facet of the room for posterity. Eventually, he and his mother are hustled back from the doorway by a policewoman. A man with a camera takes a series of pictures and I am stretchered into a waiting ambulance.

**

I am in hospital with an armed guard outside my room. I've seen Inspector Guedes a few times over the years at parties thrown by Pedro, mainly to celebrate family birthdays. He is a kind, avuncular man with a slight stutter and freckles on his bald pate.

Fortunately, Pedro had already advanced the story, both at home and in his station, of a robber studying our house, a suspicion that turned into a dramatic reality, a robbery that went terribly wrong. What Guedes can't understand is the garbled telephone call the duty officer received last night which suggested I was trying to kill my husband.

I hope my weak smile conveys an understanding of what actually transpired. As Guedes well knows, my husband was no linguist and his grasp of Portuguese was very basic. One of the robbers – there were two, a man and a woman – had gained access to the hall as I came down the stairs and is holding me in a stranglehold with a knife to my throat. The woman rushes past me. I scream as we struggled towards the lounge. My husband always has the phone at his side and must have called for help, trying to say I am being threatened by a man with a knife and we are both about to be killed.

Guedes nods knowingly and makes a few notes in his book. 'How did you get the blow on your face?' he asks.

'When the man realised Leonard was on the phone, he struck me hard on the chin. The last thing I remember is stumbling into the lounge and collapsing unconscious on the floor. He must have stabbed Leonard. I don't remember anything else until I regained consciousness.'

More notes. 'You don't recall Pedro being there and what happened to him? We have a radio message recording the presence of an intruder and he is about to enter the premises. He says your dog had been shot.'

'The dog. I forgot. Is he …? No, I don't remember Pedro being there at all.'

He raises his eyebrows. 'Your dog was put to sleep. The wound and blood loss were too severe.'

'I'm sorry. I don't want it to sound unfeeling as far as Pedro is concerned. It was just a reflex remark.'

'I understand.' He does have a warm smile. I like that. 'Do you know what they were after?'

I give him what I hope is a bemused look. 'Anything valuable, I presume. Not that they are likely to find much in that respect here. We live a modest existence.'

'It's just puzzling they left the house to go outside, confront your guard dog and remove logs from a pile in the garden. Any reason you can think of?'

I shake my head. 'We haven't touched the log pile since last year. It got damp and we keep the stock we've used over the winter under the lean-to by the back door.'

The explanation appears to satisfy him.

Sad days pass. Anna Paula insists I stay with her until I feel able to return to the house. We bury Pedro and mourn his loss. It was Kirchner's wish to be cremated. It is a harrowing hour's drive from the Algarve to the nearest crematorium in Ferreira and the brief service is conducted under the watchful eye of Inspector Guedes. This is the first time I have seen him since Pedro's funeral. There are a few leads. They have a blood sample of one of the assailants who Pedro must have shot and injured, and sightings of a Mercedes they are anxious to trace. Beyond that, it's police-speak for nothing has come to light when he says the investigation is ongoing.

I never see Inspector Guedes again. His mantle has been assumed by Daniel, who is inquisitive about every minute detail surrounding Kirchner's life, his movements, a step-by step account of everything we did on the fateful day. He is like a dog with a bone and, with all the other problems piling on top of me, he has become an irritant. I would rather leave Anna Paula's house before I lose my temper with him, and I am getting really close to that. Even his mother has told him to stop asking so many intrusive questions of me. What he suspects is a mystery to me.

My overriding problem is a lack of money to get as far away from here as I can. Kirchner controlled the purse strings and gave me whatever I needed to do the shopping or pay the bills. I have no idea if or where there is a bank account in his name or from where he sourced the money. I find sixty *contos* in twelve notes of five thousand escudos tucked in his sock drawer, but the equivalent of a few hundred Swiss Francs is not going to get me far. The house we lived in is rented, from whom and for how much I have no idea. I have to leave, but where to and with what? I'm nearly a sixty-year-old woman, with no chance of earning a living or claiming benefits from the state.

For two weeks following the so-called attempted robbery, the national and local press are full of the story including, to my despair, a grainy photo of me at Pedro's funeral. I steadfastly refuse interviews and leave it to Daniel to front the stubbornly persistent attempts to invade his mother's and my privacy. The Circle wanted us dead and they are not going to let me live. They will come back for me, of that I am certain.

The opportunity for me to escape comes by pure chance. The wizened old lady who spends her days sitting outside the doorway of the mini-market is the owner Tosé's mother. She always seems to be asleep, but Tosé says she sees everything and knows all the local gossip. I'm just about to leave with my few groceries when she tugs at my coat. 'You never check your postbox these days,' she says, looking across the road. 'The postman left a letter in it for you today. It was recorded delivery, but the lazy man signed the form himself and left it in your box rather than bring it up to your house.'

I wait until I'm back at the house before opening the letter. It is bulky and addressed to Leonard Taube at a poste restante in Brussels, from where it was forwarded to our Algarve address. The envelope inside bears the crest of a Lisbon bank I had heard Kirchner mention on a number of occasions, Banco do Carmo. I open it with a sense of excitement.

EIGHTEEN
LISBON, PORTUGAL
Tuesday, 2 May 1989

In all the years I have lived in Portugal, I have never once visited the capital city, nor experienced the energy of crowds of people milling about, the vibrancy of commercial life in full swing. I have become a country lady, aware only of the humming of the bees and the sound of the wind rustling in the trees.

The sense of panic I feel must be painted on my face; the paper with the instructions as to where I am going could be written in Chinese for all the sense it's making at this very moment. My heart is palpitating. I feel so faint. I will just stop for a minute to hold onto this lamp post until I get my breath. The young push past me, talking excitedly, disregarding those around them. Women eye me curiously, elderly men sidestep to avoid me, some even raising their hats as they pass.

A woman in nurses' uniform breaks away from a group of friends to ask if I am all right. I have to admit I'm breathless and overwhelmed. Where I live, three people is a crowd. She laughs and takes my arm. Where did I want to get to? She will take me. It's not really out of my way, she tells me. I say the 'really' means it is out of her way and she laughs again. She hands over some coins for tickets to ride the Santa Justa lift, refusing my offer to pay and insisting it's less tiring than walking the long way around to arrive at the Rua do Carmo. 'This is where the fire started,' she says, pointing at the charred remains of the Grandella Department store, now partially obscured by barriers and tarpaulins.

Of course, that is what the letter said. The text was supplied in both English and Portuguese and signed by the chief custodian officer, Doutor Manuel Pinho. It briefly described the total loss of the bank's administrative branch to the fire in August 1988 and reassured all safe-deposit box holders that there was nothing but superficial damage to the building which housed their possessions. Nevertheless, a decision had been taken by the board of directors, in conjunction with the Portuguese government, to close the facility and return the building to the original owners, the church authorities. Keyholders or their authorised agents or successors should make arrangements with the undersigned to remove their possessions as soon as possible. Discussions were underway between the bank and the relevant authorities to decide on a procedure for dealing with all unclaimed boxes, and he hoped for a speedy outcome. Leonard Taube was receiving this letter as registered keyholder of boxes H65 and N302.

I see this letter as my way out of the situation in which I find myself. Kirchner would not have a safe-deposit box without something valuable to store, and as he was always insistent a valuable could only be classed as such if you could readily convert it into liquid funds, I am hopeful my salvation is in those boxes.

Dr Pinho – do call me Manuel – was more than helpful on the telephone. Of course, many of the original keyholders are now dead. All I need is a copy of my husband's death certificate, personal identification and a statement certified by a notary of my entitlement as his sole living relative. And, logically, I need to bring the keys to open the boxes.

That is where the problem lies. As I suspect, Kirchner has used the wooden foot of the sofa as the hiding place, but there is only the key to one box, tagged as H65.

Waving goodbye to my Good Samaritan nurse, I ring the bell alongside the heavy metal doors. A security guard meets me, checks my identity and ushers me into a small reception area.

Dr Pinho is a short, slender man in his mid-fifties with a square face and a mop of unruly black hair, somehow incongruous with the three-piece pinstripe suit he is wearing. I know it's conceited of me, but I can tell from his first hesitant glance. I recognise the look from memories of Meier and Carlos – a new admirer.

We climb some stairs to an office with a view over the internal layout of the facility. The size is deceptive. Once you are inside, the area is three times larger than it appears from outside with row upon row of small and medium-size boxes, separated by curtains and a rank of private viewing rooms along one wall. At the far end, towards some steps leading downwards are a block of large and coffin-size units.

Manuel, as he insists I call him, stands behind me as I take in the view.

'Down the stairs in the crypt are more of the medium and large units. We have over fifteen hundred storage units on this site.'

'All in use?' I ask.

'Ninety per cent now. Some have been cleared out and, as the facility is closing, we no longer offer the service.'

He gives the documents I present a cursory glance and asks his secretary to make copies.

'I recognise you from your photograph.' He smiles.

My heart stops beating. My expression freezes. 'You do? How come?' I try to sound relaxed. Are the police on hand?

'Mr Taube was a regular visitor.' He shakes his head as if chiding himself. 'Have I said how sorry I am for your loss? Please forgive me. Very unfeeling.'

'You were saying, a photograph?'

'Yes. As you doubtless know, he carried a photograph of you in his wallet and made great play of showing it to me whenever we met. He was very proud of you.'

I had never seen him with a wallet, let alone a photograph of me, and the idea he would show it to someone? Well, I can only think it must have been a ploy to attempt to humanise himself in the eyes of others.

The atmosphere is relaxed if not somewhat disconcerting as he deliberately locks the door and pulls down the blinds to shield us from the view of the outer office.

'You have the keys?' he asks.

I have to admit to only having one. He opens his desk drawer and places an identical key to the one I have with N302 printed on the fob. 'I know,' he says. 'This is a delicate subject as far as I am concerned and I would crave your indulgence.'

I try to look non-committal.

'Your late husband had a safe-deposit box here for many years, one of the smaller units. This is the appropriate key.' He holds up the key from his desk. 'In May last year, my predecessor, Ernesto Braulio, was approached by someone who wished to rent one of the largest boxes. We did have one available, but as the person concerned was not an existing client, Braulio was obliged to refuse.' He looks to make sure I am following. 'I don't know the details as certain paperwork is missing, but it appears Braulio did fulfil the transaction in the name of your husband with the person concerned as an authorised co-holder.'

'And Leonard authorised this transaction? Who is this mysterious someone you keep mentioning?'

'The answer to your first question is we understand he did, although the appropriate document is water damaged and illegible. As to the second question, I regret I am not authorised to disclose this information.'

I hope I don't look as confused as I am. 'So, do I open one box or both boxes, and how do you come to have the key to Leonard's original box?'

'This is my dilemma. Legally, you have every right to open both N302 and H65. They are both recorded in the bank's records as pertaining to your late husband. My sincerest advice is to open N302 and to forget that the larger unit ever existed.'

'You have access to this unit? You know what it contains?'

'How can I put this? To the best of my knowledge, nothing that could be of interest or value to you.'

It suddenly occurs to me I might be the intended victim of an attempt to deceive me into forfeiting whatever valuables are in the box. 'Is this a personal initiative, Manuel, or does it have the bank's blessing? I notice we are talking very much in private.'

'The honest answer is both; a personal initiative on behalf of the bank. I guarantee it will achieve nothing for you.' He does look sincere, I cannot deny.

I tell him I will think about it while we go about opening the smaller of the two safe-deposit boxes.

The procedure is laborious. First, I sign a waiver exonerating the bank from any legal liability in relation to the contents of the box. Next, a second master key is released to Pinho and we make our way through the maze of corridors to row N and box number 302. It's cold and the air is heavy and musty as though it has been breathed and exhaled by every visitor over half a century.

Pinho turns his key in one of the two locks and waits for me to follow suit with the second lock. There is a hiss as the door opens to reveal a void of about fifty centimetres square. All I can see are three or four documents, nothing of any apparent tangible value. I run my fingers around the base of the box, hoping beyond hope there is something else. I sense my fingertips are touching something small, the sensation of black velvet. It's a small pouch with a string-pull around the neck.

Pinho is hovering at my back. 'If you would like to take the contents to an examination room.' It's more of an instruction than a suggestion. 'All the boxes are self-locking. When you have finished, ring the buzzer and I'll come to collect you. A word of warning. If you do replace anything in the box, it will be deemed to be unclaimed and disposed of by the bank at some future date when we have the appropriate authority to open all such boxes. Do you understand?'

I barely listen, but nod. I am anxious to see what is inside the pouch. In retrospect, I should have read the documents first. There was an envelope written in Kirchner's hand, addressed to the editor of *Die Welt* in Bonn, stamped and all but ready to post had it not been unsealed. Unfortunately, my written German, as with Portuguese and Spanish, is the weak link in my linguistic abilities. Speaking is one thing I handle with ease; writing and reading the languages, I admit my limitations.

From what I can glean, Kirchner has laid out over ten closely worded pages a history of his involvement in the Circle from inception until the incident in the railway tunnel in Bavaria. Various individuals are named and details of the make-up of the so-called cargo transported on the train. I presume he wrote it as a hold over Bauer when it looked like we were being tossed to the wolves. If so, it would be dynamite in my hands and it is going back in the box. Next, there is a receipt in French, prepared for Wiesel by some investigative agency in Brussels for services rendered, and a letter in Polish from Lew Wiesel's brother-in-law in the USA, written shortly after the war.

I open the pouch and examine the contents. My spirits lift. There are eleven cut and polished diamonds, similar to the one Kirchner sold in Darwin to pay for our escape from Australia. I can only guess they must be worth a great deal of money if I can establish a way to sell them.

We are back in Pinho's office. I have with me the diamonds and the fourth document, sheets of parchment bound together as a contract written in

Portuguese and English. I'm too excited by my find of a financial way forward to be bothered to study it, but it could have some value. I leave the covering letter in the box and take only the legal document with its fancy green tape binding and wax seals.

'I assume you know what was in the box I've just opened. You haven't told me yet how you came by the key?' I know what he is about to ask me and I need some reassurance.

'I did inspect the contents briefly, yes. Not officially, if you understand me. I can tell you the diamonds are of exceptionally high quality. If you will permit me, the world of precious stones is full of pitfalls for the uninitiated.' He hands me a slip of paper. 'The name of a dealer in The Hague, a very respectable and honest man whom I know well. I recommend you speak with him regarding the disposal of the gems. He will be expecting you and will not cheat you.'

I take the paper and put it in the pouch with the diamonds.

'Are you prepared to take my advice regarding the other safe-deposit facility?' he asks.

'Where did you find the key to the box I opened?'

'Very well. It was found in the larger of the two safe deposits, H65. I can only assume your husband intended leaving the key to the larger unit behind, but made a mistake and left the wrong key instead.'

'Why would he do that? If he had left the key he intended, he would never be able to open the box again.'

'Precisely, I believe that to have been his intention, although not strictly accurate. There is a second set of client keys in existence. People do lose keys from time to time and request a copy. The rules are very strict and every step is overseen by members of the administrative board. The keys are stored in the safe-deposit facility of another bank, of which even I have no knowledge.'

'Then you had to go through this procedure before opening H65. You must have really wanted to open it. Why?'

'A piece of fabric material was caught as the lid was closed, stopping the hermetic seal from engaging. We wrote to your husband twice to request his attendance at the bank with his key. There was no reply, so I initiated the procedure. It was fully within bank rules.'

'Well, I need to see.' It's amazing how wealth, or even the prospect of wealth, can stimulate self-confidence. 'Otherwise, I will wake up every day for the rest of my life wondering about the secret of H65.' I allow myself a chuckle.

He doesn't see the humour. 'Be it on yourself,' he says solemnly.

We are in the crypt. He pulls a three-sided curtain unit around us, deliberately placed to block the path of the camera image which flickers across the screen in his office in sequence with the various images from locations around the building. There is a central three-bar lock which holds the lid in place.

'What was this originally?' I ask.

'The tomb of some church dignitary, I believe. Our beloved dictator had little time for the church hierarchy in Lisbon and ordered all remains on site be consecrated in alternative locations.'

He takes one end of the lid, I, the other, and we ease it up from the hermetic seal. He quickly retreats and I wish I'd taken his advice. The bloated corpse on its side is almost unrecognisable – except I do. I could never forget that face. This man may be in his eighties, but the enlarged features are definitely those of Lew Wiesel. I whisper his name. The smaller man, whose disfigured body is curled up in a foetal position, I do not recognise.

As we close the lid, verifying the locks react, and reseal the unit, I turn to Pinho. 'I'm sorry. I should have listened to you. Please explain what I have just witnessed and why those bodies are still there.'

We are back in his office. 'Nobody but you and I know of this,' he says. 'And I must insist it stays that way, Senhora Krakowski. I believe that is your family name.'

I try to appear impassive, but I acknowledge the implied threat.

'I'll forget I said that, shall I? I don't know what happened, but I have had time to construct a likely scenario with the benefit of my predecessor's notes. He is the second corpse in what I will call the coffin. His name is Ernesto Braulio. I know Wiesel came here in May last year with the intention of renting one of the largest units we have. Braulio explained only clients of six months' standing could apply for safe-deposit facilities, at which Wiesel claimed he was acting as an agent for a certain Leonard

171

Taube, an old established client of the bank. He was expecting to meet with Taube next week in Lisbon and would bring him to the bank to complete the paperwork. In the meantime, he deposited a year's rental in advance, possibly with an inducement, and asked if he could put certain items in the reserved unit until the following week.'

'Did he say how he knew of Taube?'

'Not directly. However, one of the documents you glanced at in the box you opened is a receipt issued by a Belgian firm of private investigators. Logic suggests they were employed to discover your whereabouts. Possibly, the receipt was with the report which was removed, but I'll come to that.

'Go on.'

'I'm guessing Wiesel had some hold or grudge against your husband and once he had discovered your location, convinced him to meet at these premises. I'm also assuming the diamonds were somehow involved and the hiring of the large unit was intended as a coffin, but for your husband.' He checks a notebook pulled from the desk drawer. 'There is a daily report from the security guard on, would you believe it, Friday, 13 May 1988, advising his shift, rostered to end at midnight, was curtailed at nine by Braulio, who said he was working late and would stand in for the guard. I have to say Ernesto was a lovely man, but enjoyed a lifestyle way beyond his bank salary and would certainly have been open to a bribe to switch off the surveillance system whilst an unscheduled meeting took place. I understand this system glitch used to occur on a number of occasions, although I have to say now, it seems to have righted itself.'

'I can see where you're going with this, but it's all hypothesis, surely? You're saying Leonard turned the tables on Wiesel, killed him and, either by design or accidentally, also murdered Braulio. He arranged the bodies in the coffin and left.'

He nods. 'Something like that. I think he ran through the documents Wiesel had left in the deposit, removed the investigators' report and transferred the rest into his own box, N302. But if you have another theory, I'm perfectly willing to consider it.'

'I don't, but you haven't explained why the existence of those bodies has not been reported to the authorities.'

Pinho holds up the palm of his hand towards me. 'One thing at a time. Moving the hypothesis forward, it was nearing midnight, at which time the new security guard would come on station. Your husband was in a hurry to leave, placed the wrong key inside the makeshift coffin and locked the deposit with the hem of Wiesel's overcoat trapped in between the seal and the lid. It is a bank rule that all boxes of whatever size must be hermetically sealed to protect the integrity of the contents. There is a fourteen-day rule stipulating two written advices to the client, following which we can intercede. With Braulio missing, I was appointed as temporary head of department and followed our internal guidelines. I had my suspicions and handled the matter personally.'

'You opened the deposit, saw the bodies, retrieved the key, closed it again and did nothing. Why not?'

Pinho leans back in his chair and exhales loudly. 'This is a delicate issue. I alone had seen the bodies. Banco do Carmo was once a force in the Portuguese banking world, but for decades it has been gradually losing influence and custom. It is seen as a traditional bank, late to accept new technologies and ceding its status to the brash newcomers which have such impersonal attitudes to their client base. We desperately needed to raise new capital, and right at the time this incident occurred, a large share placing was about to be concluded. Negotiations had been difficult and the deal was on a knife-edge. Had it been announced that the bodies of a man once accused of alleged war crimes against his fellow Jews and of a corrupt bank official had come to light, the bank would be finished. That is why I closed the unit and why it will remain closed until orders come to open it. Hopefully, it will take years and extend way beyond my retirement.'

He picks up the two keys and jangles them in front of me. 'The bank now has the keys to both boxes and a signed waiver from you. As far as I am aware, Wiesel has no living relatives, so I propose to reassign the smaller, N302, in our records as his. The larger unit will remain in your late husband's name. As such, with the way legal processes work in Portugal, discovery and recrimination need never trouble either of us in this world.'

He was wrong, of course. It may have suited him, for he is long gone, but I am still alive. He was also wrong about Wiesel. There is a living relative, his niece Sophia Horwitz, the virtuoso cellist, although I have news for her. When they finally open N302, all hell will break loose, if I am any judge.

As for me, I have Manuel Pinho to thank for pointing me in the right direction. The diamonds proved to be flawless and colourless. They were held in safekeeping by a jolly old man in The Hague who loved both diamonds and indulging in smutty innuendoes. He would sell the diamonds one at a time, choosing his moment when the market was ready. In all, they realised a seven-figure sum and ensured a comfortable old age for me, first in a flat in Zurich and, as I became unable to look after myself, residential care close to Geneva.

I have done a great deal of research over the years and I now know more than is good for me. But it's not for me to open the can of worms. I will let Kirchner's letter do that.

Any regrets? Of course there are. I will never know my brother, Josef, and why he makes it his life's work to track me down. I don't have to worry. I was always too clever for him and always will be.

PART THREE

INTRODUCING THE PLAYERS

NINETEEN – SOPHIA
LONDON, ENGLAND
October 2018

As he raised his arm to hail the taxi, he felt the tailored shirt straining against his midriff just as the button eased out of the hole and exposed the roll of flesh around his stomach. His guess was a weight gain of seven or eight pounds since his enforced retirement the previous year, although, fearing the reality could well be starker, he hadn't yet been man enough to jump on the scales to check it out. He was prepared to defer the ramifications until another day. Better the conviction of self-deception than the prospect of an uncomfortable truth, a maxim he was grateful he had never applied to anything really important in his life.

'Do you want this cab, mate?'

'Sorry, miles away.' Hurriedly, Broadhurst clambered into the taxi, rebuttoned his shirt and took a deep breath as he gave his destination to the driver. Truth was, this stress-free, good life was beginning to show and not only around his stomach. If he had been serious about losing weight, this morning should have seen him take a brisk walk to Shepherd's Bush tube station and a Central Line train to Bank where he would change for the Northern Line service to Old Street. Too late now. He would definitely plan to start a healthier regime in the morning.

For all the years Broadhurst had worked in London, his duties as head of security had been mainly confined to Kensington Palace and the various royal households scattered throughout the United Kingdom. The City's financial district and adjoining suburbs were not areas he knew well, and he could only admire the taxi driver's skill set as they threaded through a series of side roads to avoid the traffic.

They came to a halt in front of a converted church.

The choice of venue for the meeting had not been his. A call had come out of the blue a week earlier. The woman had insisted in that tone of haughty arrogance he had come to associate over the years with secretaries who evolve into self-anointed 'confidential personal assistants', prepared to revel in any confrontation that enables them to live vicariously through their influential employers – the place and time had to be of her choosing. He must understand; she was speaking on behalf of Maestra Sophia Horwitz – *the* Maestra Sophia Horwitz. The Maestra's time was extremely precious. Broadhurst had tried to sound suitably reverent. How had she come upon his name? An unnamed impeccable source linked to the Palace was prepared to vouch for his discretion and professionalism as a confidential private investigating consultant. The Maestra wished to discuss a personal and highly sensitive issue that would command his undivided attention. There was a fifteen-minute slot in her schedule at precisely one thirty on the stipulated date.

He had done his homework. Sophia Horwitz was a name well known in orchestral circles, revered as one of the finest classical cellists of the twentieth century. Some strategically placed enquiries had also given him a detailed insight into the background of a woman whose social media profile glossed over a turbulent personal history.

Broadhurst picked up a leaflet as he waited in what had once been the narthex of the church. St Luke's had been built in the eighteenth century on marshlands with a history dogged by problems of subsidence. In the nineteen sixties, the Anglican church had been deconsecrated and allowed to fall into ruin, only to be given a new lease of life when a redevelopment project transformed the building into a community and music centre for the London Symphony Orchestra.

The receptionist looked pointedly at the clock as she noted he was seven minutes early. The Maestra could not be disturbed. She was involved in an educational programme in the Clore Gamelan Room. Her personal assistant was waiting for him in the Crypt Café. Broadhurst smiled, but he was through following instructions and sensed a little disobedience might be educational.

Down at crypt level, he dodged past the entrance door to the café and followed the corridor to his left. The double doors squeaked on their hinges. The three musicians at the front of the stage glanced up as he entered, momentarily distracted from the hunched figure who had been addressing them. The two men and one woman were seated, each with a cello between their knees, each with a bow in hand, at the ready. As the men's gaze returned to stare at the floor in what appeared to be acute embarrassment, the girl with oriental features, now red-faced, looked anxiously at the old woman who leaned forward, her arm raised.

'For God's sake, Meili!' The ratchet voice sounded like a volley of ball bearings onto a drum, harmonised with a smoker's cough, yet the dynamic effect was somehow tempered by the quiver of old age. 'Do you recognise the piece you are playing?'

The girl mumbled something unintelligible.

'How can you make Bach's Cello Suite Number One sound like the fucking 'Ride of The Valkyries'? Strangely, the profanity did not seem out of place to Broadhurst, whose presence had still not been acknowledged.

'Look here.' She used a stick to aid her climb onto the stage. The girl moved over as the old lady placed the cello so that it was to one side of her closed legs. One of the two men, a black African, looked earnestly at the pose. 'Don't worry,' she said. 'It won't affect my performance.' A smile creased her lips. 'Long time since I've had anything between them, let alone a cello.'

All three students looked bemused. Broadhurst guessed he was the only one who got the innuendo.

She touched the bow against the strings. 'Now, Meili, we are playing a piece designed to convey plaintive tranquillity, done so' – she tapped on the strings – 'with a series of bobbing chords, not as if we are playing a military march. When you play vibrato, it is not created by an upper arm movement but by the forearm. Watch and listen.'

She closed her eyes and began to play, a piece with which Broadhurst was immediately familiar. The sound was exquisite.

He knew she was well into her eighties, date of birth not specified in her bio, but references to her childhood put her somewhere between eighty-two and eighty-five. The snow white hair, pulled severely back into a knot, highlighted the pronounced forehead, now wrinkled in concentration, her entire being absorbing the sound as the bow, relaxed in her grasp, moved effortlessly across the strings. She puffed air into her cheeks, eyes opening momentarily to glance at her slender fingers as they picked out the notes.

As she came to the end of the piece, her chin dipped and she breathed deeply. Broadhurst could not resist applauding as the students tapped their bows on the body of their instruments in respectful appreciation.

Deep-set lively eyes focused on him. 'I only play before an invited audience,' she said, 'and you were definitely not invited.'

Her full lower lip seemed slightly out of sync with the words. Perhaps professional vanity had extended to plastic surgery at some time in the past, he mused. 'I have an appointment,' he said lamely.

The secretary-cum-personal assistant was exactly the person he had imagined. Plainly agitated, she rose from her chair as she saw them entering the Crypt Café, fingers fidgeting nervously with the large red baubles on an oversize necklace. Ignoring any greeting, she launched into a forceful criticism of Broadhurst's failure to comply with her instructions and exaggerated concern that precious time had been lost unnecessarily. He smiled inwardly at a change of tone so obsequious as would have made even Uriah Heep cringe when she turned to express her regret and distress that the Maestra had been disturbed.

During his many years at the Palace, Broadhurst had mastered the art of dealing with the odd temperamental royal from time to time and he had no problem in parrying the woman's broadside with a courteous, but firm response. He wondered how the old lady would deal with this control freak who plainly expected to participate in what had been described as 'a confidential and sensitive issue'. He needn't have worried.

'Alison. Be a darling and look out that Dvorak Cello Sonata with Rattle's annotations for me, would you? I seem to have mislaid it.' The old lady smiled warmly. 'I'm likely to overrun here, so keep the new batch of pupils on their toes until we've finished. I'll be along just as soon as I can.' She waited until her plainly disgruntled assistant had left the room. 'Don't pay any attention to all that,' she said, motioning for him to pull his chair closer. 'Alison's a little zealous, but she has my best interests at heart.'

'Is Maestra a formal title or a term of respect?'

'I know. I've given up trying to get her to stop using it. It's just an honorary title. I've often thought it would suit the name of an all-action adventure hero in a child's comic.'

Broadhurst laughed. 'Shouldn't it be Maestro these days? I thought it was gender neutral, like "actor"?'

'My heavens, don't suggest that to her. I will never hear the last of it. I pray one day they will elevate me to the Lords. Then, I can stop being the Maestra and start being Lady Horwitz – grand, but far less pretentious.'

A waitress appeared with a pot of tea and was about to put a plate of biscuits on the table when the old lady stopped her. 'Alison insists on the gluten-free taste-like-cardboard variety. Be a dear and bring some chocolate digestives.' The waitress gave a knowing smile and retreated.

'That's better,' she said, trying to get comfortable in her art deco chair. 'God save us from interior designers spending other people's money.' She adjusted a cushion. 'Now, Mr Broadhurst. Firstly, please do call me Sophia. I do so enjoy the sound of my name. My source tells me you were, until recently, a highly respected member of security at Kensington Palace. You have since retired and operate a small private enquiry business for selected clients whenever discretion is essential.'

He nodded. 'I act in partnership with a French associate when circumstances demand. In London, I work from home. We share a small office in Paris for international clients. My partner is a retired police officer.'

'You were at the Palace at the time of the tragedy?'

He nodded again. 'For obvious reasons, it is a terrible event which I am both bound and choose not to discuss. May I ask who recommended my services?'

'I promised no names although I suspect you will find from the nature of our conversation that the source becomes apparent.'

She rummaged inside a leather portfolio musician's case, removing a white envelope from the midst of a wad of sheet music. 'Well, would you believe it?' she said in a voice of forced amazement. 'I had the Dvorak Sonata all the time.' Her expression was impassive, but her blue eyes lit up. 'I hope dear Alison doesn't spend too much time looking for it, don't you?'

The envelope was clasped between the palms of her hand as if she were offering it up in prayer. 'Before I reveal the contents of this letter, I need to give you some relevant background information which will explain the concerns I have.' She held her cup out for him to refill. His stubby fingers wrestled to spike the lemon crescents onto a toothpick which he managed to slide into her cup.

'As you are probably aware, I am Jewish of Polish extraction. In 1938, my parents fled from Krakow to escape the tide of hate and *dénonciations* – you know the word?'

'Denouncements.'

'Denouncements, yes – so much antisemitism, even before the Nazi occupation. I was seven. My mother's maiden name was Wiesel, the youngest child of Borys Wiesel, my grandfather, who founded and expanded one of the most important industries in pre-war Europe, manufacturing rolling stock for the railways. Grandfather Borys was vehemently and, unfortunately for him, vociferously anti-Nazi. Such sentiments were considered traitorous and cost him his life. In 1939, he was attacked and killed by a group of Blackshirt thugs whilst on a business trip to the north of Portugal of all places. It was the last place he would expect to be confronted by a group of neo-Nazis.' Her eyes had begun to water, but she made no attempt to dry them. 'It was a similar fate which was to befall my parents in Chicago seven years later.'

'In Chicago in 1946?' Broadhurst was visibly taken aback. 'Surely not?'

'You need to brush up on your history, Mr Broadhurst. Many cities in the UK and America were breeding grounds for right-wing Jew hatred during and just after the war years. Many would say antisemitism is still alive and thriving in our land. I will come back to this aspect at some other time. It is not relevant to this conversation and, as my assistant indicated, time is of the essence.'

'You were an orphan at twelve.' It was a statement of surprise more than a question. None of this had cropped up during his research.

Irritated at the interruption, her expression softened when she recognised his look of genuine sympathy. 'I was away when it happened. Fortunately, my father must have sensed his family would be vulnerable. He was a successful composer and artist in his own right and had established a trust fund for me which proved more than adequate to see me through school and, with some degree of independence, into music academy.' She gave a smile of self-satisfaction. 'I was a prodigious musician from a very young age, you must understand.'

'What came of the rest of your family?'

182

'I was coming to that. My mother had three elder brothers, all of whom worked in the family business. Of course, when the Germans came, they were in fear of their lives. Lew, the eldest of the three and the new head of the company, calculated the Germans would need their factories and, more important, their expertise, to assist in the war effort. In his opinion, the family would have sufficient bargaining power to insure its safety.'

She caught her breath and inhaled deeply. 'From this time on, I have no direct knowledge of the family's involvement with the Nazis. The only thing I can tell you is when the end of the war came – Borys's widow, Lew, his wife and son and the two other brothers who were unmarried – none of them survived the Holocaust.'

Broadhurst could only wonder where this story was going and how it could concern him. After all, she was a classical musician. Was this the first movement to set the scene; a second designed to intrigue, followed by a soft refrain that would build into a rousing finale designed to embrace and captivate his interest? He would curb his impatience.

She had been sent to live with a relative in England and was studying for her A levels at a convent school in Suffolk when the publication first came to her notice. The Nuremberg trials had come and gone and public attention had centred on the Nazi hunters, most notably Simon Wiesenthal, whose objective was to trace and track fleeing war criminals and the many collaborators of different nationalities who had assisted the Germans.

A fellow Polish-born student had received a copy of an English language newssheet printed in Warsaw, entitled *Be a Patriot*. The headline, 'The Appeaser Scum who Collaborated with the Nazis', was daubed across the page, under which was an old photograph identifying her uncle, Lew, his wife, son Malik, and the two single brothers. The incendiary narrative accused the family of not only collusion with the Nazis, but denouncing fellow Jews, appropriating their property and, worst of all, betraying a resistance group who were all summarily executed in a forest outside of Lodz.

Over the following three years, she received a series of cuttings from various magazines and newspapers, all contributing to the original accusations, corroborated by eye-witness accounts which fuelled more and more violent revelations.

'Don't ask me who sent them,' she said. 'They all arrived anonymously. It suddenly stopped when I went to music academy. I have no idea why, nor do I have any basis on which to establish the truth or otherwise of the allegations. Maybe, as they say, there is no smoke without fire, but many things happen in war, many truths never come to light and many lies are told.' She drained the last remnants of her tea. 'To be brutally honest, I don't care whether the Wiesel brothers were motivated by fear or greed.' Her hand reached over to grip his. 'What I do care about passionately is that the memory of my mother and father is never tainted with the damning charges levied at her brothers. Can you understand that?'

'Yes.'

She picked the white envelope on the table and handed it to him. 'I will now turn to your assignment. Please read this and tell me what you think.'

He read and reread the two-page document. It was from a firm of Lisbon lawyers, written in Portuguese with a certified English translation. 'It seems quite straightforward,' he said. 'Following the fire of 1988 in the Chiado area of the city, which devastated the Banco do Carmo and partly destroyed the neighbouring building which operates as a safe-deposit facility, a twenty-year grace period was established by the government to allow time for accredited customers of the bank to be traced and redeem the contents of their boxes. Such an extended period had been granted in recognition of the fact that the bank and safe-deposit facility have been in operation since the nineteen twenties, and attempting to identify many of the rightful beneficiaries would be a lengthy process. You, Mrs Horwitz, have been identified as the only surviving relative of a safe-deposit box holder and have until the end of this month to prove your right to title and redeem the contents of the relevant box. If you fail to do so, the contents of all unclaimed boxes default to the State.' He looked up. 'If I'm reading it correctly. I'm no lawyer.'

She nodded.

'Do you have a problem with this?'

She nodded again. 'Needless to say, since receiving the letter, I have made several enquiries As you say, the safe-deposit facility was in operation throughout the Second World War Portugal was neutral and, as far as I understand, Lisbon was a hotbed of intrigue and illicit activities, swarming with both British and Germans along with nationals from a kaleidoscope of countries. God knows who put what in those boxes. Apparently, the building was an old church like this place and has hundreds of safe-deposit boxes, some as big as travel trunks.'

'I can imagine Lisbon was a vibrant city at the time, both exciting and very dangerous.'

She checked a fob watch hanging from her blouse. 'Had the safe-deposit box in question been in the name of my grandfather, Borys, I would happily go over and collect the loot. However, the record shows the box was registered in the name of my uncle Lew shortly before he was last heard of, and that makes me very apprehensive.'

'I'm beginning to get the picture.'

'If I were to up and go to Lisbon, Sophia Horwitz, internationally renowned and respected cellist with all the attendant publicity, only to discover Lew's treasure trove is comprised of items that confirm the allegations against him, not only do I rubber-stamp his guilt as a traitor to the Jews, but I tar the name of Horwitz with the very same brush.'

'So, you want me to go and open the box?'

'With strict pre-conditions. It is not a case of turning up there with a holdall and a smile, collecting the contents and leaving for all and sundry to see. You will go with the appropriate authority, but in strict confidence. In no way is my name to be connected with your presence. You are to make an inventory of all the items in the box, both written and pictorially, which I will review whilst you remain in Lisbon. Dependent upon the outcome, you will then arrange to remove the contents and take them to a secret location of which I will advise you at a later date. It will be my decision as to the fate of whatever is in the box. Is this something you can do for me?'

'What do you expect to find? Do you have absolutely no idea?'

'None whatsoever. It could be full of gold bars; alternatively, empty. I could not even guess. I trust you can help me?'

'I don't see why not.'

She leaned forward to squeeze his hand. 'I chose you because I have to be certain of your complete discretion. You will be the only person besides me to know what the box contains. Whatever it is, you must never tell.'

'Then I must ask: why are you prepared to entrust me with this mission? You don't know me.'

'My source told me that they believe you are already privy to information that could have great ramifications for this country and you have sworn to keep it secret until your dying day. I want you to make me the same promise.'

He stunted the urge to laugh. 'You make it sound apocalyptic. Okay, maybe a royal did once give me his PIN number by mistake, but I forgot it anyway.'

'You make light of the ability to keep a secret. It is a rare quality.'

By the time Alison had reappeared in a show of total despair that today's timetable had been completely ruined, they had discussed the practical details and the fee which Broadhurst would charge.

Horwitz rose unsteadily from her chair, waving Alison away as she moved forward to assist and accepting Broadhurst's outstretched arm. She moved closer to whisper into his ear. 'I'll get my solicitor to forward the authorisation documentation to satisfy the Portuguese authorities. Whatever happens, they must never get their hands on the contents. It could be the end of me. You only have fifteen days before the deadline. Use the time well.' She turned to face her assistant who bore an expression of indignation. 'You didn't find that score, did you?' she said, her tone full of reprimand. 'No. It seems I had it all the time.'

Broadhurst stood outside the entrance to Old Street Underground station as a stream of commuters jostled past him. '*Mañana,*' he said to himself and turned back to hail a taxi.

Horwitz had been right when she indicated he would calculate who had recommended his services. Best guess was Duncan White, the head of the Palace press office. Apart from being a passionate fan of classical music, Duncan had exactly the credentials a publicity-conscious musician like Sophia Horwitz would seek to cultivate. He was also the only one of the senior Palace employees who had calculated there was some sinister and significant reason behind Broadhurst's decision to resign from his post as head of security. To his credit, he had never pressed Broadhurst for information.

White's phone was diverted to a message service. Broadhurst proposed meeting up for a drink the following day, the place and time to suit White's diary.

As fascinated as he was at the prospect of an unusual assignment and the opportunity for a few days to swap Britain's bleak autumnal weather for the pleasant backdrop of Lisbon, instinct told him to be wary. Something about the pat storyline and Horwitz's seamless presentation was troubling. Experience told him the proposer only presented the facts to suit their own ends and omit or gloss over any aspects that could present problems. Once committed, the agent would feel obliged to complete the assignment, even when common sense suggested retreat. He was convinced. She had been hiding something crucial and he needed to find out what it was.

TWENTY - JOSEF
TEL AVIV, ISRAEL
October 2018

The lights dimmed in the banquet suite of the Carlton Hotel. The guests sitting around the large circular dining tables manoeuvred in their seats, straining to catch a glimpse of the guest in whose honour the occasion had been arranged. Net curtains at the windows swayed in a balmy breeze, occasionally parting to reveal the lights twinkling as the boats in the marina moved gently on the night swell.

Waiters moved effortlessly between the tables extending lighted tapers to bring to life each central decoration of a menorah until flames flickered all around the room. Amongst the hundred and fifty guests there was an air of anticipation. Tonight, the mood was one of respectful, almost idolatry, reverence. The room lights would not be raised; a necessary courtesy to the man whose passage into retirement would be feted with praise before his name passed from the headlines into the history books of the Jewish state. Some who knew him well feared, if appearance was anything to go by, the retirement would be short-lived, with a repeat of tonight's eulogies not too far distant as he was laid to rest.

With an attendant hovering on either side, the guest of honour shuffled unaided to his seat. Sporadic applause began and was swiftly picked up by all present. By the time he took his seat, the noise was overpowering.

It was impossible to gauge the old man's reaction. Wrap-around dark glasses with Coke-bottle lenses completely enclosed his eyes so as to dominate his face. The frames had been engineered with a small internal irrigation channel, through which passed a saline and antihistamine solution stored in the plastic pouch and electronic pump device inside his suit jacket. Every sixty seconds, a fine spray would bathe and lubricate his eyes, much as the system used in many supermarkets to keep fish and vegetables fresh. From time to time he appeared to be crying as he dabbed the excess liquid seeping from behind the rims of the glasses with a handkerchief.

Otherwise, the outward appearance was one of an old man with a balding head, the forehead covered in flat brown lentigines, a dash of white hair at the rear and a bull neck that folded into creases over his shirt collar. The sturdy shoulders were the only clue to a once stocky stature that the wasting disease had reduced to the emaciated image portrayed so widely of the Holocaust victims to which his life's work had been dedicated. The suit he wore was easily two sizes too large, but, he had insisted, why buy another? The end would not be too long in coming, and whilst there were still things to do, he could only wear one suit at a time.

Flushed and breathing deeply, the heavily built man at his side adjusted his bow tie, rose unsteadily and flicked the microphone with his index finger. The bass thud was followed by an electronic squeal that fused the guests into immediate silence.

'Esteemed guests, ladies and gentlemen, on behalf of the Derech Eretz Holocaust Survivors Society may I welcome you to our gathering this evening to pay our respects and give thanks to our esteemed friend and colleague, Josef Krakowski, who is finally sheathing his sword of justice to enjoy a well-earned retirement.' He took a long draft from his wine glass, leaving his lips glowing unnaturally red, and burped loudly.

There was another sporadic outburst of applause which he held out the palm of his hand to silence. 'Now, if we can all stand and recite the Bracha together, dinner will follow.'

'Thank you, Erik,' Josef said as they retook their seats. 'I am greatly honoured. My only regret is that Danata cannot be here tonight to share my happiness. My daughter's contribution has been no less than mine.

'Quite so. Quite so,' Erik replied offhandedly as he repeatedly tapped the base of a salt cellar and tried to attract the attention of a waiter. 'They never put enough salt in the bloody soup here. It needs something to bring it to life. Tastes like the Pope's piss.'

Josef picked his way through the five courses, feeling his way with a fork as carefully as his failing eyesight would allow and pushing most of the food to the side of his plate as he waited and watched. His initial reaction was that his fellow guests were eating, drinking and laughing together with a gusto that seemed obscene in the context of a Holocaust Survivors Society, but he banished the train of thought as unfair and irrational. Although there would always be victims of suffering, he did acknowledge the true entitlement of living as the right to love, exist in peace and seek happiness whilst doing everything possible to ensure your fellow man enjoyed the same benefits. As he looked around at the guests, it would be charitable to say they were simply enjoying this entitlement to the full.

His attention was drawn back to Erik as the society president's guffaw eclipsed the conversation at the table. Erik had a good heart, Josef admitted, but, as Danata would say, he was a real pain in the arse. Thankfully, tonight he would not be making one of his long, rambling, alcohol-charged speeches. Josef laughed to himself as he remembered his daughter's comment describing a speech from Erik as the best cure for insomnia the world had ever known. Some compliment to award her godfather.

Erik had risen unsteadily to his feet, his cheeks florid with a kaleidoscope of broken blue veins, the wine glass unsteady in his hand as he proposed the toast to the guest of honour. He stumbled as he announced the eulogy would be given by Elliott Karmi, at the same time managing to almost drop the microphone and spill Yogev Cabernet and Merlot down his shirt front as he tried to restore his balance. He sat heavily back in his seat to a reassuring pat on the arm from Josef.

Elliott Karmi was in his late forties, a slender figure with thick black hair, swept back and heavily greased. His dark olive skin, smoky green eyes and fine features ensured at least half the audience would be watching and listening intently to his comments. After thanking the president for a resounding introduction, Karmi introduced himself as an official with the National Intelligence Agency, otherwise known as the Mossad. He was attached to the department known as 'Collections' where his expertise had been concerned up until recently with war crime intelligence.

'For the best part of twenty years, my working life has been devoted to seeking out, apprehending and bringing to trial World War Two aggressors who committed atrocities against citizens of many countries whose only crime was to be members of the Jewish faith. As we meet tonight, over seventy years have passed since the war ended and time has brought closure to my work, all but for one or two loose ends.' There was some polite applause.

'Thank you. It is a cause for cheer that we in the intelligence community could never have achieved the results we did without the vital

191

support and insight of one man. His name is Josef Krakowski. For almost sixty of those seventy-odd years, Josef has worked tirelessly to avenge the millions who were cruelly slaughtered, by hunting out those who sought to flee and hide from justice. To his credit, over one hundred and fifty escapees with forged identities have been rounded up and brought to justice from all corners of the world. It's an amazing record, and even more so when you recognise that throughout all this time, Josef has barely been able to see.'

This time, there was a general round of applause and the opportunity for Elliott to sip from a glass of water. Tonight, he wasn't going to pull any punches and stick to harmless platitudes and humorous anecdotes. This bunch of bon vivants with a social conscience were going to understand the reality of what Josef had been through.

'I know most of you are familiar with the name of Josef Krakowski, but I wonder how many of you are familiar with this patriot's story.' He looked around. There was a sense of expectancy in the room. 'In 1942, the Gestapo forced his mother, father and sister from their home and transported them to the Ghetto in Warsaw. As the knock came at the door, there was just time for his sister, Rita, to hide Josef, barely seven years old, in a space no bigger than a coal scuttle between the floorboards and the cellar roof. His sister told him to wait until nightfall and then find the local rabbi to seek safety. But when the time came to move, he could not. His body was trapped, wedged tight between the timbers, his arms outstretched in front of him. Imagine how scared this little boy must have been; his family gone, in silence and total darkness, nobody to hear his whimpers or to wipe the tears from his eyes.'

Elliott had the attention of the entire room. A quick glance towards Josef and he caught sight of a slight shake of the head and a look that said: 'I know where you're going and it's not appropriate. Leave it.' Elliott shook his head in turn, as if the words had actually been spoken. Let the ice cream dessert curdle in a few queasy stomachs. Let there be some uncomfortable bums on seats. It was worth it if it brought home the real significance of the occasion.

'I said silence, I know, but I'm forgetting one thing. There was some noise … the scurrying of rats as they moved, first around him, then, emboldened by the passive form, over and across his body.'

There was a shuffling amongst the guests, gasps, a few nervous coughs, a cry from a lady with an ashen face. Nobody moved. Even the waiters stopped circulating between the tables and stood at their stations, arms folded.

'It would be callous of me to give you a blow-by-blow account of the horrors suffered by that little boy over the three days he remained incarcerated, trapped, unable to move his arms. But there he remained, clothes soiled and saturated in his own excrement, his body ravaged by rodent bites. It is a testament to that little boy's will and determination to survive that is a symbol to Jews around the world today.'

Another spontaneous burst of applause stuttered to an abrupt halt when it became apparent he had not finished.

'At the end of seventy-two hours, without food or water, the boy's tender frame had shed the few grams necessary for him to ease out backwards, but as he did so, his frail body snagged on the rough timber beams and jagged splinters pierced his skin. He cried with the pain. The tears were wet and salty, too tempting for the rats as they tore at him and severed the eyelids from his face.'

A teenage girl ran from the room, a handkerchief to her mouth. There was a collective shudder as people turned to their partners with faint smiles of reassurance, but few words. And then, there was total silence.

'I tell you this not to shock, though shocking it is, but to affirm that Josef Krakowski survived this outrage. He gained courage and strength and the child truly became the father of the man. Although handicapped by failing sight and unable to stand any bright light, Josef has dedicated his life to the one single aim of trying to make things as right as they possibly can be by holding those responsible for the atrocities they practised during the Holocaust tragedy. Physically challenged he might have been throughout all these years, but Josef, along with his daughter, Danata, who, unfortunately, cannot be with us tonight, and a small group of committed individuals, has achieved miracles. I thank you, Josef, from the bottom of my heart, and I toast your health and happiness throughout a long retirement.'

As the tone changed, the guests began to relax. Everybody stood and cheers rang out for three minutes before Elliott could round off his eulogy by a symbolic handing over of Josef's open case files to the Mossad.

It was the cue for Erik to shuffle forward to present the sash and scroll of honour awarded by the society. His arm around Josef's shoulder, he thanked Elliott and was confident that his old and valued friend could now return to his home on Lake Lugano in Switzerland and enjoy a well-earned retirement in the knowledge his valuable work would continue in the safe hands of the Intelligence Service.

Josef steadied himself as he rose to speak. His fingertips pressed hard into the starched white tablecloth as his legs fought to gain a purchase. A hand moved the microphone stand towards his bowed head. For thirty seconds, nobody spoke.

'Let me come clean,' he said suddenly, taking everybody by surprise, his voice unexpectedly forceful. 'Whilst my role ends today, I must emphasise the task is still incomplete, with work to be done by others now more able than I. You may ask why, after all these years, there are still individuals out there with explanations to give for their actions. I will tell you.'

He reached for a napkin to mop the liquid seeping from beneath the rim of his glasses. 'When I started out, my only motive was to seek a violent but plainly nebulous revenge for the death of my family at the hands of Nazi butchers. It was intensely personal and occupied not only my every waking minute, but my dreams and nightmares. And I still live with one of these nightmares that I pray will be exorcised before I pass on.'

He used no notes and although his enunciation was slow, it did not falter. 'Over time, the need for revenge went beyond my immediate family and embraced all the Jews who suffered, but I will admit to you that along this journey my attitude changed. Perhaps you will understand when I say the prospect of revenge is a far stronger emotion than that of revenge fulfilled. I came to realise those no longer with us can derive no comfort from the capture and punishment of their tormentors. That satisfaction is ours alone; we seek justice for them if only to make us feel better. Then comes a time when humanity begins to prise open the persuasion that the punishment must fit the crime, even if it never has or never could. Those crimes went beyond any punishment we could conceive.'

Murmurs of surprise and apprehension had suddenly sprung up amongst the guests. Most had expected little more than the ritualistic

194

niceties the occasion indicated: thanks to the society, to those present, to the previous speaker; a silly joke and a promise to keep his comments brief. This old man was provoking controversy, and, it appeared, he was about to walk on broken glass.

'I always assuaged my growing discomfort with the conviction my work would give to the survivors and relatives the overworked term we now use of closure. It satisfied my needs until about twenty years ago when we caught and sent to trial an elderly man who, when he was eighteen, had been a guard in the Belzec death camp. The alleged crime was that he had regularly played Russian roulette using live ammunition with various groups of slave labour children. Who could possibly try to justify such an atrocity? Was it not inhuman?'

Josef visibly inhaled at the recollection. He downed a glass of water in a single draught before dabbing his cheeks again with a napkin. 'However monstrous and heinous the crime, I found it impossible to reconcile the perpetrator with this meek, frail man straining to hear what was being said and confused as to his whereabouts. The evidence might be overwhelming, the verdict obvious, but were we trying the same man or had the passage of time already tried and sentenced him? Had it purged the evil? Were the tears that ran down his cheeks for his own plight or for the children he had so callously slaughtered? He looked like everybody's idea of the model grandfather, which, in fact, he was. He had seven grandchildren, all captured in individual photographs which he jealously guarded in his wallet. They had all written to him, endearing letters, unaware of his circumstances in custody and his past. It was at that moment I asked myself whether justice was served by incarcerating this soul until his death.'

'An eye for an eye,' a choked shout came from one of the tables. 'He needed to be punished!'

'I am not disputing your viewpoint, my friend. As I watched him be led away from the dock to obscurity, I asked myself what we had learnt as a society from the process. It was far more straightforward to react to the consequences of the past acts of one man than to proactively prepare to combat the incredible malevolent forces of indoctrination, brainwashing and radicalisation which led this individual to act as he did. In the space of that man's lifetime, barely eighty years, the blink of an eyelid – I'll excuse the analogy – in the history of mankind, these forces were so compelling that otherwise decent human beings became capable of performing outrageous acts and to not give them a second thought as they looked over their shoulders at the death and destruction they left behind.

'The problem is the forces of evil have not gone away. They are rifer in our societies than ever before and we must act. So, to finish my very last public engagement, I will tell you what we must learn from bringing these individuals to justice. I am not preaching the gospel of understanding and compassion to these bad people. Indeed, long after the last Nazi is dead, we must continue to crush crazy ideologies designed to destroy us, before they can breed. But, my friends, do not allow us to stop there. The only way to halt the spread of this fatal disease is to educate and convince the impressionable and vulnerable that there is another way. When applied fairly and firmly, acceptance and compromise are not weaknesses but strengths.'

Although over halfway through October, the night air was warm, a soft salty breeze wafting in from the ocean through the citrus garden at the rear of the hotel. Josef savoured the scent of lemon and lime in his nostrils as he breathed in deeply. Through the lenses of his dark glasses, he followed the soft glow of the fairy lamps as they swayed to and fro. The sound of laughter and chatter came from around the swimming pool where a number of guests had congregated to socialise as the night's event wound down.

Josef turned into a deserted, compact courtyard with a wooden-framed pergola set against a retaining wall where he gratefully found a seat. He waved away the two carers who had shadowed his passage from the function room and beckoned for his companion to join him. The bench rose slightly as Elliott took a seat at the far end. He knew the old man baulked at any sensation of being trapped in too close proximity to anyone.

'Are you sad it's over,' Elliott asked.

'It's not over, is it?'

The younger man looked across, his brow raised. 'They may never be found, you know. She could well be dead by now. He most probably has been for some time.'

'That doesn't mean we stop looking, try to discover the truth, does it?'

'Is that why Dana isn't here tonight?'

'Don't call her that. You know I hate it.'

'Sorry, but it's how she prefers people to know her.'

He shook his head. 'I find these diminutives so demeaning. Danata is such a beautiful name. It means an angel pointing the way. So apt, I feel.'

'Is she on an assignment?'

'Danata,' he emphasised, 'could be anywhere. She does have a life of her own, you appreciate, Elliott. She is not your concern … yet,' he added.

'But she's not anywhere, is she? You know exactly where she is.'

'And you want to know? As if it were any of your business.'

'I'm making it my business. If you don't tell me, I'll toss you over my shoulder and lock you up in HQ for the night.' He laughed. 'Fancy that, do you?'

Josef smiled. 'I give in. The thought of having to stomach Mossad hospitality, especially the food, is torture enough.'

'Okay. Spill the beans.'

'It's a long shot, I'll admit. As we speak, she's driving to Portugal. Left Lugano early today.'

'Driving?'

'It's her eco stand, she tells me. When she can avoid flying, she will. Her car is a – what do you call it? Mixed?'

'Hybrid?'

'That's the word. Hybrid. A word for the twenty-first century. She considers it justifies her actions.'

'What's in Portugal?'

'What do you prefer, the one-liner or the potted history?'

Elliott checked his watch. It would be unfair to overtire the night's guest of honour. 'My bladder's good for another half hour, I reckon. I'll let you know if I start to get bored.'

'You won't. Mine's only good for another ten minutes.'

As it was, he managed twenty-two minutes before he needed a helping hand to stand to relieve himself behind a cluster of pomegranate bushes.

Elliott had got the gist of the story.

It was back in the nineteen thirties when Salazar came to power in Portugal. In consolidating his position as dictator, he had to deal with the influence and resistance of the Catholic church. To show both his displeasure and empowerment, he had ordered the appropriation of the large crypt of a church in the downtown area of Lisbon and, much to the clergies' displeasure, leased it to the neighbouring bank at a peppercorn rent. In one fell swoop, he had sanctioned the Vatican and created an arrangement for the bank to expand its custody facilities in the heart of the Chiado district.

'The history books tell us,' Josef had told him, 'Salazar was an astute politician. He had kept Franco's civil war from boiling over into Portugal, whilst shrewdly playing his cards to keep both England and Germany at arm's length as the European war loomed large. He could pander to both sides as he moved to ensure Portugal's neutrality and the key to stimulate its economy and enshrine its banking and financial institutions.'

The crypt was deconsecrated and over a thousand burials recorded and rehoused in the Estrela and other cemeteries. The bank, Banco do Carmo, which had taken its name from the neighbouring church, was encouraged to develop the site in a unique way. Not only would all the boxes be lined in lead and airtight to protect vulnerable contents, the choice offered to the bank's select and confidential clientele was designed to range from small in size to the large coffin-size units. The bank's business flourished and over the next decade the safe-deposit crypt attracted clients from the four corners of the globe, some to secure their treasures before hostilities began, others to hide their ill-gotten gains during the conflict.

Josef shuffled back to his seat on the bench and rubbed his hands. The swimming pool area was now deserted and the breeze from the sea had chilled and intensified.

'Danata will soon be on the telephone to check I'm in my bed.'

Elliott raised the palms of his hands. 'Hold up just a minute. It's a very interesting and inviting story, but you still haven't told me what you are both up to. Don't keep me in suspense.'

'Haven't you noticed? I'm old, and I am reliably informed that old people can do what they damn well like. It's a privilege of senility.'

'Come on. Don't be evasive. We're colleagues; hopefully a lot more in the future.'

Josef looked at him out of the corner of his eye. 'You think so, do you? Well, Elliott, this is a confidential matter between the council of this society and the inner reaches of your government. However, even the Mossad can put two and two together, I would imagine. You're the detective, my boy. Look it up on your precious internet. There was a major fire in Chiado in 1988. The main bank building was badly damaged, but the church and crypt, built soundly of stone, resisted the worst of the flames.'

He rose unsteadily, gained his balance and waved over the carers to assist him. He extended his arm towards Elliott and, with surprising strength, pulled him into an embrace. 'The church has always wanted its crypt returned,' he whispered in the other man's ear. 'And now, the Portuguese government has established a date for the handover.' He released his grip and smiled. 'Just think of the consequences of that decision. There are just another ten days to go and there are many boxes still locked that must be opened.'

'And you hope somewhere amongst these boxes is a clue to Rita's whereabouts?'

'I am sure, and I must know.'

'Don't let it consume you, Josef.' He stopped to reflect upon something. 'Was Rita the motive behind that speech tonight?'

'Could there be any other reason? Tell me, how does a loving sister who risked her life to guarantee my safety turn into a figure so hated and despised for betraying her own people and condemning children and their parents to such horrors? I have to know the truth. I have to know what happened to her.'

TWENTY-ONE – DANATA
NORTHERN IBERIA
October 2018

She reached the hotel in early afternoon, hours before the ferry from Portsmouth was scheduled to arrive. Her third *café solo* was cold and untouched, the ashtray full, as the headlights from the stream of cars with UK plates snaked along the road away from the port. Several entered the hotel car park. His was one of the last, a mid-range BMW saloon in that tasteless colour of the masses. It said to her that this man, at worst, has no personality or, at best, does not enhance any positive trait by his choice of car. Hers definitely did. The bright red Alfa Spider with the chequered flag flash down the middle of the bonnet stood out strikingly amongst its bland contemporaries and gave her a surge of satisfaction as she admired it. In truth, the eco-responsible justification Danata had given her father for travelling by road instead of by air was nothing but an excuse. She just loved the sensation of speed and the meaningful glances a woman in her mid-forties could command from all those young bucks as she accelerated past them. Her car was a metaphor for the way she felt about life.

Sight of the man exiting the BMW confirmed her initial appraisal; she would be stuck for the next two days tailing a bland and uninspiring individual. His figure was hunched as he hurried across the car park, a battered briefcase held over his head with one hand as protection against the rain, a canvas holdall in the other. His suit was creased, jacket at an angle, the trouser bottoms over his shoes and soaking wet. As if reacting to her thought process, he stopped in mid-step, put down his baggage and pulled up the trousers back over his hips. Who wears a suit to go on a long journey? she thought. People without style; people who are comfortable being uncomfortable; conformists who can't react to changing conditions.

She might know very little about him, but it was sufficient. According to Josef's solicitor contacts in London, the man on his way to Lisbon was called Charles Broadhurst, a private investigator contracted by Sophia Horwitz, the niece of Lew Wiesel. He had a safe-deposit box in Wiesel's name to open and Danata intended to discover its contents – one way or the other. The only other thing she knew about him was the number plate of his BMW.

Five minutes had passed since he checked in at the reception of the Hotel Bahia Santander before she wandered casually into the car park, a large black umbrella obscuring most of her from any curious eyes in the lounge. Her room key dropped to the ground next to the BMW as she carefully bent to secure the magnetic GPS locator under the front bumper. Provided the two vehicles were travelling no further apart than thirty kilometres, she could track the BMW. The way she drove, it would be more than enough.

Her calculations misfired. She had set the alarm for six and started her morning exercise routine when she noticed the BMW was no longer in the car park. Checking at reception to learn the man had an hour's head start, she calculated the odds. He had to travel just over a hundred kilometres before a route option opened up. At that point, she would have to make a judgement. The wheels spun on the gravel as she headed towards the main road. Eyes on the mirror, her concentration obsessed with the prospect of the chase, she paid no attention to the flashy Suzuki motorcycle that slipped into the traffic stream behind her.

The rain had stopped overnight and she made good time on the A67 Autovia, ignoring the speed limits and the flashing headlights directed at the person driving recklessly behind the wheel of a fancy sports car with Ticino plates. 'Imagine what they're saying,' she said out loud to herself as one particularly irate driver was cut up and blared his horn. '"Crazy Swiss bitch!" Get a life, you loser!'

At Aguilar de Campoo, the road divided. There was still no indication on her GPS tracker, no little flashing blue dot to indicate which way he had gone. The route through Burgos would take him south on the Madrid road, then on to Toledo and crossing into Portugal at Badajoz. However, her best guess was that he had programmed his satnav for a direct route to Lisbon. This would keep him heading south-west on the A67 to Vallodolid; fingers crossed as she moved into the overtaking lane. The traffic was getting heavier as the start of the working day approached, and the rain was threatening to return.

She was just beginning to doubt her choice when, shortly after Palencia, there was a ping and the blue dot appeared. In an instant, it felt as if the adrenalin had drained out of her. She could have closed her eyes and slept. Fortunately, the blue dot was stationary. He had stopped for a rest break and she had closed in to within three kilometres of him before she, too, pulled the Spider into a lay-by and gratefully breathed a sigh of relief.

Her tactic was simple. On the route south-east past Vallodolid, onto Salamanca and towards the Spanish–Portuguese border, she planned to overtake his BMW on three occasions by stopping at rest points and waiting for the BMW to pass, leaving a passage of thirty or forty kilometres before repeating the manoeuvre. The first time she drove past at speed, catching a glimpse out of the corner of her eye that he had acknowledged her presence. On the second pass, she moved alongside him, chancing a look across. He was either on a remote phone connection or talking to himself and paid no attention as she overtook him. An Audi A4 behind her flashed his lights to pass and she settled into the inside lane two vehicles beyond the BMW until several cars had filtered past.

The traffic had been moving slowly as conditions deteriorated under intermittent heavy cloudbursts. She found herself in a queue of Portuguese cars at a petrol station just inside the Spanish border. How crazy, she thought. Free movement and the lure of a twenty cents a litre discount because the tax rates between countries varied must be driving the guy with an empty petrol station on the Portuguese side of the border out of business. As she moved forward, the BMW she had overtaken ten kilometres earlier pulled up at the pump alongside her. He had stopped his right-hand drive model too close to the concrete plinths on which the pumps were mounted and, with a car behind his, he was forced to clamber out of the vehicle through the passenger door. She caught his eye and acknowledged an embarrassed smile with an understanding nod of the head. Stroke of luck, she thought, but the feeling was short-lived. The prospect that he might also stop at the adjoining café and strike up a conversation came to nothing as she watched the BMW exit onto the highway.

Dusk was approaching as she planned her third attempt. The build-up of traffic evidenced the end of another workday and the closing of her window of opportunity. As far as she was concerned, it was vital when they finally came face to face that he made the first move to strike up a conversation. For her to take the initiative would look too contrived. She checked the GPS tracker handset. The flashing blue dot was stationary, several blocks away from the A25 trunk road that linked the mountainous city of Guarda to the south and Lisbon. He must have stopped for the night.

The Hotel Estrela was a modest three-star motel-style lodging on a hillside suburb overlooking the city. The main building, housing reception and an adjoining bar-cum-casual diner stood at the point of a road leading to a row of recently constructed two-storey terraced apartments. Danata parked the Spider two bays along from the BMW and walked back to the apartment she had been allocated for the night. From the bedroom window she could observe the entrance to his apartment. With no other restaurants in the vicinity and few guests, a casual conversation in the diner over their evening meal would finally be the ideal place to break the ice.

Again, she was to be disappointed. She hung around most of the evening, dragging out her two-course meal of the day and a half-bottle of wine for as long as possible, but he never showed. Apart from a hostile-looking young woman forever picking up her mobile to check it and then put it down, nobody else came into the dining area. Danata thought about striking up a conversation but at the sound of a ping and a hurried glance at the screen, the woman departed.

Broadhurst's car had not moved. In any case, from her vantage point in the diner, she would have seen the BMW had it left the hotel. His apartment was in darkness. He must have bought something at one of the rest stops en route. She gave one final look in his direction, exhaled deeply and cursed out loud.

This man was one of the most irritating people she had contrived, but not yet managed, to meet. Yesterday, he was away at five in the morning, so what did she do? At four thirty she was up, dressed and ready to go. Today, he left the apartment at nine. She'd almost dozed off again as the sound of his apartment door shutting brought her out of a trance. Leaving her overnight bag, she rushed for the stairs, forcing herself to slow down and amble towards the Spider.

He acknowledged her with a smile, 'If I didn't know ... Sorry, do you speak English?'

She nodded and returned his smile. Her heart was still racing from the sudden exertion.

'Good. I was about to say that if I didn't know better, I'd say one of us was following the other.'

She wrinkled her brow. 'I beg your pardon?' Did her expression convey that she had no idea what he was talking about?

'We kept passing each other on the road from Salamanca yesterday and here we are today, staying at the same hotel.'

I passed you, she thought, mentally correcting him. The way he drove that BMW, overtaking wasn't in his vocabulary. She smiled an acknowledgement. He wasn't bad-looking, she conceded, even if a little paunchy around the waist. Mid-fifties, she calculated, professional, middle class and, almost certainly, excruciatingly staid and boring. 'Yes,' she said, still trying to create an inflection of ignorance. 'Looks like an improvement in the weather today?' It's the sort of topic to which he's bound to react. The British adored talking about the climate.

'Did they fix it for you?'

The man spoke in riddles. What was he on about? 'Say again.'

'Your car. As far as I could understand him, the man indicated it was probably just a battery problem.'

What was he talking about? There was nothing wrong with her car.

'I came out when I saw the flashing light from his torch around the cars. I thought, at first, we had a thief on our hands.'

She started to grasp the implications of what he was telling her. Somebody had tampered with the Alfa. She needed to allay his concern. 'As far as my Portuguese would allow, it's been fixed,' she lied. 'I've got a message to ring him.'

'Did you know the man?'

'No,' she replied sharply. 'Why should I?'

'No reason.' He sounded more than curious.

The explanation needed to be plausible. Whoever had interfered with the car, it was none of this man's business.

Her smile was disarming. 'The hotel phoned when I told them about the problem. The receptionist said he had a contact.'

'That explains everything. When a mechanic turns up on a top-of-the-range motorcycle with no tools other than a few bits and pieces, you get your doubts.' He made to walk towards his car. 'Although, he did seem to know what he was doing.' He turned back towards her. 'You're best to check everything's all right.'

He was giving her instructions, fuck him! Tightening his tie knot and straightening his shirt collar – these were reflex actions; something he probably did after issuing a command and waiting for the result. Anyway, she already had the mobile out of her pocket. She didn't need him to tell her what to do. Only her father could do that. She moved away to make the call to Tel Aviv.

The boot of the BMW was open and he was packing away his suitcase. 'Are you heading to Lisbon?' she asked. 'Apparently, I have a problem. They are sending a tow truck for the car.'

'Lisbon's my destination. What's the trouble?'

She looked away from his curious glance and studied the ground. 'It's the alternator. It needs to be replaced. Unfortunately, the Alfa range is not particularly well represented in Portugal and the car will need to be garaged to wait for a replacement part from Madrid.' She looked back at him. 'You couldn't give me a lift, could you? I'd be very grateful.' She waited for a reaction that wasn't spontaneous. 'I'll split the gasoline and tolls with you.'

He laughed. Damn it, he had laughed at her. Nobody did that and got away with it.

'Is there a problem?' she pressed, a hint of the anger she felt in her voice.

He didn't answer immediately, but finished tidying away his luggage. 'You're more than welcome to hitch a ride and I think I can just about handle the finances. Your presence will have one big positive.' He reached for her overnight bag to stow it.

'Really? What's that?'

'I no longer have to get out and walk around the car at the toll booths. I'll hand the money to you and you can lean out of the window and pay the man.'

She was already walking to the right-hand side of the car. She stopped and turned back. 'I was forgetting. You Brits have to be cantankerous and drive on the wrong side of the road.' She shook her head in a gesture of mock frustration.

'You'll excuse me, but I think it was us Brits who set up the system, whereupon, with a few exceptions, the rest of the world decided to be cantankerous, as you put it.'

For the most part of their four-hour journey south-west to Lisbon, the atmosphere was friendly, good-humoured and relaxed. In answer to his question, her family name was Polish, a concoction of vowels and consonants thrown together in a format most people found unpronounceable. She had opted for Da Luca, her late mother's maiden name, which one of her friends had suggested matched her fiery temperament.

As they asked and parried questions with well-rehearsed lies, there was even the occasional banter. When she likened his driving speed as a practice run for his funeral, he made to stop the car and proposed she get out and walk if she thought she could get there quicker. Occasionally, their conversation strayed into more personal areas. Chas was a former SAS officer and security consultant looking for a retirement home on Portugal's Atlantic coastline, intending to use Lisbon as his base. He was well primed with all the relevant information, she acknowledged. He knew all about the various new development areas, Portuguese construction terminology and property market conditions. Done his homework, she thought with begrudging admiration. He could almost be genuine if she didn't know otherwise.

Danata's technique was based on her father's advice. If you're going to lie, stick as close to the truth as possible. She was a freelance journalist of Jewish descent, living in Ticino, the Italian-speaking region of Switzerland. Lisbon was the European hotspot of the moment and she wanted to cover various aspects of life in the capital for a series of articles. There were so many Portuguese immigrants living and working in Switzerland, she was counting on a guaranteed patriotic readership as a marketing springboard.

Hopefully, her father would be joining her sometime during her stay. It rolled off her tongue with an ease she enjoyed. How would this boring man act if she actually said, 'By the way, I've been hunting Jew haters for the last twenty-five years and I've actually participated in the death throes of five of these scum.' Stunned silence, she would imagine, and a hurried 'Excuse me. I have another appointment. I'll be in touch.' And he never would.

As it was, he suggested they meet up for dinner one night when they were both free. 'What a good idea,' she lied.

They were half an hour from Lisbon when the mood changed. It was past four in the afternoon and he had pulled into a large service area for fuel. He needed a toilet break. Did she fancy a coffee?

Five minutes had passed since she had gone for the coffees. She was standing at the bar studying the TV screen. The headline crawler announced breaking news. There had been a major explosion on the A25 just north of Guarda. The reporter stood on the roadway, smoke still rising behind her from the wreckage of what once had been a car recovery vehicle and the twisted, blackened remnants of the vehicle it had been transporting. Details were sketchy at the moment, he was saying. Drivers of vehicles in the vicinity suggested the fuel tank of the transported vehicle had ruptured and somehow ignited. The police officer from the GNR had indicated there was a casualty.

Involuntarily, she shuddered, her fingers grasping the counter top. The reporter suggested there would be little problem in identifying the vehicle that had been involved. He pointed towards the grass verge and the camera lens closed in on the image. Lying there was a section of a flame-red bonnet lid with a black and white chequered flag flash running down the centre.

'Is everything all right?' He was standing behind her.

'Fine, Chas.' She turned and met his questioning stare. 'Shall we make a move?'

TWENTY-TWO – SOPHIA
ESTORIL, PORTUGAL
October 2018

Broadhurst was visibly relieved when they reached the centre of Lisbon. The mood between them had changed on the last leg of the journey. The best Danata could manage was either some hackneyed comment or a monosyllabic response to his stream of endless banter.

She asked to be dropped off on the Avenida da Independência, alongside the Tivoli Hotel. Her 'Thank you' was sincere, even if the way she said, 'Be in touch,' conveyed exactly the opposite meaning. She collected her case from the boot and walked in direction of the hotel. He pocketed the piece of paper on which she had written her mobile number.

On a hunch, Broadhurst ignored the voice from the satnav and took the roundabout just before Rossio to return along the other carriageway of the Avenida da Independência. He put on the hazard lights. They were separated by the manicured gardens on the central pedestrian area between the two carriageways. He watched as she stowed her luggage into the boot of a cab and the vehicle pulled away in the direction of downtown and the commercial area. He was tempted to follow, but he had another twenty-five kilometres until his destination, and with the rush-hour traffic in full swing, God knows how long it would take.

It was past seven, and a ninety-minute stop-start crawl along the A5 before Broadhurst reached the famed resort of Estoril. As he stood on his balcony, looking out at the lights of the fishing vessels bobbing up and down on the Tagus, he was grateful to be away from the clinical sameness of city centre hotels.

The antique splendour of the five-star Palacio Estoril Hotel with its imposing white façade was like nothing Broadhurst had seen outside of a film set. Set between the Tamariz beach and the iconic casino, it was akin to being transported back into the nineteen thirties and the war years, when Portugal's neutrality afforded friend and foe alike an invitation into an environment where both royalty and renegade could find refuge. As he was ushered into the ridiculously large suite with its high ceilings and period decorations, he sensed the presence of the rich and famous who had occupied this very space and the ghosts of the British and German spies who had stood on the balcony, casually smoking cigarettes, as they looked at the view just like he did now and planned their next moves.

'You'll have wished you'd brought your penguin suit when you go down to dinner,' Duncan White had told him when recommending the hotel as a unique experience. Duncan had been spot on. There was a plaque on the wall of the bar recording that the hotel had been the backdrop for a James Bond movie. Thinking better of it, Broadhurst resisted the obvious temptation, guessing that the barman had smiled politely a million times before at the one-liner, and anyway, he didn't really like dry Martini. Dressed in a loose-fitting check sports jacket and a pair of creased chinos, Broadhurst was hardly the image of a fictional hardman licensed to kill.

The thought brought him back to reality. He had now seen the clip showing the remains of the car three times on the twenty-four-hour Portuguese news channel. The pieces of a jigsaw were beginning to fit together as he worked through the train of events of the last two days. He needed an early night, some quiet thinking time and more inside information. There was somebody ideally placed to help him. He would call first thing the next morning.

René Marchal had been a French police inspector based in Paris when their paths had first crossed. As Broadhurst was attempting to deal with a sex scandal involving the late Prince Albert, Marchal was pursuing a serial killer responsible for the ritual execution of a number of paparazzi journalists. Their investigations came together as they chased a lone terrorist across Europe, and a bond between the two men was forged as they dealt with the calamitous outcome. Both men retired from their posts in the aftermath of the tragedy and, although Broadhurst would carry secrets to his grave of which Marchal would never be told, a mix of energy and mutual respect had prompted them to form a partnership. The outcome was the BroadMarch Consultancy, a private investigation firm with no public presence beyond a gold-embossed letterhead which Broadhurst had insisted was fitting and Marchal considered passé and ostentatious. Both men worked from home, Broadhurst in London, Marchal in Lille, where he had relocated to spend more time with his grandchildren when his daughter and her husband had faced marital problems.

'You are in Lisbon already?' Marchal asked, amidst the sound of children playing in the background.

Broadhurst would never get used to the sound of his partner's telephone manner. Disembodied, without the accompanying smile, it sounded a mixture of irritated and censorious, and it immediately put Broadhurst on guard, as if he was about to be criticised. He dismissed the sensation. 'Enjoying a sumptuous breakfast buffet,' he replied. 'You sound like the Pied Piper of Hamlyn. How many children are you looking after, for God's sake? Sounds like a small army.'

'You phone as I stand outside the school gates. I am now waving goodbye to *mes enfants* and anxious to enjoy the next six hours of R & R; something I anticipate you are about to interrupt, *n'est-ce pas*?'

'You read the case brief I sent you?'

'I did. It sounds like a delightful assignment, full of the unknown in a beautiful city. I always enjoyed my visits to *Lisbonne*. You need me to join you?'

'Regretfully ...'

Was Marchal piqued? His mind held the image of the slender man with the brushed-back hairstyle, heavily gelled black hair turning to grey at the sides. He would be suited and booted in a dark grey two-piece outfit. The man always wore a suit. Broadhurst liked that. He would bet Marchal was even formally dressed for the school run. 'There is something I need you to do for us. It will probably involve going to Paris.'

'Go on.' The tone of voice had lost any side.

'A lady has made it her business to get to know me. I would like to know a great deal more about her.'

'Is this a personal request?'

Broadhurst ran through a summary of his journey to Lisbon coupled with his suspicions.

'You think her car was sabotaged?'

'I think somebody wants her dead.'

'You intrigue me. What details have you?'

'She calls herself Dana, but it's an abbreviation of Danata; Danata Da Luca. I'm sending you a copy of her Swiss identity card.'

'You are?'

211

Act surprised, Broadhurst said to himself. It had been a sham telephone call to the hotel in Guarda where they had both stayed. He was trying to assist a fellow guest who wanted to hire a car in Lisbon, but had lost her documents when her car had caught fire on the motorway. The receptionist knew all about it. The local news service had been full of it. Of course, he would send a copy of Ms Da Luca's registration document immediately to the hotel in Estoril, and please to transmit his commiserations to the Senhora.

'I'll give you something else, as well,' Broadhurst explained. 'She left her mobile on charge in the car while she went to the toilet at the service station. The call she made when I told her the mechanic had been working on her car was to somebody listed as Elliott on a number beginning with 9723. That code corresponds to Tel Aviv in Israel.'

'And your assessment?'

'Thus far? I think getting close to me was the objective; the assassination attempt totally unexpected, and all to do with this bank business and the safe-deposit boxes. Beyond that, I'm still working on it.'

'I will go to Paris as soon as my daughter returns from work. Give me until tomorrow morning. Call me then.' There was a difficult silence. 'And, Chas ...'

'Yes?'

'Please keep me in the loop. It's frustrating to get just bits and pieces until the case concludes. I want to know I'm relevant.'

'Of course. We'll speak every day until we meet up. We do need to know what this woman is up to.'

'I'm on the case.'

Broadhurst was lost in a rush of memories as he looked aimlessly at the blank screen of his mobile. This nagging frustration of René's was a throwback to the Prince Albert affair. They had worked as a team in tracking the terrorist, almost compromising the assassination attempt. Then, at the eleventh hour, he had sent René away, back to France, to face disciplinary action. It was only after the event when they met up and Broadhurst was able to give him a sanitised version of what had happened. René was no fool. He knew the truth was being kept from him, the facts altered to suit the circumstances. Damn it! What could he, Broadhurst, have done differently?

Hadn't he made a promise to the King? Should he ever say a word, he could bring down the royal family and sign his own death warrant. If the whole business had left René unsettled, it was no less unsettling for Broadhurst.

The waiter standing patiently to the side of his table coughed politely and held out an envelope embossed with the hotel's crest. The message was to call Sophia Horwitz later that morning. It gave a five-minute window. Seeing the name of his client on paper reminded him he had another call to make.

Most of the available data on Sophia Horwitz was standard biographical information. Feted as a child prodigy, she had arrived in England following the tragic deaths of her parents in Chicago to live with an adopted 'aunt', an unmarried music teacher who later became her legal guardian. In 1950, her prowess with the violin and cello already established, she entered a music academy in London. By the time she was twenty-one, she had met and married a young financier, Stefan Horwitz, and her future was set.

The extensive collection of information from then on was exclusively devoted to her professional and social progression as one of the world's most accomplished cellists; impressive, if not particularly helpful as an insight into the person. Before he left England, he had needed to know more.

* * *

The proposed quick late-afternoon drink with White had turned into an early evening aperitif and then morphed into a cognac to round off a bistro meal as the conversation journeyed well beyond the parameters both men had intended. Even so, Broadhurst steered well clear of any topics relating to his time at Kensington Palace, allowing White the latitude to recount various insider tittle-tattle which both men knew was designed to return them, for those few hours, to the professional relationship they once had. Broadhurst knew the press officer never had cause to doubt his integrity nor the motives at play to explain his premature retirement.

The conversation eventually turned to Sophia Horwitz. White was an avid classical music buff with a penchant for works written for stringed

213

instruments. He had met Horwitz on numerous occasions, interviewed her when a journalist with *The Times* and, unusually, once arranged for her to perform at a Palace dinner for some head of state. Her husband, Stefan, he did not know beyond a handshake and some cocktail party chatter at a few post-performance events. By all accounts, he was a very reserved man, a high-powered financier who headed up an influential private investment bank.

'As far as I am aware,' White said, 'the Four Realms Foundation has offices in London, Dublin, Amsterdam and Buenos Aires, and operates a number of equity funds and charitable institutions with noble aims. It's not my sphere of activity, so I can't tell you much more.'

'No juicy gossip?' Broadhurst laughed. 'That once was your sphere of activity, surely?'

White gave a practised hurt look. 'How could you be so cruel, Chas? You know all my sources are impeccable and beyond reproach.'

Broadhurst raised his eyebrows.

'The only aspect of their lives you might consider somewhat eccentric,' White went on, 'is that although they have been married for over sixty years, an affectionate couple who are always seen together at the right places, they apparently live *very* separate lives.'

'Meaning?'

'Whilst they have a house in South Kensington where they meet for business and social occasions, both have separate homes; hers, a mews house in Chelsea; his, an estate somewhere near Henley. Rumour has it that over the years she has had a number of affairs and, I understand on the QT, he even has a full-blown second family somewhere in Oxfordshire. Fortunately for them, they are not figures of sufficient public interest to warrant a great deal of press intrusion.'

'They have no children together?'

'No. I guess it turned into a marriage of convenience early on and they must have worked out some bizarre agreement to present a united face to the outside world. In today's social context, it seems ridiculous, but sixty years ago attitudes were not the same as they are now. You only have to look at our lot to appreciate that. Divorcee he might have been, but

Townsend would have married Princess Margaret without a by-your-leave in today's world.'

'I've been doing some digging into the history of Sophia's family, the Wiesels.' Broadhurst took a notebook from his pocket, turning to a page retained by an elastic band. 'I have never come across the name before and had no idea just how powerful this Polish family of Jewish extraction became in the period between the two world wars. In the space of two decades, Borys and his immediate family controlled the manufacture of rolling stock and rail line infrastructure throughout Poland and much of Continental Europe. I couldn't find a major rail project from Seville to Stockholm in the thirties that didn't have a Wiesel component somewhere in the mix.'

'Sounds impressive.'

'It must have been. I would have liked to have known the old man. He must have been quite a character. Did Sophia Horwitz ever talk of her family to you?'

White sat back in his chair and looked over his glasses at the ceiling. 'It's years since I interviewed her, but I do keep shorthand notes of all my published articles. From memory, I don't recall her having much to say about the Wiesel family other than to remember her grandfather as very protective towards his daughter, Sophia's mother, and to insist the family emigrated before the Nazi influence intensified in Poland. As I recall, Sophia's father – don't remember his name.'

'Vogel, I think you'll find.'

'Norman Vogel. That was it. A musician. He was one of the free-thinking intellectuals, regularly speaking out to criticise right-wing extremists.' White became more animated as the memory of the encounter was refreshed. 'I remember she was very flattering about her uncle, Lew Wiesel; a great patriot, she called him.'

'How come?' Broadhurst's brow creased. 'She could never have remembered all this or formed opinions. She could have only been a child at the time.'

White shrugged. 'How do you get to know anything about your ancestors? You gradually assimilate the memories and attitudes of your parents and adopt them as your own. I guess Sophia's mother was in awe of her brother and, once safe in the States, regularly talked of her previous life with a rose-coloured tint. Kids are impressionable.'

'I guess she had something of which to be proud. By all accounts, Lew took the business onto a new level after the father, Borys, was killed. In the event, none of the family that remained survived the war.'

White nodded. 'It's coming back to me. According to Sophia, they all died in an extermination camp towards the end of the war. When I suggested that, had they survived, certainly Lew, and possibly others, would have been tried as Nazi collaborators, she became angry and berated me for making such a heinous suggestion. In her view, they had no choice and had done the right thing.'

'I think her information was faulty. I asked a friend in the Ministry of Defence to do some digging for me. Apparently, if they did all die, as she said, it wasn't in the same place and certainly not at the same time.'

'Really? She gave me the impression they were all rounded up, taken off and executed.'

Broadhurst shook his head. 'Lew's only son, Malik, died in a camp in Poland called Potulice in the summer of 1944. The records show the daughter, Yetta, was also sent to Potulice in November, but there is no record of how or when she died. Potulice was infamous as the camp where child slave labour was concentrated and where the notorious Doctor Wolfgang Klein practised experiments in something euphemistically called Germanisation.'

'And Lew, with the rest of the family? What happened to them?'

'Lew, together with his wife, brothers and mother, was transferred to Sachsenhausen, north of Berlin, in January of 1945. Records are sparse around the time. We are talking about the latter months of the war with the Allies and Russians fast approaching the capital. Documents were being destroyed to try and protect the guilty. The best guess is they were all gassed to death in the first few days following their arrival. It is possible that Lew survived until the forced marches, but there the trail ends.'

'Why do you think Lew might have lived?'

'According to my source, the Nuremberg case files contain the testimony of one of the guards at Sachsenhausen who recalls Lew being led from the camp in April of '45. It's inconclusive. The man was trying to save his neck and could have made it up.'

White covered the brandy glass with his hand as the waiter appeared with the bottle. Compliments of the house or not, he had drunk enough. Broadhurst followed suit, excusing himself as needing a toilet break, but more as a subterfuge to deal with the bill away from the table and avoid the squabble that was bound to erupt as to who would pay.

As he returned to his seat, White leaned forward. 'You set up this meet, ostensibly to talk about my insight into Sophia Horwitz's background, but you obviously know a great deal more than I. If you're the Chas Broadhurst I remember, you have something else in mind with which you are about to regale me. Correct?'

'You've sussed me out, Duncan. I do need a favour.' They smiled at each other in unison. 'I left the client with a voice in my head telling me I had to know more about the circumstances that brought her to England and the death of her parents in Chicago.'

'Why? Is it relevant to what you're doing for her?'

'Maybe not, maybe yes. I just like to have all the facts about the person for whom I'm working. It often gives me a clearer appreciation of the assignment. There is absolutely nothing on the net. I know you must have many contacts in the US. Getting some background information shouldn't be a problem, should it?'

'Leave it with me for a day or two. I'll get back to you.'

* * *

Broadhurst was back in his room. The overindulgence at breakfast appeared to have gone straight to his haemorrhoids. He'd had the problem for years. They were itching like hell, the prelude to an uncomfortable few hours. He decided on a hot bath and was appreciating a relaxing soaking when the mobile perched in the ceramic soap tray began to vibrate.

'I was just about to call you, Duncan. I thought you'd forgotten me.'

'Far from it.' There was a silence. 'I can hear water lapping. Are you at sea or something?'

'You could say that. Are you about to give me my bearings?'

217

'Sorry, my friend. I should have known you asking for something outwardly untoward would develop into a full-scale mystery.'

Broadhurst watched the thin trail of blood as it was diffused into the bath water. 'Really,' he said. 'Do go on. I'm literally bursting a blood vessel in anticipation.'

TWENTY-THREE – SOPHIA
ESTORIL, PORTUGAL
October 2018

'A full-scale mystery, you say?' Broadhurst was back onto the call with White after a fifteen-minute delay to finish bathing, don the courtesy towelling robe and find a pillow to place under him on the seat of the leather armchair. 'You intrigue me.' He wriggled around to find a comfortable position.

'And so I will. Unfortunately, I can't be too long. Off to Vancouver for a photoshoot with son number two and his wife's extended Canadian family. He wants to put out a video Christmas card this year, no doubt to try and outdo his brother. If you recall, the wives strive for a little one-upmanship, or should it be one-upwomanship?'

'Probably one-up-personship is politically correct these days. Come on. Don't keep me in suspense.' He remembered the press chief's penchant for circling around a story to build up expectation and it seemed old habits died hard.

'I've got a good friend on the *NYT* who owes me a few favours. He's an investigative journalist through and through, and you've managed to heighten his taste buds with this enquiry.'

'Are you going to keep giving me padding or say something informative?'

'God, Chas, you are impatient. Are you like this with everything?'

'Duncan!'

'Okay, okay. Here's what I've got. We know Sophia's parents, the Vogels, died in Chicago in the summer of 1946. All the Chicago press records of the time have been transferred to in-house microfiche data files with a catalogue browser to enable staff to locate whatever it is they need to research. Sonny's first port of call was the principal Chicago dailies, the *Tribune*, the *Star* and the *Herald*. There's an inside paragraph in each which reports a firebomb attack on the home of a Jewish family in West Ridge in the northern suburbs of Chicago. The area was known as the Golden Ghetto, mainly immigrant families with a large Jewish population. The house was razed to the ground with two fatalities. A third person, a young girl, is yet to be accounted for, pending clearance of the debris. Daubed on the fence were the words *Smierc Zydow* or 'Death to Jews', the trademark of a Nazi-style Polish splinter group known to be active in Chicago at the time. No arrests have been made at this time.'

'And that's it?'

'Far from it. Three days later, there's a two-liner in the *Tribune* which reports a young girl, partially clothed, was found wandering close to Route 31, south of Muskegon in Michigan. She is believed to be the daughter of the victims of the attack in Chicago's West Ridge and has been taken to the Police Department in Holland, Michigan.'

White went on to detail the geography with Chicago, Illinois, at the southern end of Lake Michigan, and Muskegon, Michigan, one hundred and eighty miles away by road on the eastern seaboard of the lake.

'There is a ferry service across the lake from Milwaukee, way north of Chicago, across to Muskegon, which is an eighty-mile trip. How she got there remains unexplained.'

Dissatisfied with the lack of follow-up detail, White's contact, Sonny, decided to see what other coverage the fatal attack had received in the local press. After a seventy-plus-year interval, most of the publications had either ceased or, as was often the case, been absorbed into larger corporate groupings. The little additional information available was no improvement on the original police press release. One of the reports talked of the missing daughter, Sophia, as attending a Hebrew elementary school on West Peterson.

Sonny turned to the local Jewish press. The catalogue index on the server of the *Idisher Kuryer*, the *Jewish Courier*, showed extensive references to the attack and the victims, including the missing daughter, over three issues on consecutive days in August 1946, culminating in the discovery of the missing girl and a follow-up piece two days later. Sonny thought he had finally discovered a detailed record.'

'Only problem was,' White went on, 'when he asked to see copies of the papers covering the entire week the story unfolded and developed, the microfiche for each of the issues had been removed from the sequence.'

'Meaning what I think it does?'

'Exactly. There is no way we can see what was reported, as the *Courier* for that particular week no longer exists.'

'What's your contact's explanation?'

'Sonny asked the question, but the only realistic explanation is someone had the microfiche deliberately removed. The current proprietor suggested that as the publication had been suspended in 1933 and only been re-established in 1945, the organisation might have been lax and lost the original copies. It doesn't hold water. The relevant newsprint must have existed in the eighties when the individual articles were indexed into the catalogue, and the microfiche records are all number sequenced. Seven are missing from the sequence.'

'Your man is suggesting somebody deliberately removed them?'

White reacted to the tone of another mobile ringing close by. 'Your guess, as they say. I have to go now, Chas. Duty calls. You can be certain Sonny will not rest easy until he has got to the bottom of this mystery. When he has something, I'll come back to you.'

* * *

Broadhurst was ten minutes late for his meeting in the centre of Lisbon. The Banco do Carmo had its head office in the commercial area known as the Baixa, and Silvio Malato, assistant manager, was all smiles as he welcomed his guest to an office resembling a compact glass box, a desk free of any visible paperwork, and two uncomfortable-looking chairs. Malato was an intense-looking man in his thirties with thick, gleaming dark black hair, a pencil moustache and lines at each corner of his mouth which suggested a permanent smile. His role, he explained, was to oversee the decommissioning of the safe-deposit facility in the former church and the return of the property to its title holders, the Catholic authorities.

The opening of the safe-deposit boxes was a delicate matter and had to be handled with great tact and care. A decree law passed by the government and approved by EU lawyers in Brussels had provided a twenty-year grace period for the bank to trace customers.

'We are well past twenty years since the fire,' Broadhurst said.

221

'The law was not enacted until 1995, and then, as is often the case in Portugal, legal wrangling delayed the process further. Many things, especially legal issues, happen slowly in Portugal.' Broadhurst smiled. His answer was so pat, Malato must have been posed the question many times.

Sophia's lawyers had drawn up the letters of authorisation Broadhurst presented. He watched patiently as Malato carefully compared them to the series of check boxes appearing on the screen of his computer.

'This documentation' – Malato looked up with what Broadhurst could only describe as an expression of awe on his face – 'it states your credentials as senior security officer for the protection of the British royal family.' He shook his head. 'That is amazing.'

Broadhurst wasn't about to burst the man's bubble. He gave a non-committal response.

From that moment on, Malato's demeanour changed completely. Approval was a formality. Broadhurst was an ally, the man insisted: like-minded, someone who could be trusted; someone who could appreciate the meticulous detail with which this delicate business had been planned. Malato handed over a leaflet printed in several languages detailing the rules under which clients would be able to inspect the contents of their safe-deposit boxes.

'Shall we make our way to the church so you know where to come tomorrow?'

The glass doors parted, causing both men to squint as their eyes adjusted from the sombre lighting inside the bank's concourse to bright sunlight. Their voices were deafened by the sound of the traffic and the bell of the *bondi* tramcar as it made its way along the narrow thoroughfare.

'All clients will be received by appointment at thirty minute intervals over the next ten days until the end of the month, when the vaults will be closed and unclaimed boxes opened by the authorities.'

'What happens to those contents?'

'The title of any items of value will revert to the state. Personal items will be retained by the Interior Ministry for a further five years, inspected and then destroyed.

'Is it not possible a number of boxes may contain stolen property?'

'Ah …' Malato took a deep breath. 'You will read in your brochure that all boxes opened will be subject to inspection. That is why we have set specific appointments. Yours is written on the front. See? Three thirty tomorrow. Two experts and a security operative will be alongside you as you open the box, and will list the contents.' He stopped, turned and placed his hand on Broadhurst's shoulder. 'It is important we make the distinction between fiscal and criminal concerns. The Portuguese government is keen to emphasise they are not interested in any items with customs or taxation implications. What is of concern to the international community is the disposition of stolen property.'

'How are you expected to know what is legit and what isn't?'

'Good question.' He indicated a pavement café where they could remain standing by the counter and ordered two small black coffees. 'Twenty-some years is a long time to plan this event. Various institutions, museums, art galleries and respected jewellery experts were consulted and asked to prepare listings of items known to have been stolen or illegally appropriated during the forties and fifties when activity at the safe deposit was at its height.'

'There must be a million things.'

'Fewer than you might imagine, but nevertheless a substantial quantity. These have been categorised by type and value, and whatever of value is in the boxes will be compared to the listing and any photographic evidence. It has been computerised and software written to make the comparison as rapid as possible.'

'Nevertheless …'

'As you say, nevertheless.' Malato drained his cup and waited for his companion to finish. 'That is why I said clients will inspect rather than remove the contents in the first instance; that is, apart from personal items with little or no value: letters, wills – that sort of thing. Everything else will be listed, confirmed by the client and retained for the verification process. Forty-eight hours later, the contents will either be released or withheld pending further provenance examination.'

'And at the end of the day,' Broadhurst said, shaking his head, 'the client either agrees to hand the swag over or start some legal dispute in the

Portuguese courts likely to go on for decades and keep an army of local lawyers in luxuries for years.'

Malato laughed. 'I couldn't have said it better.'

'You're putting a great deal of responsibility on your experts. They must be good.'

'They are internationally renowned, but it doesn't stop there.'

'How come?'

'We have close-circuit cameras monitoring the process and a number of individuals specifically invited to watch from an inspection lounge and comment on whatever may come to light.'

'Which individuals?'

'A variety, many according to which named box is being opened and where suspicion exists. Above all, my superiors are very sensitive to the Holocaust implications, the bad press which may ensue if Lisbon is seen to be the final repository for a hoard of treasures appropriated from victims sent to their deaths in concentration camps.'

'You're talking about something that took place over seventy years ago. Surely it has no impact today?'

Malato shrugged. 'Lisbon is seen as one of the prime tourist and business convention destinations in Europe. It has a gloss which the powers-that-be are anxious to ensure is in no way tarnished by a chequered history.'

'And how do you protect this "chequered history", as you call it?'

'A confidential agreement was reached with the Israeli authorities, appointing one Holocaust survivors' group as representative of the collective interest. Senior personnel from the group and embassy officials will be present throughout the proceedings. In return, it has been agreed that any discovery with possible egregious consequences will never become public knowledge. I need not tell you how privileged you are to have this information and how we rely on your discretion, but if ...'

Broadhurst gave a knowing smile.

'... if the name of Banco do Carmo and its confidential way of conducting business were to be mentioned in royal circles,' Malato continued, his eyebrows also lifting, 'it could be of mutual benefit to both parties. We maintain several private offshore equity funds, you understand, for very selective clients.'

Broadhurst nodded. Greedy fucking bankers, he thought, the same the world over.

As they strolled along the mosaic-tiled sidewalk towards the ornate, early twentieth-century construction of the Santa Justa elevator with its delicate filigree decoration, Malato talked of the history of the bank and its occupation of the church premises.

'We even have our own ghost,' he said. 'Some employees have said they hear footsteps walking through the crypt late at night. It's probably water dripping through fissures in the stonework, but it's a good story for visitors.'

They entered the elevator cage with a group of excited Japanese tourists and the motor cranked into life as it started its forty-five-metre upward journey.

'What's the origin of your ghost?'

'During the nineteen forties, as you can imagine, the securities department was very active and the young securities manager at the time, Ernesto Braulio, was, as I understand, a very colourful character … a good rapport with the clients. It is said a little too intimate with some. However, unusual times, don't you agree?'

The elevator shuddered to a halt and they followed the group of tourists into the Praça do Carmo.

'Apparently, he came to work one day in May 1988, a month before he was due to retire on his seventieth birthday, entered the building in the morning and was never seen again. He just disappeared off the face of the earth.'

'Nobody ever heard from him again or had word of his whereabouts?'

Malato shook his head. 'Not a trace. Look.' He pointed across the road to the ruins of the Carmo Convent. 'Destroyed by an earthquake in the eighteenth century. It's a museum now. Worth a visit while you're here.' They turned right into a narrow cobbled street with a church on the far corner. 'That's where we're going.'

'You were saying, your ghost?'

'Amazing story. Never a word and nothing missing, apparently. Although rumour in the bank had it that his successor, Dr Manuel Pinho,

225

knew something of the mystery but always denied having any information. Pinho was promoted on Braulio's disappearance and served until his death in 2005.'

'The facility was still operating in 2005?'

'Barely. More as a courtesy to Pinho, who passed away at his desk. Very fitting, if you ask me. Responsibility for the safe-deposit facility moved to my branch on Pinho's death. On the rare occasions access is now required, I ask the client to make an appointment.'

Broadhurst activated the camera function on his mobile. From the outside, the church of Our Lady of Carmo and Saint Peter resembled a place of worship, albeit the plain reinforced steel front door looked decidedly out of character with the intricate Baroque design of the front aspect of the building. It was plainly intended now to keep out the unholy rather than let in the righteous. Two bell towers stood either side of the main entrance, one intact, the other badly damaged and reduced to roof-level height. Another casualty of the earthquake, Malato explained, unlike the scorch marks to the cement finish on the side of the building which had been caused by the fire in 1988. He pointed to a rectangle of land overgrown with vegetation alongside the church. It was where the old bank building had stood prior to the fire. The bank wanted to redevelop the area, but it was holy ground and required the consent of the patriarch of Lisbon, consent that would not be granted until the church was returned to the control of the Archdiocese.

Once inside the church, Broadhurst gained an entirely different impression. Beyond the electronically operated front door, which opened with a snakelike hiss and closed with a thud that reverberated in his ears, there was a small reception area with metal-clad walls, a counter and an enclosed glass cubicle with a single chair next to a foldaway metal table flap.

'The glass is bulletproof,' Malato said. 'Designed for an armed security guard who controlled the electronic screening apparatus and the lock to the internal door. It's not been manned for years. There are all sorts of alarms and sensors inside which trigger alerts both at my branch and at the security company we use.' He moved into the cubicle and flicked a plastic card from his pocket across a small screen before placing the palm of

226

his hand against the red light until it flickered green. The internal door opened with the same juddering noise as the entrance.

Broadhurst could not believe his eyes. The entire interior of the church had been redeveloped with a brick and concrete skin that followed the original Latin cross floor plan and nave. Set into the cement walls were rows and rows of gleaming silver metal safe-deposit boxes, most of a uniform small configuration with the occasional column of small suitcase-sized units. At regular intervals were sets of curtained tables, built like photo booths and designed to provide confidential inspection facilities.

Malato gestured at the floor. 'Please walk along the corridor between the two rows of LED green lights. The secondary alarms are still active and if you stray, it'll be all bells and whistles and lockdown for the next two hours and I really don't have the time to spare.' He pointed to the false ceiling. 'Effectively, they constructed a building within a building. Beyond these walls and above us is the original church architecture and fittings. There are access doors which allow the patriarch's personnel to visit and maintain the structures – all carefully controlled, of course. There is some wonderfully gilded woodwork dating back centuries, I am told. Never seen it. Come this way, please.'

'It must have cost a fortune to build this,' Broadhurst mused. 'Unbelievable. Cheaper to make something purpose-built.'

'Not only to build. It costs many thousands to maintain. Such was our late dictator's disdain for the Catholic church authorities, to spite them knew no cost.'

He led the way across the nave to a series of side chambers where Broadhurst guessed church and local dignitaries had once been entombed. Vertically mounted coffin-sized metal caskets lined the room like lockers in a giants' changing room.

Malato held his arm out as if he was about to make an introduction. 'The original incumbents were rehoused in the cemetery at Estrela when the church was originally deconsecrated. These new residents are all hermetically sealed, airtight containers and must contain God knows what. I can't start to imagine. The art treasures and objects of beauty encased within this steel will soon be revealed one way or the other. Lisbon is presently full of experts and connoisseurs desperate to see the results of this exercise. It's quite exciting, don't you think?'

'Have you never had any break-ins?' Broadhurst had seen quite enough serious artwork and finery during his years at the Palace to dismiss the prospect that so enthralled his companion.

'Seven in all, over the years. All failed. Two died falling from the roof and the rest, caught and sent to prison. It will be a blessing to hand this place back to the church.'

The tour took them through several similar-sized and equipped rooms until they entered a central space which had once been the nave of the church. A temporary three-sided, panelled structure had been erected directly underneath a glass-fronted observation room with a bank of monitors displaying close-circuit imagery from every aspect of the facility. Within the temporary structure, a security inspection unit had been installed similar to the system used at airports throughout the world.

'You will collect the contents of your safe-deposit box in a plastic container supervised by a member of our security team.' Malato pointed to the stack of trays at one end of the unit. 'You will place the contents in one of these and it will be fed into the X-ray machine, photographed from various angles with images displayed upstairs to the various individuals observing inspections.'

'The specialists and the Holocaust representatives?' Broadhurst clarified.

'Exactly. On exit from the machine, the two experts I mentioned will make a cursory separation of the items between personal of no interest and those of possible concern. You will retain photographs and listings of both categories, and after a short wait in the seating area, you will be able to leave with those personal items unless a challenge has been made by one of the onlookers and is not overruled by the two experts. There are strict conditions to protect the box holder's privacy. It will be evidence based, not argumentative. Within forty-eight hours, revised listings will be issued of those items that were retained for inspection, with the non-contentious items delivered to you and any items subject to third-party claims held in secure escrow pending a definitive solution.'

'Sounds like a recipe for legal mayhem.'

'So be it, but the Portuguese government cannot be seen to be taking any steps which might appear to facilitate the unlawful appropriation of stolen property. Every EU state has signed up to the process and all actions will be conducted in one designated Lisbon court, controlled by one stipulated circuit judge and all held in camera. A European Court of Justice appointee will also be present.'

Broadhurst took the extended hand in a firm grip. His smile could only be described as sardonic. 'Good luck with that. I look forward to seeing the process, as you call it, at first-hand tomorrow.'

His mobile was vibrating in the taxi long before he reached the hotel. He saw Horwitz's name on the screen and rejected the call. To take his client out of her comfort zone was a risky tactic, but something he felt obliged to do if he was to ever understand the underlying motivation to employ him rather than a reputable law firm. Allied to her husband's investment banking empire, there must have been a myriad choice of suitable candidates.

When they finally did speak, her irritation was more than apparent. Broadhurst recognised in her voice the mix of frustration, anger and the fear of somebody used to having total control uncomfortable at ceding that control to another.

'You were due to contact me on arrival,' she snapped, 'and I've made a number of calls you have failed to answer.'

His reaction was to offer summary explanation rather than apology, all the time reinforcing his own independence of action. There had been nothing to report beyond news of a sea and car journey. Her calls had come through when he was in the presence of other people and he had not wanted her name on his mobile screen to be visible. Everything was proceeding to plan. Tomorrow, he would be inspecting the contents of the box. The entire process was convoluted, he explained, and designed to ensure Portugal was exonerated from any possible international criticism.

He sensed her initial hostility had now been deflated into a disgruntled resignation. It was time to gauge her reaction to the two topics on his mind.

'I had the company of a young woman on part of my journey down through Portugal. Her car had broken down at the hotel we were both staying at. Conversation helped to pass the time.'

'Really?' It was one word, but it conveyed a hint of panic. 'May I know her name and the circumstances under which you came to be together?'

'You make it sound suspicious with a dash of intimacy. I can assure you it was all perfectly harmless.' He ran through the chain of events, deliberately omitting reference to the incident involving the explosion of the Alfa, which the national TV stations were now reporting as a suspected fuel tank rupture.

'Da Luca, you say, from Switzerland?' Horwitz was obviously noting the details at her end as she asked for the spelling. 'The problem, Mr Broadhurst, and something I probably don't have to tell you, is that in your unique situation there are rarely chance encounters. I have no doubt every journalist – and you can most certainly discount that nonsense she told you about an article on Lisbon's virtues – wants to get the inside track on what is going on inside the bank. The more secretive the Portuguese try to make it, the more fascinating it becomes to all manner of people in this mad world of twenty-four-seven social media. Your best course of action is talk to no one and get in, out and away as quickly as possible.'

Broadhurst explained how, because of the procedures outlined by Malato, this might not be possible.

'Let's liaise closely once you know what's in the safe deposit. We can't make plans for an unknown.' Her tone was now conciliatory.

'You will have to rely on my discretion and intuition in the matter.' Broadhurst wasn't about to be led around by the nose like a hog with a ring and chain. 'Sometimes, immediate decisions are necessary.'

She was about to say something, but must have thought better of it.

Broadhurst changed tack. 'I was intrigued at our meeting when you talked of the tragic death of your parents and the antisemitism in Chicago that persisted after the war. You were away, you told me, on that fateful day. Returning to your home must have been so distressing.'

There was a long silence on the other end of the line which Broadhurst had no intention of breaking. Eventually, she coughed. 'It's not something I ever talk about,' she said. 'It was very distressing and still brings back harrowing memories.'

'It left an impression on me too,' he said. 'That's why I was keen to understand.'

There was another pause, shorter this time. 'Well, all I can tell you is I was staying with friends in Michigan when the news came. I wanted to go back to Chicago immediately, but the police told me it would be unwise. There was still violent anti-Jewish sentiment amongst minorities of both immigrant Europeans and blue-collar Americans. As a minor with no other relatives, I was looked after by social services until friends of my parents – we called them aunts and uncles in those days, though they weren't really relatives – agreed to take me in. They lived near Buffalo and looked after me for a few weeks until a relative – more a close friend of my father in the UK – sent for me. It was a traumatic time. I hadn't even reached my teens.'

Broadhurst found himself holding the mobile to his ear long after the call had ended. Her explanation had been pat, doubtless formulated and repeated many times over the decades. The trouble was it presumed her story would be accepted at face value and no further enquiry would ensue. It was a convenient lie, more than likely designed to avoid reliving a traumatic experience, but, just possibly, to hide something far more suspicious.

TWENTY-FOUR – ISABEL
ESTORIL CASINO, PORTUGAL
October 2018

Broadhurst texted a brief message to White.

Everything was now in hand. He decided on a distraction, some time out from his assignment; a leisurely drink in the hotel bar, followed by a stroll to the Estoril casino for dinner and a twenty-euro limit playing a one-armed bandit.

'Forgive me. Broadhurst, isn't it? Chas Broadhurst?'

He looked into the mirror cladding the wall behind the bar at which he was sitting. Had it not been for the bottle-green eyes staring back at him through the thick-rimmed tortoiseshell glasses perched on that aquiline nose, he might have struggled to place her. She had aged considerably since he had last seen her, what was it … three years ago, maybe five? The smile lines around her mouth – inaptly named in her case, where they suggested a permanent scowl – had now matted into a complex marionette pattern reaching to the underside of her chin. Foundation had been heavily applied but only served to highlight the condition.

'Dame Isabel. This is a surprise. How are you?' He swivelled on his stool and indicated the seat next to him.

She remained standing. 'Don't "Dame" me, Broadhurst. You know I can't stand bloody titles. Offends my socialist roots. You will always be Chas to me and I will be Isabel to you.'

Above average height and slim, the tight, calf-length dress precluded her from perching on the stool until she had unceremoniously shimmied it up above her knees. Her face may have borne the anxieties of the troubles she had faced in recent years, but, as Broadhurst reflected admiringly, for a woman approaching sixty, she had looked after her figure.

'Although this isn't your bag, Chas, I expect you're here for the same reason as most of the guests in this hotel. Working for someone, are you?'

Isabel Solden had been named a Dame in the King's New Year's Honours list for services to the world of art just two months before the scandal broke. Appointed as Surveyor to the King's Works of Art over a decade earlier and specialising in precious stones and metals, Solden had gained a reputation as an erudite professional with a keen eye for pieces compatible with the King's priceless collection, and a skill for detecting a fake or doctored provenance. Broadhurst had met her on a number of occasions to discuss security and insurance aspects whenever items from the royal collection were to be out on loan to museums or art galleries for public view.

The proverbial had hit the fan when a fellow surveyor to the King circulated a memo from an influential auction house which alleged Solden received a secret commission whenever a successful sale was made to the royal household. As this serious breach of professional etiquette was bound to create a scandal should the accusation be made public, Solden's protests of innocence and accusations of a frame-up had gone unheeded, and she had been obliged to remain in her position in name only until a suitable period had elapsed, to avoid mutual embarrassment. Broadhurst could not remember if she was still in limbo or had now formally stepped down from her prestigious role. He decided on the diplomatic approach.

'If you're referring to this bank business that seems to be creating all the furore, I'm afraid it's just coincidence as far as I'm concerned. My interest is real estate.'

'Mmm ...' She kept it going too long. Accept the lie and get on with it was Broadhurst's maxim. She should understand he had no intention of giving her chapter and verse as to the real reason he was in town. Believe what she wanted and either enjoy his company on those terms or seek greener pastures. It was the way he intended to approach the encounter.

'Have the family interests brought you here?' he asked.

The barman was hovering. She ordered a Bloody Mary. 'No way,' she said with a dismissive shake of the head. 'Not my concern any more. Surely you were acquainted with the coup that put my head on the block?' She took a healthy swig from the glass handed to her and licked the excess tomato juice from Botox-enhanced lips. 'They waited four years before the axe fell, but I'm out now. I'm a consultant with a brief, much the same as you, I suspect.'

He didn't rise to the bait 'Would they have any interest in what's going on?'

She took another swig from the glass and repeated the lip-licking process. The guffaw that followed was for effect. 'Good Lord, Chas. What do you think? All those German and Greek family lineages? How many skeletons do you think are in the cupboard? It must be squeaky-bum time in Kensington at the prospect of what will turn up when the boxes are opened.' She drained the remnants from the glass. 'I told the barman that one was on you. If you fancy having my round and a bite to eat, why don't we get a table at the casino?'

He nodded. 'Good idea. If not you, who's here representing their interests?'

Another strained guffaw. 'You haven't bumped into that prick Justin yet? He's crawled out of a hole to present his royal credentials; staying in town somewhere where money is no object. Bumped into him yesterday at a Christie's reception. There's someone who couldn't tell a piece of jade from a Coca Cola bottle.'

'I think we'd better go before you run down the entire art establishment.'

'Not difficult.' She pulled a mobile from her purse. 'Just give me a minute.' She began to text, pressed send and looked up. 'Just letting Cartwright know where I'll be.'

'Your husband's here?' There was surprise in his voice. Isabel Solden had kept her family name when she had married Axion Cartwright twenty years earlier. It was a wise move. Cartwright liked to call himself a theatrical entrepreneur, but in police and security circles he was known as an individual with some very dubious business activities. He was cute and had never got caught, always leaving someone down the line to take the rap. White had once described him as the car driver who had never had an accident, but had seen plenty.

'Don't sound so surprised,' she said. 'The casino's full of young, pretty dancing girls, all right now listening to Cartwright telling them how he's going to make them stars, but first ...' Her voice tailed off as her eyebrows lifted. 'And good luck to him. His wandering member doesn't trouble me any more.' She threaded her arm through Broadhurst's. 'Come on, Chas. Let's go. Show me someone who knows how to treat a lady.'

It's been an interesting day, he thought, as they strolled along in the comfortable warmth and the honeysuckle scent of bougainvillea in the night air. And it doesn't look like coming to an end anytime soon.

She stumbled and squeezed his hand tight.

TWENTY-FIVE – JOSEF
CASCAIS, PORTUGAL
October 2018

Elliott reacted to the sound of the buzzer, reaching the video terminal just as Danata came down the staircase to join him. In turn, the three people at the gated entrance to the property held up their identification to the camera. Automatically feeling for the comforting touch of the Smith & Wesson tucked into his belt, Elliott released the gate lock and watched the image of the black Mercedes as it swept up the driveway.

'Some place you've got here,' the younger man said as the three guests took their seats in the spacious drawing room. His extended arm pointed to the area beyond the French windows to a garden the size of a football pitch.

'Courtesy of the Israeli ambassador for our short visit,' Danata said. 'It's his weekend retreat. If you go to the end of the property, you can look across the escarpment towards the Praia do Guincho.'

The elder of the two men, Hernando Cunha, who had introduced himself as a senior inspector with the Criminal Investigation Division of the Judicial Police, acknowledged the comment with a patronising look that said he knew all about the local geography around the affluent coastal suburb of Cascais. He glanced back over his shoulder towards the staircase. 'Will Senhor Krakowski not be joining us?' he asked.

'He is resting,' Elliott said. 'He is elderly, unwell, and the journey has tired him. The incident has also greatly concerned us all.'

'Naturally. We understand.' The prim woman from the Interior Ministry spoke up.

Cunha coughed just as she was about to continue. It said 'shut up' as plainly as if he had actually uttered the words. 'Your father's presence in Lisbon at this particular time would be an embarrassment to us if the press were to find out.' He looked straight at Danata. 'Having a famed Nazi criminal hunter in Lisbon when we are trying to damp down all the sensationalist press surrounding Banco do Carmo would just add fuel to the fire.'

237

'It would be counter-productive, I agree.' The younger man, attached to the asset recovery division of the National Directorate, added. 'We are trying to get this business over and done with as quickly as possible.'

'Don't think we are insensitive to your position,' Elliott said firmly. 'We coordinated our travel arrangements with your Interior Ministry.' He nodded towards the woman. 'We flew by private jet, using diplomatic privilege to enter your country and, to the best of our knowledge, other than people on your side who may have been briefed, nobody beyond these four walls has a clue we are here.'

For the first time, Cunha smiled. 'Under normal circumstances, the presence of Josef Krakowski in our country would be a pleasure and privilege, but these, unfortunately, are not normal circumstances.'

'No, they're not,' Elliott snapped back. 'Somebody tried to kill Krakowski's daughter and, naturally, her father is concerned enough to want to be with her and try to ensure her safety, irrespective of the embarrassment you feel it might cause.' He left his seat and walked to the French windows, turning his back on the three visitors.

Cunha ignored the outburst. His voice was calm, even-toned. 'We are still trying to establish the exact cause of the explosion. Irrespective of the outcome, the official line of a ruptured fuel line will be maintained.'

Elliott wheeled around. 'Don't give me police-speak, I beg of you. We both know what happened. Presumably you're on the trail of this motorcyclist?'

'And his accomplice.'

'What accomplice? You're not suggesting this Broadhurst character …?'

'No.' He turned to face Danata. 'I believe this tampering with your vehicle took place whilst you were dining in the hotel restaurant?'

'That's my understanding.'

'Was there anybody else in the dining room at the time?'

Danata looked up at the ceiling. 'It was late by the time I ordered. The waitress was trying to hurry me because the kitchen was about to close. An elderly couple left just after I sat down. The only other diner I remember was a young woman sitting in the corner. I didn't really see her face. She was reading a magazine. She must have already eaten because she sat with a coffee on the table.'

'Did she leave before you?'

'You're taxing my memory. As I recall, just as my meal arrived, she took a call or message on her mobile, asked for her bill and left.'

Cunha nodded. 'We think she was there to sound the warning if you left the restaurant whilst her colleague was messing with your car. There is one close-circuit camera on the side of the reception building that gives a panoramic view of the road alongside the various apartments. There are images of this woman leaving the building and joining the man as a pillion passenger.'

'Identification?' Elliott asked.

'Not at this point. Both were in full motorcycle gear with helmets. We didn't get a number plate, but we were able to identify the make and model of the bike.' He pulled a torn sheet of paper from his pocket. 'It's a Suzuki GSX 750, an expensive piece of equipment, I understand. From this, we were eventually able to establish the identity of the driver.'

'How come?' Elliott walked back to his chair and studied the policeman's face.

'If it was an explosive device, it had to be detonated, either by a timer or a remote signal. A timer was unlikely. The car could be anywhere at the chosen moment, overtaking other vehicles, alongside the school bus. Carnage could have resulted and the repercussions of the complex investigation that would be bound to follow such an act. Whoever planned this could not afford that.'

'But a remote trigger means the initiator has to be within a certain range.'

'Exactly. Our assessment is the motorcyclist was waiting at the roundabout leading on to the E802, the autoroute from the Spanish border to Lisbon, expecting to follow the Spider as it joined, heading south. The valve on the car's nearside front tyre which survived the blast was faulty, changed, presumably, to allow air to escape so that Ms Da Luca would have been obliged to pull over onto the hard shoulder. At this point, with the motorcycle trailing the car, the device could be detonated via a mobile signal.'

239

Elliott looked over at Danata to gauge her reaction. 'I get the picture. You must have passed this motorcycle as you sat in the passenger seat of your Good Samaritan's car. The would-be assassin must have sat twiddling his thumbs until the breakdown truck appears with your Spider on board, heading back towards the Spanish border. He's obliged to follow and soon realises the car is not being transported to the nearest garage where, presumably, he would have attempted to remove or disarm the device.'

Cunha nods. 'That's more than likely the case. I'm no specialist, but I understand most of these explosive devices have a sort of signature which enables those in the know to identify the probable source. Our perpetrator panics and triggers the device. Although the driver of the transporter escaped with a few cuts and bruises, there is some serious damage to his hearing. Several people in nearby cars suffered shock.'

'You were able to follow the route of the motorcycle?' Elliott pressed.

'We picked up images of the couple at a rest stop on the autovia to Salamanca. He takes off his helmet to take a call on his mobile as he pays for fuel. Interpol has him on a watch list. The name he uses is Gunter Preiss, an Austrian. He's a member of one of those black leather, tough-guy motorcycle clubs called something or other Missionaries. Interpol keeps an eye on them because of connections to FE.'

Danata gave a low, haunting whistle. 'Freies Europa – Free Europe. That's a banned outfit, isn't it? Right-wing activists?'

Cunha nodded. 'He's got form for affray, threatening behaviour and civil disobedience. All suspended sentences in Austria and Germany. The motorcycle was picked up on various cameras heading towards Madrid. We are working with the Spanish authorities. As far as his background shows, this Gunter Preiss or whatever is his real identity has no specific knowledge about bomb-making or explosives, although we could be wrong. Background checks suggest he may have links with the Baltic states and possibly roots in the Middle East.'

'So, somebody would have given him the bomb to place, a collective effort. And the girl?'

'No luck. She never came within range of the camera. All we have is a long distance image. It could be anybody. Can you remember any identifying features?'

Danata shook her head. 'In retrospect, I can only identify why she took such great pains to hide herself. Average height, average build, dark brown hair – doesn't help, does it?'

'What doesn't help?' The shaky voice came from outside the room.

Danata reacted as if she had received an electric shock. She was on her feet and out of the doorway before Cunha had time to acknowledge her rhetorical question.

'Why didn't you call out, Pappa? You know you must not take stairs without help. Anyway, you are supposed to be resting in bed.'

She assisted her father into the room, gently easing him into the armchair the woman from the Interior Ministry had vacated at Danata's prompting, carefully adjusting the belt of the flannelette dressing gown so that it no longer exposed his pyjama trousers. Once he was seated, she took the pouch and the small pump he was clasping, putting them into his dressing gown pocket. The pump appeared to respond to her action with a grateful hiss as it activated and sent a spray of saline solution into his eyes behind the dark glasses.

With rivulets of solution running down each cheek, Josef nodded to each of the visitors as Elliott presented them.

Josef looked at his daughter. 'There is nothing so tantalising as waking to hear your name being mentioned from afar by a voice you do not recognise. So great was the compulsion to put a face to the voice, I started to tackle the staircase, only realising once I was three steps down I could not accomplish the task without assistance. Thank you.'

'I apologise if I awoke you.' Cunha said.

Josef shook his head. 'Sleeping is such a waste of time at my age. Do not concern yourself.' He brushed away the droplets of liquid from his chin. 'I understood you consider my presence in Lisbon as prejudicial to the public's appreciation of what is about to take place at the bank?'

'I meant no offence.'

'None taken. I can understand the concern. It would be a journalist's dream for a dramatically concocted fake news story to associate my

241

presence with suggestions of Nazi loot. It's the stuff newspaper editors dream about. Don't worry. I shall keep a very low profile. My only concern is the safety of my daughter. There has been one attempt on her life. We must ensure there are no more.'

The woman from the Interior Ministry was perched on the edge of a dining chair. 'Is her presence really essential? Wouldn't it be wise to look on events from afar?'

'Although the Holocaust survivors' association to which I am affiliated was appointed to nominate a representative to accompany the proceedings, nobody knew who had been chosen beyond myself and the president of the association. Danata uses her late mother's maiden name, Da Luca, on all official documents and was considered best placed to complete the assignment.'

'What do you expect to find?' It was the first time the younger man had spoken since Josef had arrived. 'Do you have a specific objective?'

He was out of Josef's eyeline, but the old man made a concerted effort to move in his chair so that he could address the man directly. 'Two objectives. The first is keeping my daughter safe. In this respect, I hope to meet the man who unwittingly warned Danata and brought her to Lisbon. I don't expect he had anything to do with the incident, but I would, as you police like to say, eliminate him from my enquiries.'

'Is that wise? He might recognise you and publicise the fact.'

'Elliott has done some checking-up on the man. He was a senior member of security for the British royal family and now operates on his own account. He knows all about discretion and secrecy. Elliott will make a judgement before I make an appearance. He doesn't know of this location. Danata had him drop her off at the Tivoli where she was originally booked to stay. We know why he's here and whom he is representing. Danata and he exchanged stories and, I suspect, neither believed the other.' He smiled at his daughter.

'And the second objective?' the young man persisted.

'We are primarily interested in the contents of six boxes, one of which is the charge of the gentleman I referred to. The other five are registered in the bogus names of men long dead who committed heinous crimes against my people. Their relatives have all appointed nominees. We

242

hope to see significant property returned to the families of those to whom it rightfully belongs.'

Cunha raised himself from the sofa and took the three steps necessary to stand directly in front of Josef. 'We have taken a great deal of your time and my office needs to continue with its investigation. From what you have said, if it is in fact the case, either you or the president of your association, whose name is …?

'Erik. Erik Friedman.'

'Either you or Mr Friedman, inadvertently or deliberately, let slip your daughter was the appointee. Is that not the case?'

'Unless someone was tailing Dana's movements as a matter of course,' Elliott added.

'Also a possibility,' Cunha acknowledged, turning his attention to Danata. 'Quite a coincidence you ended up in the same hotel in Guarda with this Mr Broadhurst, isn't it? Both travelling by car, both with the same ultimate destination and both stopping at the same obscure hotel hundreds of kilometres from Lisbon; taxes the imagination, don't you think?'

'I can see why you might think that,' Danata said. 'Maybe he had an ulterior motive.'

'Maybe one of you did. Forgive me, Ms Da Luca, but I find it very hard to believe your presence to witness this process is quite as sanitised as your father would lead us to believe. I must suspect you have another agenda.'

'She doesn't. I do.' The room went silent; all eyes turned towards Josef.

Cunha smiled. 'It's finally comforting to learn I am about to know at least one of your secrets. If I have learnt one thing from this conversation today, it is that like an iceberg, nine-tenths of what I seek to learn remains hidden beneath the surface. As for my one-tenth, please …' He gestured towards Josef.

'I believe the contents of one of these boxes will lead to determining the location of the last of the war criminals I am determined to bring to justice.'

'And who might that be?'

There were tears once more on Josef's cheeks. 'My sister,' he said.

TWENTY-SIX – ENRICO (MARCELLO)
MADRID, SPAIN
October 2018

There had been severe turbulence over the Atlantic, two hours out from their scheduled landing time at Madrid's Barajas airport. The captain had apologised in advance for the inconvenience and committed to do his best to try to minimise the discomfort. It was simply not possible to skirt around the weather front. It took some believing they were over a hundred kilometres from the eye of the storm. The sudden changes in altitude as the Boeing 707 lurched up and down had provoked overhead lockers to spring open, belongings to fall into the corridors and an eerie silence amongst the passengers, punctuated by mumbled prayers interspersed by the sound of retching into paper bags. Even those infernal babies who seemed to have designed a telepathic rota for the entire flight's ten-hour duration, with one beginning to bawl out its lungs as soon as another had stopped – even those little souls had gone quiet.

As a particularly sudden and fierce movement caused the aircraft to drop and shudder, for a split second he relished the sensation of weightlessness in his stomach. The middle-aged lady seated next to him reached out with a shaking hand and grasped the ends of his fingers. 'Do you mind?' she said. 'I'm so scared and you seem so calm. It's just for a minute. In case we don't make it, what's your name? Mine is Maria.'

Where you come from, he thought, almost every woman's called Maria. The Virgin Mother. Now there was a woman who knew how to tell a story. Talk about a gullible husband. How did Joseph explain that gem to his mates? He turned his head to give her a sympathetic smile and allow himself the time to bring to mind the name on the passport alongside his photograph. He squeezed her fingers. 'Marcello,' he said. 'Don't worry. It will be all right. These aircraft are made to withstand a great deal more than this.'

As quickly as the drama had begun, it came to an end with the ping of the seatbelt release sign. She let go of his hand, a sudden movement suggesting both embarrassment and vulnerability, then a fleeting smile and polite cough as she began to fish for something in her handbag. Like the effect of a flickering flame from a candle once the electric light is restored, her attitude to his presence had reverted from dependence to irrelevance. Used and then discarded, it was a lifestyle choice he recognised, one he had once respected and put into practice and one that now seriously troubled him. The six empty cognac miniatures clinking together in the seat pocket were evidence of his solution to any impending problem.

Enrico Klaas, currently travelling as Marcello Costa, a Portuguese citizen, had been raised on a smallholding in Chapecó, on the eastern fringes of the southern Brazilian state of Santa Catarina. A Brazilian smallholding was something of a misnomer to the many European and US visitors who used to visit the family home when Enrico's grandfather was alive. A seven-hundred-acre spread might be on the small size as far as local landowners were concerned, but it dwarfed the average in most developed countries.

What little the young Enrico could remember of the main house was a constant stream of visitors, celebrations and hunting parties. Servants ran around, attending to the guest annex in what was more like a hotel than a private residence, all carefully controlled and disciplined by the master of the house. Everything had to run like clockwork, a philosophy foreign to the native Brazilians and their easy-going way of life.

Enrico's fragile memories of his grandfather were few; images of a towering figure with a booming voice and a gold chain around his neck attached to the spent bullet which would dance in unison as the old man bounced his grandson up and down on his lap and shouted profanities at an enemy vivid in his mind's eye as they charged into battle on imaginary horseback. The bullet was a lucky mascot, a sign of the man's invincibility. Somewhere during the North African campaign, it had struck the silver cigarette case in his chest pocket and ricocheted into the forehead of the man standing next to him. The mortician had been amused at his request.

In truth, repetitive lectures in German on strength of character, ruthlessness and ethnic hygiene, whatever that was, were totally lost on a highly strung seven-year-old, but Enrico had learnt enough to listen without interruption until the man sighed and ceased to talk. An interruption would easily provoke a loss of temper and a flaying hand against his cheek. Violence was never far away. There was the time, he recalled, when he overheard the two maids talking. The one with the bruises around her eyes was sobbing loudly and cursing the old sonofabitch 'who couldn't keep that large cock in his trousers'.

As far as the young Enrico knew, his grandfather had emigrated from Austria with his son, Wilhelm. Details were sketchy and there was never a mention of his grandmother or any other kin. An innocent enquiry would always provoke the same answer; the past was in the past and everyone needed to look steadfastly to the future. Learning languages was the key to success and, alongside Portuguese, Enrico was encouraged to attain fluency in both English and Spanish. The family's native German was only to be spoken within the confines of the house.

Enrico was eight when his grandfather died. There had been a hunting party in Paraguay, a two-hour drive from Chapecó. They were after wild boar, chasing a beast through dense undergrowth when a misfired shot from one of the party had claimed the old man's life. They buried an empty coffin. When the bearers went back to reclaim the body, there was nothing left but traces of bone and blood-drenched hair. The wild boars had taken their revenge.

Everything changed.

Enrico's father, Wilhelm, was no chip off the block. A quiet, sensitive and reserved man, he became even more introvert and private following his Brazilian wife's death giving birth to Enrico. A trained agronomist, Wilhelm devoted himself to the farm, spending long hours, sometimes days, away from the house, avoiding both his son and father and preferring the company of the cattle and sheep with which he seemed to have a greater affinity.

'He takes after his bitch of a mother and his sister,' Heinrich had once said within earshot of his grandson. 'A pair of namby-pamby Jesus lovers with no grasp of reality and no comprehension of the depths to which these Jew bastards have reduced us.'

Following the old man's death, the house fell silent, few visitors and no parties or hunting trips. Enrico was almost relieved when halfway through the school curriculum, two men arrived to take him away. It was his grandfather's wish that at age eleven he would be transferred to a private semi-military academy in the United States. Funds had been made available in the old man's will. It was the only time he ever saw his father shed a tear, but he raised no objection as his son turned his back on him for what would turn out to be forever. Three years later there was another tragic accident. Wilhelm was clearing a trapped log from inside the wood chipper when somebody overrode the failsafe and switched on the power. For the second time there was no body in the coffin, but it didn't matter. Only a handful of farm workers attended the funeral.

Enrico was in his thirties and thoroughly indoctrinated in the life values instilled in him at the academy in Wyoming and beyond before he learnt the truth about his grandfather.

It happened by pure chance in a dentist's waiting room in Manhattan. The copy of the New Yorker was three months old and dog-eared, but it was the cover which attracted Enrico's attention. The photo showed a grainy image of the capture of Nazi war criminal Adolf Eichmann in Buenos Aires four decades earlier, and a link which led to a montage inside the magazine of illegal but successful snatch and grab operations conducted by the Israelis against Nazi war criminals over the last half century. There, in the second group of photographs, was an unrecognisable body lying bloody and disfigured in the undergrowth. The one discernible feature was a gold chain with bullet attached around the victim's neck. The text was brutal. Heinrich Klaas was known as *Der Weisser Henker*, The White Executioner, a name attributed to the SS official responsible for road building along the Eastern Front and into the wasteland of south-eastern Russia. The slave labour chosen was doomed to either perish in the freezing conditions or suffer summary execution if unable to keep up with the punishing schedule. Alongside the stretches of tarmac were the bloodstains in the snow of over five hundred forced labour victims personally executed by Klaas.

A team of six Israeli freelancers had trailed the hunting party into Paraguay, but had been spotted by Klaas, who had died in a firefight before they could get close enough to capture him.

Learning the circumstances of his grandfather's death came as a shock to Enrico, but, by then, it didn't matter. His commitment to the white Aryan supremacy movement operated by the so-called Circle had surpassed the aspirations of his handlers to an extent that his name was amongst the first on the list for the most sensitive assignments. Those were the days.

How things had changed in a single decade. Nobody had said it outright, but after the last two operations where others had been required to clear up his mess, this would be his last chance

The wheels of the plane touched down and the woman alongside him let out an audible sigh of relief. Tourism or business? she asked, her voice now totally relaxed and in control. He was an investment banker, he explained.

With an EU passport and no hold baggage he had cleared customs way before any of his fellow travellers. The key to the left-luggage locker was in the main concourse washroom, taped to the inside of a melamine partition which hid the soap dispensers and hand dryers from view. He retrieved the small black canvas bag without checking the contents and hailed a taxi.

The inconsequential red brick building was tucked away one block from the eastern side of the magnificent Paseo de la Castellana, one of the longest and widest avenues bisecting the centre of Madrid, its twelve traffic lanes separated by reservations of verdant trees and greenery, designed to enhance the aesthetics of its eco credentials and downplay the levels of carbon emissions from the constant stream of traffic. Unlike the frontline buildings with their retail façades and prestige office complexes, the six-storey construction which interested Enrico was residential, built around the seventies, he guessed, offering trendy one and two-bedroomed apartments to the ambitious young middle-class career professionals who dreamed of a pad in the city centre. With the passage of time and surrounding development, the building had long since lost its charisma as the place to live, and a number of the apartments had been converted for private office use, probably in breach of planning regulations but a risk worth taking by some to avoid the heavy taxes applied to registered commercial properties. He glanced at the business card-sized brass plaque alongside the individual apartment call buttons outside the entrance to the building. TELA – *Asociacion Tela*, TELA – The Web Partnership, was on the third floor.

Enrico turned away from the building towards the *pastelaria* in the adjoining side road. He sipped at a coffee and chewed slowly on the *montadito* with mozzarella and vine tomato as he studied the photograph he had taken from the holdall. This so-called debrief was likely to be difficult.

The man would be both nervous and suspicious which, when aligned to his background in special forces, would make him a difficult character to deal with. Judging by the image, the man was taller, younger and fitter than Enrico, with an arrogant expression that said I'm someone to be respected. He had to be handled with care.

The bio was brief. Aziz Peetre, aka Gunter Preiss, 37, currently resident in Salzburg, was the son of an Estonian father and Eritrean mother. His parents had met when his father, a career soldier, had been stationed in Asmara during a term as a peacekeeper with the UN forces. Aziz had followed his father into the army, training with an EOD regiment in bomb disposal techniques. Two years ago, he had been deployed with UNFICYP in Cyprus when he had been arrested and tried for the rape of an underage girl in a northern town just beyond the UN buffer zone between the Turkish and Greek Cypriot states. A dishonourable discharge and Aziz was back in Tallinn, disenchanted, angry and frustrated with the establishment that his pleas of innocence had been ignored. His passion for motorcycles led him to join the local branch of the SJ Missionaries, a group of bike fanatics with extreme white supremacy credentials; just one of a thousand unofficial organisations throughout the globe with propaganda and financial links to TELA. Aziz was ripe fruit, just waiting to be plucked. His knowledge was invaluable to the group. People who knew how to disarm bombs must know how to make them. Indoctrination was easy. Aziz yearned to strike back, but he had a short temper, and affrays in Austria and Germany had resulted in a criminal record.

Enrico flipped over the page, expecting to find information on his girlfriend. There was nothing. Aziz's marital status was recorded as unattached, casual relationships only. Enrico would need to know about her.

He paid his bill and purchased the item he required before making for the toilets and a locked cubicle. What he had to do required precision. He lowered the toilet seat cover and placed the tube of sweets, the syringe and the ampoule of Rohypnol on separate sheets of toilet paper. Fuck the advancing years! He would need to use his reading glasses and kneel on the piss-sodden floor in his new chinos to see exactly what he was doing. Five minutes later he had finished, brushing the dirt from his knees and admiring

250

what appeared to be an unopened pack of mint chews with soft centres which he placed in his jacket pocket.

Enrico walked back to the entrance to the red brick building. Beyond the front door was a second security door leading to the entrance corridor and a notice in Spanish and English recording that the inner door could only be opened when the entrance door was locked shut behind the person entering. It was the system used by most security-conscious banks. Along the corridor, he could make out three rows of metal-fronted post boxes, each with an apartment name or number reference. He saw one to suit his purpose.

The buzzer was answered following the second persistent attempt. Enrico put on his best docile smiling face and held his TELA identity card up to the camera. 'I'm your onward liaison officer,' he said in English.

For a full minute there was no reaction. Aziz would be arranging the room to suit his strategy in case of a hostile reaction. A weapon would be secreted somewhere close to where he chose to sit. Enrico was patient. It wasn't the first time someone on the run had reacted to his presence with caution. The remote control in the apartment activated the door lock and he made his way into the corridor.

The postbox serving a second-floor unit was partially open, the mouth and interior jammed full of publicity and circulars going back months. He scooped the contents into a waste basket, then forced his holdall into the space. It was a tight fit, initially resisting his attempt to close the door, but a final push did the trick and the catch held. He would worry about opening it on the way out.

There were two deadlocks on the apartment door, plus a security chain. He could tell Aziz was standing to the side of the door against the wall as he released the bolts, obviously wary someone might simply shoot at him through the wooden door as he looked through the spyhole. The chain shuddered as it was thrust to its maximum aperture. Two fingers with long, dirty nails poked through the gap. 'Identification and passport.' The voice was strained and laced with fatigue.

'Is all this really necessary?' Enrico held out the documents requested. 'I'm here to organise a safe onward destination for you, for both of you.'

There was no reply. The man had angled his stance to enable him to look through the gap in the door. 'Hand me your piece, stand where I can see all of you and put your hands behind your head.'

'What is this? Do you want my help or do I turn around and walk away?' Enrico sounded resigned, ready to give up.

'Just give me your piece, hands behind your head and we're cool.' There was a plea in his voice that acknowledged he wanted to trust this man.

Enrico slipped off his jacket and twirled around slowly. 'You've been watching too many American gangster B-movies,' he said, 'but if you'd like to hear my Al Pacino impression, I'm not packing any hardware, so give me a break.' He laughed at his performance. 'How was that? Do I get the part?'

The man named Aziz released the chain and stood aside to let Enrico pass. There was a good five inches in height between them, fifty pounds of muscle and an antique Makarova semi-automatic pistol pointed at Enrico's stomach.

Enrico replaced his jacket, returning the identification documents Aziz held out to an inside pocket, his gaze fixed pointedly on the weapon. 'Where did you get that? Top some *Militsiya*, did you?' He laughed again, removing two sauce-encrusted pizza boxes from a casual chair and edging them onto a coffee table already littered with dirty crockery. 'Can't you get her to do the washing up?' he asked pointedly. It wasn't intended as a sexist remark. He needed to gauge the man, the level of chauvinistic arrogance, the frailty of his vanity.

Aziz pulled a dining chair towards him, flipped it so that the back was facing Enrico and sat astride it, his arm hanging lazily over the back, the gun pointing at the floor. 'She's good for other things,' he said, nodding towards the bedroom.

'Is that where she is?'

There was a shake of the head. 'Out. Shopping.'

Enrico gestured towards the dirty crockery on the table. 'You needed more cups and plates?'

For the first time, the man smiled, revealing a set of immaculate white teeth with two gold caps in the place of his incisors. He shook his head. 'I know how it works,' he said. 'An assignment goes wrong and somebody has to pay.' He waved his gun hand at the floor. 'I don't want that someone to be me.' His English was heavily accented, but there was no avoiding the implied threat.

Enrico could only sympathise with the viewpoint. 'Relax. You got bad intel. You can't be blamed for that.'

'That's right. Nobody told me about a boyfriend. He caught me by surprise, but I handled it good.'

The movie on the television came to an end. A loud trumpet fanfare heralded the first of a series of advertisements.

Enrico slumped back in his chair. 'Mind if we turn that off? I can't think with that noise blaring away.'

Begrudgingly, Aziz flicked the remote at the set.

'Sorry. I noticed the disapproving look. Apologies if I'm interrupting your favourite programme.' He couldn't keep the sarcasm out of his voice, but the other man didn't seem to notice.

'That's all right.' It was a matter-of-fact statement.

'Tell me everything that happened, and then we can make plans to get you out of here,' Enrico said

Five minutes later, he had the whole story and Aziz was decidedly more relaxed in his company. The 'Call me Marcello,' and subtle male bonding techniques were beginning to pay off.

'Any chance of a coffee?'

The Estonian might be warming to the visitor, but he wasn't confident enough to turn his back on Enrico as he took two fresh cups from the cupboard and replaced the metal percolator on the gas ring. He continued their conversation as he brought the coffee over, handed it to Enrico and sat down on the couch alongside. 'To answer you, Petra knows nothing. I picked her up in a disco in Setubal a week ago. She thought she was watching out for me as I broke into this rich woman's apartment to steal jewellery. She did not suspect anything.'

'I don't buy that. You stayed around all night to wait for the woman to leave. If things had gone to plan, you had to be within five hundred metres of her car to detonate the explosive. The girl was bound to realise what was going on.'

253

He gave a broad grin. The gun was wedged in between the cushions on the couch, within easy reach. 'We pitched a tent. My many charms kept Petra occupied. I wouldn't miss the woman leaving the hotel. The moment the engine started, my mobile would come to life. I told Petra I hadn't found anything worth stealing and I wanted to tail the woman to Lisbon, find out where she was staying. As to the explosion, her head was couched in my back as we rode on the bike. She would have seen nothing.'

'Let's move on.' Enrico leaned forward, closer to the man, a conspiratorial gesture. 'If we assume the worst and the man who spoke to you has provided a description to the police, we need to give you both a new identity and get you out of the country. Let me take a photo for an ID card. Twenty-four hours and you're on your way.' He pulled out his mobile, switching to camera mode as he knelt down on the floor in front of Aziz. The shutter clicked. Enrico's head reared back, his cheeks puffed. 'Jesus, man!' he exhaled. 'Your breath really stinks.' He looked across at the pizza boxes. 'What was it, garlic on garlic?'

It had the desired effect. Aziz placed a cupped hand over his mouth. 'Is it that bad?'

'Hang on.' Enrico reached inside his bomber jacket and unzipped the pocket. 'Try one of these.' He deliberately displayed the unopened roll of sweets as he tore off the outer covering. He offered the pack to Aziz who took the first wrapped pastille. 'I think I'll have one too.' He took the second. 'Here. Take another one.' Aziz did not hesitate.

There was silence as they worked their way through the crunchy outer casing and then the liquid centre.

Aziz breathed out loudly. 'Is that better?'

Enrico recoiled slightly and indicated the other sweet in the man's hand. 'Better safe than sorry.'

It was close on fifteen minutes before the drug began to take effect. The man's eyelids began to flutter as he spoke, sentences faltering as he tried to deal with the barrage of questions he was trying to answer. Total distraction was necessary to hasten the impact. Even so, Enrico was impressed. Rohypnol normally acted with five minutes. Perhaps the rape drug worked better with the conduit of alcohol than in an artificial mint gum.

Enrico glanced towards the front door. He had left it ajar so that the girl would come straight in. Any confrontation needed to be private, away from a public corridor. Where the hell was she? How long did it take to organise a few groceries?

'You ... you ... bastard.' The words slurred and faded into silence. His hand was feeling for the gun.

Enrico jumped to his feet and fell onto the man, feeling for his wrist and pulling it away from the weapon. The man lurched forwards, eyes closed, his forehead making contact with the bridge of Enrico's nose. Blood began to trickle onto Enrico's chin. '*Filho da puta!*' he exclaimed, more in anger at being caught out than in pain. '*Filho da puta!*' His fist slammed into the man's lower neck at the level of the trachea. There was a gasping, retching sound as the man struggled for breath. Enrico's bomber jacket was speckled with his blood and Aziz's spittle.

With one hand pressing a cushion against his nostrils, Enrico felt inside the jacket, undid the zipped pocket and removed the syringe and ampoule. It was a mixture of high-grade cocaine and fentanyl. Half the quantity should be sufficient, but he wasn't taking any chances. He pulled back the plunger and drained the ampoule before clenching the desperate man's hand around the syringe and injecting the contents into his forearm. The body came to rest on the floor, the laboured breathing growing shallower, the eyes open, yet glazed and unseeing. Death was fast approaching.

Enrico sat to attention. There was a noise in the corridor. Tentative footsteps. Someone was nearing the apartment.

TWENTY-SEVEN – PETRA
MADRID, SPAIN
October 2018

The closer she got to the apartment building, the more nervous she became. The adrenalin of self-righteous justification was evaporating with every step she took. Ziz would do his pieces when he saw what she'd bought. She couldn't help it. Shopping was her drug. His was popping those little pills and the smokes that were supposed to put you in a good place, love and harmony and all that crap. Trouble was, it seemed to have the opposite effect on him. He got physical, violent, like he wanted to hurt someone – her, if the last couple of days had been anything to go by. Ever since the burglary had gone wrong, he had changed, no longer the fun-loving, sensitive he-man who had picked her up at the disco in Setubal. The sex had been great but was getting rough now, a carnal lust that had left her with bruises hidden by the tattoos on her back and arms. She had a plan. She would wait for him to go to sleep, help herself from that wad of notes in the bumbag around his waist and head off back to Portugal. She had hoped that this time ... so what? In the end, he was just another arsehole, like all the other men who inhabited the world she lived in.

Petra Mendes stopped to change the shopping bags from one hand to the other. The grocery bag was heavy with the tins of food and six-pack of beer he'd told her to buy. She peeked once again into the canvas sack from the boutique with the tailored denims, ripped around the knees and with the raised butterfly design on the back pocket. They would accentuate her tall, slim, athletic figure – a bargain at sixty euros, even if it meant there was little change left from the hundred note he had given her. He really would go crazy. If she could just get his cock into her mouth before he started ranting ...

She had learnt at an early age how to react to male dominance. It still left a bad taste and, even now, occasional flashes of naked anger. Her parents were to blame. When you pluck up the courage to tell them the man who is supposed to be nurturing your natural talent as a junior athlete is in fact abusing you, and they chide you for lying and making up such evil stories about a well-respected individual and force you to go on seeing him one-to-one and insist he remains your trainer, and they never once ask questions about what he does to you or where and when and refuse to listen to your ridiculous accusations – you quickly lose all self-respect and come to the conclusion it's you that must be wrong, not them. You are ashamed of yourself. You are worthless.

The weak succumb; the strong overcome. She wasn't either; somewhere in the middle; redeemable.

At sixteen, Petra ran away from the northern Portuguese city of her birth, but not before leaving her teeth marks indelibly imprinted on his body, like a tattoo, a point in time best forgotten that lives on forever. Her tall, lithe body and soft facial features with the sallow complexion and contemptuous demeanour had taken her into the world of modelling, mainly for clothing advertised in discount store leaflets; then, into soft porn films and downward onto the streets of Bragança where the randy Spaniards crossed the border to cheat on their wives before going home with the stench of cheap perfumes on their bodies.

The epiphanic moment occurred when she stooped to look at the driver of the car and saw a man's face that looked just like her abuser. It wasn't, but it triggered redemption, a metaphoric nicotine patch telling her there was a way to escape the vice of dependence on her woeful past. She had gone back to training, pounding the streets every day; taking casual jobs waiting tables or behind bars, enjoying selective liaisons with men who enjoyed her company as well as her body and had the means to indulge her passion, or rather, obsession, for buying clothes. Aziz had picked her up at a disco in Setubal. For a few days, she had thought he might turn out to be Mister Right, the man who would whisk her away to a new life in some northern land she had never heard of, but things had started to go wrong the night he went to burgle the woman's apartment. Now, she couldn't wait to get away. His mood had darkened and shades of violence had come to the surface. But first, she just needed to get her hands on his bumbag.

She punched in the code to the apartment on the keypad and made her way up to the third floor. The corridor was in darkness. She stopped to tuck the plastic bag with the boutique logo in with the groceries. Best not to spring the news on him right away.

Petra looked up. The apartment door was ajar. That wasn't like Aziz. He was a security and control freak. The door should be locked and bolted from the inside. He would take ages before opening the door with questions such as had anybody else entered the building with her? Had anybody tried to talk to her? Was she alone? He was a fucking freak!

'You there, Ziz?' She hovered in the corridor, a sixth sense telling her something was wrong. 'Ziz?'

There was no reply.

Somebody had risen from a seat. She couldn't say why the noise seemed odd, out of place. It just did. She was aware of the thumping in her chest, a dryness in her throat. The shopping almost dropped from her grasp. Of course, such a subtle noise was one she would never normally hear. The television was switched off. Aziz never turned the bloody thing off. Even when he was fucking, he insisted in having it switched on, irrespective of the programme. He couldn't stand silence, he would say. It disoriented him. There had to be background noise for him to function.

She was about to turn on her heels when the door was flung open. Whoever it was had a hand jamming a cushion over the lower part of his head. The gun in his other hand was pointing at her midriff. The first thing that came to hand was a tin of tuna. She threw it with all the force she could muster at the approaching figure. It bounced off the cushion onto his leg. A man's voice cursed.

The plastic bag had split open, spilling cans, bottles and packets of food onto the floor. She reached to get hold of the jeans, turned and ran towards the door leading to the emergency staircase. She was just turning the first corner when the retort of his silenced gun sounded, followed by a dull thud as the bullet made contact. She kept moving, the adrenalin in her system driving her forward. Taking the stairs three at a time was no problem for her. There was only the sound of the pounding of her heartbeat as she hit the release bar on the door and careered out into an alleyway between the side of the building and a car park.

Her first instinct was to keep moving while she had the strength. Having felt the impact of the bullet, she reasoned that somewhere she had been wounded and there was bound to be a loss of blood. A cursory examination as she moved hastily between the pedestrians revealed no obvious problem, but with her luck there was bound to be some insidious impact somewhere on her body.

Reaching the Plaza Castilla, she turned left towards the metro and, hopefully, anonymity. The train heading south was jam-packed with football fans heading to the Santiago Bernabeu, the stadium home of the famous Real Madrid. She vaguely recalled the poster in a supermarket window announcing the presentation to the fans that lunchtime of a soccer star with an unpronounceable name who had just been transferred to the club for a multimillion euro fee. She joined the excited throng of people exiting the metro and making for the stadium entrance, leaving them just before the turnstiles and veering hurriedly towards the flashing neon sign above a branch of a major coffee house chain on the far side of the Avenida de Concha Espina.

It took five minutes in a locked toilet cubicle before the shaking stopped and she felt her heart rhythm return to something like normal. Afraid to look, she allowed a tentative hand to trace the contours around her lower back and buttocks, expecting at any second to acknowledge the sticky feel of blood. She lowered her hands around the calves of her legs, feeling nothing but dry skin and taut muscles.

Exhaling with relief, she picked up the new pair of jeans that had been clasped in her hand as she ran. The bullet had seared a path across the butterfly design on the seat pocket and become embedded in the leather belt wound into a spiral next to the fly. Had it struck home, it would have caught her waist high. She shook her head in disbelief. Somebody up there really did love her. And hell! The jeans already had a tear in the knee. Why not a bullet trace elsewhere? She would wear them with pride.

As the adrenalin drained from her system, Petra sat with a half cup of cold latte on the table, her face expressionless. She had made several attempts to pick up the cup since the initial swig leaving the foam moustache around her lips that had now dried into a beige outline, but her hand had started trembling again. She was afraid of spilling the contents and drawing attention to herself. Whoever it was had seen her. Probably, a member of some underworld gang who wanted Ziz out of the picture for something he'd done. They would come after her. She had to get away, and that meant money. Six euros was all she had, hardly enough to get out of Madrid and back to Portugal.

If she could make it to Lisbon … Ziz had been quite adamant; something big was going down at the place he had showed her that looked like an old church. People would be walking away with valuables worth millions, he had insisted. It would be a piece of cake. Follow the people who came out, find out where they went and, when the time was right, gain access to their property and steal whatever was worth taking. Most of the people involved would be old and unable to defend themselves even if they did confront the intruders, and as most of the stuff they would take had probably be stolen in the first place, there was unlikely to be much police involvement. She closed her eyes and saw Ziz smiling. He was probably dead, she reckoned. Pity. As far as men go, she'd known a lot worse and he had made her laugh. He also said he knew a few people in Porto who would give their right arm for some of the stuff coming out of that church. One way or the other, she would find them.

Her final move towards the coffee was successful. She drained the cup, wiped clean her lips and made for the door.

* * *

Enrico nursed the bruise on his calf. His nose had finally stopped bleeding and the torn cushion lay stained and tattered, the stuffing exposed where he had shot through it as the girl made her getaway. The sound had been sufficiently muffled not to attract attention from the neighbouring apartment. The residents were probably out at work.

It hadn't been the tin which hit him on the leg that was the problem. No, it was the shopping spreadeagled on the floor in front of him. He hadn't looked as he moved forwards after her. His ankle had twisted as he stood on a can of beer, and the sharp pain had reduced him to kneeling on the floor until the sensation had turned into a dull ache. By that time, it didn't matter. The girl was long gone.

He had screwed up again. He would sort it out. Shit! How? There would be no forgiveness, no explanations, no next time. He had seen how they sorted out apples starting to go rotten. He had even participated in two so-called 'internal reassignments'. They weren't preceded by a nice, friendly chat. He needed a drink. There was a half-bottle of vodka in the apartment.

The bottle was almost empty. He told himself not to be such a pessimist. Look for the positives. It wouldn't be a problem. They could trace almost anybody. What he needed was a name and, if possible, a visual image. All he knew from the deceased, whose body lay draped across a couch and who was now smelling decidedly worse than the supposed halitosis now his bowels had relaxed, was that her name was Petra and he had met her fifty-odd kilometres south of Lisbon in a disco.

His luck was in. Inside the torn shopping bag was a smaller plastic bag with a boutique logo and a till receipt recording a purchase that morning. There was bound to be a closed-circuit camera, either within the store, focusing on the cash register or in the street outside. An official manner and a flashed identity card should get him everything he needed.

There were just two small matters to resolve. A sanitation unit was on its way from the orphanage in Toledo. They were expecting two bodies. If they were anything like the other teams based around the world, they would be very efficient and report the discrepancy. He would need to supply an explanation that would not hasten retribution.

By tonight, the apartment would be as new, ready for the next occupant. Tomorrow, or whenever, underneath some railway arch in the suburbs where the homeless souls are known to hang out would be the remains of another victim, one more pointless death, a man who had overdosed his way into oblivion. Cursory checks would be made to identify him, a superficial post-mortem and a burial in some distant graveyard with a nameless cross sticking out amongst the weeds.

From the underground car park serving the building, they would recover the Suzuki GSX 750 and transport it to the breaker's yard in Osasuna. Subscribers to eBay would soon be able to buy pristine parts with little signs of usage, at very accessible prices.

TWENTY-EIGHT – ISABEL
ESTORIL, PORTUGAL
October 2018

She had left her visiting card propped up against the empty sparkling wine bottle on the sideboard. There was a perfect lipstick imprint of those full lips on the glass alongside, a stained cigarette butt deliberately stubbed out on the non-smoking sign on the bedside table.

Broadhurst hadn't heard her leave. Unusual. His military training and experience had imbued in him the ability to wake at any extraneous noise or disturbance. He was either losing his touch or she had demonstrated catlike stealth. Maybe she had plenty of practice.

An aversion to the rays of the early morning sun feeding in through the crack in the curtains and the gnawing pain at the base of his head told him the night had taken him well beyond his customary level of alcohol consumption. It had got off to a conventional start, not quite a friends' reunion, not quite a date; a couple of drinks at the bar while they brought each other up to date with truths, mistruths, exaggerations or downright lies about the evolution of their lives since they had last met. It was good-spirited, well intentioned, and left them feeling comfortable in each other's company as they settled into their seats for dinner and a casino variety show, easy on the eye and long enough to justify ordering that second bottle of Luis Pato Vinha Pan with its distinctive hint of violets and dried fruit.

Isabel had pried, subtly at first, into his real motive for coming to Lisbon and he had parried, countered and listened to her equally highly edited subterfuge. But, as the night wore on, the houselights came up and they tackled another small espresso and a complimentary local brandy, Isabel Solden began to let down her guard. That her less than discreet flirting had but one objective did not faze him. Only a handful of years short of her age, Broadhurst didn't really fit the profile of the younger man–older woman reputation she liked to cultivate with the media. If husband Axion could be seen around town with any one of a dozen promising starlets on his arm, Isabel would show up escorted by a clean-cut leading man half her age. If she was trying to use a one night stand with Broadhurst as today's attempt to make Axion sit up and take notice, her husband was unlikely to be impressed.

Dealing with this aspect would come later. What did impress Broadhurst was the level of malice she bore towards the royals and the Establishment in general. Her spectacular fall from favour, disgrace amongst her peers and subsequent dismissal had left her bitter and chastened. She craved revenge, the fanciful notion of a popular uprising, fuelled by a federalist revolutionary fervour intended to condemn all those who had wronged her. Broadhurst tried to stem the stream of invective and change the subject. On one occasion, she talked of her consultancy work and how she was held in such high esteem by her current clients and her work on precious metal research funded by another organisation with the acronym TELA, but in the end she always managed to veer the conversation back to her ignominy.

Tired of her rambling and barely listening to the monologue that brooked no interruption, Broadhurst suggested a visit to the casino gambling rooms. If he was honest, it was from this point on that he lost the plot. The whole night was about to turn into something totally surreal.

Isabel matched his twenty-euro stake money and suggested they try blackjack. In the space of twenty minutes, they were over a thousand euros up and hooked. A hundred-euro chip went on a bottle of champagne, but still the pile of chips grew. Isabel had abandoned her stool and leaned over his shoulder as he played, her hand nestling for support next to his crotch. She felt him react against her hand, and her lips and tongue played with his ear lobe. Everything that followed had been a logical progression.

He glanced over at the pile of notes alongside his wallet. At least she hadn't forgotten the eight hundred, her share of the final total. He didn't remember quitting the table, nor cashing in the chips, but some other, equally enjoyable, experiences did come flooding back. The woman had a lot of issues she needed to get out of her system.

The hotel brochure described his suite as 'the complete business executive experience' and it certainly was that. The anteroom had a small kitchenette with limited cooking facilities, but most importantly, a capsule coffee machine and a supply of pods with a selection of coffee varieties, all graded by strength. He chose 'Intense – 5', two capsules and a double espresso in a large cup, more as a precaution against the possible effects of last night's alcohol than medication to cure an existing condition. In fact, considering the amount he had consumed and the departure from the very sober norm of his conventional daily life, he began to feel remarkably well disposed. He skirted the inbuilt office desk and the modest inkjet printer firmly encased in the open drawer which he closed with his knee as he made his way back to the bedroom.

Isabel's card had a note scrawled under her telephone number. 'Lead us back into temptation, for thine is the power.' Very biblical, he thought, if she could only avoid divine retribution in the shape of Axion's sword of Damocles. It had become apparent that, in her husband's eyes, what was right for him was definitely not right for her, and the early hours exit from Broadhurst's bed suggested she needed to play the role of the anxious wife waiting for husband to return rather than the femme fatale image lavished on her gambling partner.

It was gone ten before he was showered, dressed and about to enter the restaurant for breakfast. Had he looked over at the corner table before announcing his arrival to the 'meet and greet' assistant on door control, he would have seen the couple and turned on his heels. Two rounds of toast and a milky coffee at a local café would have been a much better outcome than an uncomfortable reunion with last night's nemesis. In spite of a lengthy shower, he could not dispel the sensation of her scent lingering on his skin. Guilt? No. It had been a totally consensual need they had satisfied. It was more a case of not wanting to be found out, confronted with an uncomfortable truth he would have happily avoided if good sense had prevailed. But it hadn't.

Isabel whispered something to her husband and Axion waved him over, standing and extending his hand. He was smaller than Broadhurst, in his mid-sixties, with a well-maintained figure, sinewy rather than muscular, and wearing a suit with the jacket draped around his shoulders. His face was tanned with tight features, hair an attractive grey crew cut glistening with gel. His crooked smile was both practised and disarming, his eyes vibrant and bordered with crow's feet.

'It's you, sir, I understand I have to blame for keeping my wife up until all hours as you gambled into the night.' There was humour in his voice, no trace of suspicion or condemnation.

Broadhurst returned the firm handshake. 'It's difficult to quit when you're winning. Isabel brought me luck, so I couldn't let her desert me, despite her protestations.' He took the seat he was offered and smiled warmly at Isabel who wore a bemused, rather maternal expression.

'I doubt she protested too much, if at all, knowing my wife. If you have the skill to turn twenty euros into close to a thousand in the space of a few hours, then you have my permission to borrow her whenever you feel lucky.'

Was that a double entendre? Broadhurst reserved judgement. 'I think we'll rest on our laurels for the time being, don't you?'

Isabel shook her head. 'I'm game whenever you are.'

Broadhurst excused himself to make his selection from the breakfast buffet, more than anything else as an excuse to escape the seemingly pointed exchange of innuendoes parried between the couple.

Fortunately, the conversation moved on to safer topics, mutual acquaintances and experiences, life in London, politics and current affairs.

'Business or pleasure?' Axion contemplated Broadhurst's question. 'A little of both, really. While Isabel deals with her bank full of hidden treasures, I'm taking the opportunity to recruit some Portuguese song and dance talent onto my books before the Brexit door shuts and EU immigrants are no longer a favoured species. There are some very promising young artists about and taking them back to the UK with zero-hour work contracts will hopefully secure their status whilst we find opportunities for them.'

'On slave-rate salaries, he omitted to say,' Isabel added.

He shrugged. 'Most new talent will grab at the first meaningful opportunity with no heed to the reward. They soon wise up. They talk to their colleagues, come down to earth when the stardust has worn off and paying the bills is what matters. By the time you're talking about their second role, they're negotiating and talking about union affiliation as if it were their birthright.' He sounded flat, as if explaining the process was sufficient to induce fatigue. He turned to look Broadhurst in the eye, 'Look, Isabel tells me you're likely to be around for a few more days?'

266

'At least until the weekend, possibly longer.'

His hand squeezed Isabel's. 'I have to go back to London tomorrow. Stefan has asked Isabel to go up country on business over the weekend. I don't like the idea of deserting her without some local point of contact. You two are former business colleagues. Can you stay in touch while she's on the wander? I would just feel happier if I know there's somebody in the immediate vicinity with whom she can liaise. I know I'm being silly, but' – he looked into her eyes and smiled – 'she's very precious to me.'

Broadhurst was expecting a 'don't be silly' retort, a protest to insist she was a grown woman who could look after herself, but none came. Instead, she cast her eyes down into her lap, a chastened smile as if she were practising a virginal pose.

There's something decidedly odd going on here, Broadhurst thought. A piece of theatre for an audience of one. But he knew his lines. 'Of course.' He looked inquiringly at Isabel. 'I think I gave you my mobile contact? Here are my email and business details.'

Axion took the business card intended for his wife and studied it. 'The BroadMarch Consultancy. Sounds intriguing. What exactly do you consult?'

'It's a small private investigation partnership. Nothing grand. We accept very few commissions.'

'"We" being who?'

'I have a French partner – a former policeman and close friend.'

Axion caught sight of a man hovering by the entrance to the restaurant. 'Very interesting.' He rose from his chair. 'You must excuse me. Somebody is looking for me.' His attention was already totally focused on the man. 'I'll see you upstairs, darling.' He waved towards Broadhurst. 'Good to put a name to the face,' he said and walked quickly away.

'What was all that about?' Broadhurst asked. 'You don't strike me as someone who needs protecting from the big bad world.'

Isabel's loving gaze followed her husband as he walked away. 'He can be a real sweetie sometimes, can't he?'

Broadhurst left her sitting at the table. The last thing he was into was a competition for Isabel's affections. If he was grateful for one thing, it was that for both of them the events of last night had disappeared into the ether of a new day and different considerations.

A call to Duncan White was on his to-do list before he left for his appointment at the bank. He thought about it, but an eight-hour time difference would put it at close to three in the morning in Vancouver. What with that, jet lag and the demands of an immature prince and his wife, White would have enough to deal with and deserved a full day's grace before Broadhurst followed up on their last conversation.

Axion had mentioned the name of Stefan when talking of Isabel's trip 'up country'. The name had resonance with him since his review of Sophia Horwitz's background and his conversations with White. Sure, there could be many Stefans operating in influential corporate roles throughout Europe, but Broadhurst wasn't a great believer in coincidence, and a possible tie-up between the Horwitz name and a specialist in precious stones deserved some more research. He could afford a couple of hours before he left for his appointment at the bank, and he might as well get some benefit from the 'complete business executive experience'.

TWENTY-NINE – GENERAL FRANKLIN WILLIAMS (Deceased)
FOGGY BOTTOM, WASHINGTON DC, US
October 2018

'Before you go, Cristo …'

The man about to leave stopped in his tracks. Something was wrong. 'Cris' had become 'Cristo', his given name and a formality rarely used by the person addressing him, except when angry or intending to make a point. He kept facing the door. Two can play at that game. 'Yes, Mr Secretary, sir?'

'This file in my bundle?' The man had a Southern drawl, even more pronounced as he carefully emphasised each word. 'You know I do not like paperwork on topics we have not summarised beforehand, especially when your seemingly innocent FYI annotation lulls me into a misplaced sense of priority.'

'Really? How come?' Cris Hopper swung around and walked back to the oversize desk. As he straightened his tie, the shirt collar tightened against his neck and started to itch. Egyptian cotton, his wife had told him, the purest and softest money could buy, but it managed to irritate his black skin. There was a myth black people had skin like leather, but it was just the same as everybody else's and, in his case, reacted to various allergies. 'You intrigue me, Mr Secretary. I thought it was just bedtime reading.'

Secretary of State, Bo Chandler, leaned back in his chair and massaged the leg with the metal pin designed to support and strengthen his damaged femur. Both men came from way back. They had forged a lasting friendship as freshmen at the University of Alabama in the eighties. It had been little more than a decade earlier when Blacks had been permitted to enrol and their close-knit student group tended to congregate together, especially those who made it into the celebrated Crimson Tide Football Team. Bo had been the second-string quarterback, Cris, a star linebacker. Both youths were studying for degrees in political and social science, although the prospect of a professional football career seemed a clarion call for their future. A life-changing injury changed all that. Sacked whilst trying to complete a third down play, Bo was stretchered off to a waiting ambulance, two weeks in hospital following a three-hour operation and six months in physio.

His leg healed, but his head didn't. It was never in the right place, and when the coach sat him down and told him he would discover cowardice was a virtue in the world of politics but a killer on the football field, the words stung but, lucky for him, they stuck.

Bo's rise up the political ladder had been meteoric. Through municipal state legislatures and as an influential member of the House of Representatives, his work on appropriations to drive climate change, the crisis in South-East Asia and civil rights legislation had marked his card for political stardom. His last posting had been as deputy director of the CIA, where commentators predicted he would remain for some years. Yet, after just eighteen months in the post, he happened to be in the right place at election time. The surprise appointment of Bo as Secretary of State by newly elected President Brandon Williams was viewed in social media as little more than a sop to the black vote. The subsequent secondment of Cris as a counsellor to his old friend was initially dubbed a blatant case of outright cronyism. Time would be their judge.

Both appointments had since come to be seen as astute and timely. Bo's skilled brand of tough diplomacy coupled with Cris's experience as a human rights lawyer with the United Nations had underpinned the President's tenure. He was now looking for re-election as his first term of office came to an end, with Bo a possible candidate as his running mate as vice president to replace the retiring incumbent.

'Bedtime reading, is that what you call it?' Bo shook his head, causing the rolls of fat under his chin to tremor. 'It's been giving me indigestion all afternoon, something I can do without. Believe me, with three adult children living at home I can guarantee heartburn is never far away. I don't need problematic phone conversations with a foreign financier to disturb my intestines.' He flicked open the file cover to expose two sheets of paper clipped together.

'I don't follow,' Cris said. 'I sent it to you as something to be aware of, just in case. When I saw the name of the President's late father, General Franklin Williams, it flagged up. You've listened to Brandon's campaign speeches. Everything's a war: a war against terror, a war against poverty, discrimination, failing healthcare. You name it, we're fighting it, and the memory of the general is evoked at every turn.'

He waved the two sheets of paper in the air. 'Give me the background as to how this came about?'

Cris sat down without being offered a seat. 'We've already had a series of events planned to mark the seventy-fifth anniversary of significant turning points in the Second World War. Next year, there's a shitload more set to schedule and, I guarantee, at every one the President will compare his struggle to his late father's contribution to the war effort. The way he talks, you'd think the old man cleaned up the European theatre single-handed. The boss is becoming a hostage to fortune.'

Bo groaned. 'You're telling me what I know. Are you going to tell me something I don't know?'

Cris ignored the question. 'I put myself in the place of his opponent for the presidency. What would be the best way of undermining the incumbent?' He didn't wait for an answer. 'I'd have every able researcher looking for some shit to stick to the President's father. Cast doubts about the old man and you totally undermine Brandon's credibility.'

'Move on.'

'An MR report from the Pentagon came across my desk. Did you know – I certainly did not – there's apparently a whole section in Arlington paid to spend all day solving obscure crossword clues and plot Sudoku answers to compare with real-life situations using complicated algorithms?'

'What the fuck is that supposed to mean? You are the most annoying person I have ever met, you know that? Can we jettison the foreplay and hit the sweet spot on this? I've got plans for this evening and they don't include you.'

'Patience, my friend. Context is important, believe me. You gotta understand the play to make the pass, right?'

Bo checked his watch with an exaggerated gesture.

'All right. MR stands for Multiple Reference. These folk I'm talking about take a grid sequence in one part of the world and look for a similar pattern somewhere else on another grid. They match phrases and clues to pre-empt terrorist threats, uprisings and suchlike in the making.'

271

'And, in this case?'

'An operative in London, embedded in some financial institution, flagged a reference to a project entitled *Die Letzen Rechte*. That's German for 'The Last Rights', spelled as rights as opposed to wrongs, rather than rites in the religious context. This reference found some resonance with a comment in the late general's memoirs. Apparently, when summarising his wartime achievements for the glossary, he mentions helping to orchestrate the Last Rights. This was read by a copy-editor as an error by a failing geriatric and changed, but when the old man rechecked the final version, he adjusted the wording back to the original.'

'It sounds tenuous.'

'I went back to ask the nerd who originated the report to investigate further. Apparently, the London operative extracted the data from a confidential list of names and titles prepared in-house for comparison with a schedule of registered holders of safe-deposit boxes at a bank in Lisbon, Portugal.'

'How did they get hold of that? It's privileged information.'

'The schedule hasn't officially appeared yet. Clandestine negotiations with somebody at the bank are being finalised. The bank is closing the facility and the boxes, many of which have remained untouched for up to ninety years, have to be opened. It is highly unusual and needed all the wartime allies and EU members to agree before the Portuguese government could give the go-ahead. Someone inside the bank is hoping to make a profit on the side.'

Bo shook his head. 'I don't see how the general fits in.'

'Amongst the names on the London list, if I call it that, are a number of Nazi SS officers interrogated at the Nuremberg war trials. One of these officers referred to "Last Rights" in the context of a plan for a group of disillusioned Nazis and collaborators to flee occupied Germany as the war ended.'

Bo whistled and returned to massaging his leg, this time more energetically. 'Are you suggesting something in one of these safe deposits is going to pop out and bite our dear-departed five-star general, and by association his son, on the butt?'

'Our man's gonna look like the fucking prick of the century if his father isn't the pure white saviour as his picture is painted. I'd give the Pope more chance of getting caught with a hooker than Brandon getting re-elected should we discover skeletons buried in the general's casket.'

'Colourful language, Cris.' He gave himself a moment to think. 'It all kinda ties in with the call I had today. I should say two calls.'

Cris took the Diet Coke pushed across the desk and flipped the ring pull. Droplets splashed onto a memo pad at the edge of the desk. Bo shook his head and passed over a box of tissues.

'Around noon, I spoke with our senior senator from South Carolina, a rare contact from our ultra-right-wing colleague. He asked if I would be so good as to accept a call that afternoon from a contact in England, a party donor, who had a pertinent topic to discuss. He wouldn't say any more, I guess because calls are monitored and recorded, other than to suggest I have my cell phone with me.'

Cris managed to raise his eyebrows and furrow his brow at the same time.

'At five,' Bo continued, 'I did indeed take a call on the cell, from a Stefan Horwitz who is CEO of a UK-based operation, the Four Realms Foundation. It occurs to me now as most likely to be the institution in which this operative is embedded. This Horwitz and his musician wife – world-renowned as I'm led to believe – are both descendants of Polish Jews. He runs this investment business: substantial, with charitable aims and worldwide coverage. According to him, rumours have been circulating of evidence which could prove an embarrassment to the good name of the Brandon Williams family and, more pointedly, cast a smear on the reputation of the late-lamented general. It's of concern to this Horwitz character because until the mid-nineties, General Franklin Williams happened to be a non-executive director – as they call them in England – of the foundation.'

'Quite a coincidence. I've come across the breed,' Cris said. 'They turn up for lunch, say "yes", collect a fee and go home.'

'Is that it? Anyway, Horwitz is confident he can get his hands on whatever it is that might be incriminating and suppress it.'

'Why tell you? Why not just do it?'

273

'Why do you think?'

'He wants a favour from this end.'

'Precisely. It's all somewhat nebulous at the moment, but the quid pro quo is our help with a court case in Portugal he expects to be instituting sometime next year.'

'Is that it?'

'We would be asked to use our influence to bring the matter to a swift conclusion.'

'Blackmail comes in many forms,' Cris said ruefully. 'What do you propose?'

'I told Horwitz to get back to me as and when he had something concrete, at which point I'd put somebody trustworthy in touch with him. What do you suggest?'

Cris scrunched the empty cola can in half, edged his chair to the side of the desk and threw the can basketball-style into a waste bin. 'My advice is we get to grips with whatever is going on with this bank in Portugal. Get the embassy in Lisbon to put someone on the case, somebody who can act with discretion. Apparently, there are a lot of checks and balances being applied to the nature of the contents that can be retrieved from the bank and the place is crawling with a variety of groups with vested interests. The Israelis are bound to be heavily involved. It may well be our people are already plugged into the event.'

It was an hour later and Bo had read the memorandum three times before calling for transport back to the secure condo he lived in whilst away from the family home. He had already dismissed involving the embassy. Using diplomats to become embroiled in re-election issues had already nearly cost one presidency, and the prospect of walking into the nest of vipers of House indictments and Senate trials definitely did not appeal. Cris would have to be personally involved, but he also had another idea.

Back in his CIA days, he had a number of one-to-one meetings in Jerusalem with Erik something or other. Need to check his surname. Erik was a former member of the Knesset and had chaired an intelligence committee for some months. His penchant for good living was partly financed by a covert retainer from the CIA in exchange for regular briefings on Israeli security details. It would have been far-fetched to describe him as an agent or spy in the sense that most Israeli intelligence activities were coordinated with the knowledge and input of the US, but it helped to understand the thinking of various influential politicians behind the scenes and Erik was an astute observer.

Friedman – that was his surname. Erik Friedman.

In the end, Friedman's excesses with alcohol and escorts had cost him his political career, but by the time Bo had left the CIA, the man still had some influential posts in a number of NGOs and could well prove useful in this instance. The suggestion of a case of a decent Montrachet could well convince Friedman to seek out somebody in Lisbon who could fulfil a confidential brief.

Bo made a note to follow up his idea in the morning. Right now, he was looking forward to an armchair before an open fire, a plate of his favourite pasta and the warmth of Reagan, his black Labrador, lying atop his slippered feet.

THIRTY – ELLIOTT
CASCAIS, PORTUGAL
October 2018

She looked good, he conceded, even with no make-up, hair dishevelled and her body enveloped in a white, towelling dressing gown, three sizes too big, with a hemline soiled where it had dragged along the ground. Though he was outwardly a verbal advocate of all forms of sexual equality, Elliott recognised the hypocrisy of his brand of closet chauvinism. He could hardly excuse his basic response to the ins and outs of a voluptuous female form as an appreciation at some aesthetic level. In his experience, most women with bodies to excite knew exactly to what primal instincts they were appealing and Dana, along with all her many qualities, had plenty to offer in that direction, even if they were currently camouflaged in a shroud.

The truth was Dana had been the one and only woman he had admired, not as a possible sexual conquest, but as someone he could first relate to and laugh with and whose company he found stimulating away from the bedroom. Not that she had ever shown any serious interest in him as more than a friend, except, perhaps, just that once when she had let down her guard. Elliott was besotted by the prospect of a more serious and intimate relationship but knew himself well enough to understand why he did not force the issue. The prospect of her rejection stirred a kind of aggressive reaction inside him that he did not like and could not rationalise. Seemingly beyond his control, his hackles would rise whenever he watched her in social interplay with other men, however benign the outcome. He berated himself for his schoolboy immaturity, but the passion to possess her never subsided.

Whether she was aware of his intense feelings, he could not tell. Unlike her father, she certainly seemed oblivious to the level of attention he paid her whenever their paths crossed. Josef, however, had his measure. Elliott had been seconded three years earlier to compliment the operation evolved under Josef's auspices over five decades and to bring to a conclusion the dozen or so open files remaining of claims against Nazi war criminals still believed to be alive. Prior to Josef's scheduled retirement, he was the liaison between the so-called Krakowski Bureau in Ticino, Switzerland, and the Mossad headquarters in Tel Aviv.

Initially, he had spent a great deal of his time around Josef's home on Lake Lugano, where he had first met and developed his friendship with Dana, or Danata as Josef insisted on correcting him. Josef had soon picked up on the reason Elliott insisted on inviting himself to meetings whenever his daughter, a vital member of his investigation group, was to be present and encouraged her to attend social events where they might end up alone in each other's company. Josef, damn him, seemed to find it amusing.

'Got a thing for older women, have you, Elliott?' He sounded like a schoolmaster.

'Come off it, will you? We're only friends and, anyway, what's four years these days? There are twenty-year gaps between some couples.'

'And you fancy the idea of a couple, do you?'

'I'm not saying that, you prying old man. Anyway, what's it got to do with you? You want your daughter to be happy, don't you?'

And Josef would laugh, but behind the laugh Elliott detected a sadness. 'She's too good for you,' he would say, and then, 'Only joking.' But he wasn't, and both men knew it to be true.

She had reached the bottom of the stairs and was studying him. 'Is there something wrong?' she asked.

He shook his head, more to clear it than as an answer to the question. 'No, I was just thinking about something. You've slept well. It's nearly midday.'

'I did, thank God. I was shattered. Didn't realise just how much. I'd better get a move on. First clients are due at the bank in an hour or so. Drive me in, will you? We won't disturb father. He had a restless night, I know. You come back and set up the video link. He'll be up and around by this time and I'll speak to him from the observation room.'

She retreated back up the stairs, turning to smile at him as she reached the top. 'Are you all right?' she queried.

'Fine. Just remembered. I got a message to contact Erik at two p.m. local time in Israel. That will be one here. I'll give him a call after I drop you off. He needs me to do something.'

278

However important it might be, mentioning Erik was an excuse. He could hardly blurt out he wanted her so much it left an ache in the pit of his stomach. How could he deal with the suffering? At some stage, he would have to make his feelings known and reap the consequences. In a month, his secondment would be over. Right now, he was supposed to be in Ticino with Josef, closing up the office; not sitting in a safe house in Lisbon, intent on protecting the woman he loved. There, he'd said it. The end of the year. He'd give himself until the end of the year to convince her he was the one for her. And if she didn't play ball? Well, there was always the secret. He must be able to use that to his advantage.

It had been two years ago at the Dream Island Resort in Yoav, a weekend convention on covert detection techniques organised under the name of some private investigation group as a cover for Mossad and a group of its new intake. Elliott had been asked to handle one of the class lectures and had managed to convince Dana to assist him and provide some practical examples for the candidates to analyse. Reluctantly, she had agreed.

Suffering from a cold, no appetite and, in the bar after dinner, one too many rounds of brandy, necessary he assured her for medicinal purposes, she had ended up sprawled on a lounger on his terrace. As he massaged her feet, she wanted to talk. It was all about work, realities, and nothing about her feelings and emotions that he hoped would open a path for him to hint about the way he felt. As much as he probed and prompted, she would not be drawn. It seemed her only emotional response was concern for her father's health and well-being. He was obsessed with the prospect of finding his sister. He was convinced she was alive. She was concerned that his mental deterioration would prejudice his physical condition.

And then, she told him. He must promise never to tell another living soul, especially not Josef. He must never know. She knew Rita Krakowski was alive and had a good idea how she could be located, but Dana had been sworn to secrecy by the one person she would never betray.

PART FOUR

DISCOVERY

THIRTY-ONE
LISBON, PORTUGAL
October 2018

A discreet tap on the door diverted Broadhurst's attention from the screen he had been studying earnestly for the past two hours. Three o'clock. He was late. This must be from the concierge to tell him the taxi he had booked was waiting. He grabbed his coat and briefcase. Arriving late for the appointment might mean losing his slot at the bank and having to reschedule. That must not happen. He sprinted past the startled bellboy and headed for the lift.

It had been easy to become engrossed in the numerous browser entries for Stefan Horwitz and the Four Realms Foundation. The story had started in the late forties when a charitable organisation was incorporated in the American state of Delaware. The founders were hidden behind two firms of corporate nominees, ostensibly because the donors did not wish to be identified as benefactors to the tune of twenty million dollars, a fortune equivalent to ten times that sum today.

The objectives of the foundation were noble and, in many respects, before their time; ethical investments in corporations and entities designed to enhance social cohesion and eradicate all impediments to the health, growth and development of strong bonds between the progressive elements in society. The original administrative committee selected to oversee investment and disbursement strategy included an array of well-respected figures, church and business dignitaries, headed by a non-executive chairman who had been feted as a hero during the war, General Franklin Williams.

For taxation reasons, the Delaware Foundation remained a non-trading organisation, divesting investment and disbursement decisions to a network of private investment banking subsidiaries with a holding company in Buenos Aires, Argentina: TELA – *Asociacion Tela*, TELA – The Web Partnership. As far as Broadhurst could tell, TELA now had branches in more than a hundred countries.

Little of note was recorded in the intervening years until 1961, when a young assistant director in the London branch, Stefan Horwitz, was appointed as Chief Executive Officer of the group. According to the magazine *International Money Management,* as unexpected and surprising as the appointment was, his first act as CEO to move the head office from Buenos Aires to London was both timely and astute.

Stefan appears to have had the Midas touch. Despite opening branches around the world at breathtaking pace, the foundation's latest annual report had three pages listing a spectrum of community and business projects receiving grants and soft loans during the year, yet maintaining and controlling capital funds of investments approaching half a billion dollars.

Now, nearing eighty-seven, Stefan was still on the board as honorary president and his photograph on page three of the report displayed a man who could have been taken for someone fifteen years younger.

As to the possible link between TELA, Isabel and precious stones, Broadhurst had barely started to investigate when the knock came at the door. All he had seen so far was a pie chart showing fifteen per cent of the group's total investments were in gold and precious metals. Stefan's address to shareholders appeared biased towards a green investment strategy intended to encourage a reduced dependence on oil and the development of battery power.

* * *

The taxi slowed to a halt outside the church building. A sprinkling of individuals lined the pavement behind a police tape, to the front of which were two press photographers, an RTP outside broadcast van and a young lady talking earnestly into a microphone as she looked into the camera. Shutters clicked as Broadhurst waved his client pass at the policeman and made his way towards the entrance door which opened as he stepped forward.

There was no sign of Malato. A security guard verified his identity and reached into a box file to retrieve a key with N302 written on the fob.

'How did you come to have the key?' Broadhurst asked the guard as an elderly couple stepped forward to join them. The old man introduced himself as a partner in Sotheby's Zurich office and the woman as consultant to the president of the World Jewellery Confederation in Milan. Broadhurst

284

shook hands dutifully as the man explained that the key had been delivered into the bank's safekeeping thirty years earlier.

'Shall we proceed?' The woman said.

The process was remarkably efficient. The security guard opened one lock as Broadhurst opened the other. The box was empty save for a few documents which Broadhurst extracted, placed on a portable X-ray machine and which were then photographed. A copy of the print with an annotation on the back confirming there were four documents was handed to Broadhurst, who was then asked by the guard to confirm the box was empty and to sign a statement releasing the bank from any further liability.

'I can't see any problem,' the elderly man whispered to Broadhurst as he was led to a waiting room, 'but we have to go through the motions. You do understand?'

The motions were obviously a lot more complex than Broadhurst or the man could have imagined. An hour passed and still no one had come to speak with him. His patience was beginning to wear thin enough to provoke him into action when the door was thrust open and a portly, middle-aged woman bundled into the room. 'We need your consent to something to overcome a little difficulty that has arisen.' She pulled a paper tissue from the sleeve of a knitted two-piece to wipe the perspiration from her forehead. 'Bloody hot in here, don't you think?'

Broadhurst found himself studying the woman standing legs apart in front of him. Her face was dominated by a double chin obscuring her neck and a large keloid above her top lip protected by a cluster of stubble. Her grey-blonde hair was thin and receding, her complexion sallow and the clinging two-piece did nothing but enhance the rolls of fat around her stomach.

'You would be?' he asked.

'Jardim. *Doutora* Fernanda Jardim. I am a lawyer instructed to help in this matter.' Her English was enunciated precisely in an outdated upper-crust accent, as though she had digested the collected works of PG Wodehouse.

'May I ask what matter, precisely, and for whom you are acting?'

She ignored the question. 'It's trivial really. A party in the observation room would like your permission to examine the documents you

285

have retrieved and have them delivered to you in the morning. I take it you would have no objections?'

'Where are the documents now?'

'They are in the hands of bank security.'

'You avoided my question, so I have no idea whom you are acting for and I have no intention of allowing them into the possession of any third party. My instructions are to retrieve the documents and deliver them unseen direct to the heirs of the original box holder. My position is crystal clear. In the circumstances, I need to advise Senhor Malato accordingly. It was explained specifically to me that the concern of the authorities relates only to stolen valuables. Documents of the kind I inspected could not possibly be construed as falling into this category.'

She studied him over her glasses. 'It's the response I expected. I'll pass the message on,' she said and turned on her heels.

Ten minutes later, the original documents were in his briefcase and Broadhurst had made his way out of the building. The throng beyond the cordon had filled out. They were now two or three deep, straining to see whoever was entering or leaving the bank. Before him were a group of reporters and the woman from the television station, anxiously waving a microphone in his direction. He sidestepped the media contingent with a hurried 'no comment' and ducked under the tape a policeman had kindly held up for him. A hand from the crowd settled on the corner of the briefcase, tugging hard to pull it away from him. He swivelled around, using his free hand to push the arm away, at the same time bringing the briefcase upwards to rest pinned against his chest. He was staring directly into the face of a determined-looking young woman, lips pressed tight together, hazel eyes blazing intent. He shook his head, moved his shoulder towards her and nudged her back into the crowd as he stepped towards the cobbled sidewalk.

The Google Maps app was already set to the destination he required; a ten-minute walk was indicated. He did it in seven. The stationers had everything he needed.

There were three messages waiting for him at the hotel: one to ring René, the second from White saying he expected to have some further news in two or three days, and the third, a chaser from Sophia Horwitz. The text reply to René advised he would call back in an hour or so.

The call to Sophia Horwitz was brief and to the point. He described the documents in his possession. It was like talking into a void, the sense of anticipation on the other end of the line somehow eerily detectable in the total silence.

'I can scan them over to you, if you like.'

'No. No copies, as I stipulated. Just one thing. Are you certain that with the letter from the lawyers there is no contract document in Portuguese or English?'

'Absolutely certain.'

She let out a discernible sigh. 'Dear, dear,' she said. 'Never mind. I'll send a courier to collect what you have tomorrow. Expect a call.' She thanked him for his cooperation and told him to send the account for his services.

He was about to close out the call when she spoke. 'One thing: did anybody try to stop you getting the contents of the box?'

'Apparently so. A local lawyer by the name of Jardim asked me if I would leave the documents overnight for inspection, presumably by one or other of the observers. Obviously, I refused. I have to say the documents appear to be innocuous.'

'They most certainly will prove to be so. Regrettably, there are still people around who wish to paint my uncle Lew as a collaborator, even though he was acquitted. They cast around for anything to lay their hands on if they feel it would help their cause.'

The conversation left him feeling decidedly uneasy. Everybody was lying. Even he was. Nobody was showing their hand. What was it all about? He couldn't fathom the answer. Common sense and René would tell him not to get involved. He had done what was asked of him. All that remained was to hand over the contents of the box, go home and get paid. So, why couldn't he do just that?

He laid the four documents on the table. Using the courtesy coffee-making facility, he steamed open an envelope addressed to *Die Welt*, removed a series of sheets that looked as though they had been ripped from a writing pad. There was tightly spaced writing in German on both sides of

287

eight pages. He put them in between the pages of a Gideon's Bible to straighten them out and resealed the envelope using several blank sheets of paper in place of those he had removed. He repeated the process with a carefully folded one-page letter from the US with a postmark of 1946 and signed by somebody named Norman. The text was in a language he did not recognise, vaguely eastern European if he had to guess. For now, whatever it said could wait.

The two single sheets presented more of a problem and required some thought, although the process for both would follow a similar pattern. Taking the receipt from the investigative agency in Brussels, he folded the page to hide the name and contact details of the source at the top, leaving only the detail of the service provided, namely 'consultancy services', and the cost visible. On his tablet, he found the website of a South African private investigator, printed the page header logo and, after several attempts at modifying and reducing the size of the image, produced an A4 sheet with the name and address at the top. The final step was to line up the visible content on the original receipt under the new header and produce a copy. It wasn't perfect, but at first glance it would serve to send any unauthorised reader off on the wrong tack.

He repeated the process with a letter from a firm of Portuguese solicitors based in Coimbra, dated September 1939 and addressed to Borys Wiesel, simply recording the enclosure of a signed and notarised copy of the contract and indicating that they remained ready to provide their services in the future. He chose the logotype of a firm of lawyers in Seville and aligned the text of the original onto an A4 copy.

Some black smoke from a waste paper fire mixed with a butter pat in an ashtray was intended to discolour the copies, sufficient to satisfy a cursory glance and avoid immediate detection. Satisfied, he fed the two envelopes and loose pages into the manila envelope the bank had provided and locked them into the safe installed inside the wardrobe compartment. All the originals, flattened as best he could, were sandwiched in the middle of the inkjet printer's paper tray.

'I thought you had forgotten me,' René said as he acknowledged Broadhurst's greeting wave on the Skype video link.

'Apologies.' Broadhurst ran through the events of the day and what he described as his amateurish attempt to recreate a dummy set of documents. 'If my hunch is correct, the best I can achieve is to satisfy initial curiosity with a cursory examination and to put the bank on the spot so I can't be challenged.'

'I don't get you.'

'Let's see how it plays out over the next twenty-four hours and I'll explain in more detail.'

To his credit, René didn't push it. 'I've got the information you asked for. Danata Da Luca, real name Danata Krakowski, is the daughter of famed Nazi war criminal hunter, Josef Krakowski. She is also part of his organisation. They live on Lake Lugano in the Italian-speaking area of Switzerland. Krakowski is in his eighties and recently announced his retirement; reluctantly, I understand.'

'He wants to carry on? How many Second World War criminals are still alive?'

'His bugbear is he never found out what happened to his elder sister, Rita. She became the partner of an SS officer and was sought to answer charges as a collaborator. He is also on the wanted list. They were both last heard of in Valparaiso, Chile, in 1962 and subsequently disappeared off the face of the earth. There have been a number of alleged sightings of the man, Kirchner, in both South America and Europe, but nothing has materialised. Of her, there is no trace. The assumption is she passed away under an alias, but this theory does not appear to have satisfied brother Josef.'

'If we accept that Danata engineered our 'accidental'meeting, they must believe there is something in the papers I retrieved from Lew Wiesel's safe-deposit box to point them in the right direction.'

'And is there?'

'No idea. There's only one document in English. The other three are in German, French and a language I don't recognise; I'll guess Polish, considering the provenance.'

'Scan them over to me and I'll get any I can't personally deal with translated by a discreet agency we worked with when I was with the police.'

Broadhurst nodded. 'I will, but I suggest you redact any names in the documents just to be on the safe side. By the interest generated, there could be something quite telling.'

'Understood. Anything else I can do?'

'This is a long shot given we're thirty years on, but you'll see a receipt from the Grand-Place Détective Privé France et International in Brussels for a consultancy assignment carried out on behalf of Lew Wiesel. If it still exists, can you see if there is a copy of the report they provided on file?'

'That really is asking for something. Nobody was making digital copies in the eighties, and the possibility of locating a paper copy, even if the firm still exists, well ...'

'I know. Give it a shot, anyway.'

It was just after five when the call ended, time enough for Broadhurst to realise he had missed lunch and eaten nothing since the uncomfortable breakfast experience with Isabel and Axion. He had noticed an attractive fish restaurant on the coastal road facing the estuary. A fifteen-minute stroll was just what he needed, both to clear his head and to work up an appetite for a decent-sized sea bass.

THIRTY-TWO
ESTORIL, PORTUGAL
October 2018

Petra watched from a high-backed chair in the hotel's meeting area as the senior receptionist put the new trainee through her paces. Verbal instructions were followed by a series of deft movements on a touchscreen and a look of relief on the face of the trainee. A few minutes later, following a stand-alongside session when the young girl dealt with a client's enquiry as the senior receptionist hovered, ready to pounce, the opportunity arrived. Five minutes, Petra heard the woman say. She would be back in five minutes.

It was the time of day when reception was quiet, an hour before the post-working day check-ins began and at a point when existing guests were out sightseeing or back in their rooms. Petra waited until an anxious-looking Japanese tourist exited the elevator and began to make his way to reception. Petra arrived at the counter just before him. The girl looked nervously from one to the other.

Petra spoke up. 'Can you tell my stepfather, Mr Broadhurst, that his daughter is in reception?' The girl was barely concentrating, distracted by the Japanese man leaning across the counter to check if anybody else was available.

'I'll be with you in a minute,' the girl said to him. The man stared blankly at her. 'Sorry, what name was it?' she said, turning back to Petra.

'Broadhurst,' Petra said testily. 'Can you please tell him I am here?'

'No reply,' the girl said after holding on for thirty seconds. 'He is not in his room.'

The man was now unfolding a street map and spreading it across the counter.

Petra tut-tutted. 'He must be around. He's expecting me. Tell you what' – she slung the knapsack from her shoulders – 'Get someone to take this to his room, will you? I'll try and find him.'

'Sintra,' the man was saying, studying the street index. 'No see Sintra.'

'It's not in the city centre,' the girl said. 'And it's not a street. It's a town. Just wait a minute and I'll show you.'

'My bag!' Petra emphasised.

'Sorry.' The girl pressed a key on the telephone. 'Can you send someone to take a bag to 418?' she said, obviously harassed but trying to appear in control.

'Thank you.' Petra smiled. She made as if to walk out, but doubled back around the terrace and back inside alongside the elevator serving clients using the swimming pool and spa.

Ten minutes passed before the bellboy arrived with the knapsack. She watched from her hiding place along the corridor and quickly followed him into the room. 'Gosh,' she said, sounding surprised. 'You got here before I did. How did you do that?' The boy smiled, obviously impressed. 'I've only got a euro in change. Hope you don't mind.' Her hand lingered on his as she pressed the coin into his palm.

She was in. She had watched Broadhurst walk out the hotel and turn down towards the seafront. If he had gone to dinner, she had an hour; if for a stroll, say twenty minutes. There had to be something of value he'd recovered from the safe-deposit box. Her search was meticulous. The briefcase was open and empty, save for some unused stationery and a glue stick. Whatever of value he had was in the safe. A four-number combination. There had to be a master code. She tried a dozen numbers before resorting to a dinner knife that snapped into two as she tried to prise the door open.

Damn! It should have occurred to her. His credit card holder was on the bed. If he'd gone to dinner, he must realise and turn back. Unless he paid in cash – who paid in cash these days?

The door to the room slammed shut. She wheeled around. 'What the fuck!' she said in English.

'So glad to discover I have a stepdaughter. If I had a wife, she would be thrilled as well. You understand what I'm saying?' Broadhurst stood in front of the door, barring her way.

She nodded and thought about attempting to push past, but gave up the idea. He was getting on in years and she was very fit and agile, but there was something about the way he carried himself which suggested some disarming skills and, anyway, he didn't seem particularly angry or upset.

'Why don't we sit down and have a talk? If you can help me, I will see what I can do for you.'

'I'm not like that,' Petra said. 'I'm not some bloody whore if that's what you're thinking.'

'Don't sound so self-righteous. Are you suggesting what you came into my room to do is more morally acceptable than being a bloody whore?'

'Do I look like one to you?'

'I've no idea. I'm not overly versed in the appearance of ladies of the night.'

'What?'

'Forget it. Sit down. Do you want a drink?'

She looked taken aback but sat perched on the edge of a chair, studying his face, waiting for him to make a move. It never came.

'I asked if you wanted a drink?'

'I like limoncello.'

'Is that a drink or a piece of music?'

She managed a sarcastic laugh. 'You're out of touch with the cocktail scene. Limoncello's an Italian spirit. You should try a Tuscan Pear. It's a stunning drink.'

'See if there's one in the minibar over there. If not, pick something else. And hand me a scotch.'

They sat facing each other in the lounge area, his, a scotch on the rocks, hers, a coke.

'Two easy questions to start with: who sent you and what are you after? One thing you should remember; I've spent years listening to people tell me lies. If you do, I'll know. Every lie, I'll knock ten euros off what I intend to give you when you leave this room.'

'Eh?'

'Let's play a game. We'll pretend you're a whore and, instead of sex, I want information; the works – no holding back, no made-up stories. When you're done, I'll pay you the escort's going rate. How's that?'

'Are you on something?' She looked at him askance.

'That's the deal. Take it or leave it. Of course, if you leave it, I'll feel obliged to summon the manager and have you arrested for attempted theft.'

'You are going to be disappointed. What do you think? Mr Big sent me and told me to steal the crown jewels?'

'I'm used to being disappointed. Try me.'

'I heard something about people going to the bank and coming away with all sorts of valuables. My idea was to select a mark, chat up one of the security guards for a name, wait until they came out, then follow him or her, and break into their place to recover whatever was worth taking.'

'Recover? Don't you mean steal?'

'My understanding is that most people won't know what is in the boxes. The stuff has been there forever. Whatever they find, they didn't have it yesterday; they didn't expect to have it today; so, they won't miss it if they don't have it tomorrow.'

'And that's your justification, is it? You cannot miss what you have never had?'

'It means I won't lose any sleep.'

'Who told you about what was going on at the bank?'

'Ziz.'

'Sorry?'

'Ziz, my boyfriend.' She looked down at the floor. 'Probably my ex-boyfriend. He was involved with some serious people and I think he might have screwed up and paid for it.'

'What serious people?'

'No idea, but bad enough for me to get shot at by one of their heavies.'

Broadhurst looked her up and down. The story seemed convincing enough to be the truth. 'Your English is too fluent to have come off the blackboard. You're not Portuguese, are you?'

She shook her head. 'Mum's from the Czech Republic. My dad is English, working as an engineer in Prague when they met and started living together. I came along early on. Mum and I took a holiday in Portugal when I was twelve. Dad was busy. They weren't getting on by this time. Mum's sweet, but she could never keep her legs closed. There's this Portuguese waiter, André. She falls head over heels for him, ditches Dad and we move to Portugal. They actually get married and change my name to his. Instead of Petra White, I'm Petra Mendes. Working in Portugal is a no-no. Wages are shit. When I was eighteen, I moved to the UK and came back when Mum took poorly. That's my story. Satisfied?'

Broadhurst stood up and stretched. 'I don't know about you, but I'm starving. There's a fish restaurant I like the look of. Fancy it?'

'You're not coming on to me, are you?' She pushed her head down into her neck as if recoiling at the idea.

'I ask you,' he said. 'Who comes on to their stepdaughter?' He held the door open for her.

The call came as they were halfway through a fish and shrimp *cataplana*. Broadhurst's raised eyebrows and sardonic smile as he recognised the caller's name on the screen confirmed it was an initiative he had expected.

Malato sounded nervous as he stumbled over a hurried apology. The bank's lawyers had noticed some inconsistencies in the documentation submitted to support both Sophia Horwitz's right to the contents of the safe-deposit box and Broadhurst's authority as her agent. In the circumstances, he urgently needed to recover the contents of the box and hold them in escrow until the matter could be regularised. They were waiting in the reception of the hotel for his return to fully explain the matter.

Broadhurst put his hand over the mobile's microphone. 'Fancy a dessert?' he asked, motioning to the phone and giving her a broad smile. 'You choose, and order a brandy with my coffee to follow.' He released his hand. 'I'm just starting dinner, Senhor Malato. I could be some time.' He winked at Petra. 'Perhaps you can give me some idea what the problem is?' He placed the mobile on the table, turned the speaker function on and the sound down to avoid disturbing the neighbouring diners. He reached for the bottle of the Douro reserve red wine and topped up their glasses. 'This could take some time,' he whispered.

'You want me to run through everything?' Malato asked.

'If you wouldn't mind,' Broadhurst said, bending to speak into the microphone. 'I shall need to explain it to my client.'

'There are a number of documents submitted on behalf of your client that are in English or Polish with Portuguese translation. In the first place, we have an affidavit sworn by Sophia Horwitz attesting her right as heir, being the only living descendant of Lew Dawid Wiesel. In support of this affidavit, there is a copy of Sophia Horwitz's birth certificate, a declaration from the Polish authorities to confirm Sophia's mother was the legitimate, whole sister of Lew Wiesel, and a copy of Lew Wiesel's birth certificate. Is that clear? Mr Broadhurst, did you hear me?'

Broadhurst hurriedly swallowed a mouthful of crème caramel and bent towards the phone. 'Absolutely. Do carry on.'

'All the signatures on those documents were recognised by either a British or Polish notary, and everything was translated into Portuguese and certified by an official translator.'

Broadhurst replaced his hand over the microphone. 'That cheesecake you chose looks excellent. May I try a spoonful?'

Petra pushed the plate towards him. 'You're paying. Help yourself.'

'Sorry?' Malato said. 'I didn't hear what you said.'

'I said please make the documents available for inspection.'

'That's not all,' Malato continued. 'Further, there is a declaration from the public records office in Warsaw, listing the remaining family of Lew Wiesel as his wife, Magda, two children, Malik and Yetta, plus two unmarried brothers and a mother. Again, this has been notarised. Finally, there is a statement from the Holocaust Commission in Virginia certifying extracts from the various concentration camp records that all those listed appear in camp assembly details, and, in the light of no other substantive evidence, this constitutes proof of death. Accompanying all this is a power of attorney from Sophia Horwitz in your favour with limited rights and obligations.'

Broadhurst pushed away the empty dessert plate and wiped his mouth. 'Seems pretty belt and braces to me, Senhor Malato. Can't imagine what else you would want.' A nod of the head to the waiter acknowledged the espresso and balloon brandy glass placed in front of him.

Malato hesitated before he spoke. 'The problem is that before these documents can be recognised in Portugal, they require an apostille. Most can be done in Gibraltar, the American document in The Hague. It can be done quickly; a day or two is all Doutora Jardim requires.'

Broadhurst ran the brandy around inside the glass. 'Really? Doutora Jardim doesn't act for Sophia Horwitz. Why would she get involved? And what is this apostille anyway?'

There was a shuffling noise. 'Jardim here,' the angry voice said. 'Are you going to be long, mister? We need to resolve the problem. We are waiting for you.'

Broadhurst reached for the mobile and switched off the speaker. 'Madam, forgive me, but I didn't ask you to come to my hotel tonight nor to act for my client, nor to construct this trumped-up piece of nonsense.'

'An apostille is not nonsense. It is a certification by a recognised authority that the document concerned is fit for legal interpretation in another jurisdiction. In simple language, it enables the Portuguese authorities to accept it. Your lawyers overlooked it, and to overcome the problem, I agreed to help.'

'If that is the case, and I see no reason why you include the Portuguese authorities in your argument when it is the bank's administration that has to be satisfied, I am happy to remain as trustee of the contents of the safe-deposit box whilst the formality is concluded.'

There was a delay before the reply, the muffled sound of voices. 'I am afraid your offer is unacceptable. The contents have to be under the bank's control until all proof of entitlement requirements are met. That is the agreement between the bank and the Portuguese government which you find dubious.'

Broadhurst gestured to a waiter for the bill. 'I'll be back in due course. See if we can sort this out.' He rang off before Jardim had a chance to reply and sat back in his chair. He watched Petra play with her coffee cup. 'Now, tell me all about yourself and how you came to end up in Lisbon.'

THIRTY-THREE
ESTORIL, PORTUGAL
October 2018

They were in the bar, spread around a table in the corner. Malato and Jardim sat to one side, talking together. The old man in the wheelchair wearing dark glasses and wrapped in a synthetic fur coat nursed a glass in between gloved hands. Standing just behind him was another man conversing on a mobile, who had the appearance of a bodyguard. They all looked up as the newcomers threaded their way through the seating to reach them.

Jardim had an 'about time' look on her face as she trundled forward, arm extended.

Broadhurst sidestepped an armchair, leaving Jardim's hand flaying in mid-air. 'I won't apologise for keeping you all waiting as I wasn't expecting you in the first place.' He looked at Malato with what he hoped was an expression intended to chide an errant schoolboy. 'Nor a reception committee.' He turned around to face the man in the wheelchair and his bodyguard.

Malato made the introductions. Josef Krakowski was identified as a client of the bank and consultant to the observation group; Elliott Karmi as a friend of the family. Broadhurst acknowledged the old man and extended his hand towards Karmi. '*Shalom aleichem*,' he said, waiting for the reflex response of '*Aleichem shalom*'. Mossad, he thought. Has to be. Late forties, muscular figure, works out, stereotype Israeli secret service operative.

'This is Petra,' he said. 'She likes to be known as my stepdaughter.' Petra gave a demure wave. 'Now, how can I help you?'

Malato went to repeat the explanation, but a gloved hand stopped him in mid-sentence.

'I don't know if you are aware of my background, Mr Broadhurst.' Krakowski cleared his throat. 'If not, save to say I am trying to trace the whereabouts of my sister, Rita, who has been evading discovery for over seventy years. I believe the papers stored in the safe-deposit box attributed to Lew Wiesel may provide some clues as to how I might find her. Perhaps you are in a position to confirm this or otherwise?'

'I have no idea what they contain. My brief is to recover the documents and deliver them to my client. You, presumably, know who that is and, if so, why not approach them and make your request direct?'

'Stefan and Sophia Horwitz may have good reasons that escape me, but they have already declined a request from the Holocaust organisation I represent. I am asking you, in good faith, to give me sight of the documents. All today's delaying tactics and this initiative tonight to hold up things further is simply an attempt to convince the authorities at bank and government level to redraw their guidelines to allow us proper scrutiny.'

Broadhurst nodded. 'I appreciate your honesty and candour. All I can say is that it is not within my fiduciary responsibility to comply. In fact, quite the contrary. I have been specifically asked not to open or divulge any detail, other than to my clients. You must understand my position.'

Elliott moved from behind the wheelchair. 'I understand Mr Broadhurst is interested in the real estate market in Portugal. I don't doubt if there was a meeting of minds, we might be able to help in that direction. We enjoy a great deal of influence within certain strands of the Portuguese property market.'

Broadhurst avoided the ham-fisted suggestion of bribery with a patient smile. 'For the time being, I suggest you perform your delaying tactics until and unless one or other of us gets some clarification or a determination. I've made my position clear. I'll get the documents.'

'May I accompany you?' Malato asked. 'For the sake of good order.'

'Be my guest.'

Malato spent the journey time to Broadhurst's room apologising profusely for the disruption and inconvenience. Broadhurst put a finger to his lips. 'Please. Try not to sour our relationship even further.'

'Repeat, please.'

'It doesn't matter.' He opened the safe and retrieved the four fictitious documents, putting them in a larger envelope and sealing it before appending his signature once at each end of the adhesive tape. 'I am relying on you to ensure this envelope is not opened until the issue is resolved. I'll know if it's been tampered with.' He took a blank sheet of paper from the desk. 'Write me out a receipt, please, identifying you have taken possession of the contents of safe-deposit box N302.'

As they made their way back into the bar, the mood had changed. Danata had arrived and was whispering in a huddle with Elliott and her father. She looked up as Broadhurst entered, a confused and quizzical expression on her face.

'How's the real estate hunting going?' she asked.

'About as well as the journalism, I shouldn't wonder,' Broadhurst retorted.

'Petra here introduced herself as your stepdaughter. I was under the impression from our journey together you weren't married?'

'It's how she describes herself. I've never been too concerned with family relationships.'

'That sounds like a way of saying mind your own business.'

'Your construction, not my intention.'

Petra had gone to the bar and was sitting on a stool with her back to them.

'Her face seems familiar,' Danata said. 'I get the feeling I've seen her somewhere.'

Elliott attracted her attention. 'We should be going. There's nothing more to achieve here and your father is tired.'

Danata nodded and turned to face Broadhurst. 'I tried my hardest today to stop the release of those papers. I almost managed to convince one of the experts. I'll have another crack tomorrow. Josef said you won't give him permission to examine them.'

'Wrong. I would happily let you read them, but it's not in my gift. I have orders to follow very specific instructions.'

She picked up her coat. 'I will get my own way on this. You can rest assured.'

'I hope you do. Take it out of my hands and I'll look on from afar.'

'Enjoy your stepdaughter. You are certainly a man full of surprises.'

'Touché,' he said as he watched them leave.

THIRTY-FOUR
ESTORIL, PORTUGAL
October 2018

Petra had seemed reserved, almost reticent to talk as he walked her back to his room. Her comment, 'I've taken the ring out, but I think she recognised me,' begged further investigation, but right now his unenviable task was to explain the situation to Sophia Horwitz. He sat Petra down in front of the television and retreated to the bedroom, shutting the door behind him.

Much to his surprise, Sophia Horwitz took the news calmly, merely asking who had been present when the bank reclaimed the documents. He made no attempt to explain the fact that the envelope contained fake papers and the originals were safe in his possession. For the time being, he needed the opportunity to understand exactly what was going on and why he had the nagging feeling he was simply being played as a pawn in a bigger game.

There was a gap in the conversation while he scanned across the receipt signed by Malato.

'I assume you don't want the lawyer Jardim to arrange the apostilles? She's guaranteed to take forever.' Broadhurst had a pen ready to take down the information.

'This is Stefán Horwitz. We've not spoken before.' The words were carefully enunciated, the tone lacking any emotion. 'I have just spoken with my solicitor. He will make contact. You say Krakowski was concerned with locating his sister. Do you believe him?'

'I have no reason not to. He came over to me as a man conducting a quest he needs to complete before he dies.' Broadhurst weighed his words. 'He said you had vetoed his request to look over the contents of Wiesel's safe-deposit box. I found that somewhat strange; your wife having told me of a Jewish upbringing, she could surely appreciate the motive for his wanting to know.'

'Nobody did that,' Horwitz snapped back. 'My wife explained to you the delicate nature of the matter. Clearly, we have a right to be the first to see the contents, primarily to understand if there is anything which could sully the Wiesel name and possibly prejudice Sophia. What I told the Holocaust Foundation Krakowski hides behind is that if there was anything to identify the whereabouts or what had happened to his sister, or any other person of interest come to that, I would give him the detail.'

'His daughter seems bent on convincing the experts to allow her access.'

'The woman is a loose cannon, dangerous and unpredictable. Her methods, legal or otherwise, are determined by whatever needs to be done to achieve the objective.'

'Somebody else must think like that. They tried to blow up her car with her inside.'

'Really? So, we can discount the idea of a petrol tank explosion, can we?'

Broadhurst was taken aback. 'A car fire in Portugal made the news in the UK? I am staggered.'

'I have an extensive press cuttings service, Mr Broadhurst. This week, for obvious reasons, I am very interested to know what is going on in Portugal that could be of possible interest. Can we just recap on the four documents present in the safe-deposit box?'

'It's exactly as I described to your wife. Two letters, one with significant bulk, sealed and addressed to a German newspaper, date of origin I could not say beyond very old. According to the postmark on the second, it was sent in February 1946 from Chicago, Illinois, addressed to Lew Wiesel at an address in Nuremberg. The letter was open and I did look at the signature in order to tell your wife who had sent it, although the content is in a language I assume is Polish. The signature says "Norman".'

'That will be Norman Vogel, my wife's father and Lew's brother-in-law. They wisely emigrated to the US before the war started.'

'Apart from that, there is a receipt from a detective agency in Brussels issued in 1989, addressed to Lew Wiesel, and a letter from a firm of lawyers in Coimbra, dated 1939, addressed to Borys Wiesel. It's the only document written in English and talks about enclosing a contract which was not with the letter. That is the sum total of the contents.'

The line went quiet again for a full minute before Horwitz reacted. 'You didn't happen to see when was the last time our box was opened by someone ?'

'As a matter of fact, I did. The security guard had the register with him in which I had to print my name. He had trouble with the spelling. The previous occasion was on the thirtieth of April, 1989, opened by *anonima*, indicating an anonymous female, and countersigned by Pinho, who I am told was the previous manager of the safe-deposit facility. Prior to that the box was opened on two previous occasions, but the page was smoke damaged and the writing illegible.'

Horwitz had partially covered the microphone and was talking to someone. His wife's voice sounded brittle and irritated. 'In the circumstances,' he said, finally, 'you will probably have to wait two days to satisfy this apostille requirement. I take it you're convinced the contact at the bank won't weaken and provide access to the documents?'

'He's a dotted "i"s and crossed "t"s man. Whatever his superiors say, he'll do what he's told. The only instance would be if Krakowski's daughter gets the green light.'

'She won't. My lawyer will see to that. If my contact touches base with you, tell him where things are at. He's expecting to collect the documents, so he'll need rerouting.'

'Anything else?'

'Ye-e-es.' He drew the word out as if thinking time was required. 'It's apparent to me the previous visitor to the box was Rita, Krakowski's sister. You've got a couple of days waiting around; see if there are any clues as to where she might be. If we can help the old man find her, it will take his mind off my paperwork and do him a good turn.'

Great minds thinking alike, Broadhurst mused as they ended the call. It was already an issue he had brought sharply into focus.

The television was tuned to a Brazilian soap opera with a group of wailing women at a hospital bedside. He checked to see Petra asleep, curled up in the foetal position on the sofa, the remote clasped in one hand. As he removed it, she stirred and turned, but remained asleep. Whatever she had to say could wait until morning. He found a spare blanket in the wardrobe and carefully laid it over her. He was feeling exhausted himself and his haemorrhoids had started aching just before he made the call to Horwitz. A long, hot bath and an early night were exactly what was needed.

The tap on the door came as he tested the temperature of the water in the bath and was about to get undressed.

'All right if I come in?' Isabel had a wine bottle in her hand as he opened the door. 'I thought you might like to know what went on in the observation room today. It got quite testy over your little haul.'

He remained with the door partially closed, barring her entry. 'It's somewhat inconvenient tonight, if it's all right with you, Isabel. I was just about to take a bath and go to bed.'

For a second he thought she was about to react badly, but her lips parted in a smile. 'You are a dark horse, Chas. You've got a guest in there. Did I give you the taste for it again?' She laughed. 'She won't be up to my standard, you know that, don't you?'

What would be the point of denying and weaving some fabricated excuse? It wasn't worth it. Let her believe what she wanted.

'Appearances can be deceptive,' he said instead. 'And you're absolutely right. After wearing gold, who would settle for silver?'

'Pig iron, more like,' she said, 'if it's that little creature I saw you with in the bar. Join me for breakfast around eight-thirty and I'll fill you in.'

'Perfect.'

She turned with a sweep of her dressing gown. 'Watch your blood pressure,' she said. 'Don't want a corpse on our hands, do we?'

Gratefully, he closed the door. The woman had some stamina, he'd give her that. Petra had not stirred.

He closed the door to the en-suite bathroom. Slowly, he lowered his bottom into the hot water. He definitely needed the operation.

THIRTY-FIVE
THE ALGARVE, PORTUGAL
October 2018

Riding the afternoon Alfa Pendular express rail service from Lisbon south to the Algarve was quite an experience. As the train crossed the Tagus on the railway line engineered under the road bridge named '25 de Abril', the date of Portugal's revolution of 1975, Broadhurst relaxed into the three-hour journey to Faro. At least he understood the parameters of the task on which he was now embarked – namely, find out what had happened to Rita Krakowski.

During the night, Petra had partially undressed and placed the cushions from the sofa onto the floor, presumably for more leg room. Broadhurst had already showered and shaved and was halfway out the door for his breakfast appointment with Isabel when Petra stirred. Half asleep, she asked if she could use the bed, hardly waiting for confirmation before she staggered into the bedroom, draped in her blanket. He guessed she would be asleep again before her head touched the pillow.

Isabel patted the seat alongside her as they caught sight of each other. He dutifully sat down. Wet lips lingered on his cheek close to his ear a second too long. 'I hope one or other of you benefitted from last night's experience,' she whispered.

'Having been united with a stepdaughter, your train of thought is entirely inappropriate.' He got up to go to the buffet.

'That's what they call themselves these days, is it? Hardly original.'

'Can I get you anything?' he asked.

'Another coffee, small and black. Hurry back. I have to be off in ten minutes.'

He settled on a slice of watermelon, two croissants with blackcurrant jam, and orange juice.

Isabel stirred the coffee absent-mindedly. 'Do you know much about this Elliott Karmi?'

'Why do you ask?'

'I was in the observation room with the rest, including the Da Luca woman I saw you talking with in the bar last night. Everything was going swimmingly well up until your paperwork appeared on the scene. We'd seen a few pieces of jewellery, a couple of vases, some second-rate oil paintings, nothing controversial up until then. I couldn't see any possible reason for objecting to a couple of letters and some loose sheets. The basis for any challenge is quite specific, exclusively a suspicion of theft. Nevertheless, Da Luca did raise a question of the possible historical value of a letter written by an indicted war criminal to a German newspaper, suggesting it was intended for public disclosure. Truth to tell, she didn't appear to have fully convinced herself.'

Broadhurst frowned. 'How did she know who had written the letter? There was no indication on the envelope.'

'Don't know. Nobody asked the question. It was at that point she was called out to speak to someone.'

Broadhurst put the last mouthful of croissant into his mouth and washed it down with the orange juice. 'Need a coffee,' he said. 'Anything for you?'

'Another coffee, small and black.' She hadn't touched the last one.

She pushed the cold coffee out of the way and concentrated on the cup he put in front of her. 'I was walking to the powder room when I overhead Karmi going berserk at her. She had to get hold of the letter, he was saying. It was vital. It could have repercussions internationally. Any idea what he was talking about?'

'No.'

'He was pacing up and down like a man obsessed, saying to her if only he could get into the room and speak with the two experts who held sway over the decision. She asked what was so important and he gave her some waffle. I have to admit, when she did come back to the observation room, her pleading was sufficiently impressive to get the woman expert wavering on her side. Karmi called her out a second time and when she came back, her objection changed to a suspicion of theft in that a letter from an indicted German war criminal was found in the safe-deposit box of a third party. It suggested to her that the letter had been stolen. I thought it was flimsy and so did the male expert who managed to convince his colleague to release the papers to you.'

'Interesting.'

'So, was there any dynamite in the letter? That's what I want to know.'

'No idea. The envelope was sealed and if it was written in German, I wouldn't understand it. Anyway, I don't have it any more. It's back in the bank's possession.'

'Don't tell me they accepted her argument?'

'No, a problem with the client authority.'

She spurted a mouthful of coffee onto the table. 'Sorry. Not very ladylike. They are so transparent, it's laughable.'

'It should be resolved by tomorrow.'

'Judging by Karmi's attitude, he'll have got his own way by then, however he goes about it.' She pulled over his wrist to check the time. 'I must be off. Don't want to miss today's adventure. It's the weekend tomorrow. I have to go up country, hush-hush business, but I should be back Sunday afternoon. Fancy checking out the gold standard?'

The suggestion was still ringing in his ears as he made his way back up to the room. Petra had found a towelling dressing gown and was back in front of the television, remote in hand as she surfed through the channels. 'Nothing good on in the morning, unless you want to decorate your house or rustle up some nouvelle cuisine, neither of which rattles my cage.'

He suggested she switch it off and tell him what she had meant last night when hoping Danata had not recognised her.

'I mentioned my boyfriend, Ziz, didn't I?'

'Briefly.'

'I think that woman must have arranged to have him killed.'

'What are you talking about? Does she know this man, Ziz, you call him?'

'Aziz is his name. He's from somewhere near Russia, one of those countries.'

'Sounds like it,' he said, the words laced with sarcasm.

'No. I mean his dad is from the Arab world, don't ask me where, but they live in Austria now, I think. We met in a disco and it sort of gelled. Anyway, he's part of a group that turns over rich people, real pros apparently. His job is to plant tracking devices on cars so that the ones who do the robberies have got an exact idea where the people live whose houses they plan to rob. We were tailing this woman to a hotel in the north of Portugal and I had to sit in the restaurant and make sure I could warn Ziz if she left before he had finished. It was the woman in the bar last night. It all worked out and he finished before she left. Mind you, we had to camp out overnight to be able to tail her in the morning.'

'And did you tail her?'

She shook her head. 'I never saw her or the car again. The woman had a zippy red sports car and she must have lost us. Ziz said he saw which road she took and knew from that where she was going, so we didn't have to bother tailing her. I did think it was a little silly, sleeping out all night, just to forget about her, but I was with Ziz and that was all that mattered.'

'Ziz was driving what, exactly?'

She looked at Broadhurst as though he was mentally deficient. 'I told you. He was part of a group. All of them are nuts about fancy motorcycles. Ziz has one of the latest shiny models. Don't ask me which one.'

'What does the group call itself?'

She laughed. 'I should know that; spent enough time pressed up against the writing on the back of his leather jacket to shield me from the wind. They are known as the SJ Missionaries.'

Something clicked in Broadhurst's memory. Right then, he couldn't place it. 'Strange name,' he queried.

'Great minds, et cetera. I said that to him. Apparently, they started the group in some abandoned monastery in Estonia called Saint Joseph's. Ziz would laugh. Monks were sent out to do God's work. His group are missionaries for the devil. That's how they got the name.'

'So, where did you go, if you didn't follow the woman?'

'Ziz had to meet somebody in Madrid. He had the use of an apartment. We waited for a day or two. I went out shopping and as I returned, somebody came out of the apartment and started shooting at me. I can only assume the woman had eyeballed Ziz and sent somebody to see to him. I was petrified, but if there's one thing I can do, it's run. Believe me, I did. I don't know what to do now she's seen me. I need to get out of Lisbon. You know that money you talked about?'

Broadhurst reached for her hand. 'I don't know if you are in danger or not, but I can assure you there is nothing to fear from Danata. She didn't send anybody after you, I can guarantee. I guess somebody wanted Aziz out of the way and you were considered collateral damage. Right now, until I can find out what is going on, your best move is not to move. Stay here. When the time is right, I'll give you some cash to go away somewhere.'

She pulled her hand away. 'Why are you doing this for me?'

It was a spur of the moment decision and one he would always regret. 'You can help me with something.'

'Oh, yes?'

'You speak Czech, right? There are similarities with German? You share a land border, after all.'

'A few words, perhaps, but nothing more. Czech is Slavic and German is Germanic. They may have been the same once, but now all we have are some German words in the language. Though I did study German for a few years at school. It was compulsory.'

'Turn your back and don't look until I say so.' He went to the printer tray and removed one of the handwritten sheets in German. 'Can you make sense of this?' He offered the paper to her.

Two minutes later and the page was back in his hand. 'It's difficult enough trying to decipher the handwriting,' she said, 'let alone try to understand the words. I can see the writer mentions something about a circle and comments about after the war, but the rest is meaningless.'

He made her turn around again, removed the paper tray and replaced the single sheet. 'I'll have to wait a little longer,' he said. 'Now, get dressed and go down and get some breakfast before the restaurant closes.'

It was just gone midday when the hotel phone rang on the desk where he was working on his laptop. 'I tried your mobile,' Marchal said, 'but it went straight to message.'

Broadhurst checked. The battery was out. He plugged in the charger. 'Out of juice. Do you have something for me on the translations?'

'Not yet. This is to do with the receipt from the investigation agency. We've had a bit of luck on that score. Apparently, the Grand-Place business was absorbed into a French company, Quatre Rois, in 2008. Quatre Rois is closely involved with Europol on a number of cross-border

311

investigations and they are currently quoting for a major consultancy assignment with the Police Judiciaire.'

Broadhurst bit his tongue. Typical René, he thought. I'm getting the explanation as to how he got the explanation. Please get on with it, he said to himself.

As if reading his mind, Marchal continued. 'Anyway, you will understand how I came to get the information so quickly. They are very keen to help the police – I may have given them the wrong impression as to whom I was – and so, to demonstrate their efficiency—'

'And so?' Broadhurst couldn't help himself.

'Are you in a hurry, Chas?'

'Not at all, René.'

'When the merger took place, they digitalised the Grand-Place historic case files in detail back only as far as 2000. Before that, they made a bullet-point summary record of each case and destroyed the paper file. The receipt you hold was for an investigation on behalf of Lew Wiesel to locate a German national, Heinrich Kirchner, who was a former major in the SS. Kirchner was cohabiting, or had cohabited, with a Polish national, Rita Krakowski.

'The target was believed to be living on the Portuguese Algarve. He had applied for a fiscal number with the tax office in a place called Loulé, using the name Leonard Taube. His address is shown as care of Tosé at the mini-mercado Girassol. The only other notation confirms suspects located and observed.'

* * *

The express ran over a series of points outside a station signposted Grandola. The scenery had started to change. Broadhurst returned to the present with a jolt. The large advertising hoarding alongside the track bade them welcome to the Alentejo, a region of rolling hills, clusters of cork trees carefully sliced and identified with white paint, plantations of olive trees and fields of vines, now drastically pruned to await new growth in the spring. Cattle and horses roamed amongst the trees, the only signs of life in this vast expanse of countryside. Occasionally, the train ran past a farm or smallholding before it began to climb towards the gentle sierra backdrop to the Algarve and descended to swing east to run parallel to the sea towards Faro.

He picked his way through clusters of backpackers and taxi drivers bustling around the small station concourse and made his way by foot in darkness towards the marina and the Hotel Eva, where he had a reservation for the night.

It had been the warning in the guidebook that had deterred him from driving the BMW from Lisbon. According to the reviews from contributors, tourists should avoid the EN125, the main road traversing the Algarve from the Spanish border to the Cape of Saint Vincent, branded the most dangerous and accident-prone road in Europe. In heeding this advice, he had opted to hire a left-hand drive model locally and had happily paid the premium for the 'no excess' insurance option. As he made his way cautiously in the small hatchback to the town of Loulé, he came to two conclusions. One, compared to the overstated prospect of a highway requiring drivers with dodgem car reflexes, the reality was of far more sedate and conventional driving conditions. Secondly, and more critically, the idea in his mind's eye that he would find out what he needed to know by asking a few questions in a rural town where everybody knew everybody else, was beyond naïve. The task would be immense.

The district of Loulé stretched across an area of almost three hundred square miles, from the coastline of the affluent Golden Triangle in the east to the border with Albufeira on the west and north into the mountains of the sierra. God knows how many mini-markets were spread around the region, but it must run into hundreds and he was looking for a business operating thirty years ago, before supermarkets and hypermarkets had squeezed out local traders.

His initial enquiries centred on the town hall, the local civil registry and the central police station, all of which proved fruitless. The name of Taube appeared nowhere within the system and Broadhurst managed to test the temper of a number of public officials unwilling to spend time trying to satisfy a foreigner's curiosity. He drove around the backroads, stopping at any local store where the proprietor could be approached to establish if they

313

had heard of the mini-market 'Girassol', which he learnt meant 'sunflower'. Nobody had.

Disheartened and tired, he made his way to Vilamoura. He had decided to spoil himself with a night at the five-star Tivoli hotel on the marina. The name reminded him of the hotel in Lisbon where Danata had left him as they ended the drive from Guarda. It seemed more like weeks ago than a handful of days. He was prompted to check in with Petra. There was no answer from the room phone and he had forgotten to take her mobile number. She hadn't tried to ring him, so there was little more he could do than leave a message saying he would be back the following late afternoon.

There were few tourists at this time of year and most of the restaurants spread around three sides of the marina were closed. He decided on a Chinese meal, which meant following the signs away from the marina towards a residential area. The House of Sun was both open and literally next door to the local police station. It was a part-time, mainly seasonal facility, and the overweight, middle-aged policeman was about to close up for the night.

'Never heard of it,' he said in answer to Broadhurst's enquiry. His English was heavily accented and laboured. 'Which zone of the *concelho* is it in?'

'I don't know and it's somewhere that existed thirty years ago.'

'Most of my colleagues in Loulé are from outside the district and there is no one I know with thirty years' service. There is one person who may be able to help you. Inspector Rodrigues is with the Judicial Police in Faro. He used to be a *cabo* and then a *sargento* in a post we had at one time in Boliqueime. He knows the area very well and could help. I'll find his mobile number for you.'

Broadhurst found himself to be the only diner. Food ordered, he played with the slip of paper in his hand. No time like the present. He dialled the number.

'Inspector Rodrigues?'

'Sim.'

'Do you speak English?'

'Yes. Some.' The voice was gruff, as if he had just woken up.

'Sorry to disturb you on a Saturday, but I am looking for information about somebody who lived in the area thirty years ago.'

Broadhurst explained who he was and gave the name of the mini-market.

'What did you say was the name of the person you are looking for?'

'Taube. Leonard Taube and, more specifically, the woman with whom he lived.'

There was silence on the line. 'Who did you say you were?' The voice was alert, totally focused.

He repeated the introduction and reason for the call.

'Where are you?' Rodrigues knew the restaurant. 'I'm on the night shift, starting at midnight. Stay where you are and I'll be there as soon as I can.'

The choice from the dessert menu between a banana roll or fried ice cream was on Broadhurst's mind when the restaurant door opened and the man walked in. My saviour, he thought. The one thing I shouldn't eat with my problem is some sickly, sweet pudding.

'I'll skip the dessert,' he said to the waiter. 'Just a coffee and whatever my visitor would like.'

Rodrigues was small in stature, around fifty, with a receding hairline and a serious limp that made him walk in a slightly lopsided fashion. He shook his head and waved away the waiter.

'Daniel Rodrigues,' he said and held out a hand, the palm creased with ingrained dirt, as were his fingernails. He edged onto a seat. 'So, you're looking for Leonard Taube?'

'You know of him?'

'I did. They were neighbours, Leonard and Angela. For many years. She taught me everything there is to know about horticulture and beekeeping. I was fascinated by her as a child, as a youth, even as the man I am today. Do you know where she is, what happened to her? Over the years, I've tried to find out in my own small way, but my resources are limited and now, with this …' He slapped his leg.

'What happened?'

'Chasing a felon. I fell – or, rather, I was pushed – off a scaffold. I fell from the second storey of a building into a container. It wasn't like you

315

see in the movies where the hero falls onto a mattress conveniently placed there. My container was full of cement and reinforcing rods. I spent three months in hospital. Now, I do a desk job until they can pension me off.'

'Tell me all you know about the Taubes and I'll let you know where I'm up to.'

Rodrigues began the narrative of growing up with Angela as a neighbour and mentor, developing his interest in plants and bees, and the tragedy of the so-called attempted robbery that cost the life of Leonard and his father, Pedro.

'Leonard is buried in the local cemetery. Shortly after the funeral, Angela said she had to go to Lisbon to tidy up her husband's affairs. She left and I never saw her again.'

'You said "so-called" robbery. How come?'

There was a strained look on Daniel's face. 'It didn't seem right to me. Leonard was stabbed, yet my father was shot. The attackers were a couple, a man and a woman. That's weird. Leonard made a phone call to the police, supposedly saying Angela was about to kill him. That was deemed erroneous. Explaining it away as a robbery appeared to me a convenient answer to a suspicious event.'

'You were probably correct.'

He stared at Broadhurst for the first time. 'How come?'

'Taube wasn't their real name.'

'I guessed that.'

'Leonard was a former SS major during the war named Heinrich Kirchner, a concentration camp commander, wanted for various crimes. Angela was also to be tried as a collaborator. Her name is Rita Krakowski, a Polish Jew. You can be certain many people wanted to see them dead.'

Daniel began to rub his thighs, a grimace on his lips.

'Are you all right?'

'I get cramp in both legs.' He pinched the back of his legs. 'I knew there had to be a backstory.'

Broadhurst called for another coffee. 'You never heard from Angela again, you say?'

'I didn't say that.' He finished his massaging and fished inside the inner pocket of his jacket. 'I said I never saw her again.' He pulled out a crumpled cashier's slip with the Western Union logo. 'My mother never really recovered from my father's death. She was never the same happy-go-lucky, vivacious woman I remembered. In 2010, she was diagnosed with an aggressive form of bone cancer, given six months to live. There was a medication to prolong life developed in the States, but it was not authorised for participation in Portugal.'

'What does that mean?'

'The drug was super expensive and the Portuguese health authority refused to put it on their approved list of medicines for which they paid a proportion of the cost. So, if Mum wanted a monthly course of treatment, we had to find five thousand dollars to pay for it.' His eyes began to fill. 'Out of the question, I'm afraid.'

Broadhurst waited for the other man to wipe his eyes and blow his nose.

'I don't have any idea how Angela came to know of Mum's illness, but she did and wrote her a letter. It's a personal document addressed to Anna Paula and I was never allowed to read it while Mum was alive. What Mum did tell me was that Angela had sent enough money for six month's supply of the drug to Western Union in Albufeira, and I should go along with her identification and an authorisation to receive the money.'

'Did the letter bear any identification as to from where it was sent?'

'No. I quizzed the teller at Western Union as to the origin of the money. His information was an anonymous sender from Thonon-les-Bains in Switzerland It's on Lac Leman, almost halfway between Montreux and Geneva. I often thought about going there, but the opportunity never presented itself.'

Broadhurst checked his watch. The man would have to be going. 'Did you eventually get sight of the letter?'

'No. She tore it up, but I know what was in it. As she lay dying, her mind started to wander and she rambled on about nothing in particular, speaking to non-existent people or a real person who wasn't there. She talked to Pedro. "We'll have to tell him one day he's not ours. He must never know it was Angela who left him for us."'

Broadhurst sighed. 'I assume if I find her alive, you want to know where she is?'

317

'I'd like to visit her when you do. I wouldn't like to see her on my own.'

'You have my word.'

THIRTY-SIX
THE WHITE HOUSE, WASHINGTON DC, US
November 2018

'Of course I'm going.' President Brandon Williams sipped carefully from the glass of bourbon and cast a casual eye on the television news channel, sound muted, the headlines running across the bottom of the screen. 'Why wouldn't I? It's the anniversary of the liberation of Auschwitz. Think of the Jewish vote if I appeared to snub the occasion. It's a no-brainer.'

Bo Chandler wheezed at the effort of uncrossing his legs and leaning forward to convey the gravity of his next comment. 'If you end up standing on a podium delivering a speech that touches on your father's contribution to the war effort and the liberation of the camps, just as a news story breaks with the contents of that letter, your re-election chances are toast. Believe me.'

The President carefully replaced the glass. 'Two things, Bo, you seem to be forgetting. One, you tell me the original letter is now under your control, so how could it get out to the press? Secondly, my father was not acting on some personal mission. If what the letter describes is correct and there is nobody alive to corroborate this fanciful story, its veracity can easily be questioned. And even if it were to be true, he would have been acting on official orders.'

'True or otherwise is irrelevant. Attitudes change. It may have been politically acceptable to invite enemy doctors and engineers with dubious practices to come to the US after the war, but it's certainly something we shouldn't boast about now. Sommer is known as the butcher of Potulice, and to ascribe his salvation as US citizen, Peter Winter, to the efforts of your father would be political poison.'

'It was the policy at the time.'

'Clandestine, even so, and, according to the letter, the general instigated a massacre of a troop of German soldiers and civilians and allowed two lorries filled with gold and God knows what to be diverted so that a band of Nazi war criminals could live in comfort for the rest of their lives with enough left over to plan the next Reich. Were those orders, as well?'

319

'That's bullshit. He would never have done any of that. It's all lies.'

Bo watched the rain cascading onto the outside terrace. So thick was the glass of the bulletproof windows, he could not hear a sound beyond the President's heavy breathing. 'Shit sticks to a blanket, as you well know, sir. Agreeing to participate until we have confirmation there are no copies would be foolhardy.'

'And when will that be?'

'Hopefully, soon. What we do know is the courier secreted the originals and returned some dummy paperwork to the bank in Lisbon. There is no trace of any copies in his room and he only had the originals in his possession for under twenty-four hours before he left the hotel.'

'Plenty of time.'

'Maybe, but we've verified there is nothing on his mobile, nor did he use any significant upload capacity via his SIM cards. That leaves the hotel IP address. There were uploads during the twenty-four-hour period from the address sufficient to account for a data transfer in excess of that necessary to copy the documents, but we are talking about a hundred-room-plus hotel with ninety per cent occupancy.

'And this courier? To whom could he have sent copies?'

Bo took a prompt card from his pocket. 'The courier is out of the picture. Most likely recipient would be his business partner in France. My contact, Stefan Horwitz, is sending somebody to check him out. Alternatively, he is also friendly with the head of the press corps that looks after the royal family. But this guy has been on an assignment in Canada and is unlikely to be the intended recipient. We are giving him the once over, all the same.'

Williams downed the rest of his bourbon, closing his eyes as he savoured the experience. 'I think it's best if you send one of our own, strictly between us, to keep an eye on developments. I'll need to say something by early January about my visit. We need to be abreast of the position.'

'I'm already on it,' Bo replied. 'I've arranged for Cris Hopper to travel to Paris in the morning. He'll avoid the embassy and any official channels, liaise with Horwitz's contact and recover the letter. The brief is to establish if a copy exists, recover or destroy it, and to sanction any collateral action necessary to preserve secrecy.'

'That sounds like a euphemism.'

Bo struggled to his feet, massaged his leg and made his way to the door. 'With all due respect, sir, if it is a euphemism, you do not want to know anything about it.'

THIRTY-SEVEN
LISBON, PORTUGAL
November 2018

She had been a woman of few words. It was one of the qualities Broadhurst had admired in his ex-wife. She never wasted a syllable on waffle or trivia, always straight to the point, irrespective of the effect of what she said on the other person. For somebody who survived in a hierarchy where politics, innuendo and nuance were everyday weapons of survival and advancement, he found her brutal candour an exhilarating relief; except the once, that was.

'I'm divorcing you, Chas,' she had said. 'The only love in your life is the SAS, a selfish mistress who demands and gets more of your attention than I could ever hope for. My new partner offers the prospect of not only love but companionship, and the only competition for his affection is a dog. Goodbye.'

It had been cut and dried. Was it? If she was so set in her ways, why had she come back to talk to him in this monotone with so many words and hardly taking a breath?

'Come quickly. I told you he was waking up. Now do you believe me?'

A hand began to massage his, each finger kneaded in turn between hers. It was rather erotic.

His eyes clicked open as if a child's doll. His lips were bone dry and the stench inside the mask was of stale breath. He coughed and felt the pull of the drip tube feeding into his hand as he moved.

'Welcome back.' The voice was Isabel's, not his ex-wife. 'There were a couple of days when we thought we'd lost you.'

As his senses returned, people arrived. A doctor and various nurses fussed around his bed, checking machinery, adjusting dials, temperature, blood pressure, five mils of this and that.

It was like walking back through a time tunnel, from the last thing he remembered to leaving the coach at Oriente bus station and hailing a cab.

He had gone to the bank. Malato was on edge. Clients, experts and observers were all getting difficult to handle, he had said. Family heirlooms were being cited as stolen treasure, niggling arguments erupted between experts and observers, tempers were frayed and he couldn't wait for the whole business to end.

Broadhurst asked if he could check the records to see if there was a safe-deposit box registered in the name of Taube. Then came the apology. It was the lawyer, Jardim, who had insisted on the apostille, not he or the bank's management. They were satisfied. He would get the envelope back shortly, another day at the most. Lawyer Mello had intervened on behalf of Senhora Horwitz.

What name was it? Taube. Yes, H65. It was one of the largest. No reaction from the client to the series of statutory notices that had been sent; typical for about forty per cent of the boxes. Letters were sent to a postbox in Brussels. The bank would probably end up having to open it.

It was late afternoon when he arrived back at the hotel. There was a selection of messages awaiting him in reception: requests to call René and Duncan White; four reminders from Isabel about getting together; a note from Danata to say she had called by to see him and would call again; and a request from housekeeping to remove the 'do not disturb' advice to allow daily cleaning. He asked for a spare key in case Petra was out.

The room had been ransacked. Cushions had been ripped open and tossed onto the floor, along with the contents of all the drawers; clothes had been ripped apart and cast aside. The printer tray had been opened with blank sheets of paper littering the floor. The contents of the safe-deposit box had gone.

'Petra!' he called. 'Are you there?'

Water was running in the shower. He pushed open the bathroom door. A sodden towel hampered his entry. The towel rail had been ripped from the wall. Spatters of blood dotted the floor. Petra was in the shower cubicle, fully dressed. She sat in the tray, her back propped against the wall. There was a bullet hole in the centre of her forehead. Water sprayed around the body, the skin now blue and wrinkled. Her hand clutched one end of the towel rail.

Broadhurst straightened his body, just as he sensed somebody was behind him. He turned and ducked, moving forward as if to make a tackle in a rugby match. The butt of the revolver aimed at his head cannoned into his shoulder blade instead. The pain was sharp and dynamic. His left arm was now useless. He drove his fist into the middle of a black T-shirt, using his good shoulder to bundle the man back into the bedroom. They fell onto the floor, the hand still grasping the barrel of a silenced revolver. Broadhurst reached for the butt and trigger guard as they struggled on the floor. A tanned hand with a gold signet ring twisted at the barrel, wrenching it out of Broadhurst's grip. His hand followed it, the roles now reversed. The assailant strained to bring his finger around the trigger as Broadhurst pushed the barrel out of the line of fire. The man was now using both hands to direct the gun at Broadhurst's head.

With the attention centred on the weapon, Broadhurst had an opening. Lurching sideways, he headbutted the man with all the force he could muster. There was a grunt lost in the man's throat as he finally tore the gun free from Broadhurst's restraint. Blood was seeping through the material of the black balaclava that hid his face. He was cursing in a language Broadhurst did not understand.

Three things happened all at once, he recalled. They were the last three things he remembered. There was a tap on the door. 'Are you there, Chas? I hope you're not decent.' Isabel's mobile rang. 'I'll just take this and be with you in a second.'

The gun broke free of Broadhurst's grip. The barrel swung around towards him. He made one desperate lunge with his hand as the sound came of a cork popping.

There was darkness.

* * *

The police inspector made a few more notes before he spoke. Broadhurst had forgotten his name. Possibly, he had never said what it was.

'You're lucky to be alive,' the policeman said. 'You are also fortunate the bullet that grazed your skull clipped a vein and dislodged some bone fragments.'

'Doesn't exactly sound like good luck.'

'Believe me, it is. You were a mess, blood everywhere, bits of bone. I'm certain your attacker would have finished you off if he didn't think you were already dead. As it was, he made a clumsy attempt to make it look as though you had killed the girl, leaving the gun in your hand, but he had to flee the scene before your visitor returned. Lucky she was around. Saved your life. You would have probably bled out.' He checked his watch. 'Look, the doctor says I can only have ten minutes this morning. I'll check in again later this afternoon or, at latest, tomorrow morning. Your attacker will be long gone, but we will get a detailed description from you, check it with some closed-circuit images from outside the hotel and see if we can identify the suspect.'

Broadhurst closed his eyes. 'How long have I been here?' he asked.

'Four days. I'll need all the background information from you. Everything to do with the bank, whatever it was that the assailant wanted he was prepared to kill for, and the girl's role in all this. Try and get it straight in your mind.' He handed Broadhurst a card. 'By the way, I didn't introduce myself. I'm Inspector Hernando Cunha. I'll be looking after the case.'

He looked down at Broadhurst and shook his head. 'I told my superiors this business of opening all the safe-deposit boxes would bring untold problems onto our heads, but nobody took me seriously. And now, this.'

Broadhurst watched as Cunha stopped for a word with the policeman guarding the room. They both laughed as they turned to look at the patient.

As the novelty and pain wore off, the days in a foreign hospital began to drag.

Gone was the urgency; the critical care became a gradual process of recovery, the progression from an operation to restore an area of damaged bone, to another, to graft skin from his thigh onto his hairline above the ear to disguise the wound. Waiting and monitoring were now the watchwords. Repercussions with serious head injuries could manifest themselves in a myriad of ways.

Gone were the repetitious questions from Cunha and his young sergeant about the information contained in the missing documents, the reason for his visit to the Algarve, constant probing to which he provided the same sanitised answers. Some of it was easy. He couldn't explain what was in the letters because he didn't understand. Some of it was hard. When he

326

had to deal with queries about Petra's presence – the bubbly personality, the smart alec comebacks, the disarming smile – it hurt like hell. It was his fault she was dead and she had suffered. By accident, the sergeant had let it slip during one particular question and answer session that she had been subjected to torture before she was executed. How long had she held out? She wasn't stupid. When he had gone to the printer paper tray to retrieve the page he had shown her, she must have recognised the sound. If he had been twenty years younger, he could have easily taken that evil bastard.

Gone was his assignment. The only contact he had with Sophia Horwitz was a sympathy card with a trite 'Sorry things turned out this way', a cheque for the balance of the agreed fee and a thank you for his cooperation. Case closed. Only, it wasn't. He had a young woman's death to avenge.

For the first three days of convalescence, Isabel was a frequent visitor. She was helping the police with her enquiries and trying to make some of her own, he guessed. One gratuitous piece of information she offered was that her visit to the north of Portugal had been to Guarda, the very same town where he had stayed overnight and first met Danata. Coincidence maybe, but it sparked his curiosity. What was so fascinating about Guarda? She had to check on a mining operation, she had told him.

On the last of the three days, she looked disappointed. Axion had insisted she return to the UK immediately. She was her normal acerbic self. He probably had no more young starlets to screw and was running out of clean underpants. He might be able to stage a complex theatrical production, but he claimed he didn't know how to turn on the fucking washing machine.

With a furtive hand under Broadhurst's bedsheet to check the bullet hadn't ricocheted and a kiss on his cheek, she was gone.

He woke up at three in the morning, anxious and sweating. How stupid had he been not to realise? How the hours dragged by until the young nurse with the boyfriend who delivered pizzas came onto the ward. A call to the concierge at the hotel and a hefty tip to the delivery boy got the work mobile from the glove box of the BMW into his hands just after lunch.

The call was answered at the first ring. 'Thank God,' Marchal gasped. 'I have been going frantic trying to get news of your condition. The only information came from the hotel. You had been taken to hospital with a life-threatening condition. At the hospital, there has been a total lockdown, even to the point of refusing to confirm you were actually a patient. What has been happening, and how are you?'

Broadhurst gave him a potted version of events. There was total silence at the other end of the line. 'That's why I've been so stupid, just thinking about myself. You must be in danger.'

'I must?'

'If those letters were worth killing for, they must put you in the line of fire. You know what they contain, presumably?'

'Yes. They are inflammatory, I accept, but without corroboration the allegations are at best circumstantial and might make a few waves, but no more. They could easily be discredited. Shall I fill you in?'

'No. Leave it for now. Your analysis may well be right, but one person is dead and I only made it by the skin of my teeth. If whoever wants the letters enough to kill for them, the thought is bound to occur that I may have made a copy and sent it to someone, you being the likeliest recipient. Fortunately, I used this mobile to scan the documents and nobody has this number on their radar. I wouldn't be surprised if my personal mobile is bugged.'

The relief in Marchal's voice at finally establishing contact with his partner had changed to concern. 'I'll take the necessary steps to secure the position. I'm in Lille. I left Paris a couple of days ago.'

Broadhurst waved as one of the nurses passed the door. 'You do that, and watch your back,' he said earnestly. 'Tell me, what would be the ramifications if someone was alive who could corroborate whatever is in Kirchner's letter?'

'The political ramifications would be earth-shattering.'

'That's doubtless their Achilles' heel. Listen, as it would be wise to absent yourself from your normal routine for a while, can I suggest you leave your personal mobile, the number shown on the firm's letterhead, somewhere far away from where you will be. They are bound to have a trace on it. Get a new number, let me have it, and leave the partnership mobile with the scanned images and any hard copies you made with your lawyer with one of those "in the event" letters.'

'You are cheerful.'

328

'Just a precaution.' Broadhurst went on to explain the Taube identity adopted by Rita Krakowski and the starting point for locating her at the Western Union counter in Thonon-les-Bains in Switzerland. 'It's from where she sent the money to Daniel's mother, circa 2010. She would have been in her early eighties at this point, having, I imagine, abandoned the transient lifestyle and living somewhere within the Lac Leman region. I'll join up with you as soon as they let me out of here.'

Another week passed before Broadhurst was prompted to contact Duncan White. Broadhurst was in a physio class, learning to walk properly. For some reason, the head wound had provoked a physical reaction in his legs. When he tried to walk, he would inadvertently lean to his left, creating an irregular movement which gave the impression he was about to start a game of hopscotch. The impulse to lean over was so strong he would break into a sweat with the effort of concentrating to right himself. For three hours every day, he would grimace at the physio nurses as he strained to correct his posture. It was at the end of a session when one of the nurses asked him if he had heard about the argument over Christmas cards in the British royal family. It was that moment which triggered his memory.

He used the encrypted Kensington Palace email service to contact Duncan White. The message was short and to the point. Organise a new burner mobile and ring me on it.

'What's all this cloak and dagger burner business, Chas?'

Broadhurst ran through the events of the preceding fortnight and his fears that White might be suspected of being in the document loop.

'What do these letters say, exactly?'

'I don't know the detail as yet. As far as René is concerned, it's a Nazi SS officer's insurance policy to protect him from betrayal by his own side and it names names with contemporary political ramifications.'

'That's interesting and puts into perspective a call I took the other day. I didn't think anything of it at the time, being engrossed in the containment of another one of son number two's attempts at one-upmanship, but it could be related. Stefan Horwitz called me out of the blue asking if I had heard from you. I said you hadn't been in touch since before I went to Canada and I had been trying to reach you without success.'

'Did he accept that at face value?'

'He appeared to, and from what you say he must have been aware of the attempt on your life and the hospitalisation, but said nothing. In fact, he made it sound as though he thought I might be able to help him locate you. Strange, don't you think?'

'Did he say anything else?'

'Yes. He asked me if I had ever come across an American journalist by the name of Sonny Gerbitz. I said the name rang a bell and asked why or if there was something I could do to help. He ducked the offer and asked if it was possible you knew of the man. What could I say? Of course it was possible, but I very much doubted it. You hadn't operated in similar spheres.'

'Has Sonny come up with anything else? When we last spoke, he had traced the discovery of Sophia wandering around after the death of her parents, somewhere in Michigan, wasn't it?'

'Muskegon, the other side of Lake Michigan. That's right. I mentioned Horwitz's call when we last spoke and he just said 'Jesus. This stinks.' I asked him why and he said he'd tell me after he'd done a little more research.'

'And did he?'

'No. We haven't spoken since and I've been up to my neck. But he did send me a copy of some paperwork.'

'Can you bring me up to date with what it contained?' The anxiety in Broadhurst's voice was apparent.

Papers rustled. 'Right, got it. Four years ago, an old brewery building in the industrial zone of Milwaukee – hadn't been operational for years – was subject to a compulsory purchase order under a city ordinance. The area was rescheduled for residential development and the other property owners around were only too glad to take the big bucks the city was prepared to pay as compensation. Industrial sites worth little suddenly became very valuable once the area was zoned as residential. However, the owners of the brewery site raised objections, fought tooth and nail to avoid the compulsory purchase order. They came within a whisker of winning until the state governor interceded. The property owners had a history of making substantial donations in support of the Republican ticket and with a staunchly blue Democratic governor in power, the order went ahead.'

'Why object?'

'They were willing to see the property transformed into social housing, but they insisted on being allowed to carry out the redevelopment themselves rather than hand over the land to the city. In the end, they lost.'

'I suppose you can understand the profit motive. It's a fascinating story, but I assume it's going somewhere?'

'Absolutely, and it's possibly why Sonny has come to the attention of Stefan Horwitz. The owner of the brewery site in Milwaukee was a corporation called Eagle Distillers Corp, now defunct, which just happened to be a subsidiary of what was then a fledgling operation, TELA – The Web Organisation. Coincidentally, the newspaper with the missing microfiche of the editions published around the time Sophia reappeared, the *Yidisher Kuryer,* was owned briefly by TELA from 1984 through 1987.'

'That's Horwitz's company?'

'I said Sonny was tenacious. He says it was a convoluted path back through various offshore dummy companies, but the ultimate holding company turns out to be the Four Realms Foundation, the charitable investment bank headed up by Stefan Horwitz.'

'Is he suggesting there is some relationship between TELA and the disappearance and reappearance of the young Sophia?'

'As I told you,' White replied, 'he didn't want to tell me what else he had discovered until it could be verified with some further research. It's unlike Sonny, but he was really circumspect about saying anything else. I got the impression he's concerned about personal safety. He told me he's got a young wife and two infant kids to think about these days. His days of bravado investigations are now tempered by common sense. I've never heard him talk like that. I don't know whether someone has put the frighteners on him.'

'For God's sake.' Broadhurst sounded concerned. 'Tell him to back off. It's not worth it. This business has already resulted in one death, two, possibly, almost three if you count my near miss. All I was after, originally, was some background data on Sophia. I have no interest in stirring up a hornet's nest when we are unable to calculate the risks we are taking.'

331

'I'll pass on the message, but he's like a dog with a bone. His teeth may not be so sharp and he may look around more often to see who's lurking behind and take his time, but you can bet he won't stop until all the marrow has been sucked out. And don't forget, there's a hell of a story for him in this, especially if he can rely on your contribution.'

Broadhurst pressed his colleague to relay whatever Sonny discovered as soon as he had it. He thanked White for his help. 'I've got a nasty feeling there is still some way to go before this human tragedy plays out,' he said.

THIRTY-EIGHT
GARE DU NORD, PARIS
December 2018

Marchal was certain he was being tailed. The doors on the metro train on Line 4 north were about to close as he made out to be searching for something by patting the pockets of his clothes. At the last moment, he boarded the train, conscious out of the corner of his eye of the man in the dark bomber jacket two carriages along mirroring his action.

Good. He could relax. It would not be in vain. Seven stops from Châtelet to the Gare du Nord and just after the morning rush hour, plenty of seats. As anticipated, the man in the bomber jacket followed him at a discreet distance onto the station concourse. His was the eleven o'clock regional service to Amsterdam, scheduled arrival time just after five. He could have taken the high speed Thalys service and saved almost half his journey time, but he was in no hurry and it would be fun to keep his tail guessing.

At Brussels, he changed onto the Antwerp service and, there, onto the Rotterdam link. At precisely four fifteen he boarded the final leg to Amsterdam. The train was crowded and he found a seat alongside a frayed-looking business man with an open collar and loosened tie. The man's briefcase was in the overhead rack. The external document pouch was empty and as he organised his overcoat alongside the case, René slipped his reformatted mobile with volume muted into the bottom of the pouch. He had used a fully charged XL battery to ensure a seventy-two-hour standby life.

As the train pulled into Amsterdam Central, he looked around to establish there were no suspicious eyes on him, reversed the overcoat to the light-brown rainproof side and pulled the baseball cap from the pocket. He was one of the first out of the carriage, through the ticket barrier and onto Stationsplein where he sidled to the front of the taxi queue, apologising in gasping sobs to those in front that he was late for his flight.

Confident he had not been followed off the train, he sat back in the taxi and relaxed. His flight was scheduled to leave in two hours. Three days earlier, he had couriered his suitcase to the hotel in Geneva. A text on his new mobile told him it had arrived safely. He smiled as he caught the driver's eyes glance disinterestedly at him in the rear-view mirror. Somebody was set to spend a fruitless day or two monitoring the signal of a decoy mobile.

THIRTY-NINE
ESTORIL, PORTUGAL
December 2018

The dinner invitation came out of the blue.

Broadhurst had been discharged from hospital four days earlier with an instruction to rest up for a week and to avoid travelling, especially by plane where the possible variations in cabin pressure could have an adverse effect on the medication he was taking and increase the risk of a cerebral aneurysm. An appointment was made for him to complete a series of final tests in mid-December. Even with the all-clear, he was strongly advised to schedule his return to the UK by car in short daily mileage tranches over a week. Avoid stress at all costs was the stern advice.

After two weeks of convalescence, there was one thing to do that weighed heavily on him. He had taken the coach service to the northern town of Chaves and the cemetery where Petra had been buried. It was bitterly cold with a biting wind and the temperature just hovering above freezing. He called on her mother and stepfather, humble people, busy trying to eke a living out of a little restaurant on the edge of town. He explained how Petra had been helping him as a translator for an assignment he was working on and how distressed he was about the assault and robbery which had claimed her life so tragically. They said little, asking no questions, barely acknowledging his attempt at a eulogy. He guessed, like him, they had regrets, their own cross to bear. Naturally enough, Petra's mother knew something of her daughter's lifestyle, and the way she looked at him clearly questioned his motives for being there. Even so, both she and her husband expressed their gratitude for the thousand euros he left with them, the fee he said he had agreed to pay for her services. He didn't bother to mention that through the undertakers he had arranged for a polished granite ledger cover and headstone for the grave.

The visit hadn't been the cathartic experience he might have expected. As he sat on the coach back to Lisbon, his anguish was greater than ever.

The invitation from Danata advised that a car would pick him up at seven. He reluctantly accepted he could do with a distraction, something to stop the constant round of recriminations and regrets that triggered his depression.

Danata greeted him at the door to the villa. She gave him the full 'you poor man' sympathetic treatment. From anybody else, Broadhurst would have seen the concern as genuine. In Danata's case, he couldn't tell whether she was for real or a damn good actor, projecting a façade to hide an involvement in what had taken place. Initially, he was prepared to give her the benefit of the doubt.

Josef was already seated at a circular dining table in a conservatory leading onto a manicured lawn. His lips spread into a smile as he greeted his guest. 'Good to hear you are on the road to recovery, Mr Broadhurst.' The sound was the hiss of the small pump as saline solution was sprayed into his eyes behind the dark glasses. 'You should know at the outset, as much as we are interested in the content of Kirchner's letter, Danata and I had absolutely nothing to do with the pointless death of the young lady and the attack upon yourself. However anxious I was to achieve an objective, I would never resort to such gratuitous violence.' Liquid fed onto his cheek as if he were crying. 'I hope you accept my affirmation.'

Before Broadhurst could answer, Danata appeared with a bottle of chilled *vinho verde* and three glasses. 'Thank God, that's all over,' she said. 'I suggest we raise our glasses to the Banco do Carmo and look forward to an end to this drama. The sooner they get to open the unclaimed safe-deposit boxes, the better for all concerned.'

'Will you return for that?' Broadhurst asked.

'Of course. I've set a few days aside at the end of January.' She gave him a sympathetic smile. 'Apart from your desperately awful incident, the rest of the appointments proceeded without too many disputes. There was a tantrum over a pair of silver and enamel medals struck from dies prepared by the renaissance artist Francesco Faria, which turned out to have been looted during the war from a museum in Bologna, and a tussle over a Georgian set of pink topaz jewellery, supposedly once the property of Maria Isabella of Spain. Beyond that, a dozen or so objections, but little of importance. Gratefully, tomorrow we head off to Lugano and I can't wait to get back.'

Broadhurst looked over her shoulder towards the hallway. 'No bodyguard any more?'

Danata looked askance. 'Who?'

'He means Elliott,' her father said. 'No, he was called away on some assignment. Mossad business, I imagine. It's just father and daughter, the way I like it.'

A maid appeared carrying a tray of chicken salad, baked potatoes and zucchini tempura. Broadhurst relished the change from hospital and hotel fare, and accepted a second helping of both the food and the free-flowing wine.

'May I ask an indelicate question?'

Danata raised her eyebrows and stifled a smile. 'With your background,' she said, 'do you know how to?'

'Believe me, at times royal behaviour can be very indelicate.' He looked over at the old man. 'When did you lose your wife?'

Josef cleared his throat. 'It will be seventeen years next spring. Safira was an artist, a sculptor in metal of no mean talent. She had commissions that took her around the world. That was our downfall. She caught meningococcal disease from a carrier who had returned from the Haj in Saudi Arabia to Holland and had commissioned a sculpture to evidence his devotion. We thought Safira was on the road to recovery, although she was more lethargic, spending far more time in her studio at home, avoiding the socialising she had once loved so much. In 2002, she developed sepsis and within two months had died. God bless Danata, who cared for her with such commitment during those last months.'

'Why do you ask?' Danata queried.

'No ulterior motive. When I first heard it, the name rang a bell. I was just curious.'

'What about you, sir? Never married?' Josef asked.

Broadhurst smiled. 'Once. Briefly. She said I was married to the regiment and could not support two wives. I regret she was right. I've never contemplated remarrying; not seriously, anyway.'

'You travelled to the Algarve, I understand. I can only assume your trip was connected to locating my sister?'

'My clients asked me if I would be of whatever help I could to you.'

'Did they really? I am amazed. Their charitable foundation might well be altruistic, but I've never known the Horwitzes to be particularly sympathetic, especially when you consider they were born into the Jewish faith.' He hesitated. 'Although, I suppose it's right to say they have never followed the faith – not demonstrably, anyway – and they have certainly shunned my activities.'

'Are you saying Horwitz did not approve of your work?'

'Our paths have crossed from time to time. He does the American administration's bidding and sometimes our objectives don't marry, especially if US interests might be prejudiced.'

'Thirty pieces of silver?'

'Something like that, though far more subtle. I don't want to speak too unkindly. They do give a great deal to many charitable causes.'

Danata moved to fill Broadhurst's glass a third time, but he covered it with his hand. 'Medics told me two glasses of wine is the limit until the wound heals properly.'

She moved to refill her own. 'They didn't tell you how big the glass should be though, did they?'

'Isn't that where the unspoken communication between people comes into play?

'Depends whether you're a self-deluding alcoholic or not.'

They both laughed. Josef would have joined in had he not started a coughing fit, which sent Danata into nursemaid mode. He waved her away as the cough subsided and he regained his composure. 'Do you know where my sister is?' he asked.

'Getting closer. My partner is on the case. Tell me, has anybody tried to sell you Kirchner's letter?'

Josef shook his head. 'Kirchner doesn't interest me. He will be long dead by now.'

'I believe that to be the case,' Broadhurst said. 'Circa 1989.'

The old man did not react. 'Proof is always essential,' he said, 'but I have to admit the time has passed when I'd already be out of this chair and shaking you bodily to make you give me details. As I have said repeatedly, the letter is only of interest if it gives a clue to Rita's whereabouts. If you are as close as you say, even that loses its relevance, provided you are prepared to tell me where she is when you do find her.'

'All I can promise is I will ask her and, if necessary, try to convince her to meet you and her niece.' He watched Danata react, her body stiffen. 'I will advise you accordingly.'

Danata shook her head. 'I want more than that.' Josef grunted a query at the remark. 'Once you reveal her identity, she will be in danger.' She looked over at Broadhurst's expressionless face. 'If whoever is prepared to kill you and the girl to find out what Kirchner had to say, they must be concerned he shared his secrets with her. I want you to bring her to our house in Ticino. The property is alarmed and protected against intrusion. There were times when death threats against Josef were almost daily occurrences. Nazi sympathisers were lining up for years to witness his death. We live in a virtual fortress.'

'I see the logic, but I would point out we have not located Josef's sister yet. She could have passed away, and even if we do locate her, my partner and I will be bound by her wishes.'

'When you find her, please convince her,' Danata pleaded. 'We need to keep her safe.'

Broadhurst weighed up whether he should reveal what else he knew. It would be interesting to get their reactions. 'There is one more thing,' he said. 'Somebody is joining me when and if we do locate Rita to fulfil a maternity test. He claims to be your sister's biological son, your nephew, and Danata' – he turned to face her – 'your cousin.'

Josef's mouth opened, but no words were uttered. The silence was shattered by Danata. 'He's a fraud,' she shouted. 'He must be. Rita was sterilised in the camp. She couldn't have children.' Her eyes flickered between the two men. She had overstepped the mark. She reached with one hand, straining for a chair to sit down.

'What do you mean?' Josef asked, leaning back as if to distance himself from her. 'How could you know if she was sterilised or not? We know nothing about her life. There is no record.' The words tailed off as he wrestled with the outburst.

Dig yourself out of this one, Broadhurst thought.

And she did. It was as convincing as could be, given the circumstances. 'I didn't mean to be categorical,' she stammered, desperately trying to regain her composure. 'Of course, I don't exactly know, but it was commonplace in the camps to sterilise women who would be sent off to the German whorehouses. Rita ended up as the concubine of an SS officer. She must have been sterilised.' She looked around, craving acceptance. 'That's all I meant,' she added lamely.

FORTY
THE FOUR REALMS FOUNDATION OFFICES, LONDON
December 2018

'I'll take the call in my office,' Stefan said to the secretary. 'Steady my elbow, will you?' With a walking stick in one hand and the woman at his side, he shuffled along the carpeted corridor to the room facing him at the end. He returned her smile. 'Don't get old,' he said. 'For the fortunate, the mind ages gracefully along with the body. For those less blessed, the indignity is that at a certain point in time, your persona freezes, at twenty or thirty, forty, whenever, and then has to witness your physical descent into helplessness. It's very challenging.

'It's called retirement,' the middle-aged secretary replied curtly. 'Time to allow the mind to savour what the body cannot. With respect, something you should do.'

'Have I told you you're fired?' he said.

'Every day for the last twenty years. One day I'll take you up on it.'

'Don't you dare,' he said, allowing himself to fall backwards into the leather padded chair. 'Who did you say is on the line?'

'Cris Hopper from the White House.'

'Sounds like an insect. Put him through.'

He flexed his fingers and picked up the receiver from the retro handset on the desk. 'Mr Hopper. Good of you to call. How may I help you?'

'Secretary Chandler suggested you would be able to assist in a delicate matter concerning the President.' The voice was a rich golden brown with an accent that said Deep South and slavery. 'I'm in Paris. If necessary, I could hop on a plane to London to touch base.'

'Touch what? Oh, yes. Base. Is it not something we can deal with over the phone? I was fully briefed by Secretary Chandler on the circumstances. Coincidentally, it was already a subject of interest to me before our paths collided. I have people involved.'

'Me too. I have been in touch with our asset on the ground.'

'Your what? "Asset on the ground"? You mean a person?'

341

'Yes.'

'Forgive me. An asset to me is something inanimate, tangible or otherwise, that sits on a balance sheet, either fixed or current. The popular jargon sometimes defeats me. Secretary Chandler told me the statement prepared by Kirchner is in safe hands, is that not so?'

'The original, yes. I need to establish if copies exist and, if so, where. Any leaks involving the general's alleged wartime activities could prove highly embarrassing for my boss.'

'He can't be held responsible for his father's acts. We would all be damned, wouldn't we?'

'We don't all go around extolling our father's virtues at every opportunity, either. We are confident if the information leaked, the poll figures would drop ten points on day one and the media storm would keep the issue alive until polling day. We would be sacrificing a right-wing Republican for a lefty Democrat who wants to open the immigration floodgates. We must do everything possible to stop it.'

'As much as I sympathise with the viewpoint, my interest is in locating an individual who might well be able to corroborate Kirchner's account of events. At this point, our interests are wholly compatible, so what would you require of me?'

'To put it bluntly, I need to ensure no copies of Kirchner's exposé exist and to guarantee any other source could be closed down. Whatever is necessary to achieve these aims will be undertaken. I need an operative with the relevant skills.'

'Forgive me, but didn't you say you had an asset, as you call it?

'More a blunt instrument. What may be needed is the surgical ability to extract information. A professional would be desirable.'

'I do have somebody who has been off on a wild goose chase these last two days. I'll put him in touch with you. He knows what he is doing ... most of the time.'

'Can you get him to meet me in Geneva?' He gave the name of the hotel. 'Tell him to ask for Mr Blackwood.'

The only sound on the line was Stefan's heavy breathing. 'Why Geneva?' he asked.

'I have it on good authority your Mr Broadhurst is narrowing in on the location of Rita Krakowski. When he finds her, she is expected to be transferred to Josef's lakeside villa south of Lugano in a place called Paradiso.'

'How fitting. You have been busy.'

'I understand you have a sanitation unit to clean up after unfortunate incidents.'

'My good man, how would I expect to know of such things? When our colleague contacts you, ask him to contact TELA in Zurich. They may possibly know what you are talking about. Is that all?'

'Thank you. By the way, Bo sends his regards.'

'How very nice, I'm sure. Mr Hopper?'

'Yes.'

'No loose ends.'

The line went dead.

Stefan looked up at the array of clocks on the wall. In Buenos Aires, it was just after three in the afternoon. He used a private messaging app to support the call encryption to the head of South American human resources. The call was accepted on the second ring. Hearing the background noise of animated conversation and the chink of cutlery, Stefan guessed the woman was at lunch in a busy restaurant. He apologised for the disturbance and waited whilst she moved out of earshot of her table companions.

'More than a little disappointed with your operative's performance so far,' Stefan said. 'Madrid did not go as expected.'

'Partially,' she replied. 'He claims bad intel; or rather, lack of intel.'

'A good operative never allocates blame. If he omits to do something, he gets on and corrects the omission. I understand he's just spent nearly two days being played by a retired policeman. Hardly inspires confidence, does it?'

'We have been watching him. Until recently, his track record was impeccable. I have suggested we let him finish the assignment and then retire him.'

'Be it on your head. He's become a liability. Incompetence incurs retribution at all levels. Understood? We cannot afford any more mistakes.'

There was an echo on the line. Momentarily, her voice came over in disjointed syllables.

'What did you say?' he prompted.

'I take on board what you say. You know the Madrid omission was corrected.'

'Really? That's news to me. When?' There was an uncomfortable edge to his voice.

It was the woman's turn to sound confused. 'The female in the PI's hotel room. Surely you heard about it?'

'That was the same woman? I had no idea. What was her connection to the man?' Uncomfortable had changed to disturbed. 'Was she a plant?'

'Not that I'm aware of, but the incident did not involve one of ours. I suggest you follow it up at your end. Whoever holds the document will have the information.'

'I expect you to perform,' Stefan said in Spanish. 'Whatever has to be done, it would be desirable from all standpoints if everyone connected with this fiasco suffers the same fate as the woman, if you get my meaning?'

'I understand.'

Stefan passed on Hooper's contact name and details of the hotel in Geneva. He ended the call by clicking on the menu option to delete the record.

The woman walked over to where her guests could see her, offered a shrug of the shoulders and made a 'T' symbol with her two index fingers before retreating back to the corridor leading to the toilets. She used the same encryption service to make the call.

Enrico sighed as he saw the coded caller ID on his mobile screen. More aggro, the last thing he needed.

'I have instructions for you,' she said. 'Go to video, please.'

Enrico hesitated. 'A little inconvenient at the moment.'

'Do as I say.'

The image came to life. He had made a point of showing her he was sitting on the toilet. 'Happy now?' he said.

She ignored the sarcasm. She wrote the names of a person and a hotel on a piece of paper with her lipstick baton and focused the camera on the wording. 'Can you read it?'

'Yes.'

'Make contact. He will point you in the direction of the people who have the paperwork you require. You will also have backup.'

'I prefer to work alone.'

Her video feed showed a white expanse of ceiling as paper rustled, followed by the sound of clothes being adjusted. Her next view was of the spout of a soap dispenser accompanied by the noise of running water. 'Are you listening?' she queried.

Eventually, his smiling face filled the screen. 'I said I prefer to work alone.'

'No option. Dissatisfaction with your performance to date has been expressed. Your assignment is in jeopardy. The memory of El Salvador is still fresh in certain minds.'

'We've been all through that,' he said angrily. The image of the human rights lawyer in the cross hairs of his rifle sight flashed in front of his eyes. He had thought the cheap glasses would help, nothing too serious, a correction diopter of merely 1.25. The close detail was certainly sharper. He was sweating, more from the humid heat than the occasion. The sequence was to exhale deeply and relax as he squeezed the trigger, just like he had been taught. The lenses immediately fogged up. He couldn't see a thing. The bullet caught one of the safe-house minders in the side of his neck. All hell broke loose. He was lucky to get away with just a torn ankle.

'I'm using contact lenses these days,' he said, but forgot to add they were still in the original packaging somewhere in his suitcase. He still preferred using glasses for close-up, detailed work. 'I'll find the girl, don't worry. I'll finish this. I've got some leads.'

'Too late. Somebody has dealt with the problem.'

Enrico's brow furrowed, nose pinched between his eyes. 'How come?' he managed to say with obvious amazement. 'You've put somebody else on the assignment? That means ...' The sentence tailed off into silence.

'Hold up. Let's say it was a fortuitous coincidence. There is an extension to your brief. As you see, important interests are now involved in ensuring a satisfactory outcome.'

'This guy's contact details you've given me – he's government?'

'The highest level. At the end of the day, we have no time for finesse. Whoever could be in the know has to be removed.'

'How many are we talking about?'

'Five or six, I guess. Maybe I should organise assistance.'

He moved closer to the mobile so that all she could see was his face. 'I've told you, I work alone.'

'I will make that judgement,' she said, and before he could respond she ended the call.

FORTY-ONE
VEVEY, SWITZERLAND
December 2018

'I take it you have finished reading my story.' She watched intently as he carefully organised the last four pages into a square on the table and focused the camera on his mobile. The shutter clicked.

'What do you propose to do with them?' she asked.

'Haven't decided yet,' Marchal said. 'I'll wait for Chas to arrive. He should be here any minute. We'll probably store them on the cloud for the time being.'

'The cloud. Is that for my benefit?' she asked.

'How come?'

'When I pass away, I shall be able to look for the fluffiest white cloud and consult them. Although, in my case, you would need to make them fireproof and send them downstairs.'

'I don't read it that way. It's not only your version of events which can be called upon to support your claim for justice in the next world.'

'You have somebody who would bear false witness?'

'I've read Kirchner's statement. He says categorically you were tricked into cooperating with him in misleading the parents into agreeing to part with valuables in order to secure the freedom – in inverted commas – of their children. You were blameless.'

'What I imagined; what I knew; what I suspected – these thoughts are jumbled in my head. But blameless? No. He is simply attempting to demonstrate that under a thick and ruthless skin, he had something resembling a conscience.'

'You read his letter?'

'No. I saw it when the small safe-deposit box was opened. I knew he had written something as an insurance policy when he began to suspect Bauer was not totally on his side. Australia, if I remember correctly. Pinho counselled it was wiser for me to have nothing incriminating on my person now I was about to pursue my future under the name of Taube.' The breath rattled in her throat. 'You never did tell me what gave me away and allowed you to find me?'

347

Marchal laughed. 'The clue's in my profession. I'm a detective, remember, and detectives detect.' He saw the flash of impatience cross her eyes. 'All right, I was following a lead Chas gave me. You sent money to a friend on the Algarve.'

'Anna Paula.'

'Yes. The remittance showed the location of the source even though you sent it anonymously. I guessed at your age you would need residential or nursing care and would likely have opted for a location somewhere within a local taxi ride of Thonon-les-Bains. The rest was just legwork and a cooperative taxi firm.'

'I loved Anna Paula. She was taken too soon.'

'How did you know she was ill?'

'I use a lawyer in Brussels with an office on the Algarve. I receive a quarterly report, primarily to monitor Daniel's progress, but it talked of my dear friend's terminal illness. There was always a photograph of my son, sometimes with Anna Paula by his side.'

Marchal watched the BMW come to a halt in one of the visitor's parking spaces. Chas looked older and had lost weight since they last met. The baseball cap was pulled down firmly over one side of his head as he went through a series of stretching movements. His expression was drawn and tired.

'You look as though you have been through – how do you say? – the wringer,' Marchal quipped.

They hugged each other. 'It must be the onset of old age,' Broadhurst said. 'I never used to take death so personally, even when it was somebody in the squadron. Now, I can be thinking of something quite alien and suddenly her face pops into my head. Such a tragic loss.'

It was mid-afternoon before Marchal had brought his partner up to date with the content of both Kirchner's statement and Rita's narrative. She had just awoken from her afternoon nap and was waiting to meet the new arrival.

Broadhurst was pensive. 'Do you think the Americans are somehow involved in this?' he asked. 'Kirchner's confessional could be highly embarrassing for the President. Danata and co were desperate to get their hands on the document, far and beyond its value to the Holocaust organisation.'

'You think her father is implicated?' Marchal asked.

'No. My assessment is his vision is totally blinkered. His objective is exclusively focused on finding his sister. As for the daughter, she knows something she is not telling. What it is, I can't fathom. Maybe there is a US link.' He looked over the papers spread across the table. 'What was in the letter from Wiesel's brother-in-law? I had a glance at it, but it was written in Polish.'

'Dynamite as far as the Kirchner–Wiesel relationship was concerned. Norman Vogel, Sophia's father, confirmed Lew's son, Malik, had never arrived in the States. The photograph Lew's family had received was a fake and the couple photographed outside the building with the Swedish flag were Nazi sympathisers who had since been hanged. There was no evidence Malik had ever left the camp in Germany. It appears Lew had been coerced into handing over a fortune in diamonds for nothing.'

'I can't imagine how desperately Lew must have wanted his revenge. No wonder he hired the private investigators. His intention in luring Kirchner to Lisbon was, without doubt, to recover the diamonds and kill him.'

Marchal nodded. 'If Rita's recollection is sound, Kirchner managed to turn the tables and kill Wiesel along with the bank's custodian, an unfortunate witness to murder.'

'Did Vogel say anything else in the letter?'

'Only that he suspected his family were being watched. He didn't know by whom, but there were some sinister forces at work in the States and he was seriously thinking of moving the family to the Midwest.'

Broadhurst stood back as Marchal made the introductions. Rita had decided to remain in bed. She had been coughing more than normal today, so Matron had been summoned and had suggested that with all the excitement of so many new visitors, she needed to rest.

Rita tut-tutted her disdain at the suggestion as the door closed behind the woman. 'Now, who is this person?' she asked Marchal.

Broadhurst dutifully stepped forward to be met by a studied head-to-toe appraisal.

'Good to meet you,' he said. 'I've heard a great deal about you.'

She continued her examination for several seconds before acknowledging his remark. 'I expected you to be younger, fitter, a more athletic man; someone who could compliment René's detective skills with some brawn. Clearly, I misunderstood the relationship.'

'I must have other talents if my physical appearance disappoints.'

She winced at the remark.

'Are you all right?' Marchal sounded concerned.

'"Disappoints" is the wrong word. The opposite would be "pleases". You could do neither, as far as I am concerned. It was a simple observation, not intended to offend.'

Broadhurst smiled. 'No offence taken. Whilst René has been with you, I have been in Lisbon at the Banco do Carmo. I understand you refer to a visit to the bank in your memoir?'

She feigned disinterest in the remark, but he could tell he had her attention. 'A bittersweet experience as far as you were concerned. I had the opportunity to meet your brother, Josef, and his daughter, your niece. Ill health and old age have forced him into retirement, but he still has one ambition in life.'

'To see me brought to justice for the crimes of which I am accused.'

'You are wrong. His only desire is to meet you again before it's too late, nothing more. I have his word.'

She raised her eyes to meet his. 'Before it's too late, you say. Let me tell you, young man, it was too late seventy-odd years ago when I opted to sacrifice an honourable death for a subservient and undistinguished life.' Her voice was quivering. 'What purpose would it serve? I have already explained how I feel about it to René. He understands me.'

Broadhurst glanced around at his partner, who was standing at the foot of the bed.

'If lending a sympathetic ear and saying nothing constitutes understanding, then I plead guilty,' Marchal said. 'If I remember correctly, I said I had read nothing which could brand you as a collaborator, much less a traitor. Above all, I believe, as you do, Rita, if I may call you that, it is too late to tell somebody how you feel after they have gone. I know this from personal experience.'

'You do,' she said, her head bowed as if contemplating her two clenched fists on the bedsheet. They were trembling, making a scratching sound on the starched surface.

Broadhurst sensed her resistance was wavering. 'Whatever Josef has been led to believe as to what you did or became, the only thing he actually knows for certain is that in giving him the chance to save his life, you sacrificed your opportunity to escape and, ultimately, your freedom to live a normal life. He recognises that.'

'He does?'

'He as much as told me so.' Broadhurst glanced at Marchal, his expression pleading forgiveness for the white lie.

She closed her eyes. 'I need to think. Would he come here?'

Broadhurst shook his head. 'We think it's too dangerous. His presence here might alert others. What you remember could get you killed. Josef and your niece, Danata, have a house on Lake Lugano. He has asked if you would visit him there. It is a more secure location. He says you can stay for as long as you want. He lives in a suburb called Paradiso.'

'I know,' she said. 'Can you leave me now? I would like to think.'

The two men were discussing the route they would take to Lugano by car, a circuitous journey covering over twice the straight-line distance, either north-east via Bern or south into Italy; either way, a minimum of four hours travel time to reach their destination. Marchal had just indicated a preference for the Bern route when Broadhurst's mobile sounded.

'Unknown caller,' he said, walking to an area out of earshot of the care home staff. As he returned the mobile to his jacket pocket, he motioned his partner over. 'That was somebody who described himself as "attached to the US government Washington corps", though he added he was here in a private capacity. He wants to meet us urgently.'

'I can guess why,' Marchal said. 'Who is it?'

'A guy named Cristo Hopper or, as you might expect from an American keen to make friends, "Call me Cris – no 'h'." He claims to be aligned with the Secretary of State, whatever that's supposed to mean. He's in Geneva, obviously with intel as to our movements. Do you want to join me?'

'When's the meeting?'

'I said we could make it this evening. I'd let him know the time.'

Marchal fell silent, glancing back towards the entrance to the nursing home. 'You go. I promised I wouldn't leave her side until it was safe to do so. If she's agreeable, I will make plans to set off with her in one of these' – he pointed at the three quasi-ambulance-style transit people carriers in the car park – 'tomorrow morning and meet up with you in Lugano.' If you're in Geneva tonight, your best bet is to take the Italian route and arrive from the south.' He looked at the BMW. 'Anyway, we would never get her comfortably into that for a four-hour drive.'

'I understand,' Broadhurst said. 'It makes sense, but I don't relish the fact circumstances contrive to keep you on the sideline of this assignment.'

'Believe me, I don't feel that way at all. In fact, I think I might well be right in the eye of this particular storm.'

As he crossed the square in Geneva's Old Town, the cafés and restaurants were full of revellers on pre-Christmas dinner dates, a mix of groups from tables of four to large office party gatherings. Terraces were boxed in against the chilled, dry night air by clear plastic awnings, within which lamp post-style gas heaters pumped warmth around the enclosed space. An invitation to calamity, Broadhurst thought, as he watched someone back a chair into the base of a heater.

He climbed the flight of stairs in front of the mottled grey stone façade of the Hotel Les Armures and made his way to the adjacent café, which the plaque on the wall described as 'Geneva's oldest coffeehouse'. The athletic-looking man rose to greet him as he entered the bustling interior, hand extended. 'Glad you could make it, Chas. Can I call you that? I'm Cris.'

Broadhurst unbuttoned his overcoat. Compared to the temperature on the street, the heat inside made him feel nauseous. 'Can I help you with that?' Hopper asked, taking the coat and folding it carefully over his arm. 'I took the opportunity of booking a table downstairs in the Carnotzet. I understand it means wine cellar, but they serve a wonderful cheese fondue, if you're into that sort of thing. I'm an aficionado.' He led the way.

Despite its claustrophobic feel and rustic appearance, the temperature was pleasant and the tables well-spaced, the conversations between the guests muted. Hopper walked towards a corner table. 'I think you've met Elliott Karmi,' he said, as the man seated at the table rose to greet him.

'I didn't realise this was a joint US–Israeli initiative,' he said, handing his overcoat to a waiter. He offered his hand to Elliott who grasped it firmly. Broadhurst looked down at the bronzed hand and the band of white flesh on his finger where a ring had been.

'We maintain a close relationship, Chas,' the American said. 'Sometimes the US and Israel have a mutual interest in a particular policy objective. Now, let's get right down to the important business. What do you guys fancy to eat? I've already made my choice. I'm following in the footsteps of three famous Americans, the presidents who have already stayed in this wonderful hotel.'

The conversation was forced into an uncomfortable bout of trivia, led masterfully by Hopper who refused to be sidetracked from topics comparing menu or wine list selections to extolling the glories of the hotel and Geneva's tourist attractions.

Broadhurst turned to the Israeli. 'Does Josef know you are here?'

'Why should he?' Elliott sounded dismissive. 'His objective is personal, to locate his sister; mine has a strategic political aim, vitally important. The short answer is "no". I left them in Lugano this morning.'

'And does your strategic political aim involve having someone break into my hotel apartment and murdering whoever happened to be in there?' Broadhurst sensed his body tense as did the other man's.

'Guys. Please.' Hopper reached out, a hand on each of their arms. 'Let's hold back on the accusations and retaliations.' He spoke to Broadhurst. 'I can assure you, neither the US nor Israeli authorities had any part in the attack in your hotel room and the unfortunate death of the young lady. I give you my word we are not implicated in the tragedy.' A waitress with the wine hovered at his shoulder. 'Let's leave the where and when and concentrate on the here and now.' He acknowledged to the waitress to pour the wine, and raised his glass.

Broadhurst scraped back his chair and made to get up. 'I didn't come here on a blind date and I have no appetite to humour you and play charades while we pretend to be old friends, when I really would prefer to wring both your fucking necks for being involved in something that gets a totally innocent person killed and intends I suffer the same fate.' His raised voice had started to turn heads in the room.

The hand that had never left his arm applied a pressure stronger than he could have imagined. 'Sit down, please,' Hopper insisted. 'God, you Brits are so touchy. Don't be so thin-skinned, Chas. You walked into this assignment with both eyes open. You must have realised it was not going to be a straightforward mailman's role. I'm asking you to sit back down, listen to what we have to say, enjoy your meal and a glass of wine like a civilised person, and we can all go to our chosen destinations.'

They ate their meals in a half silence, punctuated by Hopper's seemingly endless banter and apparent indifference to the fact that both his guests were reacting to his banal questions with stone-faced, one-word answers wherever possible.

Coffee was served. 'Okay,' Broadhurst said. 'I've suffered the ritual at your request. Can we now get down to what you invited me here to discuss?' He smiled in response to Elliott's ice-cold stare.

'My niece studies in England, Chas,' Hopper said. 'She has a place at Cambridge. She reckons you English are lousy lovemakers; no foreplay, straight in for the kill. Don't you enjoy socialising, getting to know people, understanding what makes them tick? It must be the American way.'

'I suggest you tell your niece she's mixing with the wrong people. Socialising is one thing; hypocrisy is something else.'

Hopper reacted as if he had just reached a conclusion, straightening his back and placing the palms of his hands on the table. 'We have a right-wing, Republican president in the US, an honest man, keen to preserve the integrity and reputation of the fifty-two states. He is coming up for re-election next fall and patriots want this strong man with his no-nonsense policies to carry on his programme for another four years. This is where I'm coming from.'

'I'm listening,' Broadhurst said.

'As far as foreign policy is concerned, he has ruffled a few feathers, but his unequivocal support for Israel has ensured a stabilising force in a notoriously volatile area of the world.' Hopper proffered a smile to Elliott. 'In my opinion and in that of most free-thinking Americans and Israelis, should President Williams lose in November, the alternative is an ultra-left-wing liberal with flower power credentials, a proponent of unchecked immigration, international appeasement and Daffy Duck domestic policies; in short, a disaster.'

He indicated to the waitress to bring another coffee.

'As you know, the polls are set fair at the moment with a healthy lead projected for our man, but with social media, the popular press and 24/7 news coverage, attitudes can change in the blink of an eye, especially when we enter the last few months of campaigning and the real mudslinging starts. That is where I need your cooperation, Chas.'

'How so? I have no particular interest in domestic American politics, nor can I or would I choose to try and influence them.'

'That's good to hear. The problem is the reputation of the President's late father. There are no skeletons in the President's cupboard, merely a penchant to constantly extol the virtues and wartime achievements of his father, the general. If documents or copies of documents exist which allege the old man was involved in facilitating the escape to America of the family of a German doctor with a heinous reputation and diverting funds captured from the enemy to facilitate the escape of high-level Nazis, well …'

'It could destabilise everything,' Elliott interrupted.

'Possibly.' Hopper moved his head from side to side. 'Even though the source could be discredited as a deceased fugitive war criminal, at best it could prove embarrassing, and at worst, derail the campaign.'

'So, what do you expect me to do?'

'Chas, is it not apparent? You and you alone know if copies were made; if so, where they are and how many. For all I know, at this very moment details could be winging their way around the world on Twitter, sitting in the inbox of influential newspapers or, as I would hope, contained by you either in digital or paper form somewhere safe. If the former, we'll finish up dinner and my tactics will change to react accordingly. If the latter, we can carry on talking.'

Elliott coughed. 'I think it's also relevant to point out Kirchner's statement is not your property. You held it in trust for the safe-deposit holder, as you do, indeed, for any copies you made in direct contradiction to your instructions.'

'I've thought about that,' Broadhurst replied. 'The legal right to the document is certainly not the heirs to Lew Wiesel, irrespective of the fact of where it was discovered. If anybody, it belongs to Kirchner's only legitimate heir, his common-law wife who, by the way, is in a position to corroborate or otherwise the content of the document.'

There was a low groan from Hopper as he pushed his chair back to stretch his legs. 'So now you're telling me I don't only have to worry about the work of a deceased fugitive war criminal, but a living fugitive from justice as well? Saints alive.'

'Perhaps neither. There is a scanned copy on two mobiles and a hard copy used for translation. They are all within my control.'

Elliott leaned forward. 'You've located Rita Krakowski?'

Broadhurst nodded. 'Tomorrow, I'll explain the situation to her and your request. I can see that the current president should not be judged by the sins of the father, but the ultimate decision is up to her. If she agrees, I will undertake to destroy the sections of the statement which deal with the general, although there are other aspects within the document which still interest me. As soon as they are put to bed, I will destroy everything. Does that satisfy you?'

'As encouraging as that sounds,' Hopper said, 'you have made the whole thing suddenly sound far more intriguing than I imagined. Any clues?'

'Only that it's nothing that could seriously influence your campaign.'

Elliott shot the American a glance. 'What do you propose to do if the old lady refuses?'

Broadhurst shrugged. 'Whatever she deems appropriate. I can't see why she would want to put anything Kirchner said into the public domain, can you?'

356

Hopper called for the check. 'I'll take that at face value, Chas. Two things I ask of you. Whatever her decision, you agree to call me before any action is taken. Irrespective of the outcome, if common sense and fairness prevail, it needs to be kept a matter between us. Also, the US administration would be unhappy if a copy remained in existence for any length of time.'

A heavily pregnant woman was on the CNN news roundup complaining about the lack of Medicare for her family as Hopper muted the TV volume and rose to pull the weighty velvet curtains together across the bay window. It was the same suite Clinton had used when he stayed, so the receptionist had assured him. Not a bad achievement for a black boy who grew up in a wooden shack in the backwoods of Alabama with an alcoholic father and a mother who cleaned house for the folk in Madison.

He was revelling in this unaccustomed bout of self-gratification when the secure call came through. As he heard the familiar drawl, he supressed the urge to say to Bo right away, 'Hey man, guess where I'm sleeping tonight?' Instead, he said, 'Everything is going to plan. The information is secure.'

'How many?' Bo asked

'Five.'

'Jesus! That will create a shitstorm. Is it really necessary?'

'It's Stefan's call. He firmly believes we can never be confident something will come out of the woodwork unless action is taken. You gotta take his point of view seriously if you recognise he's talking about two people of his own faith with stellar reputations. I'd be happy to take the risk. My inclination is to believe the Brit. He's one of the honour-bound, "my word is my bond" generation, but I guess he can't speak for the others.'

'How is it going to be presented?'

'I expect Stefan has already written the draft copy; spurned lover with mentally unstable history, that sort of thing.'

'Make sure you're well away from the action. We can't let the US appear to be mixed up in this. What about the original? When do you get your hands on that?'

'It was entrusted to a consultant, some titled dame working for Stefan who was staying in the hotel. It must be in London by now. I'll collect it on my way back through to DC.'

There was a pause on the end of the line. Finally, Bo spoke. 'One thing I can't quite get a handle on with all this, is trying to grasp why Horwitz appears so committed to the project. I get the Israel angle and wanting to preserve a presidency committed to maintaining a strong ally in the area, but there's a voice in my head telling me he's in this for something else. He never expected the exposé by the Nazi guy to be in the safe-deposit box, so what was he expecting? I don't know.'

'Do we care?'

'Maybe not, but it's always elucidating to understand the other guy's motivation.'

'I can do some digging.'

'Best to keep your own counsel and get yourself a stone-cast alibi. Organise a briefing with the ambassador in London. Say you're instructed by me to prepare a report on the UK economy, now there's no more EU.'

'Anything else?'

'Yes. Put on a sad face when the news breaks!'

FORTY-TWO
PARADISO, LUGANO, SWITZERLAND
December 2018

'This must be it,' Broadhurst said to himself as he pulled the BMW into the entrance to the solid double gates in front of the property. The motion-activated camera moved to focus on the passenger seat and then turned fractionally to bring the driver into view. He waited for a voice to ask him who he was or a motor spring to life and the gate begin to open.

Nothing happened.

There was no buzzer or bell to ring to summon the attention of someone inside. The movement of the camera must activate some way of alerting the residents to the presence of a visitor. He walked ten metres in each direction, but a high wall with iron stanchions and strands of razor wire at the top restricted any view of the interior of the property. Two further cameras scanned the length of the perimeter. If they were at home, somebody must know he was there.

Beyond the end of the wall, he could make out the rays of the late afternoon sun dancing on the waves of the lake and, in the distance, following the curve of the bay, a group of low-rise buildings within Lugano city limits.

As he closed the driver's door, his business mobile blurted the message alert from inside the glove compartment. The screen identified an anticipated mail from Duncan White. He would open the message and attachment later. He drummed his fingers impatiently on the steering wheel.

He had spoken with White the previous evening, the last of three calls he had made as he settled into his space capsule of a room in the budget hotel in Annemasse, just east of Geneva on the highway through to Chamonix and Italy. He had surveyed the chipboard furnishings, ruefully concluding that Clinton had certainly never stayed in this establishment; but then again, Broadhurst wasn't paying north of five hundred euros a night for the privilege. He had even seen some change out of a fifty-euro note.

His first call was to Marchal. The old lady had relented and reluctantly agreed to tackle the four-hour drive to meet her brother. They would set off first thing in the morning. She insisted Marchal be at her side at all times, even when the face-to-face confrontation took place, and that he would promise to stay with her until they agreed he could leave or she returned to the home in Vevey. Marchal had accepted the open-ended ultimatum with reluctance once he realised there was no alternative. A driver would be provided and they intended to make several stops en route to make the journey more bearable for her. It was left for Broadhurst to text Danata and advise her and Josef to expect his sister around late afternoon. Broadhurst would time his arrival to more or less coincide with Marchal.

Next, came a duty call to the Portuguese mobile. He didn't really expect Daniel to be in a position to react to the information that the woman he knew as Angela Taube was in a residential nursing home in Vevey, Switzerland. The man lived on a salary barely above the minimum wage in a decidedly less affluent member state of the EU and would have little opportunity for discretionary expenditure on travel and subsistence in one of the most expensive countries in Europe. As Broadhurst expected, Daniel's reaction was low-key as he took down the details. He thanked Broadhurst and promised to be in touch.

Duncan White had an excited edge to his voice. Sonny was being secretive, he said, but reckoned something had come up which could open a real can of worms. He needed to arrange a Zoom video link when the three of them could talk. Until then, he was saying little. Sonny admitted he was concerned about safety, more for his family than for himself. He had the uneasy feeling he was under surveillance and could not work out whether it was genuine or just paranoia.

There was one thing he could share at this time. Trawling the media, his persistence had paid off with the discovery of a file photograph stored by the local Holland, Michigan daily, the *Sentinel*. It was of a demure-looking Sophia Vogel saying goodbye to the local police chief on the day she left for Buffalo in 1946. White would email the photograph as soon as Sonny had got hold of a copy. This must be the attachment that had just arrived on his work mobile.

Broadhurst was about to accept that nobody was at home, when the motor on the gate hummed into action. The driveway was no longer than fifty metres before it opened out into a courtyard with a turning circle around a small circular flower bed with a life-size metal sculpture in the

360

middle. The interwoven strands of caramel and chestnut brown metal formed the image of a young girl in distress, hands with half-metre long, copper-coloured pointed fingers stretching skywards as if pleading for relief. Broadhurst found the image deeply disturbing yet strangely compelling.

The hacienda had a meandering single-storey frontage with an extended flat roof over a portico decorated with a series of arches inset with casual furniture either side of a ranch-style front door. The brickwork was painted a light mustard colour with a relief in white and the windows were in leaded glass protected by decorative antique cast-iron grills which Broadhurst assumed were by the same artist who had fashioned the sculpture.

Broadhurst parked the BMW alongside a silver Mercedes Estate with a disabled badge parking timer nestled against the windscreen.

Elliott stood hovering at the front door, appearing to check if a second vehicle was about to follow the BMW into the property.

'You beat me to it,' Broadhurst said.

'After speaking with Dana, I came back in a hurry last night. By ten, most of the Swiss are in bed. The roads were almost deserted.'

'Quite a place,' Broadhurst said, looking around. 'I wouldn't mind retiring to somewhere like this.' He pointed to one end of the building where the single storey became two and the tiled roof was scalloped to imitate a Chinese-style effect. 'You must get a stunning view of the lake from up there,' he suggested. 'Quite something.'

Apparently satisfied no one else was about to arrive, Elliott motioned him to walk to the end of the building and a pathway leading alongside the house to the rear. 'There's a spectacular view of the lake from every aspect,' he said as they emerged onto a neatly trimmed lawn which ran down to a jetty where a small fishing boat with an outboard motor and roofed centre console was moored.

Broadhurst could not fault the comment. The portico design with arches also featured along the length of the rear of the building, but the interior rooms were defined from the portico by three sets of concertina glass doors designed to integrate inside and outside during the summer months. The lawn extended for fifty metres down to the lake, giving way at the perimeters of the property to bushes and fruit trees which partially hid the mesh metal fence with more razor wire and close-circuit cameras from view. A swimming pool with a paved surround, shower and changing facilities occupied the area at the far end of the building, with a circular metal staircase leading up to a sunbathing terrace on the flat roof.

Elliott pushed one of the concertina doors open just enough for them to enter, closing it as Broadhurst stepped into the lounge. He rubbed his hands, reacting instinctively to the gentle heat coming from the gas-fuelled log fire in the centre of the room. There were two sets of sofas and armchairs, one set closer to a wall-mounted large-screen TV, the other in a more private corner alongside an extensive bookcase and antique scroll writing desk. Open newspapers and magazines were scattered across the furniture. In the far corner, Broadhurst noted a staircase with a guide rail for a stairlift bolted to the wall, obviously installed to assist Josef to get to the bedroom area on the upper floor. It appeared that the various coffee and side tables, along with any flat surface, had a small bronze or metal decoration as its centrepiece.

'Quite a place,' Broadhurst repeated. 'I didn't realise catching Nazi war criminals paid so well.'

Elliott managed a laugh. 'It doesn't. It was Safira, his late wife, who had the money. She was at the top of her game, with creations worth a fortune. Believe me, I could retire and live in luxury for the rest of my life just by selling what you see around you.'

'Tempting,' Broadhurst joked. 'Especially as the owners are not in the room at the moment.'

'They had to go out. They shouldn't be too long. When can we expect your partner and Rita Krakowski?'

'Any time now, I would guess. I'm surprised they didn't arrive before me. I imagine she's very nervous about meeting her brother after a lifetime's separation.'

'Josef certainly is, I know that.'

Elliott led the way as they walked from room to room, the contemporary-style dining room – undoubtedly Danata's influence – the office with the two partners' desks, the dark oak-stained bookcase and the battered three drawer filing cabinet – undoubtedly Josef's influence – when the discreet light in the corner recess began to flash on and off. The muted tinkle of wind chimes briefly sounded, followed by the screen of a monitor on one of the two desks coming to life with an image from the camera at the front gate. A transit with the logo of the nursing home was waiting to enter.

The old lady looked remarkably healthy, Broadhurst thought, as the hydraulic tail lift lowered her wheelchair to the gravel. For the first time her cheeks were pink, eyes vibrant, and what little hair she had, positioned strategically to maximum effect. She was looking around urgently until Broadhurst advised her brother was not at home.

'Not very considerate of him, is it?' she asked no one in particular. 'What does he intend to do, make some grand entrance like Julius Caesar? Who are you?' She directed the question at Elliott.

Elliott introduced himself and added, 'I have been helping your brother for some time, but I live in Tel Aviv.'

The old lady gave him the critical up and down look she had first given Broadhurst. He moved behind the wheelchair. 'Let me show you the house while you're waiting,' Elliott said.

As they moved to the passageway which led through to the rear of the house, Broadhurst caught Marchal's arm as he went to follow. 'Are you all right?' he asked. 'You look tired.'

Marchal gave an apologetic smile. 'Slept badly last night and just couldn't relax on the journey. She slept like a baby; woke up once for a toilet break and went straight back to sleep; asked if we could stop and buy her an ice cream, got chocolate all over her face and then went back to sleep yet again. Woke up for a third time, demanded we stop while she applied make-up. It was just like travelling with a child. Have you met up with the brother?'

Broadhurst shook his head. 'No. They've gone out, apparently. Did you talk with her about the reference to the President's father in Kirchner's statement?'

'Yes. She doesn't care. It's up to us what is done, she said. That also applies to her own memoirs. She prefers that I make the decision for her.'

'My goodness, you have made an impression. So, what's your position?'

'I take your view, Chas. I don't want to get embroiled in US politics any more than you do. The trouble is it doesn't stop there, does it?'

363

'Having met the US contingency and Elliott here, I don't see the motivation to have killed the girl and the attempt on my life. There is something else in play beyond General Williams and his wartime antics, something equally as important, and I think we are close to the answer. I calculate that Messrs Broadhurst and Marchal are inconveniently in the way.'

'You say we're close?'

Broadhurst waved his hand in the maybe, maybe not fashion. 'Something is not right about this place. The hairs are standing up on the back of my neck. I don't know what it is, but we have to act with caution.' He watched the wheelchair and Elliott turn in the distance. 'Let's keep up with the house guest and see if we can find out where the householders are.' He began to walk to the rear of the house.

'What's not right, exactly?' Marchal persisted.

'Nothing I couldn't reasonably explain away, that's the problem. They've gone out shopping according to Elliott, but not in the comfortable car with the disabled parking facility. That's parked over there. And remember, Danata's car was blown up in Portugal.'

'They could have more than one car each.'

'I agree. Inconclusive. There's no sign of the two guys who take care of Josef and look after this place while he's away.'

'Gone shopping as well?'

'Quite possibly. There's a stairlift in the lounge going to the bedrooms on the upper floor, presumably to transport Josef up and down. The lift chair is not at the bottom where you would expect it to be if the person who uses it had just gone out. I looked up the staircase while I was on a guided tour of the ground floor. It's at the top.'

'He walked down the stairs or the lift is broken. Coincidence?'

Broadhurst put his arm around Marchal's shoulder. 'Feasible, of course. As my army buddy would say, if you want to stay alive, treat one coincidence as suspicious, two as a conspiracy, three as an impossibility.'

They speeded up to close the gap between them and the wheelchair which Elliott was about to push through the concertina doors into the lounge. 'Stay close to your charge. If something starts to go down, get her to safety.'

364

Marchal's return stare was part concern, part incredulity.

Rita was subjected to the guided tour around the ground floor which Broadhurst had received, before the wheelchair was positioned in front of the gas fire and Marchal had attended to adjusting her seat position and arranged the blankets.

Rita smiled at Broadhurst. 'Quite a mother hen he's become, don't you think? I'm thinking of employing him.'

'At least the pay will be better than with this one,' Marchal said, nodding at Broadhurst.

Elliott motioned them to sit down, but he remained standing. 'It's mid-afternoon on the East Coast now,' he said. 'I promised Cris an update for onward transmission before close of business today. Can you tell me where we stand?'

Broadhurst went to speak, but Rita's shaking arm reached upwards, telling him to remain still. 'As I recall, the General Williams whose existence in that railway tunnel you wish to deny was a fresh-faced man, I would guess in his forties. That fateful night, he presided over or orchestrated the mass murder of a carriage full of soldiers and civilian prisoners, forced into service on pain of death. On his way to secure the safety and transfer to the US of a concentration camp doctor who had once attempted to neuter me with a red-hot poker, he happily witnessed the murder of a German officer by a ten- or eleven-year-old girl, the said doctor's daughter. This much I witnessed.' She stopped to regain her breath, her hand still raised. 'I later learnt that of the trucks loaded with stolen Nazi treasures taken from the train, two were diverted to assist with the funding and sustenance of fugitives from justice. I can certainly vouch for that as one of the recipients of the general's largesse.'

Elliott and Broadhurst were listening intently to her story. Marchal was nodding from time to time as if certifying the facts.

'What are you saying?' Elliott looked concerned. 'That this information should be in the public domain?'

Rita spluttered a cough into her handkerchief. 'Wait!' She took a minute to compose herself. 'Maybe it should, if it could do any good. What I am being asked to condone concerns the son of General Williams who was not even born when this deadly incident took place. I have no doubt the general sat an impressionable young boy on his knee and told him wondrous stories of his bravery and valour during the war, stories which the son is happy to repeat at every opportunity. The sins of the father should not settle on the shoulders of the son, in respect of whom I know nothing. Let him be judged on his own actions, not those of which he had no part.' She relaxed back into the wheelchair, exhausted with the effort.

'I think your answer is obvious,' Broadhurst said as he looked for a confirmatory nod from Marchal. 'We will redact all references to Williams from the copy we retain until we have finished the outstanding issue to be resolved. The other digital copy on the mobile and the hard copy in René's office will be deleted-slash-destroyed, as will the copy on my phone, in due course. You have our word.'

'I'll pass the information on,' Elliott said. 'It's good enough for me, but they may require physical confirmation in some form.'

Broadhurst shrugged his shoulders. 'In what form? It seems pointless. You are prepared to take our word as to the number of copies, but not as to their destruction. It makes no sense.'

'I'm just thinking out loud,' Elliott said. He turned to the old lady. 'You have a written version of what you told me?'

'I do,' she replied.

'I shall require that.'

'We will do a similar redaction in that document,' Marchal said. 'It is much more an account of a girl's struggle to survive in horrendous circumstances than an incriminating revelation as far as the general is concerned. References to an American presence at the time can be easily eliminated.'

'That's not acceptable,' Elliott said, his voice now edgy. 'We need to be in possession of all the relevant documentation.' He glanced towards the staircase. 'Any decision as to what happens to it has to be up to us.'

'Who is "us"?' Marchal said. 'You make it sound like some private initiative. Whoever "us" is, let's get one thing clear. You're not in a position to negotiate and our offer is non-negotiable.'

'Where is the document now?'

'In a safe place that doesn't concern you.'

There was a lull in the conversation as the stand-off heightened the tension in the room. Before anyone could speak, there was the sound of a loud thump on the ceiling from the floor above and the stifled scream of a female.

'You told me everyone was out,' Broadhurst said, aggression in his voice as he took a stride to sidestep Elliott and reach the staircase. 'What's going on?'

Elliott moved to block his path, a hand moving under the tail of his jacket. The red laser beam was activated as he grasped the butt of the Concealed Carry Smith & Wesson 442 and the point centred on Broadhurst's chest. 'Back off, Mr Broadhurst. Don't force my hand.'

Broadhurst was almost on top of the man, no more than a metre from the end of the snout-nosed barrel. Should Elliott fire, the .38 would make a sizeable hole in his chest. The natural reaction, and that which Elliott would anticipate, was for Broadhurst to raise his hands in surrender. Once raised to their full extension, he would be unable to react without signalling his intention.

Broadhurst began to extend his arms. As he did so, he stepped to one side and moved forward, closing his right hand over both the short two-inch barrel and the chamber, twisting and driving Elliott's gun hand down towards the floor. The fingernails of his left hand bit into Elliott's palm, forcing his wrist in the opposite direction and causing him to release his grip. The revolver tumbled onto the tiled floor, beyond the reach of either man.

Unarmed, there was no question as to who was the fittest of the two. Elliott had the advantage of age and twenty pounds less good living around his midriff, plus regular visits to the gym to sharpen his response. His first move was to dislodge the grip Broadhurst had on his arm which stopped him from moving to retrieve the gun. The older man was surprisingly tenacious with a strength that belied his years. Elliott turned his body to face Broadhurst, made a fist with his free hand and swung his arm. Moving out of reach cost Broadhurst the grip on the other man's forearm. Elliott had broken free and was diving to his left to retrieve the gun.

As Elliott focused his attention on the weapon, a brown suede Hush Puppy, size nine, kicked the gun across the floor out of his reach to nestle under the footstall of the wheelchair. He winced with pain as the foot turned and stamped on his outstretched hand. A knee was pressed tight against the small of his back. His arms were being prised behind him forcing his head downwards to press tight against the floor.

'Thank you,' Broadhurst gasped, taking the necktie Marchal offered him. 'If you could bind ...' He never finished the sentence. Marchal collapsed in a heap on the floor alongside the wriggling figure of Elliott.

Broadhurst turned his head to see the barrel of a gun inches from his forehead.

'Enough heroics for now,' the man said, 'don't you think?'

Darkness.

FORTY-THREE
PARADISO, LUGANO, SWITZERLAND
December 2018

Nobody was talking.

He must have blacked out. For how long he didn't know. The doctors had said excessive stress and heightened blood pressure needed to be avoided in the recovery stage. He sensed the bile in the back of his throat, but the urge to vomit had passed. The wound on the side of his head where he had had the surgery throbbed. He tried concentrating on opening his eyes. His eyelids fluttered as if he had learnt from finishing school how to react to an unexpected compliment.

There were three of them, plus the old lady. She looked on as if a spectator at a tennis tournament, her gaze moving intermittently between the man standing and the two seated alongside each other. Broadhurst was one of the two, his wrists bound by plastic ties to the arm of a carver chair somebody had brought in from the dining room. Marchal was similarly bound in the adjoining chair. His forehead and one cheek were spattered with blood, but he was conscious, his attention focused on the man standing alongside the fire.

Broadhurst didn't recognise the man. He was swarthy, late forties probably, about seven or eight years younger than Broadhurst, conventionally handsome in a nondescript sort of fashion, medium build and height, and blonde hair cut in a short, military-style fashion. There was no sign of the gun. Instead, from the sheaf attached to his belt, he had removed a stiletto blade which he held by the hilt between his thumb and index finger as if he were about to allow it to drop. From time to time, he would swing it backwards and forwards using the pressure of his two fingers to hold it.

The man walked over towards Broadhurst with a glass of water which he held to his lips. Broadhurst gulped greedily. He was now fully conscious, the pain in his skull now a dull ache that pulsed in tandem with the beat of his heart. Water dribbled down his chin and onto his neck as he spoke. 'What is all this? Why are we being held captive?'

'I will do the talking,' the man said in heavily accented English. 'You will listen and I will talk. Is that clear?'

Broadhurst said nothing. He looked over at Marchal and received a collegial smile that said 'hold your peace'.

'I asked you if that was clear?'

Broadhurst looked at the man and shrugged.

'I will take that as a yes.'

There was the sound of ice clinking in a glass coming from the kitchen. The man looked around to follow the sound. 'As you can see, Elliott's attempt to secure the required result without coercion has failed miserably. Broken bones in his right hand are all he has to show for his efforts which I advised at the outset would not succeed. He wanted to do the decent thing by the Krakowski family and appeal to your sense of fair play. I don't play fair.'

'Three questions,' Broadhurst interrupted. 'What has happened to Josef and his daughter? Who are you and who are you working for?'

The man walked forward, the stiletto oscillating to and fro until the tip of the blade came to rest on Broadhurst's cheek just below the left eye.

'For God's sake, man,' Broadhurst continued, seemingly unmoved by the threat to him. 'You act and sound like a second-rate actor who didn't get the part of a Bond villain. Don't make speeches. Tell us who you are and what you want.' A thin line of blood began to trickle down his cheek.

The man withdrew the stiletto, cleaned the tip against the sleeve of Broadhurst's jacket and returned it to the sheaf. He appeared to be considering his response. 'Very good, Chas. May I call you that? You may know me as Marcello. I'll skip the Bond villain if you abandon the muscle-man tactics. The introduction was simply to let you know that I am not here to appeal to your better nature. My methods are far more straightforward.' He hesitated. 'Vulgar might be a better word to describe them.'

'You could start by answering my questions.'

'Josef and his daughter have been restrained but are otherwise unharmed. That is, apart from the bruising the lady received by casting her body from the bed onto the floor in an attempt to attract your attention. She appears intact. I have told you my name. That will have to satisfy your curiosity.'

The noise came from Marchal's chair as he tried to edge it around to face his partner. 'This guy isn't interested in the American angle. He wants what Rita left in the safe at the nursing home.' He reacted to the look of alarm on Broadhurst's face. 'Don't stare like that. I didn't tell him. Rita did. She made her position quite clear to me from the start. She doesn't intend to be obstructive and suffer the consequences. There are no sides now as far as she is concerned, no moral stance.'

'I want to see Josef,' she said in little more than a whisper.

'And you will. In good time. Let's not involve your family in an issue which concerns only you three.' Marcello pointed the stiletto at Marchal. 'René is almost right. I do have more than a passing interest in assisting with the preservation of an American president, but unlike Elliott' – who had just walked back into the room clutching a tea towel filled with ice cubes around his right hand – 'my main concern is a document you were expected to find in the safe-deposit box, but was not there. When this came to light, the only conclusion was that it had been removed by the last person to open the safe-deposit box, namely Ms Krakowski here, back in 1989.'

'I'm confused,' Broadhurst looked around at his partner for clarification.

'Don't you see?' Marchal's voice was tinged with frustration

'We've been played, Chas. You were hired because the Horwitzes wanted somebody who could be relied on to react according to the outcome once the safe was opened. If the documents were intact, you would complete your courier duties and deliver them into their hands. If something was missing, it would mean locating Rita and you would need little encouragement to do this. All they had to do was send somebody to monitor your movements, and sit and wait for today's outcome.'

'Why not come themselves? My investigative tactics weren't exactly rocket science.'

'Their man here can probably tell you.' Marchal nodded towards Marcello. 'My guess is it would have raised public awareness of their interest in what was in the box and would probably have provoked a much more dramatic objection from the Krakowskis on behalf of the Holocaust Foundation. Stefan Horwitz is quite obviously a lapsed Jew with little time for Josef and his methods.'

371

Marcello broke off from the whispered conversation he was having with Elliott. His foot trod on the remains of a mobile smashed into pieces on the floor and he kicked them out of his way.

Marchal explained. 'He took our mobiles with the digital copies of the letter, put the SIM cards in the waste disposal and trashed the phones. He has the keys to the office in Paris where I left the hard copy.'

Broadhurst nodded. He glanced down at his hand. It was white through lack of circulation, the surface glazed and creased like snakeskin. He imagined the sensation he would experience when the tie was cut. The silhouette of the man standing in front of him cast a shadow on his trousers.

'Unfortunately, my plans have changed,' Marcello said. 'Our intention was for Elliott to return to the nursing home and retrieve the documents from the safe whilst we amused ourselves here. Unfortunately, the injury to his hand means he cannot drive. In the circumstances, I must go and, to keep me company, Chas, you will be my chauffeur. Before we leave, there will be a toilet break, one at a time, no locked doors. Elliott will get the rest settled down for the duration. All being well, we will be at the home by eleven and back here in the early hours of tomorrow morning.'

'And then what?' Broadhurst asked.

'We reach an understanding whereby it will not be necessary for me to seek any of you or your family members out at some future date because of an unfortunate indiscretion, if you get my meaning.'

Rita did exactly as she was told, but with great difficulty. The call to Matron was punctuated by a serious coughing fit, several pauses and stuttered sentences, but, finally, the message was understood. She would need the documents which had been put into the safe shortly prior to their departure. The second man who had come to visit her would pick them up. Matron sounded concerned. Was she all right? She sounded in some discomfort. Was it wise to have left the home? Would it be better if she returned?

The questions were parried with expertise. Broadhurst was impressed. A lifetime of dealing with prying questions, often innocently posed, he imagined, had produced an ability where it was more natural for her to lie than tell the truth. Matron could rest assured. Rita would send for the vehicle to take her back as soon as she had seen her brother.

'Satisfied?' The question was directed at Marcello.

'Perfectly.' He looked around, his gaze coming to rest on the overcoat and beret which Marchal had draped over the armchair on arrival. 'Yours?' he asked.

Marchal nodded.

'Don't mind if I borrow them, do you?' Marcello picked them up. 'I'm not equipped for the night-time chill.'

'Not in a position to object, am I?'

The motorway traffic was light and with one stop for petrol close to Lucerne, they were drawing up at the home just after ten thirty. There had been little conversation on the journey. Marcello sat in the back of the Mercedes Estate, behind the passenger seat, the butt of a Glock 25 protruding from a shoulder holster. Broadhurst had made various attempts at conversation, all parried with silence or one- or two-word answers. The only exception was when asking how Marcello had managed to come by a semi-automatic, military-grade weapon, illegal in the gun-crazy US.

'It's not treated that way in certain South American countries,' Marcello had said. 'It's perfectly legal. They don't make such hypocritical distinctions between guns for sporting purposes and personal protection.'

'Is that where you're from, South America?'

There had been no answer.

Apart from a low-power bulb in the entrance hall, the home was in darkness. The Mercedes came to a standstill in one of the car parking spaces marked '*Visiteurs*' at the side of the building alongside those signed '*Personnel*', where another four or five cars were parked. With no cloud cover, the air was chill and watery moonlight illuminated the scene. Broadhurst stretched and slapped his arms across his body to generate some heat.

Marcello exited the car with the Glock in his hand, aimed at Broadhurst's forehead. 'Ground rules,' he said. 'I won't hesitate to use this if there is one wrong move inside. Do you believe me?'

'I certainly do.' He raised his arms as if in surrender. 'I know the type of person I'm dealing with.'

Marcello indicated for him to move forward. As Broadhurst led the way, he trod on a piece of frozen, compacted snow, slid and staggered to regain his balance. Marcello stood to one side and waited, the gun trained on the prone figure.

The front door was locked. Broadhurst pressed the bell push. After fifteen seconds, there was the glow from a ceiling light in a corridor beyond the reception area. A tall, slender figure, slightly stooped, clad in a red uniform with a white pinafore, walked briskly to the door. Broadhurst remembered her as the night matron, a woman with a scrubbed appearance, an abrupt manner and a permanently displeased expression as if honed on sucking lemons.

She gave a cursory nod and opened the door. The hall fanned out into a large reception area with a small counter at one side and various pieces of Swedish-style seating where visitors could wait. In one corner, a TV screen shone in the gloom, tuned to a twenty-four-hour news channel. Two or three inmates sat in the darkness either watching or dozing in armchairs.

The woman walked smartly to the rear of the counter. With a practised disdain, she retrieved the document case from a shelf and placed it purposefully onto the varnished surface. 'This is most irregular,' she said. 'We close the doors always at ten.' She selected the words in English as if considering each one before she carefully enunciated it. 'We only reply to emergencies after ten. Had Ms Taube not been one of the foundation members, such an irregularity could not be permitted.' She produced the manila envelope which she placed on the document case by meticulously lining up the corners. 'Especially not for casual paperwork.'

Broadhurst apologised for the inconvenience and thanked her profusely as he picked up the case and envelope. Marcello hovered in the shadows by the entrance door, out of range of the camera trained on the counter, but within earshot.

'Will that be all?' she said, making ready to leave.

'Thank you.' Broadhurst said.

She stopped in her tracks and sighed. 'By the way, there was a gentleman waiting to speak with you. I told him you were on your way here.'

374

'Thank you,' Broadhurst repeated.

'A polite man,' she said. 'I told him he could not wait inside. It was approaching ten. I insisted he wait in his vehicle. I do not know if he did. Perhaps he left. Please close the door firmly.'

'Who were you expecting?' Marcello asked.

Broadhurst turned and studied the woman's face, silently imploring her not to contradict him. 'I organised a newspaper contact. He was to do an article based on these' – he pointed to the document case which he had handed to Marcello along with the envelope – 'for publication after her death. I intended to have a preliminary chat with him to establish some ground rules. I had suggested nine thirty. He must have tired of waiting.'

They were at the front door, the matron holding her ground, watching their exit.

'I just hope everything is all right with Elliott,' Marcello said loudly and pointedly. 'His unbalanced attitude worries me.'

'Sorry,' the woman said, 'are you talking to me?'

Marcello ignored her. 'I just don't trust Elliott's mental state.' He opened the door for Broadhurst to pass in front of him. 'He's a loose cannon.'

The door shut behind them and Marcello ushered Broadhurst towards the car park and into the front passenger seat whilst he sat in the back.

'Journalists and memoirs of a life on the run,' he said, a humour in his voice Broadhurst had not witnessed before. 'That's an article that won't be happening,' he added absent-mindedly. His attention was focused on the unmarked envelope set alongside the document case. He peeled out a stapled bunch of parchment papers and glanced at the first sheet. The staple had rusted and streaks of brown marked the document where it had been folded. The musty smell from decades of concealment permeated the atmosphere inside the car.

'Game, set and match,' he said, replacing the paperwork in the envelope.

'What was that outburst about Elliott intended to achieve?' Broadhurst asked.

'More than you could ever imagine,' Marcello joked, as he opened the rear door and stepped out of the car.

The rush of chill night air made Broadhurst shiver. At least, he thought it was the cold night air.

FORTY-FOUR
PARADISO, LUGANO, SWITZERLAND
December 2018

The Mercedes pulled into the gated drive just after three thirty in the morning. Marcello operated the remote control and they parked alongside Broadhurst's BMW. He leaned over from the driver's seat and cut the two plastic ties that bound his captive's wrists to the arm rest. As he did so, Broadhurst stirred and awoke, momentarily unsure of where he was or why every bone in his body ached.

As soon as they had reached the autoroute, Marcello had opted to drive, once again saying little nor explaining the motive behind his strange outburst as they left the home. 'Just something on my mind,' was the only explanation he was prepared to offer. Broadhurst soon tired of his initiatives to create some form of understanding between them, to appeal to some sensibility that would provoke a reaction. The hypnotic effect of the beam from the headlights on the road ahead was overpowering enough to dull the sense of foreboding and allow him to succumb to the weariness and drift into sleep.

Apart from a light in one of the upstairs rooms, the villa was in total darkness. As they alighted from the car, the motion sensors reacted to the movement by activating both the security lights and the motor driving the adjacent surveillance camera.

The front door was ajar. In the lounge, all was silent. From the flickering glow of the fire, Broadhurst could make out the silhouettes of the old lady asleep in the wheelchair and Marchal tied to the carver as he had been nine hours earlier. His chin rested unmoving on his chest.

From the foot of the staircase came the sound of raised voices from the bedroom above. Elliott was pleading and Danata was shouting. Marcello climbed six stairs to ensure his voice was heard above the argument. Momentarily he was out of Broadhurst's eyeline.

On the floor alongside the last stair were two dinner trays, the remnants of two meals piled onto one plate and one tray untidily balanced on the other. Broadhurst bent and retrieved a serrated dinner knife from the

377

top plate, moving a soiled napkin across to hide the remaining cutlery. He slid the knife into his trouser pocket.

Marcello's voice ordered the twosome to shut up and demanded that Elliott secure the Krakowskis and come downstairs. Danata stopped in mid-sentence and there was silence.

'I was just—' Elliott went to explain.

'Not now. Not here. Restrain him,' Marcello said, indicating Broadhurst. 'Here are the ties. Then, join me in the kitchen.'

'Did you get what you were after?' Elliott said.

'I believe so. I have a call to make in a few hours.'

'Why bother to keep them tied up? We've got everything we came for. I can report we've gone as far as we can on containing the release of the Williams material, if you accept the assurances these gentlemen have given us. You have secured the paperwork retained by Josef's sister. Our assignment is complete.'

Marcello walked over and took the plastic ties back from Elliott. He bound Broadhurst's wrists to the chair. 'All in good time. As soon as I have confirmation, we can wrap up this business.' He smiled at Elliott and put his arm around the other man's shoulder as he led him towards the kitchen. 'Let's get some more ice on that swelling,' he said.

'What is going on?' Marchal whispered.

'Nothing to help us. I've got a very ominous feel about this.' Broadhurst summarised the events of the journey to Vevey and back.

'What do you make of it? Why the outburst about Elliott?'

'It was put on intentionally. He wanted to be overheard. He's planning something. Why borrow your coat and hat? He stayed in the shadows whilst I talked to the matron. It could easily have been you. This is not intended to end well. Tell me, what happened here?'

'Elliott was apologetic, said he regretted having to tie us up but it had to be. He cooked some burgers; released us to eat, one at a time, Rita first. She's quite amazing, incredibly stoic with a strange fatalistic attitude to this bizarre happening. He wheeled her over to the toilet and tried to help her. She told him to back off in no uncertain fashion and, somehow, managed to look after herself.' He leaned over to look at the woman asleep in the wheelchair. 'All that concerns her now is to meet her brother and niece.'

'Why are they being kept upstairs?'

'I've thought about that. Two reasons, I believe. One, I think they know who Marcello is working for and if they participated in the conversations with us down here, it would have added confusion and disarray to his plans. Secondly, I guess Marcello calculates Elliott's resolve is weak and if Danata was in close proximity to him, he would start to waiver.'

'He was right. We arrived back at the tail end of that confrontation.'

'It kicked off when he took the dinner trays upstairs for them. She started shouting at him. He tried to explain the ordeal would soon be over and it was all necessary for the good of the State of Israel and relations with the US. It made no difference. He couldn't leave it. A few hours later, he collected the dinner trays, brought them down and then went back up to try and reason with her. You heard the result.'

'Do you believe it or was it play-acting for your benefit and she's not what you think, but an accomplice in this charade?'

'Difficult to accept that hypothesis. It seemed real enough to me.'

'Listen.' Broadhurst explained there was a knife in his pocket. 'Elliott hasn't tied your wrist as tightly as mine. You have some play in your hand. See if you can get the knife between your fingers and take it.'

For five minutes, they struggled to bring their chairs closer together, to manoeuvre Marchal's hand nearer to Broadhurst's pocket, but with no success. Both men were breathing heavily with the exertion as they sat back.

'What are you two up to?' Rita's disembodied voice sounded from beneath the blanket almost covering her head.

'I am trying unsuccessfully to get something from my pocket into René's hand.'

She let the blanket slip to chest height. 'Maybe I can help. They don't bother to tie my hands. I am no threat.'

'Could you?'

As she tried to steady herself on the arms of the wheelchair, the blanket slipped to the floor and her hand quivered with the exertion as she reached across to the chair in which Broadhurst was trapped. She stood, body stooped and wavering in front of him, her free hand feeling roughly in his pocket. The knife appeared, the blade clasped tight in the palm of her hand, a thin trickle of blood appearing between middle and index finger. 'Now what?' she said.

'Place the handle of the knife, blade pointing backwards into René's hand so that it is concealed below the arm of the chair.'

She took a step to the right and carefully eased the knife into Marchal's hand as instructed.

'Thank you.' René winked at her and gave a broad smile.

As she moved back the two steps to the wheelchair, her body began to sag and she landed heavily in the seat, forcing the wheels to strain against the handbrake with a loud screech.

Marcello was at the door of the kitchen. 'What was that?' he said, advancing towards them.

'I've got cramp, you fool,' she said. 'You keep me sitting here all this time with no regard for my condition. I can't move and my blood doesn't circulate any more. I tried to stand up for the pain to pass, but I could not make it. You're a disgrace.'

Marcello stood in front of the three of them, his gaze going from one to the other. He checked the ties around Broadhurst's wrists and turned to Marchal just as she spoke. 'For God's sake, man, at least rub my leg, will you? The pain is unbearable. Look at the muscle. It's knotted.' She held out the thin spindle of a leg. 'Please. Be gentle.'

His expression softened as he turned towards her and bent down, adjusting the leg onto his thigh and beginning to massage her calf muscle.

When thirty seconds had passed, she said something to him in Portuguese and he replied in Spanish: '*Gracias.*'

'What time is it in the UK?' Marcello asked.

Broadhurst heard the question as he came out of another bout of fragile sleep. His mouth was parched. Light was streaming in through the concertina glass doors, the view of lawn and lake so tranquil and at odds with the tension inside the villa.

'An hour behind Continental Europe,' Elliott replied. He checked his watch. 'Seven thirty there.'

Marcello and Elliott were sitting on a sofa facing their hostages. Marcello was twiddling a dinner knife around in his hands. 'Recognise this?' He looked at Broadhurst.

Marchal mumbled an apology. Broadhurst gave an understanding nod towards his partner. The Frenchman's face was gaunt, cheeks hollow and pallid. He looked on the point of collapse.

'I have to admire your ingenuity, Chas, and that of your lady friend in so competently distracting me.'

Broadhurst turned his head towards the old lady. She was awake, staring straight ahead, as if mesmerised. 'Are you all right?' he asked. She did not react.

'Unfortunately, it slipped from René's hand before he could do any damage. Lucky for him, I suggest.' The mobile vibrated with a loud hum. 'At last,' he said, breathing out deeply. He laid the dinner knife on the sofa and fished in his pocket for the phone.

The conversation was brief and mainly conducted by the caller. Marcello's contribution was restricted to a 'yes' on three occasions. There was some thinking time as he finished the call, studied the screen and purposefully returned the mobile to an inside pocket. His hand remained there.

'Good to go?' Elliott asked.

Marcello nodded.

'Let's get out of here and let these people sort it out. I'll get Danata from the bedroom.' Elliott went to get up.

'Sit down,' Marcello said. His hand had reappeared from inside the jacket, holding the Glock.

'What are you doing?' Elliott looked bemused.

Broadhurst shifted in his chair as much as the ties would allow. His haemorrhoids had flared up. 'Don't be naïve, Elliott,' he said. 'He's got no intention of any of us walking out of here today. We pose too much of a threat. You, as well.'

Elliott swung around, his expression one of disbelief. 'What's he talking about?'

'Nothing, just stirring up trouble, or trying to,' Marcello said, the Glock centred on Elliott's midriff. 'Your weapon, please.'

'What?'

'Give me your gun. Do it slowly.' The Glock moved up and down in his hand.

Elliott reached behind him.

'Don't you see, Elliott—'

'Shut up.' The Glock moved around to point at Broadhurst.

Broadhurst ignored the order. 'He has to silence us all, Elliott, including you, I regret. What is it you've become? Oh, yes, a loose cannon, I remember was his outburst …' He hesitated. 'At least' – he turned to René – 'it was your outburst, René, standing there in your hat and coat in the shadows. I should be careful, Elliott.'

It was too late. Marcello snatched at the Smith & Wesson as Elliott withdrew it from his belt, dropping the Glock onto his lap. In one move, he swapped the Smith & Wesson into his gun hand, held it to Elliott's temple and, releasing the safety, pulled the double-action trigger. The sound reverberated around the room. Blood and bone spattered over Marcello's extended arm and sprayed the sofa. Elliott's body lurched into the air and keeled sideways, the expression on his face still one of amazement as the final beats of his heart muscle pumped blood out of the gaping wound.

Marcello pocketed the Glock and turned to face Broadhurst as he carefully removed and folded his jacket. 'Good try,' he said, rising from the sofa, taking care not to disturb the body. 'Don't mourn his passing too much. He's the guy who was in your room and killed the girl. Even with his mask on she recognised him, and by laughing, exposed his fragile ego. She could identify him to you and the police. He waited to see if he could frame you for her death. Very embarrassing.' He had a smile on his face. 'I expect you thought it was me?' He waited for an answer, but there was silence. 'Believe me, had it been me, you wouldn't be here now.'

'I knew it was him, from the mark of a missing ring on his tanned finger.' Broadhurst returned the smile. 'By the way, it was your first mistake. He's right-handed, so you shot him in the right temple. Makes sense. Only problem is his right hand is out of commission where René stamped on it and broke the bones. I doubt those swollen fingers will even go through the trigger guard. He would have used his left hand to commit suicide.'

Marcello levelled the revolver in Broadhurst's direction. His expression momentarily registered apprehension. 'We'll overcome that problem, I'm sure.'

'That's a five-shot chamber, four bullets left; five of us to deal with unless Danata is part of this.'

Marcello's brow creased. 'That's desperation talk. I am sure I can teach Elliott to be equally proficient with the stiletto.'

'I'm curious how you propose to frame Elliott for mass murder when your face must have been caught by every security camera in the place.' Broadhurst tried to smile. 'For all you know, you could well be a star on social networks already with thousands of hits and a face as famous as a pop star.'

'Now who's in a Bond movie, Chas? What is it? Keep the villain talking until you can fashion a miraculous escape? Sorry, but I'm bringing the conversation to an abrupt conclusion.' Marcello gave himself leg room to prepare to fire at a distance of two metres. 'It has to look spontaneous, maniacal.'

'They switched it from monitored to local before you arrived,' Marchal spoke up, one eye on Broadhurst, the other on the gun. Marcello changed direction to face him. 'Elliott told me while you were absent. He convinced Danata yesterday it would be better not to have Rita's visit taped and stored in case of repercussions. Apparently, they've done it before with a couple of sensitive meetings here. You switch the system to local. It disarms the Wi-Fi connection, prompting the security company monitoring the place to call, ask for a name and password, and to confirm you want to go offline and for how long. With the local switched on, you can record in-house, if required, or run simple transmission as a security alarm with no backup. That's what's operating now. There's no record of what has been going on since yesterday afternoon.'

Two things happened simultaneously. As if waiting for the prompt, the motion alarm signal chimed out from the office. A figure had emerged from the shrubbery at the perimeter leading down to the lake, advancing across the lawn towards the area of the swimming pool and garage before disappearing from view.

At the same time, Marchal thrust his right arm upwards, severing the remaining threads of the plastic tie he had already partially cut through with the knife before it was discovered. On his feet, but with his left wrist still bound to the arm of the chair, he pitched forward, thrusting the chair, legs first, towards the outstretched arm that held the revolver.

Marcello took a step backwards and moved to the side. One of the legs struck him heavily in the pelvis just as he fired the Smith & Wesson. The gun jerked in his hand as the laser beam centred on Marchal's head, then pitched towards the ceiling. Plaster dust sprayed into the air. The second shot hit its target.

As if in slow motion, Marchal collapsed onto his knees, an expression of astonishment on his face as his eyes fixated on the wound. Head and shoulders first, he pitched forward onto the floor, his arm, still bound to the chair, pointing upward in a bizarre gesture as if a child at school attempting to attract the teacher's attention. A trickle of blood began to form into a pool under the still body.

There was a yelp from the old lady. Another motion alarm signalled, this time with a staccato peel. Marcello hobbled to the sofa, pocketed the Smith & Wesson and massaged his thigh. 'They're here,' he said. The Glock was in his hand now.

'Who?' Broadhurst said. 'The police?'

There was the sound of footsteps pounding on the flat roof above.

Marcello started to hobble towards the stairs. 'You wish,' he said. 'I thought at the time that man from the newspaper story was rubbish. They must have been waiting for us at Vevey and trailed the car here. I'll let them finish the dirty work. I'm supposed to be in the victim count. They can think again if they imagine I'm hanging around for the execution.' He disappeared out of view.

Rita had slid from the wheelchair and was lying on her belly, inching her way towards Marchal. She reached him and placed a hand against his collar bone. The blood seeped slowly through her fingers. 'Hold on,' she said. 'You can't die before me. I won't allow it, René. Do you hear me?'

To Broadhurst's surprise, Marchal nodded, his eyes still closed.

Danata descended the stairs, Marcello directly behind her, the Glock pointed at her back. She looked around with scared eyes, her gaze coming to rest on the slumped figure of Elliott Karmi, his head buried in the arm of the sofa, fingertips languidly grazing the floor. She gave an involuntary yelp. It was impossible to say whether it was a reaction to the scene she was witnessing or the dig she received into her shoulder blade from the revolver.

'What have you done?' She sounded angry more than distressed. 'What has this all been about?'

The sound erupted of glass screeching. 'They're on the roof,' Marcello said, his voice anxious but controlled. 'They know I've seen them.' He prodded her hard again. 'Get moving, exactly as I said.' They exited the lounge along the corridor towards the far end of the building.

Broadhurst waited and watched. They emerged, hunched and running by the changing area alongside the swimming pool before veering off onto the path through the trees and shrubs at the perimeter of the property. Marcello held the Glock in one hand, the manila envelope in the other. There was no gunfire, no sniper's bullet finding a target appearing intermittently between the trees and bushes. Whoever had their sights on the couple was surely waiting for them to make the last final dash across the stretch of lawn at the water's edge towards the jetty and the fishing boat.

Looking from the lounge, the topography of the lawn meant Broadhurst could barely see the crouching figures as they moved. From the roof, they must be able to pick them off with ease, but there was no gunfire. Danata clambered onto the vessel and moved to the controls. Marcello released the mooring line from the jetty and used his hands to grip the boat rail and vault onto the deck. The outboard motor fired into life and the boat moved out into the lake.

'How is he?' Broadhurst asked.

'If I press as hard as I can, the blood flow almost stops,' she said. 'I have no strength to keep up the pressure. The wound is just below his shoulder. The blood is venal, not arterial.'

There was the sound of a window opening on the floor above.

'Can you reach the knife?' he said.

She looked over at the sofa. The dinner knife was next to Elliott's body, where Marcello had been sitting.

385

There was the sound of footsteps in a bedroom, metal tips ringing on the ceramic floor.

'I'm sorry,' she said. 'If I try to crawl over and reach it and return to you, the bleeding will start again and he has already lost a great deal. Even if I managed to reach you, I have no strength in these wrists to cut your ties. By that time ...'

Broadhurst nodded. 'You stay where you are.'

A muffled conversation was taking place upstairs. Broadhurst could not make out who was talking or what was being said.

The ring of metal-tipped shoes began to get nearer, stair by stair.

FORTY-FIVE
PARADISO, LUGANO, SWITZERLAND
December 2018

From Rita's position on the floor, she had the best view of the stairs up to the first floor. Broadhurst needed to crook his head to see, but even so, his field of vision took in only the bottom three stairs. There was no point in taxing himself.

Marchal was now unconscious and the strain of holding her skeletal hand against the wound was beginning to tell on Rita's face. 'If we are to die,' she said, 'it will be together.' There was no reaction.

She looked up as the figure came into view, wiped her eyes with her free hand and gasped. 'You,' was all she said.

Broadhurst swung his head around. 'It can't be,' he said. 'Daniel! For God's sake, cut me free.'

'Is there anybody else down here?' His eyes fixed on Elliott's body.

'No. Please. Quickly.There's a knife on the sofa.'

Rita's eyes followed his every move. Broadhurst grimaced with pain as the ties were cut and frantically massaged his wrists. He wobbled unsteadily on his feet. 'There's a mobile in the BMW, in the boot well, under the jack. Call for an ambulance and the police. He tossed the keys onto the table by the front door.'

Daniel returned, holding the mobile, a look of disbelief on his face as he passed it to Broadhurst. 'They're on their way.'

Broadhurst had taken over stemming the blood flow from Marchal's wound. Rita lay on her back on the floor, her hand and arm soaked in blood, her blouse covered in droplets.

'Can I help you into the chair?' Daniel said.

'Leave me,' she replied. 'Just hold my hand like we used to do all those years ago and let me look at you. Get a cushion for my head.'

He crouched on his haunches next to her and began to massage the hand free of blood she held out to him. 'You are my mother?' he said.

Her body tensed. 'No,' she said tersely. 'Don't call me that. It's not correct. I may be the biological reason you exist, but your mother is the wonderful woman who nurtured you from birth, guided you through your

387

formative years and loved you with every fibre of her being. For her, you became the man of whom, together with the memory of your father, she was so proud. As for Pedro, he was fine and honest. By being present at a time when I was in danger, he helped to save my life – much as you have done today. Like father, like son, and I have been twice blessed. Do not lose perspective.'

He squeezed her hand. 'I won't, I promise.'

The sounds of sirens grew louder. Broadhurst pointed Daniel in the direction of the front gate release switch on the wall.

'There's an old guy upstairs,' Daniel said. 'He's been restrained. I untied his hands, but he's in a bad way. Keeps asking for Danata.'

'Point the medics in the right direction,' Broadhurst said. 'Did you see anything? Was she forced or did she go of her own free will?'

'I have no idea. I had seen a partially open window in one of the other bedrooms. That is how I managed to get in. I heard the noise down here and crept along the corridor. The old man was on his own.'

'I won't ask you right now how you came to be here, I'm just glad you are.'

'Me too. I saw the woman standing at the window as soon as I started to make my way up from the lake. She was gesturing for me to come nearer. By the time I got to where she had been, she was gone.'

'The sight of you certainly spooked the guy who was about to kill us. He'd been so cool and calm until then, but there was something unsettling about him, something below the surface about which he was very wary. He was convinced there was more than one of you.'

'These steel-capped police issue boots certainly make a noise.'

'Thank God,' Broadhurst said.

FORTY-SIX
PARADISO, LUGANO, SWITZERLAND
December 2018

For the umpteenth time, Broadhurst fumbled for his mobile to check the time. Four o'clock. As drained and exhausted as he felt, sleep would not come. He pulled on the towelling robe and made his way in the darkness from the smaller of the two guest bedrooms, down the stairs and across the lounge. From the kitchen, where he must have spent most of the afternoon and early evening, there was a soft fluorescent glow and the sound of a chair creaking.

'Come in and join me,' Danata said, reacting to the half-whispered curse as Broadhurst hit his knee on a coffee table in the lounge. 'Grab a glass. The only alcohol in the house is some kitchen brandy, but it's half decent. I couldn't sleep. Still getting used to the idea of having a grown-up cousin, I guess.' She motioned to him to sit down on the stool next to her. 'At least, after the first glass, it starts to grow on you.'

The pair of thick, flannelette pyjamas she was wearing had the design of a bear and a bull, both standing on their hind legs, about to embrace each other. The jacket was buttoned up to the neck.

'Those two look really uncomfortable,' Broadhurst said, pointing at the design with his glass. 'A collision about to occur. You got a friend on Wall Street?'

'Well spotted,' she said, 'But actually it was someone from the Bursa.' She recognised the enquiring look. 'It's the Tel Aviv Stock Exchange, but, more appropriately in this case, a metaphor for the collision of two intransigent personalities.'

Broadhurst shook his head. 'Too much information for this time of the night.'

She smiled an acknowledgement.

'I didn't hear you come back. How was Josef when you left him?' He refilled her glass.

'They transferred him from IC back to a general ward after the examination. His blood pressure had normalised and the heart murmur was under control. He's in a general ward, the same as your partner. They said

René's problem was principally loss of blood; the wound itself was not life-threatening. He was sleeping like a baby. I wish my father had been, instead of bombarding me with questions and not waiting for the answer before he asked the next one.'

'Understandable, in the circumstances. He must have been worried about you.'

'You would think so, but he was more concerned with Rita's state of health. They still haven't met, you know?'

He nodded. 'My understanding is she won't meet him without René being present. Anyway, once Elliott's body had been removed and René and your father had been taken to hospital, the lounge and study were sealed off as crime scenes, along with the main bedroom. They took Daniel off – to the police station, I imagine. I don't know if he came back or not. When the ambulance service eventually accepted Rita was not going with them for a check-up, thanks to her cry of "once they get an over-eighty in those places, the only way you come out is horizontal in a box", they kept us here in the kitchen until forensics had finished. We were interviewed individually, with our sanitised version of the truth.'

'What does that mean?'

'Maintaining Rita's true identity a secret; avoiding conjecture about your boyfriend's inconsistent behaviour until we understand the motivation.'

'My boyfriend? You mean Elliott? Are you joking?' She shook her head and made a popping sound with her lips as the air escaped.

'He murders a girl in cold blood, yet labours under the mistaken belief Marcello would let us all happily walk away as soon as those wretched documents had been recovered. It was naïve.'

'I can tell you why,' she blurted in reply. 'I was really angry with him. I went for him, something I now regret. He was blindly following Marcello's orders, under protest sometimes, I accept, but always in awe of a ruthless streak he did not have in him. He tied up me and Dad because Marcello said so. The deal was he would get you together with Rita and convince you to part with all the documents and copies. If he did this, everybody would be free to go. Marcello agreed, but never had any intention of keeping his word. We knew that. Elliott couldn't see it ... rather, he didn't want to see it. That's what we were arguing about when you came back from Vevey. The trouble was, he had accidentally killed the girl ...'

'Accidentally?' Broadhurst said, his voice an octave higher than normal. 'You're saying he didn't mean to kill Petra?'

She held up the bottle and he let her serve what in an English bar would have been a quadruple. 'You're right,' he said. 'The taste does get better as the story becomes more fanciful.'

'He said so and I tend to believe him. Elliott was no field operative with the kill-or-be-killed philosophy. He was an analyst; give him a set of facts or figures and he would plot a course of action. Once upon a time, he may have had some basic training in armaments and person-to-person combat, but he had spent too many years looking at a screen and chewing the end of a pencil to have remembered how to kill in cold blood.'

'So, what did he say happened?'

'The top Mossad brass in Tel Aviv had been contacted by a retired agent who knew Elliott was in Lisbon with a request emanating from the White House. He was to look out for some paperwork surfacing from the bank which mentioned the President's late father's activities during the latter stages of the war. Elliott was told a lot rested on Israel's status with the US if he could oblige. He took the bait, hook, line and sinker. He gave me hell on the day you were in the bank to secure possession of the contents of Wiesel's safe-deposit box when he saw the scan of the envelope of Kirchner's letter intended for the German press.'

'But you weren't successful. I had the originals. And, as far as he knew, I had given them back to Malato when you came to the hotel with that cock and bull business about an apostille. He must have bribed Malato to see what was in the envelope.'

'He did, so I found out during our shouting match. It was an expensive price to pay for a few sheets of toilet paper, wasn't it? I take my hat off to you. That was a cute move.'

'Deadly, as it turned out.'

She hesitated. 'Yeah. Bad choice of phrase. You didn't leave him any alternative, did you? He wasn't expecting the girl to be there. He mistook the room service waitress for the turn-down service and held the door open for her as she exited the room. The girl appeared from the bathroom ready to eat, only to find she had a companion whom she recognised from the previous evening. Even so, he said she would come to no harm if she told him where you had hidden the originals.'

'And?' She appeared taken aback at how he could make one word sound so hostile.

She reached out to place her hand over his. 'I understand how you feel about this kid, but don't put me in a "them and me" camp. I'm trying to explain it for your benefit, not condone Elliott's actions. I'm just repeating his courtroom defence before execution of the sentence.'

He nodded, but removed his hand from under hers. She left hers there, on offer, it seemed to him.

'Elliott was a complex man, thin-skinned with amazingly little self-confidence for somebody in that job. I was probably the only person who could make fun of him and get away with it. The girl was way too savvy for her years, sensing his weakness and beginning to goad and make fun of him. She started to play a game, teasing and prodding at his lack of manliness. The mood changed when he slapped her; not once, but a series of blows, demanding she stopped talking and do as he asked. But she kept puncturing that thin skin as if she enjoyed the pain.'

'Come on. This is—'

'His words, not mine. He was out of control. In the end, she pointed at the printer and, as his attention was distracted, went to grasp the gun he was holding. There was a struggle, and the rest you know.'

'Very convenient. And the shot fired just happened to catch her in the middle of the forehead, execution-style?'

She shrugged and pursed her lips together. 'Unfortunately, we will never know. When the enormity of what he had done hit home, he got some fanciful idea he would try and frame you when you got back. He had to hang around for a day and, by that time …'

Through the kitchen window, he saw the eerie, grey hue that announces the dawn in a cloud-filled sky. 'I need a coffee. You?'

She accepted the offer. For a while, they sat at the kitchen table, nursing their cups, either unwilling or unable to broach the silence.

'I can't work you out,' he said eventually. 'I am almost inclined to think you might be batting for both sides.'

'What does that mean?'

'You appeared to willingly facilitate Marcello's strange exit and escape. You take him in the boat to the other side of the lake – where was it?'

'The jetty at Bissone. Go on.'

'He lets you go unharmed, so you can point the police in his direction. For all we know, you could have dropped him off somewhere totally different.'

'Go on. Anything else?' Her face was drawn, her eyes boring in on him.

'Yes. You obviously know a lot more about Rita than you let on. All that bullshit when we last met about sterilising all the would-be sex slaves in the camps as an excuse for your knowing what had happened to her. Instinct tells me you are hiding something. I also believe Elliott knew what it was and could have used it as a hold over you.'

She gave a wry smile. 'Fanciful. Your problem, Chas, is you're looking at a mole on my skin and calculating my entire body is racked with cancer. Let me put you straight.'

She stopped and looked towards the kitchen door. 'Don't hang about, come in,' she said. 'Join the late night drinks party or the crack of dawn coffee set, whichever you prefer.'

In a superfluous gesture, Daniel tapped on the door to announce his presence. 'Hope I'm not disturbing anything,' he said. 'I woke up when she started coughing, but she went back to sleep. I couldn't, and thought I'd get a glass of water.'

'Okay. It's not the dawn coffee set but the wet nurse water brigade. Welcome. There's some Evian in the fridge, I think.'

'Water from the tap is fine.' He sat down heavily on a chair in between them.'

'I didn't realise you were back,' Broadhurst said. 'They took you to the police station? Why?'

He nodded, a tight-lipped expression on his face. 'They're a heavy lot. I showed them my Portuguese police credentials – the documents I tried to show you as you stood at the window,' he said to Danata, 'and I was immediately manhandled into a car and taken to Lugano. It took hours;

393

verifying my credentials with Faro, accepting I was not conducting some covert operation without Swiss police authority – they made it sound like a crime that outstripped murder - and finally, coming to understand the reasons for my actions yesterday, including the theft of a kayak.'

'I'd welcome an explanation,' Broadhurst said.

He spoke in short, clipped sentences, as if he were giving evidence in court. Daniel had realised it was now or never if he was to reunite with Rita, or Angela, as he knew her. When Broadhurst had called from Lisbon to say he was leaving for Geneva, he had asked for time off, cashed his savings and flown to Geneva. As soon as Broadhurst had told him where Angela was staying, he had hired a car and driven to Vevey.

'Some haughty matron told me Angela was absent for a few days, but you were expected at the home shortly. As it was nearly ten and the doors would be locked, I would have to wait in the car park. I woke just as your car pulled up, and was about to get out and attract your attention when I saw you slip and the guy wave what looked like a gun at you. I stayed where I was, watched, and then tailed you back here. I knew I couldn't appear at the front door, and the place looked like a fortress.'

'Why not call the police at that point?' Broadhurst asked.

'What was I going to say? I thought I saw a gun. I needed to do a reconnaissance first, establish who, what and where. I saw the lake as the only access point. There is a kayak club on the foreshore, just where the buildings end. The guy had just unchained a bunch of kayaks and was in a shack talking to half a dozen kids in wetsuits. I moved one of the kayaks out of sight and paddled around the headland towards the jetty where your boat is moored.'

'I admire your initiative. I'm certain we wouldn't be here today without it.' He looked at Danata for confirmation, but all he got back was a stony stare.

Daniel acknowledged the comment with an embarrassed nod. 'It's a darn sight more difficult than it looks. The water in Lake Lugano is freezing and my trousers got soaked!'

'Please, go on.'

'At first glance, the terrain leading up to the back of the house from the lake is totally exposed to view. I stuck to the shrubbery and trees on the perimeter when I saw I was being watched by a woman on the first floor.'

Broadhurst looked around at Danata. The stony stare was still in place.

'She looked scared. The only thing I could do was take out my warrant card and hold it up. There was no way she could read it, let alone barely see it, but she seemed to understand. I tried to get nearer and mouth some questions, but she shook her head and pointed at the far side of the building. I thought I'd blown it.'

He exchanged a smile with Danata.

'I waited. Two minutes later, she reappeared at the window, showed me her wrists bound together in front of her body and then a pillowcase with words written in lipstick. The writing was very shaky, but it said there were five hostages, two gunmen, and to get onto the roof and come and free her. I could see to where she pointed, the only access to the flat roof was at the far end of the building near the garage and swimming pool. I made a dash across the lawn, hoping I was not seen, and climbed onto the roof. Unfortunately, my steel-capped work boots made quite a noise. Eventually, I worked my way along to the first floor, climbed onto the terrace and looked into the bedroom where I had seen the woman. She wasn't there any more; just an old man, lying in a bed. The windows were locked shut from the inside. As I climbed over the terrace wall to one of the smaller bedrooms where a window was partially open, I turned to see the woman and a man I thought was the same guy I had seen the previous evening. They were together in the garden and running towards the jetty where I had ditched the kayak. I watched the boat take off and the rest, as they say, is history.'

'I suppose I should apologise.' The words were conciliatory, but belied the look on Broadhurst's face.

'But you still have your doubts?' Danata said.

'Can I understand what's going on?' Daniel interrupted.

'Chas is dubious as to my motives for seeming to aid and abet our captor.'

'Really?'

'Is that not so, Chas?'

Broadhurst cupped his hands under his chin and rubbed the stubble on his cheeks. 'For the aforesaid reasons, although I take on board what Daniel has just told us.'

'I don't owe you any explanations, Chas, nor will it trouble me in the least if your doubts remain, but I will tell you both a few things, primarily so that my relationship with a cousin I did not expect to meet can get off on the right foot.'

She indicated to Daniel to bring her a glass of water. 'Marcello arrived here with Elliott the morning before you. It didn't take long to realise their agendas were not the same, nor their differing methods to secure these objectives. Marcello said they were working to identical ends on behalf of different masters, but he was much more preoccupied with the arrival of Josef's sister than the prospect of convincing Chas and René to part with various copies of Kirchner's statement. He was clearly a suspicious man prone to violence, but he was far from comfortable with the assignment. His breath forever smelt of alcohol, any strange noise would prompt him to react by assuming some intruder was on the premises. He strained to look into the distance, stubbornly persisting even though he had at least two pairs of glasses that I saw. He was highly strung and, in my opinion, capable of erratic and ruthless behaviour. It came as no surprise when, shortly before Chas arrived, he overrode Elliott's protestations and forced Dad and me into a bedroom where he ordered Elliott to bind and gag us. We stayed that way until you were here and I managed to throw myself onto the floor, dislodging the gag and screaming. I took a kick to the stomach for my trouble.'

'Did you think your life was in danger?' Daniel asked.

'I knew it was. None of us were likely to get out alive. He was at breaking point, but it was only when we were on the boat that I understood why.'

'He told you?' Broadhurst asked, the disbelief in his voice apparent.

'He was rambling, talking incessantly, not specifically to me.' She fired the words at Broadhurst. 'Initially, when he intended to escape by boat and needed me to take the controls, my only concern was to get him away from the house as quickly as possible, before his paranoia dissipated into a realisation that a hit squad had not appeared to usurp his role, just a lone ranger with no weapon and a big heart.' She beamed a smile at Daniel. 'Risking my life to save five seemed worth taking, so I played my part. I kept the tension up by indicating I could hear noises from various different points around the house. He was more than prepared to believe there were two, maybe three, sent to get him.

'Once he was on the boat and away from immediate danger, his mood changed. Out came the hip flask and a show of bravado. "They'll all be dead in there by now. I've been on three of these ops – IRs, they're called: Internal Reassignments. You don't take prisoners, just a photo of the operative you were sent to liquidate plus confirmation no witnesses remained."

'After I feigned distress at the prospect of you all dying – I did it pretty convincingly, even if I say so myself - I asked whether he thought they would come after him. There was more rambling, talk of operations he had been involved with, how they didn't value his record and commitment, threats of revenge and restitution. He then picked up the manila envelope and waved it at me. "What I've got in here, they want desperately. I'll do a deal and settle down somewhere far, far away, out of reach, where I will be no trouble to anyone."

'As we pulled into the berth at Bissone, he holstered his gun, turned and said, "I'd do the same yourself if you've got any sense. Go back there and they will kill you." The last I saw of him, he disappeared into the crowd, clutching his envelope.'

Broadhurst raised his eyebrows. 'The redemption of the malefactor, is that it? You should write a novel.'

'Maybe I will,' she retorted. 'I'll write a part for someone cynical and arrogant, shall I? You might recognise him.'

Daniel raised his hands. 'Now children, let's keep it civil, can we?'

Danata's cheeks flushed. 'Okay, let me answer his second accusation, on one condition you must both agree to.'

The two men exchanged a glance.

'I mean it. On no account are you to repeat to anyone, especially my father, what I am about to tell you. Is that understood?'

'If you say so,' from Daniel, a nod from Broadhurst.

'I nursed my mother during those last months. Most times, the morphine took away the pain and her senses and she would talk to herself, disjointed, unintelligible, mostly incoherent utterings. One day, she refused the medication and insisted I listen. She had made a promise, and I was bound by it, not to reveal the fact she had received a visit from Rita Krakowski at the studio. Rita knew Josef was travelling. She asked after him, personal details, habits, personality; every possible snippet of information. Mum showed her photos of them together from the time they had met until the present, photos of me from childhood.

'Rita had said Josef must think of her as a bad person. She had just finished writing the story of her life, those pages in the document case you hid in your car just before the police arrived. Mum read them over two days. She gave me a precis. That's how I know so much about my aunt. Rita was old and Mum knew she herself was dying. They made a pact of silence. It didn't stop Mum using her wiles and subtlety to try and influence Josef without giving the game away and, of course, she knew Rita must live somewhere relatively close. She was a frail old lady by this time and would hardly be gallivanting around the continent.'

'You knew about me?' Daniel asked.

'Of course, but I had to pretend it was nonsense and nearly got myself into hot water with Josef when I talked about sterilisation. Does that satisfy you, Mr Private Investigator?'

'It's quite a burden to have to carry with you,' Broadhurst said, 'especially when you are so close to your father.'

She ignored the comment and stood up. 'I think we should try and get a few more hours' sleep. The hospital expected Josef to be released from hospital this afternoon. After nearly eighty years, today, at last, they will finally get to be reunited.'

FORTY-SEVEN
BOULEVARD DE CLICHY, PARIS
December 2018

'What time is he coming?' Broadhurst edged around the rectangular meeting table towards Marchal. 'There's hardly room in this place to swing a cat. More than four people at any one time and you'd have to take it in turns to stand up to avoid the danger of intimacy or assault.'

'Don't exaggerate, Chas. My office, a meeting room and access to a communal toilet in a prestigious building. What do you expect for nine euros a day? It's half the going rate because I know somebody in the judicial police happy to do us a favour.'

'It's half the going rate because it's plumb next to the Theatre of Two Donkeys which many clients might consider an apt metaphor for our little concern.'

'That's unkind. This is the beating heart of the city. The *Théâtre des Deux Ânes* is all about teamwork.'

'Have you walked around at night?' Broadhurst said in feigned amazement. 'Attentions in this neighbourhood are directed to body parts a little south of your beating heart.'

Marchal laughed. 'It's all about danger, passion and, above all, discretion; our credentials in your nutshell.'

Broadhurst eased himself into a chair alongside his partner. 'Two thirty or three thirty? I don't remember.'

'Two thirty. He has to be away by three, a plane to catch. The conference call is at three thirty. Reminds me, I've got to speak to my daughter. The kids are in a school Christmas pageant tonight. I promised I'd be back in time. I'll be in the office if you need me.'

With nothing better to do, Broadhurst skimmed through the apps on his mobile with the dotted symbols. The emails were mostly spam, the Facebook notifications about people he didn't know or didn't care about, and he could not fathom why Instagram would indicate new, unopened activity on a dormant account he had once been encouraged to open but never used. Curiosity got the better of him. The photograph on the screen was a shot from a hotel foyer showing Daniel supporting Rita, alongside a smiling Danata with her arm around the shoulder of the stooped figure of Josef, his face barely visible, but a hand held out with a thumbs-up sign. The caption said: 'After almost eighty years, a family Christmas in prospect.'

Broadhurst smiled at the memory. What everyone believed would be a momentous reunion had turned out, in the best possible sense, to be a somewhat low-key affair.

***

Rita was radiant; dressed in a full-length maroon velvet dress and made up expertly by Danata, she was propped up by cushions in a high-backed armchair on the rear terrace. With Daniel in attendance alongside, she looked to Broadhurst the epitome of an Edwardian dowager duchess, chatelaine of a minor stately home. All she lacked was a King Charles spaniel to complete the set. Broadhurst could not resist posing her for a number of takes on his mobile camera.

Danata ushered a rather haggard-looking Josef, his wrists bandaged where he had been bound, onto the terrace.

'I'm sorry to say René cannot be with us. The doctor insists he spends another night under observation. He is still very weak ... but cheerful,' she added. 'I know you wanted him to be present,' she said to Rita, but the old lady's attention was elsewhere.

Brother and sister just stared at each other in silence for what seemed like an eternity. The chairs had been arranged so that Josef sat directly opposite his sister. Danata sat balanced on the arm of Daniel's chair and draped her hand around his shoulder. Broadhurst stood to one side.

'*Pan śmierdzące pierdy,*' Rita said with a straight face that made it sound like a rebuke, but Danata chuckled.

'*Starsa siostra,*' Josef replied. 'Not a day has passed when I do not think of my big sister. I hope her memories of me transcend an unfortunate nickname.'

'They were the last words I ever said to you as I pushed you into your hiding place. Do you remember?'

'No. Were they?'

'I said, if anybody comes close, you must try not to let them know you are there. I was afraid your *pierdnięcie* would give your position away.'

Josef leaned forward and reached for both of her hands. He drew them towards him and clutched her fingertips. 'I have so longed for this day, even at the expense of being reminded you used to call me Mr Smelly Farts.'

'It wasn't me who came up with the name,' she said in mock indignation. 'It was Mother who began to call you that when you were still in nappies.'

The mention of their parents sparked their conversation in Polish, animated and excited by common memories, they talked on and on. At no time did he let go of her fingertips, gently massaging one at a time until a passage in their conversation reached a critical point, when he would grip them tight again.

Later in the evening, after a buffet dinner from a local restaurant had arrived and been consumed, when the exertion and excitement of their day had taken its toll on the old couple, they were escorted to their beds. 'When will we talk again?' Josef had asked as he sat on the chairlift.

'When you have read what I took the trouble to write, just for you. Then we can speak of other things.'

He nodded, and pressed the button to activate the motor.

Danata, Broadhurst and Daniel were back in the kitchen, occupying the same seats as they had earlier that day.

'They seemed to get on well,' Broadhurst ventured, 'though I didn't understand a word of what they were saying. It's a hell of a language.'

'I'll second that,' Daniel said.

A bottle of Evian was passed around. 'They trod carefully,' Danata said. 'There is still a minefield to get through and Rita thinks it will help if he reads her memoirs first.'

'I think she's right,' Broadhurst said.

'They talked of life in Krakow before the war. Josef was too young to remember, but he was desperate to soak up everything she had to say. In turn, she was riveted to his adventures of managing to get through the war without being caught. It was fast forward then, to their lives over the past thirty years. There's a huge void in the middle called "Kirchner" which has yet to be dissected and explained. It will take some time, but they have learnt today how to relax into each other's company. I am encouraged.'

* * *

Marchal walked back into the room. 'Our visitor is just getting out of a taxi,' he said. 'Let's see what he's got to say for himself.'

FORTY-EIGHT
BOULEVARD DE CLICHY, PARIS
December 2018

'Good to make your acquaintance, René. You don't mind me calling you René, do you?'

Hopper used both his hands to grasp Marchal's, at the same time revealing an engraved cufflink with precious stone inset, manicured fingernails and twenty thousand dollars' worth of Blancpain Villeret with Roman numerals on his wrist. 'And to catch up with you again, Chas.' He released Marchal's hand to raise his palm in acknowledgement to Broadhurst on the other side of the table. 'Compact operation you've got here. I'm impressed.' His overenthusiastic attempt to push back a chair produced a hollow thud as it made contact with the partition wall. 'Yes, sir. Keep a tight control of the overheads; I can see that.'

Broadhurst pushed several A4 sheets of closely printed text across the table. 'You came for this. There are no other hard copies and you are probably aware our mobiles ... cell phones ... were destroyed by your operatives last week.'

'Let me assure you, gentlemen, I have no operatives or associates on this mission. It is not US government-sponsored, merely a private initiative on behalf of the President's re-election campaign. I would not have it any other way, rest assured.'

'Even so,' Broadhurst said, 'the man sitting next to you at dinner just over a week ago was brutally executed whilst serving your quest.'

'Hardly.' Hopper gave both men a resigned and sombre shake of the head. 'Elliott's death was a tragedy. His interest was on behalf of the State of Israel, which fortuitously dovetailed with mine. It's my understanding that the rogue killer who committed the murder and held you captive was not interested in this' – he waved the sheets of paper in the air – 'but in some other document in your possession. Have they caught him yet?'

'Not to our knowledge,' Marchal said.

Hopper checked his watch. 'Don't want to miss my flight. I have to be home in time to prepare for Christmas. Can I take it, between us three and your source, we can consider the matter closed?'

Broadhurst moved his head from side to side. 'As far as the historic records of events are concerned, you can be assured our word is binding. You've just touched on the other problem.'

Hopper sat back in the seat he was about to push back. 'That being?'

'Your principal could likely suffer what, in the words you used to me when discussing the death of Petra, is termed collateral damage, if and when issues pertaining to the document in the hands of the assassin come to light. You may be forced, again using your words, into a state of containment outside of our control.'

'Really? Are you sure?'

'It's hypothetical. I'm just warning you of a possibility, not putting you on notice something specific will occur.'

'Can you give me more details? I like to know what I'm dealing with. You make it sound very John Le Carré.'

'We don't have all the information at our disposal, and it is not in our gift to control the progression of the research, or how or whether it is divulged.'

'And even if you did, you wouldn't tell me.'

'That's about it,' Broadhurst said.

Hopper got up to leave. He hesitated at the door. 'Pick the side you are on. You should tread carefully, gentlemen. I've enjoyed doing business with you and I wouldn't want to see you or your sources prejudiced by an error of judgement. But remember, you are up against extremely powerful people and institutions, and it's in nobody's interest to have a Watergate every time a president is elected. Believe me, to avoid this, the forces of democracy can be channelled into a far more covert and lethal force than can be mustered by any dictatorship. Take extreme care.'

'That sounds like a threat,' Marchal said, looking at his partner.

'Don't confuse friendly advice with a commination,' Hopper said.

The door closed behind him.

FORTY-NINE
BOULEVARD DE CLICHY, PARIS
December 2018

'We could always take his advice and leave well alone,' Marchal said. He had been sitting quietly on his own since Hopper had left. 'After all, Horwitz has Kirchner's statement and the promise of the contract or whatever it was that Marcello considered so vital as a means of survival; Josef and Rita were reunited and we were paid for our assignment. It's a fair result.'

'Is that how you want to leave it?' Broadhurst asked. 'It's a perfectly reasonable request and if you insist, I'll bow to your decision. For me, the only trouble is it ignores two factors.'

'I imagine it does.'

'Firstly, in ten minutes or so, we are due to speak to an American reporter who, according to my former colleague who will also join us on the call, has a potential storyline which he describes as a ticking time bomb. Saying to him, well done, now shut up, forget it and go away, is unlikely to cut any ice. His story will break whatever we consider is best for us. Once it does, a lot of press interest will generate more investigations into the past, and General William's wartime antics, true or insinuated, will be totally exposed, probably in concert with a major financial scandal.'

Marchal nodded.

'Secondly, a professional assassin is on the loose out there who was complicit in the death of an innocent girl which weighs heavily on me. If I can convince myself I have done everything possible to right that wrong, maybe I won't be so troubled by my conscience.' He held his palms together as if praying. 'Somehow I don't think my conscience will let me off so easily.'

The screen split into three locations as Broadhurst and Marchal joined the video conference call. The backdrop to Duncan White's smiling face was his office at Kensington Palace which Broadhurst knew so well. The monarch's picture was still hanging slightly off-centre on the wall. Sonny Gerbitz was in a child's bedroom backed by a wall papered with clouds, rainbows and prancing unicorns. 'Apologies,' he said. 'When the kids are awake and playing in the lounge, it's the quietest room in the house. We haven't graduated to a place big enough for me to have an office, but one day we hope to move from this condo.'

'Maybe this story will get you there,' Broadhurst said.

Sonny turned away from the webcam, avoiding a retort. Broadhurst guessed the young man was in his mid-thirties, fresh-faced with an unruly mop of tight, curly jet-black hair. His shoulders were hunched into a black leather jacket and he nursed an electronic vape in his hand which from time to time he clicked nervously between his teeth but did not smoke.

'Let's set out the facts,' White interjected, 'and see where we get to. Just to recap, Sonny was trying to establish a link with the disappearance of Sophia from the family home in Chicago with her reappearance three days later the other side of Lake Michigan in Muskegon. One of the possible routes took her north from Chicago to Milwaukee – we're in the state of Illinois now – on a ferry across the lake to the Michigan side where she was found wandering around. Sonny discovered that the ownership of a former brewery in Milwaukee and the Chicago Jewish newspaper which reported the incident could be traced back to TELA and the Four Realms Foundation, now run by Stefan Horwitz. Correct?'

'Right,' Sonny said.

'We have to question TELA's motives; one, for missing microfiches covering the period of Sophia's resurrection and dispatch during the period they owned the publication, and two, fighting a long and ultimately futile battle to retain possession of the brewery site when expropriated by the local authority. Where do we go from there, Sonny?' White asked.

There was a long and audible drawn-out breath on the audio feed before Sonny spoke. 'Last year, the city's contractors got around to demolishing the building and excavating the foundations for the new development. A digger pulled up a selection of human bones that had been there for decades. The chemicals used in the brewing process had seeped into the ground over the years and contaminated the skeleton, making it difficult to complete a full DNA comparison test. The head was missing, ruling out a dental check.'

'Presumably, the police tried to identify the remains?' Marchal interrupted.

'They got a low-grade DNA sample which, unsurprisingly, had no data match, given the body had been there for decades, and a pathology report which confirmed the skeleton was of a young female in her teens.'

'You don't seem particularly exhilarated by this discovery, Sonny?' Broadhurst said. 'Does the obvious hypothesis not enthral you?'

'Around forty young girls are reported missing in Illinois every year and never discovered,' Sonny said flatly. 'Probably, a similar count would apply for Michigan. It's all highly circumstantial and any suggestion of a link with Sophia Horwitz would have to be couched in so many caveats, it would lose traction.'

'Who's got to you, Sonny?' Broadhurst said. 'This thread is red meat to an investigative reporter. You are scared of something or somebody. Does this have anything to do with the American connection and the fact that General Williams was a non-executive director of the Four Realms Foundation until the mid-nineties? We've already had threats from friends close to the President suggesting René and I take a holiday and lose our memories.'

'Let me do the talking, Sonny,' White said. 'I've had the benefit of being privy to this information for a couple of weeks now, while you two gents were swanning around in Switzerland enjoying the scenery.'

Broadhurst couldn't supress a guffaw in protest. 'That's us,' he said, '*bons vivants.*'

'You're right, Chas.' White had adopted a serious tone. 'Sonny's wife was in a shopping mall with their kids a few weeks ago when a woman approached her. She was effusive, full of compliments about the children, asking their names. As she went to leave, she whispered in Sonny's wife's ear the fact that they knew where the kids went to school and if Sonny didn't drop the story he was working on, the kids might not make it back home one day. Same thing if the police got to hear about this conversation. With that, she was gone. You can understand the state Sonny and his wife are in.'

'Sure.' Broadhurst looked at René. 'Threats create a state of mind both uncomfortable and difficult to deal with. Duncan, you presumably have a suggestion?'

'Let's assume for the sake of argument that the real Sophia Horwitz, née Vogel, was murdered in Milwaukee and her place assumed by the

407

current Sophia Horwitz, née Vogel, found wandering in Muskegon. The real Sophia Vogel disappeared in Chicago, Illinois and reappeared across the lake in Muskegon, which just happens to be in Michigan. She refused to return to Chicago, which was perfectly understandable, and claimed a so-called aunt as the closest person to a relative in England. The federal system in the US means that the states act independently and what might be of interest to the law in Illinois has no import as far as the authorities in Michigan are concerned. They were probably just glad to see the back of her. I have to say it sounds reasonable. Nobody who might have known her was asked to identify her. Why would they be? Does it sound logical?'

'Perfectly,' Broadhurst said. 'My question is, how do you intend to get Sonny out of the picture and make a series of allegations which will get the best libel lawyers in London licking their lips in anticipation?'

'Following my trip to Canada with my royal charges to resolve their Christmas card dilemma, I have set in train the same security protocols to provide a safe and discreet hideaway for Sonny and family for the next two months or so, while he works on a new project. Subject to the outcome of this meeting, he is all packed up and ready to go. Right, Sonny?'

'Our luggage is parked by the front door, just waiting to load.' For the first time, Sonny smiled.

'How do you suggest putting the allegations into print?'

White nodded. 'It depends exactly what you and René are bringing to the party, Chas. That's what this is all about. The bare bones are these: the last time we talked, you mentioned your quest to find the Krakowski woman and the revelations contained in her memoirs. This seems to me like the best medium on which to concentrate our efforts. We get Sonny to convert the memoirs into a six-part serialisation, "Rita's Diary – A Holocaust Survivor", or some such title, to run in tandem with the events marking the anniversary of the liberation of the concentration camps from next year. I've sold the idea to an affiliate of Maclean's in Canada, who would take the lead and syndicate the series around the world – the US rights ceded at no cost to me, acting on behalf of Sonny. Into this series, we feed in whatever the lawyers say we can about the Sophia Horwitz story and the TELA operations. How does that sound?'

'Thinking aloud,' Broadhurst said, 'it sounds feasible. It will mean getting Rita's consent – that's René's speciality – and ensuring she is safe and out of harm's way.'

'The last I heard from Danata,' Marchal said, 'was that they plan to take her to Israel in the New Year while she is still able to travel. The Holocaust Foundation has a home for veterans in Jerusalem and a place has been arranged for her. Josef is selling up in Switzerland and is planning to move to be close by his sister. The doctors say she has a few months at the most and he won't be far behind her.'

'What do you expect to say about the TELA operations?' Broadhurst said.

'Things are quiet in my sphere at the moment,' Duncan replied. 'The royal family is off to Sandringham and, beyond the Christmas Day speech, we have little to do. My people are making some discreet enquiries and digging up info on a number of the donations and loans which TELA makes to various organisations listed as promoting good causes.'

'Sounds as though you've been busy.'

'The sixty-four-thousand-dollar question, Chas, is what information do you have which can transform allegations into accusations?'

Broadhurst smiled and reached for a folder on the table. 'I think I can give you just enough to put a time bomb under TELA and the Four Realms Foundation.'

FIFTY
OFFICES OF PATRICIO BRITO & ASSOCIATES, LONDON
March 2019

'Thank you all for coming.' The lawyer made a claw of his fingers on one hand and ran it back through his mane of fine grey hair, at the same time adopting a facial expression as if he had just relieved himself of some enormous mental burden. He flicked visiting cards around the table in poker fashion. Broadhurst, White and their lawyer followed suit, as did Stefan and Sophie Horwitz together with their two female attorneys. Broadhurst carefully placed all the cards he received in a small plastic bag which he transferred to his jacket pocket.

'My name is Silvio Ramos. Unfortunately, my colleague and senior partner, Patricio Brito, is unable to attend and has asked me to chair this meeting in his absence. He will be available at a later occasion.' He turned to the woman sitting next to Stefan Horwitz. 'You wished to address the meeting, Doutora Weiss?'

The woman peered over a pair of iron-framed glasses. 'My clients understood the purpose of this meeting was to discuss the progress of their request to seek performance of a contract. They do not understand nor agree to the presence of these two gentlemen who are in no way connected to the transaction under consideration.'

Ramos gave a respectful nod and played with the designer stubble above his top lip. 'As you know, Doutora, my firm acts for the Portuguese government; in this instance, the legal department of the Ministry of the Environment. These gentlemen, Senhores Broadhurst and White, have been specifically requested to attend on its behalf.'

'I can't imagine why,' Weiss said dismissively. 'These men are no more than private investigators hired by my client to perform a task which they singularly failed to do correctly.'

She looked at Stefan for direction.

'Very well. We accept their presence under protest and only as it is relevant. As and when we discuss matters outside of their remit, we request that they withdraw.'

'Absolutely,' White said. He turned to Broadhurst with a sarcastic grin. 'I expect we've got plenty of' – he pursed his lips – 'private investigating to be doing?'

Ramos turned his attention to the designer stubble on his chin. 'To recap, through her solicitors, Hausmann, Weiss and Associates, Senhora Horwitz has requested performance of a contract entered into in 1939, between the Portuguese government and Borys Wiesel, to explore and commercialise the reserves of lithium in the country. As we all know, as battery power becomes more prevalent, lithium is a valuable component; and although Portugal's reserves are dwarfed by Chile, Australia and Argentina, it so happens Portugal has a particularly high-grade variety derived from the pyroxene known as spodumene. It is the only source available in Europe. Known reserves in the north of Portugal are estimated to be worth in excess of a billion dollars.'

White gave a long, low whistle.

'Quite so,' Ramos acknowledged. 'There is no dispute as to the fundamentals. I understand Ms Horwitz's consultant, Dame Isabel Solden, has visited the area on a number of occasions to provide an appraisal. The contract Senhora Horwitz seeks to enforce contains an all-embracing commitment to extend the terms of the contract to the discovery of any additional reserves of lithium, which, I understand, is not beyond the realms of possibility. Although this contract cannot be assigned to a third party, the terms specifically refer to the rights of successors in title to both parties, namely the heirs of Borys Wiesel or to future Portuguese governments, during the period of the contract, which runs for one hundred years from 1939.'

'Precisely,' Weiss interrupted. 'My client contends that as she is the only living descendant of Borys Wiesel and as the terms of the contract are legally binding for another twenty years, she intends to enforce the agreement.'

'Quite so,' Ramos said, matter-of-fact. 'It is in the Portuguese government's interest to contest the validity of the contract for a number of reasons. Firstly, the royalty payable to the State is based on commercial conditions in 1939 and is barely five per cent of the rate which it presently receives from the current operator, the successor contract holder.'

'The illegal contract holder,' Weiss interrupted, turning to Stefan Horwitz triumphantly as if waiting for a cry of 'hear, hear!'.

'We are not in the courtroom now, madam,' Ramos said. 'I am simply summarising my client's position. Secondly, we have argued that the contract should be considered null and void for non-performance during nearly eighty years, which was clearly not the intention of the parties and satisfies civil code precedent regarding an obligation to perform. Nevertheless, to avoid protracted legal proceedings, my client did make an offer, without legal consequence, to settle the matter.'

Weiss held out her hands. 'Which my client refused as derisory. We attended this meeting on the understanding a further offer would be forthcoming.'

'It is,' Ramos confirmed. 'The original offer of two million euros is withdrawn and the revised offer is one euro.'

Stefan Horwitz stiffened in his seat, returning Weiss's confused look with a glare. 'Is this some sort of a joke?' she said.

'No joke,' Ramos smiled benignly. 'Both parties accept that, whatever its defects, the contract has no value if one or other contracting party no longer exists.'

'What has that got to do with anything?' Weiss asked.

Ramos turned to White. 'Perhaps you would explain.'

White looked over a pair of tortoiseshell glasses directly at Sophia Horwitz. 'You are probably aware that over the past three weeks, the Canadian magazine *People and Places* has been summarising the memoirs of Rita Krakowski, a Polish Jew and a survivor of the camps, who was ensnared during her lifetime by a ruthless concentration camp commandant. The series has been syndicated around the world. I'm sure you understand.'

There was no reaction from the other side of the table, just fisheye stares at the speaker.

'In tomorrow's edition, Rita talks of an experience she witnessed in a railway tunnel in Bavaria at the end of the war, where, amongst a series of brutal acts, she watched as a young girl was encouraged to kill a captive German officer by slicing his throat. It is Rita's belief the girl was somehow hypnotised.'

413

'Fascinating, I'm sure,' Weiss said. 'But I don't see the relevance of this horrific story to our discussions today. Can we talk sensibly about a deal?'

Ramos put a finger over his lip and turned back to White.

'We have passed on to Mr Ramos a signed statement from Rita Krakowski, confirming the identity of the girl in the tunnel as Gretchen Sommer, daughter of a notorious German doctor and war criminal. In her statement, Rita also refers to a girl whose photograph appears in the pages of a Holland, Michigan, newspaper, the *Sentinel*, in October 1946, in which she is described as Sophia Vogel, only survivor of a firebomb which destroyed her family's Chicago home. Rita identifies this girl as the very same Gretchen Sommer. As you will see from the photographs appended to the statement, there is very little physical similarity between the school photo of Sophia taken at the end of the academic year in July to the *Sentinel* photo of Sophia taken in October.'

'What absolute rubbish!' Weiss said. 'You are attempting to make some ridiculous utterings from a dementia-ridden old lady support a preposterous contention that my client is not who she says she is. Shame on you and your scandalous behaviour. Now, can we talk a deal or not, Ramos?'

'We have no alternative but to take this initiative seriously and reserve our client's position until further investigations have been undertaken. I regret no further discussion is warranted; unless, of course, you wish to withdraw your proposed action.'

Broadhurst leaned forward and spoke for the first time. 'There is a simple means of refuting Ms Krakowski's allegations.' He addressed his remarks to Sophia. 'As I'm sure you will claim to have long forgotten how to speak Polish, I suggest you agree to a DNA test.'

'Why on earth would I do that, you interfering man? You have been nothing but trouble since I stupidly hired you. I am who I say I am and have nothing to prove to anybody.' She hesitated. 'Anyway, I am the last surviving member of the Wiesel family and there is no available source with which a DNA sample could be compared.'

'If there were, would you agree to submit to the test?'

414

Stefan's voice rumbled like thunder in the distance and getting closer. 'I see no point in protracting this meeting if we are about to descend into the realm of hypothesis.'

'I wasn't,' Broadhurst said. 'On February the second, the Banco do Carmo got around to opening the safe-deposit box H65, one of the largest units remaining and registered to an alias used by an SS major named Kirchner, whom I will describe, exclusively for legal purposes, as the common-law partner of Rita Krakowski. Inside they found the remains of two individuals, still in reasonable condition, given the hermetic sealing around the unit and the relative lack of exposure to the atmosphere. One of the bodies was confirmed as that of Lew Wiesel, with ample examples of DNA available for comparison. For internal security reasons, the Portuguese government has exercised its right to classify this information as secret, but you can take my word for it.'

'It's my understanding,' White said, 'that the DNA shared between an uncle and his niece is around twenty-five per cent, so the result, one way or the other, would be pretty conclusive.'

Weiss visibly bristled. 'These allegations are nothing short of defamatory, and should they appear in print tomorrow, as you suggest, they will be dismissed as libellous and redress sought from all parties concerned.' She turned to Stefan Horwitz. 'We will take immediate steps to place an injunction on the publication of this shameful and malicious material and seize all copies in course of distribution. I propose we leave immediately so I might begin. Time is of the essence.'

Stefan Horwitz placed a restraining hand on his lawyer's arm. 'What other libels do you intend to print in this article?' He indicated for the lawyer to make a note. 'And, whose byline is associated with it?'

'It's attributed to me and Mr Broadhurst,' White said. 'As to additional historical material, our only interest is to establish the truth.'

Stefan Horwitz adjusted his glasses as if focusing on Broadhurst. 'Exacting your pound of flesh, Mr Broadhurst, can cut both ways. You and your associates would do well to remember that. An ill will can have serious repercussions.'

The entourage headed by Weiss was ready to leave. Stefan extended an arm to help his wife to her feet, holding back as she shuffled to the door which White rushed around to hold open. 'I wouldn't want you to take any of this out of context,' White said to Sophia. 'I always have been and will continue to be a dedicated admirer of your musical genius.'

Sophia Horwitz sucked in loudly and spat in White's face.

FIFTY-ONE
OFFICES OF PATRICIO BRITO & ASSOCIATES, LONDON
March 2019

'I think we deserve a sherry, don't you?' Ramos said to his guests as he returned from ushering White's lawyer into the elevator. 'On behalf of the Portuguese government, I can only thank you for your intervention. I found it most refreshing to be present as a virtual bystander.'

'You still might have to do a deal with them,' White said, gratefully accepting a glass.

'I doubt that would now be countenanced. You have created the prospect of a legal maelstrom from which no one will emerge victorious for, most likely, somewhat longer than it takes to extract the last vestiges of lithium from the ground. The Portuguese government is a past master in the art of protracting legal proceedings beyond the patience of a saint, believe me.' He made a point of clinking glasses and took a mouthful of sherry which he savoured like a mouthwash between his cheeks. 'I'm intrigued,' he said, eventually. 'Are you able to expand, in confidence, on where else your investigation is taking you? It might well impact on the advice we provide to our client. I am also confused as for what reason a plan would be conceived to substitute the identity of a child with a profound Nazi family background for that of a Polish Jew. As much as I subscribe to the pronouncement of your witness, it is an element which will ferment doubt in any judgement.'

Broadhurst nodded. 'What better cover for disguising Nazi ideals than an establishment notionally headed by a man married to the descendant of a family of Polish Jews. Nobody would dream to suspect. It was a dilemma which Rita and Josef helped to clarify for us. Just prior to the outbreak of war, Portugal was a hotbed of suspicion and rumours, perpetuated by intelligence agents from both friend and foe alike. The disposition of natural reserves was critical, and the Portuguese dictator, Salazar, maintained the country's perceived neutrality by sanctioning an exploration contract for the lithium reserves with Borys Wiesel, a respected industrialist from a buffer state between Germany and Russia. The war effectively meant the contract was sidelined, but its existence assumed a new importance after the war, when the fate of the Wiesel family came to light. From the end of the war until his reappearance in Poland years later, Lew Wiesel was believed to be dead, along with all the remaining members of his family—'

Ramos didn't allow him to finish. 'Except Sophia Vogel, his niece.'

'Precisely. The whereabouts of Lew's remains and the contract were unknown at the time and of secondary consideration. The Ratlines, which by this time had morphed into Four Realms and TELA, mistakenly assumed Poland would emerge from Soviet occupation as an independent country, and the wealth and industrial power once exercised by the Wiesel family would generate a claim for restitution and compensation running into millions. Of course, it never did; or at least, not until the eighties, when the USSR collapsed.'

There was a nod of comprehension from Ramos. 'When Lew Wiesel resurfaced, interest in the lithium contract was restored. It all makes sense.'

'Even more so,' Broadhurst resumed. 'When Kirchner reported in 1988 that Lew had made contact, the Circle ordered Kirchner to attend the meeting, secure the contract and kill Wiesel. He realised Wiesel would be out to seek revenge for his family, so he struck first. However, suspicious of the Circle's attitude to him and, especially, to Rita, he decided to avoid handing over the contract and kept it in the safe-deposit box as a bargaining chip.'

Ramos checked his watch. 'Are you gentlemen free for lunch? It's on me. There's a pretentious Italian where they serve a magnificent seafood risotto on Portland Place. I need to hear the rest of your tale.'

It was after four when Broadhurst and White emerged into the watery, fading sunshine to hail a taxi. Ramos had stayed behind, ostensibly to settle the bill and finish his third Graham's Vintage Port 2003, but more to think on the likely ramifications of everything he had heard over their extended lunch.

Their agreement had been only general conversation until the main course plates had been collected and they had the dessert menus before them. It was White who took up the story, explaining the role of Sonny in developing the exposé of Sophia Vogel. He told how Sonny had turned his

418

attention to the background of a man called Ludo Horwitz in the years following the end of the Second World War.

Living in a modest home in a suburb of Laramie in Wyoming, Horwitz had been a successful businessman in a partnership with a fellow German of a similar Jewish background. Horwitz had disavowed his faith when his partner had accused him of stealing from the business, and his pleadings had been dismissed by the local Jewish community which had ostracised him and his family.

In Sonny's opinion, although the police were never involved, the probability was the accusations were well founded. Ludo's teenage son, Stefan, was suffering from glioblastoma, a fast-growing, aggressive tumour that forms on the supportive tissue of the brain. The medication he needed stalled the advance of the growth and was extremely expensive. His weekly trips to the university hospital in Cheyenne ran into thousands of dollars and had forced Ludo into selling the large homestead he had owned when a partner, downsizing to a modest house in the suburbs and employment as an assistant at a local supermarket.

It was at the university hospital where Ludo met and became friendly with a certain Peter Winter, a research fellow with a specialist facility on the campus dealing with applied life sciences. They became friendly, socialising together and, more importantly for Ludo, integrating Stefan into one of Winter's experimental groups which meant the medication he required would be supplied at the university's expense.

As Stefan's health declined, he became a permanent resident in Winter's facility. The situation changed dramatically in 1950. According to university records, Winter was given compassionate leave of absence to deal with the sudden and unexpected death of his own son, Andrew, from a brain haemorrhage. The death certificate was signed by the resident physician at the Institute for European Reunification in Denver and was followed by a private family cremation.

In a newspaper article which appeared a few weeks later, there was a rare photograph of Peter Winter alongside a smiling Stefan Horwitz who attributed the gradual reversal of his degenerative condition to the exploratory treatment he had received. Winter was quoted as saying that

Stefan's recovery went a long way to putting aside the sadness he felt about his only child's death.

White came to the end of his explanation. 'Sonny sent a Freedom of Information request to the federal government to establish that Peter Winter was, in fact, the name adopted by Dr Sommer when he moved to the US in 1945, but, as you might expect, the request was denied on the grounds of classified information. Rita did confirm that the man in the newspaper photograph bore a close resemblance to the man she knew as Sommer and that, from what she could recall, Stefan could well have been Sommer's son, Anders, but nothing is conclusive.'

'You're saying Sommer's daughter married her brother, who became head of the Four Realms Foundation?' Ramos sounded flabbergasted.

'It would explain why they have lived very separate lives,' White said.

'But you can't prove it?'

Broadhurst lifted the plastic bag from his pocket. 'I am reliably informed that it may well be possible to extract DNA from the surface of the visiting cards handed to us this morning. It depends upon sweat and skin cells. I took the liberty of taking the cards handed to you, Silvio, as well as asking your secretary to collect the water glasses they used under sanitised conditions and bag them up for us. I'll pop by and collect them. Hope you don't mind.'

'Siblings share about fifty per cent of the same DNA,' White added. 'If we can establish that match, plus no relationship to the Wiesel family, it may not stand up in court, but it will make great press.'

'What else would you like to know?' Broadhurst said jovially, downing the remnants of his port. 'Perhaps we can let you into some secrets about the Four Realms Foundation. We have to go now and get the cards and water glasses into the hands of the specialists, but I'll leave you with a teaser that could well be explained in this weekend's edition of *The Sunday Times* by their Insight team.'

'Please do so,' Ramos said.

'What do you think the name of the Four Realms would be if it were a German organisation?'

420

'I'm not up on German, I'm afraid.'

Broadhurst grinned. 'Me neither, but I think it would translate pretty much as the Fourth Reich.'

EPILOGUE

Broadhurst tutted at the sound of the second ring on the doorbell and, with an audible sigh, allowed the open broadsheet to slide from his knees and come to rest on the floor in front of his armchair. Who could possibly be interested in disturbing him at ten on a Sunday morning? It was a fifty-fifty chance between a delegation from the Jehovah's Witnesses or a contractor with an Irish accent who was just passing and thought the drive could do with a new lick of tarmac. Whoever it was would soon be on their way.

This was the second week of revelations from the Insight investigators into the history and workings of the Four Realms Foundation, and it made chilling reading. Two Sundays previously, the first exposé had dealt with the origins of the organisation, funding lines through a morass of offshore and dummy organisations which led back to post-war Switzerland and Argentina, clandestine characters associated with the Nazi regime and the famous Ratlines escape routes with links to stolen Nazi gold and treasures. The mix of fact and innuendo picked up on the characters involved, the early members of the administrative board and, of course, the involvement of General Williams, whose position was subtly linked to the mysterious Allied officer in the Bavarian tunnel revealed in the serialised memoirs of Rita Krakowski. The climax to that week's article was the question concerning the parentage of Stefan Horwitz and his wife, Sophia. The investigators had seen evidence which, the investigators alleged, confirmed their real identities were those of Anders and Gretchen, children of the Nazi 'Doctor of Death', Wilhelm Sommer, clandestinely taken to the States to live and work and given immunity from prosecution as the war criminal he undoubtedly was.

The furore created in international press circles was immense, and both *The New York Times* and *The Washington Post* were quoting reliable sources which Broadhurst knew could only mean they had got to Sonny Gerbitz and Duncan White. Like Watergate and Nixon, it was only a question of time before General Williams and his president son would be in the spotlight.

423

Broadhurst and White had agreed not to resume contact until the clamour had subsided, to avoid embarrassment that might well be caused if White's role at Kensington Palace surfaced in the press.

The following week there was a hiatus in the revelations as several injunctions were served, with various firms of renowned legal standing and the Royal Law Courts kept busy for days as attempts were made to still future publication. Late on the previous Friday the injunctions had been lifted and promises of more astounding revelations on Sunday had stimulated public expectancy.

Broadhurst was halfway through today's exposé when the doorbell rang.

The investigators had turned their attention to the list of benefactors of the foundation as detailed at the insistence of the Charity Commission in the last annual report. Under the title 'Donations and Investments by TELA – The Web Organisation – The Foundation's Social Distribution Arm in More Than a Hundred Countries Throughout the World' there were four pages of good causes listed with a stamp-sized photo or emblem against each one.

'We have researched six of these supposed charitable organisations,' ran the article. Broadhurst had read down to number three.

'The Saint Joseph Overseas Missionaries' was the title. An inset showed a brochure cover of a figure dressed as a nun, extending her hand to a smiling black child sitting in the centre of a mud hut, with the description, 'Faith and Guidance to All'. A watermark cross had been drawn across the cover and underneath was a picture of three grizzly looking individuals aboard motorcycles, the words 'SJ Missionaries' printed on the back of one rider's leather jacket. 'The Real Saint Joseph Overseas Missionaries', ran the subtext. 'Groups of fanatical right-wing agitators sent around the world to generate hatred and unrest directed at the weakest and most vulnerable.'

'The Circle of Friendship' ran the next column. The crossed-out brochure cover showed a group of homeless individuals sitting in a circle, holding hands, all staring up lovingly at a bearded man suggestive of Jesus. 'Providing help where help is needed' was the description. Underneath was the drawing of a smiling Nazi soldier holding a block of gold in the air with

424

a speech bubble coming from his lips, saying, 'Ensuring the survival of fascism throughout the world.'

Broadhurst had just read an inset feature which read '*Hacer Correr La Voz*' – 'Hear the News and Spread the Word' – with two jolly men of Latin appearance standing next to an ageing printing machine and holding the cover of a magazine depicting the nativity. It had also been crossed out in favour of a photograph showing a closed bible in one frame, and then, when opened, a printed page headed 'The Holocaust Lie', under which was a report detailing how the Argentinian printing organisation specialised in producing inflammatory literature for distribution throughout the volatile states of South and Latin America, blaming the Jews and LGBT communities for poisoning democracy and propagating poverty amongst the masses.

He had just had time to glance at the concluding paragraph of the article, which castigated the 'Fourth Reich' foundation as nothing better than a fascist organisation run by the son of a Nazi war criminal, with the single aim of undermining liberal and free-minded societies throughout the globe.

His mind absorbed, Broadhurst opened the front door without thinking.

* * *

The late-night connection on Line 2 of the Metro de Caracas terminated at Zoológico. Through a haze of sugar cane spirit, Enrico vaguely remembered trying to work out what 'Furg' and 'Rezig' meant amongst the vocabulary of graffiti language plastered across every available space on the walls, windows and ceiling of the carriage. Perhaps there was a dictionary. He would ask the first guy he saw with a spray can.

He wasn't supposed to be here. He should have alighted at La Yaguara and walked to the motel where he was staying. Now, it would mean a forty-kilometre cab ride back. What the hell! He had plenty of money. Old Stefan had really wanted to get his hands on that contract. Three hundred thousand dollars safely tucked away in a Curaçao bank account. He had just returned from there three days ago and was enjoying a short vacation, experiencing the night spots of Venezuela's capital. He was taking it easy though. Three hundred K would not last forever, even with the favourable exchange rate in this shithole.

Enrico went to get up. He couldn't. His legs would not react. His eyes focused. There was a syringe attached to his thigh, the needle embedded in his muscle. Sobriety returned with the panic. He tried to lower his hand to remove the syringe, but it would not respond to the command of his brain. He was paralysed. What was it? Curare? He felt the saliva running down his chin.

The two men seemed to be wearing black plastic bin liners. It suited their black faces, he thought. They were carrying him. He was having trouble breathing. His lungs seemed to have gone to sleep. He heard the trumpet of an elephant in the distance.

They laid him on some straw. It was damp, and the stench – his sense of smell had not gone, he realised – was so vile he would have retched if his body knew how. What was that sound? It was something he recalled from his grandfather's smallholding. That was it. He knew exactly what it was. The wild boars were grunting frantically in expectation of their next meal.

* * *

Rita Krakowski died peacefully in her sleep at a hospice in Jerusalem on the twentieth of May 2019. Her brother, Josef, niece, Danata and biological son, Daniel, were at her bedside as she passed on. Those early months of the year had been so eventful, but she never tired of the novelty of the fame she had acquired. Her serialised memoirs had spawned a Facebook account with over half a million followers, and hours of television documentaries.

In April, the International Institute of Holocaust Remembrance Foundations issued a statement commending the strength and fortitude of Rita Krakowski, and formally requested that all warrants issued for her apprehension by various government authorities be immediately rescinded; as indeed occurred.

During their last conversation, Josef had asked her how she had managed to survive in the camps. He smiled at her answer. She said she had Yodel and Tillie, bullets and bread dough to thank for that.

426

The woman who stood on the doorstep seemed vaguely familiar to him. The taxi was double-parked alongside Broadhurst's BMW, the driver standing away from his cab at the pathway leading to the house. He held a mobile in his hand, but not in use. The expression on his face was of concern.

Her hair was dishevelled, the winter coat fastened only by the top button. As it flared open, Broadhurst could see streaks of blood across a white, tight-knit cardigan and in the lap of a floral skirt. She had used her left hand to press the doorbell; the right remained in her coat pocket. Blood from her fingers now smeared the bell push and the lacquered paintwork on the front door. She walked up a step and used her outstretched foot to stop him closing the door. 'You got what you wanted, you evil man.' She spat the words at him.

The sound of her voice triggered his memory. Alison, the Maestra's devoted assistant. She used her knee to force the door, but his own leg, pressed against the inside, restrained the forward movement. He glanced towards the sand wedge propped against the wall as a precaution against unwanted callers.

'What do you mean?' he said.

The pressure on the door eased momentarily. 'She was due to give a virtuoso recital in advance of Maundy Sunday. I called around to collect her at nine. They were in the music room. Dear God' – she was talking in a monotone – 'they had slit their wrists. There was blood everywhere. I tried to save her, pressing that frail body to mine, breathing life into her mouth, but she left me. He was collapsed against the piano, blood all over the keys. The lid of a tin was still in her hand. You have destroyed something so precious, and now ...'

She had started to move away. Momentarily he was off balance. Then, the door came swinging towards him, knocking him onto his back as his feet lost traction on the mat.

Four things happened at once. The woman came crashing through the doorway, a metal paper knife in her hand. His hand closed around the

427

head of the sand wedge. There was the sound of heavy footsteps on the path, and the wail of a police siren abruptly stopping.

Instinctively, he made to grab her wrist.

Her face was almost on top of his. He recognised the perfume she was wearing, but could not put a name to it.

ACKNOWLEDGEMENTS

I would like to extend my thanks to my editor, Nicky Taylor, for her professionalism, support and dedication to detail in appraising and correcting my manuscripts. I sometimes tell her that my many mistakes are deliberate, designed to try and catch her out, but I would be fibbing. Nothing escapes her scrutiny, and her suggestions for improvements are always erudite and pertinent.

My thanks also go to Andrea Orlic, whom I have now worked with on cover designs for both *Deaf Wish* and *The Last Rights*. Andrea is a talented and versatile artist, whose compositions encapsulate so well the themes of the novels in such eye-catching fashion.

The idea for *The Last Rights* came to me as I read a book that charts the build-up, execution and chaos surrounding the greatest robbery of all time – the aftermath of a last-gasp attempt by a defeated Nazi regime to ship the gold and treasures stored in the Reischbank from Berlin to Munich in April 1945. *Nazi Gold* by Ian Sayer and Douglas Botting is an extensively researched and detailed reconstruction of an intriguing chain of events culminating in a criminal cover-up on an unimaginable scale. It is well worth a read.

Whilst *The Last Rights* is a fictional narrative, wherever possible it has been grounded in contemporary historical fact. Although our train *Falke*, the Hawk, is a creation, two trains did leave Berlin on the fourteenth of April: *Adler*, the Eagle, and *Dohle,* the Jackdaw, both packed with gold and currency. Having said that, it is worth recording that vast amounts of time and money have been spent in recent years searching for a third train, allegedly buried in the wilds of Lower Silesia, now part of southern Poland but during the war under Nazi control. Thus far, no luck.

I am also indebted to David G Marwell's excellent recounting of the story of the 'Angel of Death': the life and times of Josef Mengele, the infamous concentration camp doctor on whom my Dr Sommer is loosely based. Marwell deals extensively with Mengele as a fugitive from justice after the war and his use of the Ratlines to effect an escape from Germany through Italy to Argentina. I have drawn heavily upon the detail he provides and, especially, the adoption of a false domicile in the South Tyrol (Italy's

Alto Adige) to secure travel permits to South America. The publication, *Mengele: Unmasking the 'Angel of Death'*, is a fascinating read.

I have tried wherever possible to blend the historical detail from third-party sources, admittedly with some poetic licence, into the storyline. However, I was present in Lisbon in 1988 on the day following the fire in the department store in Chiado and witnessed the devastation caused to the surrounding area. To the best of my knowledge, no bank or church was in the path of the fire, but it provided a useful conduit to further my plot.

Just a sombre note to finish: reading and writing about the Holocaust and the treatment of young women (*House of Dolls*, Ka-tzetnic 135633 and *Cilka's Journey*, Heather Morris) is a stark reminder of the product of fanaticism, prejudice and division in society barely ninety years ago. When mutual respect between individuals is eclipsed by a collective hatred, we should all fear the consequences.

Geoff Cook – October 2020

Geoff Cook

Geoff grew up in South London, the latch-key child of a widowed mother who struggled in post-war Britain to turn a place to live into a loving home. And she succeeded. Love you, Rita. RIP.

Geoff has had a varied commercial and financial career, living and working in countries with a Latin flavour (South America, Southern Europe) as well as London and the Welsh Valleys in the UK. His experiences extend from professional accounting, investment banking and pop music management to running a ceramic tile factory and retail outlets, managing a leisure complex, operating a restaurant ship, and owning and cheffing in restaurants on the Portuguese Algarve.

As a child, he opened a street lending library and developed an interest in literature and writing, turning his hand to numerous articles and projects over the years. In 2010, he published his first full-length novel as an e-book and has gone on to write a number of plays and novels of which *The Last Rights* is his latest offering.

Novels: Pieces for the Wicked – 2010 (e-book)

The Sator Square – 2017

'You should read it and follow the loops and tangles' – Booklore

Deaf Wish – 2019

'Twists and turns make this an interesting whodunnit' – Goodreads

The Last Rights – 2020

Plays: The Painful Truth – 2015

The Last Chapter – 2016

Current projects include *Octogen*, a futuristic novel about life in 2060 without oil and the internet, and *Deguello*, a thriller set in Korea with a man who keeps on discovering surprising facts about his recently deceased wife.

For more information, visit www.geoff-cook.com

DEGUELLO

**An extract from Geoff Cook's next release
(Scheduled publication – late 2021)**

ONE
London – 2018

Penelope Forbes-Hunter flinched at the sound of the office door slamming shut behind her. Didn't know her own strength, did she? Funny thing: she only pushed it shut so forcefully on her way into the building, never on the way out at the end of the day. Why? Damn it! Of course, she knew why. The realisation displeased her. Keeping up the pretence that everything was all right for eight hours, five days a week, was so draining. It was only after the door closed behind her to mark the passing of another groundhog day that she could breathe a sigh of relief and kid herself as to just how much better tomorrow would be.

Her repertoire of telephone excuses for the delay in settling supplier accounts centred around the inefficiencies of a non-existent accounting department, imaginary personnel absences attributed to debilitating sickness or the death of yet another aged relative. She knew that the person at the other end of the call had already heard several versions of today's excuse and would respond politely, not because they believed a word of what she was saying, but because of who she was – or rather, what her family name had once represented in the world of publishing. She longed for the courage to yell into the mouthpiece: 'There are a thousand reasons we can't pay you. The first is we don't have any money and the other nine hundred and ninety-nine don't matter.' But she couldn't. Not yet. The frustration of keeping up appearances was really getting to her. Dabbing her eyes with the sleeve of her jacket, she knew there was now a smudge of mascara on her brittle, veined cheek that hadn't been there before.

The sound of shuffling told her she was not alone. Turning her head away, she took a second to compose herself before acknowledging the presence of the intruder.

The young girl standing in the middle of the deserted reception reminded her of a newly born animal separated from the pack by a predator: vulnerable, unsure, ready for flight yet glued to the spot.

'The porter let me in,' the girl mumbled into her blouse.

'You would be …?' Penelope asked in the haughtiest tone she could muster. It was a rhetorical question. She already knew. The girl's sycophantic letter begging a placement had reflected, paradoxically, initiative and yet the inability to demonstrate originality. The girl must have trawled in depth through the publishing house's website with the many images of its owner and principal, Penelope Forbes-Hunter, photographed in a variety of traditional poses at the head of every page. The pleading letter was full of quotes from the site, regurgitated to appear as if displaying originality, but failing lamentably with countless misspellings and phrasing best described as a grammatical car crash.

Still, never mind. Penelope gave an in-body, indiscernible sigh. Against her better judgement, she had been bullied into accepting the girl. At least she was for free, work experience, paid for by the government. Whatever literary knowledge the girl expected to acquire, her skills would be mainly concerned with identifying the words 'Nescafé' and 'semi-skimmed' on the shelves of the kitchenette over the course of the next six weeks.

'Roberts, Miss,' came the halting reply. 'Administrative assistant. Work experience.'

'Do you know any sentences or just a limited selection of words?'

'Sorry?'

'Never mind. Do you have a Christian name?' Lips caked in dark red lipstick pursed together.

'Xania,' the girl replied.

'Spell that.' She waited, arms crossed, as the girl stammered a reply.

'Never heard of that name before. Where's it from?'

'My mum.'

'No, I didn't say from whom, I said from where. Never mind. Sounds like a medication for treating diarrhoea.'

'Sorry?' There was a blank smile prior to comprehension. 'Oh, you mean … Spain. She was in Spain.'

'Congratulations. You've managed a sentence, albeit simply framed around the verb "to be". The origin of the name is Spanish, you say? Which province? The "X" suggests a Basque influence.'

'I don't know where she was – on holiday somewhere. She was pregnant with me. Saw the name advertising some product on TV just as her waters burst. She thought it was a good omen.'

The answer stunned Penelope into silence. She closed her eyes. Was there any future for the human race? People used to name their children after famous people, both contemporary and historical. There was pride in a well-used name. It had all changed in her sixty-two years on this earth. Her parents, founders of Forbes-Hunter Publications, had named her after Penelope Delta, a famous Greek author of children's stories who had so influenced their literary aspirations. As they had often said, their hope was that the name would inspire her to see their fledgling business grow into a force for advancement in the literary world. Nowadays, parents sought originality in the child's first name, something to set their offspring apart from the run of Johns and Janes, something that would stamp a personality on the child in the naïve belief that the simple choice of a name would set them apart from the rest.

She looked at the girl, standing there, the toes of her shoes seemingly glued together, obviously unsure of whether to speak or to remain silent. What chance for this girl with a name probably derived from a brand of Spanish toilet rolls? Come to that, what chance for Penelope Forbes-Hunter? Like everything else, the world of publishing was changing. Technology favoured the brash new entrants with toilet roll names and paper-thin pedigrees, discarding as it did the double-barrelled dinosaurs who fed on the printed page and sturdy binder's board covers. Penelope had refused to be bulldozed into a world she despised, and now her future and that of the business which bore the family name hovered on the brink.

The silence was broken as the office door opened and groaned slowly to a close. Forbes-Hunter recognised the overpowering scent. It reminded her of the weedkiller she used to keep the cracks between the crazy paving in her garden free from unwanted growths.

'Morning, Hannah.'

The only permanent staff member of Forbes-Hunter Publications ignored the greeting and moved forward, hand extended. 'Welcome to our little team, Xania,' she said, grasping the feeble appendage hovering limply in mid-air. 'I'm sure you will be of great value to us. Don't you think so, FH?'

Penelope glared over her thick-rimmed, half-moon glasses with what could only be described as disdain at the inappropriate use of an

437

acronym to identify her, albeit regularly used between the two women in a more private setting. She pinched the nostrils of her slender nose together with both index fingers. It was a habit she had acquired to show disapproval and, by the disingenuous smile with which it was met, easily recognised. Penelope raised her eyebrows. 'Of course, you know my assistant, Ms Barton, from your interview. I will rely on her judgement.'

Hannah Barton was some twenty years her employer's junior and had worked for the business, initially with Penelope's father, since leaving Warwick university with a mediocre 2:2 degree in English literature. Now in her mid-forties, she was the mainstay of the day-to-day running of all administrative and legal matters, leaving Penelope, as the figurehead, to deal with their dwindling list of authors and relations with the publishing world. Hannah was a dumpy woman with tightly curled, mousy hair and heavy features that had never led to her success in attracting much attention from the opposite sex. Few had got close to appreciate the warm-hearted and bubbly personality, and her current on-off relationship was with a former CID officer who had been pensioned off after suffering a serious acid attack during a domestic violence incident. She knew he was a depressive and totally self-centred, but he liked to cuddle and so did she. He had a nice way with his hands, she had confided.

As Penelope talked, Hannah's eyes ranged across the half-dozen envelopes in her hand that constituted the morning's post: mainly bills and circulars.

'Of course,' Penelope was saying, her staccato voice rising and falling in a theatrical manner, 'as a front-line publishing house, we constantly receive submissions from literary agents and authors to publish their offerings but we have to be very selective in order to preserve our reputation.' She moved closer to Xania as if about to impart a secret. 'You will remember that we do not accept any sample manuscript for consideration unless it is prepared in Times New Roman, 12 point, double-spaced on white, unbound A4 paper and is accompanied by a query letter and one-page synopsis. If it does not meet those criteria, my girl, you may immediately bin it.'

Xania looked confused. 'Do I print off the attachments to the emails?'

Penelope's brow creased. 'What do you mean?'

Hannah stepped forward. 'What Ms Forbes-Hunter is saying is that most of our current publications are cookery books and historical reference works which do not lend themselves to digital submissions. Initially, we insist on a hard-copy through the post.'

Xania giggled.

'Why are you laughing?' Penelope looked offended.

The girl was still smiling, slowly gaining self-confidence. 'Mum said I would probably get to meet Jackie Collins, Martina Cole or Jilly Cooper. She didn't say anything about the Hairy Bikers.'

'What are you talking about?' Penelope was shaking her head.

Hannah sensed they were in grave danger of losing their free helper even before she'd had the chance to discover where they kept the coffee mugs. She took the initiative. 'And you probably will meet all these people,' she said. 'But before you can run, you must learn to walk and this is probably one of the best places to get to grips with all the basics. When you leave here, you can go to Pergamon or any other mainstream publisher and get a job by simply saying "I was trained at Forbes-Hunter". They'll be falling over to employ you.'

Xania looked impressed. 'When do I get to meet the rest of the staff?' she asked.

Hannah looked askew at Penelope, who was about to speak, but once again got in first. 'All in good time. This is our compact executive suite,' she went on, her fingers metaphorically crossed. 'There's just the conference room directly behind you, Penelope's office to the left and mine to the right, next to the kitchenette and toilet. You'll sit at the reception desk to greet our visitors.'

'Everything is to go in the diary.' Penelope was keen to wrestle back control of the situation. 'Who have I got first today?'

Hannah thumbed through the diary. There was only one entry. 'Michael Renton. At nine thirty. I'll get his manuscript.' She walked over to a filing cabinet and pulled open the third drawer.

This was the opportunity Penelope had been waiting for, the chance to reassert her authority with this young wisp of a thing. 'God save us from the Michael Rentons of this world,' she gasped loudly in mock desperation.

'He fancies himself as a novelist. I've had to put up with the rambling nonsense he produces for the last ten years, one piece of garbage after another.' She shook her head. 'And you know why I do it?' She continued without stopping. 'Why I'm kind and gentle and tell him to work on this or that, show, don't tell, change the tense? Well, I'll tell you. His wife is ... was, one of our bestselling authors. Poor cow, married to that loser. She was brilliant, not only a renowned human rights lawyer but a sensational cook. The Korean and Vietnamese recipes in her books, those photographs – good enough to eat on their own.'

'She's dead?'

Forbes-Hunter nodded. 'Tragic circumstances. A heart attack whilst working in Seoul. She was half Korean by birth, on her mother's side. Her father was a Yank, I think, but they lived in the UK. Parents were hounded out of Virginia prior to the Lovings' verdict on interracial marriage. They came to the UK. Ha-yoon was her birth name.' She laughed to herself. 'We affectionately called her "High Noon". We published her cookery books under the Taiwanese name she preferred, Mei-Ling.'

'I'll ask my mum if she's heard of her. She likes cooking tikka masala.'

Penelope was about to react but Hannah tapped her arm. 'Here it is,' she said, handing over a sheaf of papers in a brown folder. 'As pristine as the day he brought it in.'

Penelope guffawed loudly. 'You didn't expect me to read this rubbish, did you? I'll give him the usual runaround and get rid of him.'

'Be a little circumspect, please,' Hannah pleaded. 'We will need his authority to produce an in memoriam compendium of her recipes, a posthumous souvenir of her best. Remember, she kept all the rights. They pass to him now.'

'Don't worry. I'll tell him he's produced a literary masterpiece, just a few tweaks needed.' She checked her watch. 'Should be here by now. He's always punctual. Maybe he's forgotten or not coming.' There was the sound of exhilaration in her voice. 'In any event, let's have a coffee. Will you show Xania where we keep the beverages?'

The girl's hand shot up as if responding to a question in school. 'No need,' she said, 'I already found everything.'

440

'You did?' Penelope stared at Hannah. 'How come?'

'The gentleman followed me in and said he had an appointment. I asked him if he wanted a coffee and he said yes, so I went to find out where things were.' She pointed to the open door of the conference room. 'He's waiting in there for you.'

Printed in Great Britain
by Amazon